Joliffe took my face in his hands and said: "Jane, there has never been anyone like you."

"I only want to be with you," I answered.

We kissed and I had never dreamed that there were such kisses. I was in a state of euphoria and the transition from terror to bliss was too sudden. Everything seemed unreal. I was in love with a man I had so briefly known and we were here together half clad in this room which for me had always seemed like part of a fantasy.

I expected to wake at any moment to find that I had dreamed of that flickering light and I would find myself seated at my window where I had dozed off.

But no, I was here, and Joliffe's arms were about me and he was telling me that he loved me and he was urging me to love him completely and utterly.

"Come to my room . . . or I'll come to yours. . . ."

Fawcett Crest Books
by Victoria Holt:

VICTORIA HOLT

The House
of a
Thousand Lanterns

FAWCETT CREST • NEW YORK

A Fawcett Crest Book
Published by Ballantine Books
Copyright © 1974 by Victoria Holt

ISBN 0-449-20498-7

This edition published by arrangement with
Doubleday and Company, Inc.

Alternate Selection of the Literary Guild
Selection of the Doubleday Bargain Book Club

Manufactured in the United States of America

First Fawcett Crest Edition: July 1975
First Ballantine Books Edition: June 1983

Contents

Roland's Croft

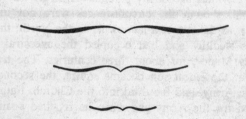

When I first heard of The House of a Thousand Lanterns
I felt an immediate curiosity to know more of a place
with such a name. There was a magical, mystical quality
about it. Why was it so called? Could there be a thousand
lanterns in one house? Who put them there? And what
significance had they? The name seemed to belong to a
fantasy from something like the Arabian Nights. Little did
I realize then that I, Jane Lindsay, would one day be
caught up in the mystery, danger, and intrigue which was
centered in that house with the haunting name.

My involvement really began years before I saw the
house, and I had had my share of heartbreak and adventure even then.

I was fifteen years old at the time my mother became housekeeper to that strange man Sylvester Milner who was to have such an influence on my life and but for whom I should never have heard of The House of a Thousand Lanterns. I have often thought that if my father had lived we should have gone on in a more or less conventional manner. I should have led the life of a well-bred though rather impecunious young lady and would most likely have married and lived happily, if less excitingly, ever after.

But the marriage of my parents was in its way unconventional, though the circumstances were not unusual. Father was the son of a landowner in the North; the family was wealthy and had occupied the ancestral home, Lindsay Manor, for about three centuries. The tradition was that the eldest son became squire, the second went into the Army, and the third into the Church. Father was destined for the Army and when he rebelled against the career chosen for him he fell into disfavor and after his marriage he was completely estranged.

He was an enthusiastic mountaineer and it was when he was climbing in the Peak district that he met my mother. She was the innkeeper's daughter, pretty and vivacious; he fell in love with and married her almost immediately in spite of the disapproval of his family, who had other plans for him concerning the daughter of a neighboring landowner. So incensed were they that they cast him off and all he had was an annuity of two hundred pounds a year.

My father was a delightful man, charming, and interested in any form of art; he knew something about almost everything in this field. The one thing he was not particularly good at was earning a living, and as he had been reared in the utmost comfort he was never really able to adjust himself to circumstances other than those in which he had been accustomed. He painted in a manner which could be called "quite well" but, as everyone knows, to paint quite well very often means not quite well enough. He sold the occasional picture and during the climbing season worked as guide. My earliest memories are of seeing him set off with a party, armed with crampons and ropes, his eyes alight with excitement, because this was what he wanted to do more than anything.

He was a dreamer and an idealist. My mother used to say to me: "It's a mercy you and I, Jane, have our feet firmly planted on the ground, and if our heads are often in these Derbyshire mists they're never in the clouds."

But we loved him dearly and he loved us and he used to say we were the perfect trio. As I was their only child they contrived to give me the best possible education. To my father it seemed natural that I should go to the school which the female members of his family had always attended; as for my mother she believed that my father's daughter must have only the best, and so from the age of ten I was sent away to Cluntons', that very genteel school for the daughters of the landed gentry. I was a Lindsay of Lindsay Manor and although I had never seen the place, and was in fact banished from that holy ground, I still belonged to it.

Financially uncertain but secure in our love for each other and having Father's annuity and his sporadic earnings to help us, we struggled gaily on until that tragic January day. I was home for the Christmas holidays.

The weather was bleak that year. Never had I seen the Derbyshire mountains so menacing. The sky was a leaden grey, the wind icy and some five hours after my Father and his party set off, the blizzard began. I never see snow without recalling that terrible time. I still hate that strange white light which permeates the atmosphere, I hate the silent snowflakes falling thick and fast. We were shut in a weird white world and somewhere up the mountain was my father.

"He's an experienced climber," said my mother. "He'll be all right."

She busied herself in the kitchen baking bread in the enormous oven beside the fire. I always connect the smell of freshly baked bread with the tragedy of those dreadful hours of waiting, listening to the grandfather clock ticking away the minutes, waiting . . . waiting for news.

When the blizzard subsided the snow lay in drifts in the lanes and on the mountains. The searchers went out; but it was a whole week before they found them.

We knew though before that. I remember sitting there in the kitchen, the warmest place in the house, with my mother while she talked of their meeting and how he had bravely defied his family and given up everything for her. "He was the sort who would never give in," she kept saying. "In a minute he'll be back. He'll be laughing at us for being afraid."

But if he could defy his family he was no match for the elements. The day they brought his body home was the saddest of our lives. We buried him with four members of his party. There were but two survivors to tell the tale of endurance and suffering. It was a common enough tale. It had happened many times before.

"Why do men have to climb mountains?" I demanded angrily. "Why do they have to face dangers for no reason?"

"They climb because they must," said my mother sadly.

I went back to school. I wondered how long I should be there, for without Father's annuity we were very poor indeed. With her accustomed optimism my mother believed that the Lindsays would take over their responsibilities. How wrong she was! My father had offended the family code and when my grandfather had said he would be cut off he had meant it. They did not own us.

My mother's great concern was to keep me at Cluntons'. How, she was not sure, but she was not one to wait for something to fall into her lap. When I came home after that term she told me of her plans.

"I have to earn some money, Jane," she said.

"I too. So I must leave school."

"Unthinkable!" she declared. "Your father would never hear of it." She spoke of him as though he were still with us. "If I could find the right sort of post we'd manage," she added.

"What as?"

"I have my talents," she answered. "When my father was alive I helped him run the inn. My cooking is good; my household management excellent. In fact I could enter some household as a housekeeper."

"Are there such posts?"

"My dear Jane, they abound. Good housekeepers don't grow on trees. There will be one stipulation."

"Shall you be in a position to make stipulations?"

"I shall enter the household on my terms, which are that my daughter shall have a home with me."

"You set a high price on your services."

"If I don't no one else will."

She was self-reliant. She had had to be. I thought then that had she been the one to die suddenly my father would have been completely lost without her. She at least could stand on her own feet and carry me along with her. And yet I thought she was asking too much.

I had another term at school before we should have to face the embarrassment of considering whether we should be in a position to pay the bills and it was during this term that I first heard the name of Sylvester Milner. My mother wrote to me at school.

My dearest Jane,

Tomorrow I am traveling down to the New Forest. I have an interview at a place called Roland's Croft. A gentleman by the name of Mr. Sylvester Milner is in need of a housekeeper. It is a large establishment I gather and although my condition of accepting the post has not exactly been agreed to, I have stated it and am still asked to attend for the interview. I shall write to you to tell you the result. If I am accepted my remuneration should be enough to keep you at Cluntons', for I shall need little, as I shall have bed and board provided, as you will during the holidays. It will be an admirable solution. All I have to do is convince them that they must employ me.

I imagined her setting off resolutely for the interview, ready to fight for her place in the sun—not so much for herself as for me. She was a very small woman. I was going to be tall for I took after my father and was already several inches higher than my mother. She had rosy cheeks and thick hair, almost black with a touch of blue, the sort of color one sees in a bird's wing. I had the same kind of hair but my skin was pale like my father's, and instead of her small twinkling brown eyes I had my father's large deep-set grey ones. We were not in the least alike—my mother and I—except in our determination to sweep aside all barriers which prevented our reaching the goal we had set ourselves. In this case, particularly when so much depended on the outcome, I felt she would have good hopes of success.

I was right, for a few days later I heard that she was settling into her new post at Roland's Croft, and when the term ended I went to join her there.

I traveled down to London with a party of girls from Cluntons' and there I was taken to the train which would carry me to Hampshire. When I reached Lyndhurst I was to board a local train. My mother had written the instructions very carefully. At the halt of Rolandsmere I would be "met" and if her duties prevented her from coming in the trap, she would see me as soon as I arrived at the house.

I could scarcely wait to get there. It seemed so strange

to be going to a new place. My mother had said nothing about Mr. Sylvester Milner. I wondered why. She was not usually reticent. She had said very little about the house except that it was big and set in grounds of some twenty acres. "You will find it very different from our little house," she wrote unnecessarily really, because I certainly should. Oddly enough she left it at that and my imagination was busy.

Roland's Croft! Who was Roland and why a croft? Names usually meant something. And why did she say nothing of Mr. Sylvester Milner, her employer?

I began to build fantasies around him. He was young and handsome. No, he wasn't, he was middle-aged and had a large family. He was a bachelor who shunned society. He was tired of the world and cynical; he shut himself away at Roland's Croft to keep from it. No, he was a monster whom no one ever saw. They talked about him in whispers. There were strange sounds in the house at night. "You take no notice of them," I would be told. "That is just Mr. Sylvester Milner walking."

My father used to say I should curb my imagination, for at times it was too vivid. My mother said it ran away with me. And as it was accompanied by an insatiable curiosity about the world I lived in and the people who inhabited it, these made a dangerous combination.

I was therefore in a state of high expectancy when I reached the little haunt of Rolandsmere. It was December and there was a faint mist in the air which obscured the wintry sun and gave an aura of mystery to the little station with its name worked in plants on the platform There were very few of us to alight and I was seen immediately by a big man in top hat and a coat frogged with gold braid.

He strode along the platform with such an air of authority that as he came to me I said: "Are you Mr. Sylvester Milner?"

He paused as though with wonder at the thought and

let out a roar of laughter. "Nay, miss," he cried. "I be the coachman." Then he muttered to himself, "Mr. Sylvester Milner. That be a good one. Well," he continued, "these be your bags. Just from school, are you? Let's get to the trap then." He surveyed me from head to foot. "Ain't like your mother," was his comment. "Wouldn't have known you for hers."

Then with a sharp nod he turned and shouted to a man who was lounging against the wall of the little booking office. "Here, Harry then." And Harry picked up my bags and we made a procession, myself behind the coachman who walked with a swaggering gait as though to indicate that he was a very important gentleman indeed.

We went to a trap and my bags were put in. I scrambled up and the coachman took the reins with an air of disdain.

"Tain't like me to drive these little things but to oblige your ma . . ."

"Thank you," I said. "Mr. er . . ."

"Jeffers," he said. "Jeffers is the name." And we were off.

We drove through leafy lanes that edged the forest where the trees looked darkly mysterious. It was very different country from our mountainous one. This, I reminded myself, was the forest in which William the Conqueror had hunted and his son William Rufus had met his mysterious death.

I said: "It's odd to call it the *New* Forest."

"Eh?" replied Jeffers. "What's that?"

"The New Forest when it's been there for eight hundred years."

"Reckon it were new once like most things," answered Jeffers.

"They say it was built on the blood of men."

"You got funny ideas, miss."

"It's not my idea. Men were turned out of their homes to make that forest and if anyone trapped a deer or a wild boar his hands were cut off or his eyes put out or he might have been hanged on a tree."

"There's no wild boar in there now, miss. And I never heard such talk about the forest."

"Well, I did. In fact we're doing Anglo-Saxon England and the Norman invasion at school."

He nodded gravely. "And you're spending the holiday with us. Surprised I was when that was allowed. But your mother stuck her foot down and it had to be. Mr. Milner gave way on that, which surprised me."

"Why did it surprise you?"

"He's not one to want children in the house."

"What sort of one is he?"

"Now that is a question, that is. I reckon there's no one knows what sort of man Mr. Sylvester Milner is."

"Is he young?"

He looked at me. "Compared with me . . . he's not so very old but compared with you he'd be a very old gentleman indeed."

"Without comparing him with anyone how old would he be?"

"Bless you, miss. You're one for questions. How would I be knowing how old Mr. Sylvester Milner be."

"You could guess."

" 'Twouldn't do to start guessing where he were concerned. You'd sure as eggs come up with the wrong answer."

I could see that I should get little information about Mr. Sylvester Milner through him, so I studied the countryside.

Dusk of a December afternoon and a forest which my imagination told me must surely be haunted by those whom the Norman kings had dispossessed and tortured! By the time we had reached Roland's Croft I was in a state of great anticipation.

We turned into a drive on either side of which grew conifers. The drive must have been half a mile in length and it seemed a long time before we reached the lawn beyond which was the house. It was imposing and elegant and must have been built round about the time of the early Georges. It struck me at once as being aloof and austere. Perhaps this was because I had been imagining a castle-like dwelling with battlements, turrets, and oriel windows. These windows were symmetrical, short on the ground floor, tall on the first floor, a little less tall on the next and square on the top. The effect was characteristic of eighteenth-century elegance removed as far as possible from the baroque and gothic of earlier generations. There was a beautiful fanlight over the Adam doorway and two columns supported a portico. Later I was to admire the Greek honeysuckle pattern on these but at the time my attention was caught by the two Chinese stone dogs at the foot of the columns. They looked fierce and alien in comparison with so much which was English.

The door was opened by a maid in a black alpaca dress and a white cap and apron with very stiffly starched frills. She must have heard the trap pull up.

"You be the young lady from school," she said. "Come in and I'll tell Madam you're here."

Madam! So my mother had assumed that title. I laughed inwardly and that pleasant feeling of security began to wrap itself around me.

I stood in the hall and looked about me. From the ceiling with its discreet plaster decorations hung a chandelier. The staircase was circular and beautifully proportioned. A grandfather clock standing against the wall ticked noisily. I listened to the house. Apart from the clock it was quiet. Strangely, eerily quiet, I told myself.

And then my mother flashed into sight on the staircase. She ran to me and we hugged each other.

"My dear child, so you've come. I've been counting the days. Where are your bags? I'll have them taken up to your room. First of all, come to mine. There's so much to say."

She looked different; she was in black bombazine which rustled as she moved; she wore a cap on her head and had assumed great dignity. The housekeeper of this rather stately mansion was different from the mother in our little house.

She was a little restrained, I thought, as arm in arm we mounted the staircase. I was not surprised that I had not heard her approach, so thick were the carpets. We followed the staircase up and up. It was constructed so that from every floor it was possible to look down into the hall.

"What a magnificent house," I whispered.

"It's pleasant," she answered.

Her room was on the second floor—a cosy room, heavily curtained; the furniture was elegant and although I knew nothing of these matters at that time I later learned that the cabinet was Hepplewhite as were the beautifully carved chairs and table.

"I'd like to have had my own bits and pieces," said my mother, following my gaze. She grimaced ruefully. "Mr. Sylvester Milner would have been horrified with my old stuff, but it was cosy."

It was beautiful and elegant and right for the room, I realized, but it lacked the homeliness of our own rooms. Still, there was a fire in the grate and on it a kettle was singing.

Then she shut the door and burst out laughing. She hugged me once more. She had slipped out of the dignified housekeeper's role and had become my mother.

"Tell me all about it," I said.

"The kettle will be boiling in a jiffy," she answered. "We'll chat over our tea. I thought you'd never get here."

The cups were already on the tray and she ladled out three spoonfuls of tea and infused it. "We'll let it stand for a minute or two. Well!" she went on. "Who would have thought it? It's turned out very well, very well indeed."

"What about him?"

"Who?"

"Mr. Sylvester Milner."

"He's away."

My face fell and she laughed at me. "That's a good thing, Janey. Why, we'll have the house to ourselves."

"I wanted to see him."

"And I'd thought you wanted to see *me*."

I got up and kissed her.

"You're settled then, and really happy?" I said.

"It couldn't have been better. I believe your father arranged it for us."

She had believed since his death that he was watching over us and for this reason no harm could befall us. She mingled strong occult feelings with strict common sense and although she was firmly convinced that my father would guide us as to the best way we should go, at the same time she put every effort in arranging it.

It was clear that she was happy with her post at Roland's Croft.

"If I'd planned a place for myself I couldn't have done better," she said. "I've got a good position here. The maids respect me."

"They call you Madam, I notice."

"That was a little courtesy I insisted on. Always remember, Janey, that people take you at your own valuation. So I set mine high."

"Are there many servants?"

"There are three gardeners, two of them married, and they live in cottages on the estate. There's Jeffers the coachman and his wife. They live over the stables. The two gardeners' wives work in the house. Then there's Jess and Amy, the parlormaid and housemaid; and Mr. Catterwick the butler and Mrs. Couch the cook."

"And you are in charge of it all."

"Mr. Catterwick and Mrs. Couch wouldn't like to hear you say that I was in charge of *them*, I can tell you. Mr. Catterwick's a very fine gentleman indeed. He tells me at

least once a day that he's worked in more grand house-
holds than this one. As for Mrs. Couch, she's mistress of
the kitchen and it would be woe betide anyone who tried
to interfere there."

My mother's conversation had always been gay and
racy. I think that was one of the characteristics which
had attracted my father to her. He himself had been quiet
and withdrawn, all that she was not. He had been sensitive; she was as he had once said like a little cock sparrow
ready to fight the biggest eagle for her rights. I could
imagine her ruling the household here . . . with the exception of the cook and the butler.

"It's a beautiful house," I said, "but a little eerie."

"You and your fancies! It's because the lamps aren't
lit. I'll light mine now."

She took the globe off a lamp on the table and applied
a lighted match to the wick.

We drank the tea and ate the biscuits which my mother
produced from a tin.

"Did you see Mr. Sylvester Milner when you applied
for the post?" I asked.

"Why yes, I did."

"Tell me about him."

She was silent for a few seconds, and a faint haze came
over her eyes. She was rarely at a loss for words and I
thought at once: There *is* something odd about him.

"He's . . . a gentleman," she said.

"Where is he now?"

"He's away on business. He's often away on business."

"Then why does he keep this big houseful of servants?"

"People do."

"He must be very rich."

"He's a merchant."

"A merchant! What sort of a merchant?"

"He travels round the world to many places . . . like
China."

I remembered the Chinese dogs at the porch.

"Tell me what he looks like."

"He's not easy to describe."

"Why not?"

"Well, he's different from other people."

"When shall I see him?"

"Sometime, I daresay."

"This holiday?"

"I should hardly think so. Though we never know. He appears suddenly . . ."

"Like a ghost," I said.

She laughed at me. "I mean he doesn't say when he'll be coming. He just turns up."

"Is he handsome?"

"Some might call him so."

"What sort of things does he sell?"

"Very valuable things."

This was unlike my mother who was usually the most loquacious of women and my first impression that there was something strange about Mr. Sylvester Milner was confirmed.

"There's one thing," said my mother. "You might see a strange-looking man about sometimes."

"What sort of a man?"

"He's Chinese. He's called Ling Fu. He won't look quite like the other servants. He travels with Mr. Milner and looks after his private treasure room. No one else goes in there."

My eyes sparkled. It was growing more mysterious every minute.

"Is he hiding something in this treasure room?" I asked.

My mother laughed. "Now don't you get working up one of your fancies. There's a simple explanation. Mr. Milner collects rare and costly things—jade, rose quartz, coral, ivory. He buys them and sells them, but he keeps some of them here until he finds a buyer. He's an authority on them and Ling Fu dusts them and looks after them.

Mr. Milner explained to me that he thought it better for Ling Fu to do this and none of the other servants to be involved."

"Have you ever been in the room, Mother?"

"There's no reason why I should. I take care of the household. That's my business."

I looked into the fire and saw pictures there. There was a face which looked genial at one moment and as the coal burned it changed subtly and was malevolent. Mr. Sylvester Milner! I thought.

My mother showed me my room. It was small, next to her own and it had a window which reached from the ceiling to the floor. It was discreetly but tastefully furnished.

"You can look out on the gardens," she said. "You can't see very much now but they are very well kept. The lawns are a picture and the flowers in the spring and summer have to be seen to be believed. You can just see how the house is built—with a wing either side, like a letter E with the middle strut not there. Look, over at that wing. You see those two windows. That's Mr. Milner's Treasure Room."

I looked and was excited.

"You'll see it clearly in daylight," said my mother.

She was very pleased with herself. She had managed her affairs admirably.

We went back to her room and talked—how we talked! She caught me up in her mood of exultation. Everything had turned out as she would have wished.

It was in a state of euphoria that I spent that evening, but my first night at Roland's Croft was an uneasy one. The wind soughing through the trees sounded like voices and they seemed to be repeating a name: "Sylvester Milner."

It was an interesting holiday. I soon was on good terms with the servants. It was fortunate, said my mother, that

Mrs. Couch took to me and Mr. Catterwick had no objection to my presence.

I was to the fore when the gardeners cut down the fir tree and we dragged it into the house. I was there for the cutting of the holly and mistletoe.

There was a wonderful smell in the kitchen and Mrs. Couch, whose rotund figure, rosy cheeks, and cosy look fitted her name, was making innumerable pies and fussing over the Christmas puddings. Because I was already a favorite of hers I was allowed a little of what she called the "taster." It was the happiest day I had known since my father's death when I sat near the kitchen range, listening to the bubbling of the puddings and then seeing Mrs. Couch haul them out by a long fork hitched through the pudding cloths and set them in a row. Last of all came the small basin which contained the "taster." Then I sat at the table and ate my small portion while I watched Mrs. Couch's face—apprehensive, hesitating, and then expressing gratification.

"Not as good as last year's, but better than the year before that."

And all those who had been privileged to share the "taster" protested that the puddings had never been better and that Mrs. Couch couldn't make a bad pudding if she tried.

For such compliments we were all rewarded with a glass of her special parsnip wine and there was a glass of sloe gin for Mr. Catterwick and my mother, which I suppose denoted their superior rank.

Mrs. Couch told me that in the old days there had been the Family and nobody was going to make her believe— not that anyone had tried to—that it was right and proper that houses should pass out of families and go to them that had no what you might call roots there.

This was an oblique reference to Mr. Sylvester Milner.

"And will he be home for Christmas?" asked the wife of one of the gardeners.

"I should hope not," said Jess the parlormaid, who was promptly reproved by Mr. Catterwick while I felt that shudder of something between fascination and fear which the name of Mr. Sylvester Milner always aroused in me.

My mother, like Mr. Catterwick, kept somewhat aloof from the servants. One had to keep up one's position, she told me, and the servants respected her for it. They knew that she had "come down in the world" and that I was at Cluntons' where Mrs. Couch informed them one of the ladies of the Family had gone.

"Of course," said Mrs. Couch, "when the Family was here, the housekeeper's daughter wouldn't have gone to the same school as one of its members. That would have been unthinkable. But everything's different now. He came . . ." She shrugged her shoulders and lifted her eyes to the ceiling with an air of resignation.

I would not have believed I could have enjoyed a Christmas holiday so much without my father. There was not only the strangeness of it all but the overwhelming mystery of Mr. Sylvester Milner.

I tried to find out everything I could about him. He never said much I gathered, but he had made it clear that he wanted everything done his way. He had changed the house since he took over from the Family. He had even had those heathen-looking dogs put on the porch. The Family it seemed had fallen on hard times and been obliged to sell the house. And he had appeared and taken it. He crept about the place, said Mrs. Couch. You'd find him suddenly there. He talked in a sort of gibberish to that Ling Fu. They were often shut in the Treasure Room together. And Mrs. Couch thought it was a heathen thing to do, to keep a room locked against Mr. Catterwick and let a foreigner have the key.

I suppose it was helpful that our first Christmas without my father should be so entirely different. There was less nostalgia for the past. I said it seemed like a miracle but my mother explained that my father was arranging it;

he had guided us here because he was looking after us. It seemed so, for everything was going well.

We were very merry decorating the servants' hall with holly, ivy, and mistletoe, and even Mr. Catterwick smiled wryly at our antics and only gently reproved the maids for their exuberance. The carol singers came on Christmas Eve and sang by the portico, and my mother put a shilling in their tin on behalf of the house.

"Of course when the Family was here," said Mrs. Couch, "they was brought into the hall and the Master and the Mistress and the rest of the Family served them with hot punch and mince pies. That was how it had been done for generations. It's a pity times have to change."

She had a rocking chair in the kitchen and she liked to rock herself to and fro after a heavy baking. It soothed her. Since I had come she liked to talk to me and as I was so interested I was glad to listen. I spent quite a lot of time in the kitchen with Mrs. Couch. My mother was pleased to see that we had become friends for there was no doubt that the cook was a power in the house.

She talked a great deal about the Family, and how it had been in the old days. "A *proper* household," she said, implying that there was something rather improper about it in its present state, "they had been, the Master, the Mistress, and the two daughters. They came out," she went on, "as young ladies should and they might well have made good matches in due course. But the Master he was a gambler, always had been . . . and his father before him. Together they gambled away their fortune."

"And then they sold the house," I prompted.

She leaned close to me. "For a song," she hissed. "Mr. Sylvester Milner is a true businessman. He bought when the Family had no other way but to sell."

"What happened to the Family?"

"Master died. Shock, they said. Mistress went to live with her family. One of the young ladies went with her and the other I heard took a post as governess. Terrible that were. She who'd had a governess of her own when she was young and been brought up to expect to employ one for her own children."

I wondered fleetingly what I should do when I grew up. Should I become a governess? It was a sobering thought.

"He asked me if I'd stay on and I said I would. The house had always served me well. Little did I know . . ."

I leaned towards her. "Know what, Mrs. Couch?"

"That there'd be such change."

"Life's always changing," I reminded her.

"Everything had gone on here in the same way for years, as you'd expect it to go. We had our differences. Mr. Catterwick and I didn't always get along, same as now. But it was different then."

"What happens when *he's* here?" I asked.

"Mr. Milner? Well, he'll have friends to dinner. And they'll go up to the Treasure Room like as not. Talking away. Talking business, I suppose, being in business. Well, it's not what I expected, nor did Mr. Catterwick for that matter. I'm used to gentry and so is Mr. Catterwick."

"You could always leave and go to a place where there's a family which hasn't gambled away its fortune," I suggested.

"I like to settle, and I've settled here. I'll put up with a bit . . . for he's not here all the time."

"Does he ever talk to you?"

She put her head on one side and then she said: "He was never one to come down to the kitchen and give me the menu as you'd expect with a family."

"When his friends come to dinner . . ."

"Then I'd go to his sitting room and knock on his door bold as brass. 'Now, what's for dinner, Mr. Milner,' I'll say. And he'll answer: 'I'll leave it to you, Mrs. Couch.' And how am I to know whether these friends of his have any special likes or don't-likes. He's not like the Family I can tell you. He's rich though, must be. He bought the place didn't he. And he keeps us all here."

"And is hardly ever here himself."

"Oh he'll be here between spells of travel."

"When is he coming back, Mrs. Couch?"

"He's not one to give you warning."

"Perhaps he wants to come back suddenly and see what you're all doing."

"And I wouldn't put that past him."

And so we talked and I always contrived to lead Mrs. Couch from the Family to the present owner of Roland's Croft.

On Christmas Day there was duckling followed by the Christmas pudding solemnly carried to the table by Mr. Catterwick himself and encircled by mystic brandy flames which were watched lovingly by Mrs. Couch. My mother sat at the head of one end of the big table and Mr. Catterwick at the other, and all the servants and their families were gathered there.

I had the sixpence from the pudding and the three wishes to which that entitled one. I wished that I should see Mr. Milner before I went back to school and then the Treasure Room and the third wish was that my mother and I should go on living at Roland's Croft.

I thought that if only my father were there it would have been the best Christmas I had ever had, but of course had he been alive we shouldn't have been there.

After dinner everyone had to do "a turn" except my mother and Mr. Catterwick whose dignity saved them and Mrs. Couch whose bulk excused her. There were songs, recitations, and even a dance; and one of the gardeners and his son played their violins. I recited *The Wreck of the Hesperus* which, Mrs. Couch whispered, I did so beautifully that it brought tears to her eyes.

During the evening my mother sent me upstairs for her shawl and as I came out of the servants' hall and shut the door on the lights and gaiety I was suddenly aware of the quiet house closing round me. It was almost like a premonition. That warm servants' hall seemed a whole world away. In a sudden unaccountable panic I dashed up the stairs to my mother's room, found the shawl and prepared to come down again. I stood at her window and peered out. The candle I had brought up with me showed me nothing but my own face reflected there. I could hear the wind in the trees and I knew that not far off was the forest which long long ago men had said was haunted by the ghosts of those who had suffered for it.

Desperately I wanted to go back to the comfort of the servants' hall, and yet I had an irresistible urge to linger.

I thought then of the Treasure Room which was always locked. There is something about a locked room that is intriguing. I remembered a conversation I had had with Mrs. Couch. "They must be very precious things in there, to keep it locked," I had said. "They must be." "In a way it's like Bluebeard. He had a wife who was too inquisitive. Has Mr. Sylvester got a wife?" "Oh, he's a strange gentleman. He's giving nothing away. There's no wife here now." "Unless she's in the secret room. Perhaps she's his treasure." That had made Mrs. Couch laugh. "Wives have to eat," she said, "and wouldn't I be the first to know if there was someone being fed." And that overwhelming curiosity which my father had always said should be curbed took possession of me and I longed to peep inside the Treasure Room.

I knew where it was. My mother had told me.

"Mr. Milner's apartments are on the third floor, the whole of the third floor."

I had made an excuse to go up there one afternoon when the house was quiet. I had tried all the doors, and peeped into the rooms—a bedroom, sitting room, a library; and there was one door which was locked.

And now clutching my mother's shawl, deeply aware of the darkness and silence of this part of the stairs, I forced myself to mount to the third floor.

I held the candle high. My flickering shadow on the wall looked odd and menacing. Go back, said a voice within me. You've no right here. But something stronger urged me to go on and I walked straight up to that door which had been locked and turned the handle. My heart was thumping wildly. I was expecting the door to open and myself be caught and drawn into . . . I did not know what. To my immense relief the door was still locked. Grasping my candle firmly, I fled downstairs.

What a comfort to open the door of the servants' hall, to hear Mr. Jeffers singing a ballad called *Thara* slightly out of key, to see my mother put her fingers to her lips warning me to wait till the song was finished. I stood there glad of the opportunity for my heart to stop its mad racing, laughing at my fancies, asking myself what I'd expected to find.

"You've been a long time, Jane," said my mother. "Couldn't you find the shawl?"

On the second day of the new year there took place a little incident which left a mark on my memory. Amy the housemaid was getting something from the top shelf of a cupboard and in doing so pulled down some holly.

I was in the kitchen at the time—just the two of us, and she said to me: "It's been in the way ever since it was put up and so's that on the dresser. It's time it came down. You help me, Jane."

So I held the chair while she climbed up, and when she had taken it down, I said: "It looks unfinished now. If that comes down all of it should."

So we began to take it down and as we were doing so Mrs. Couch came in. She stared at us in horror.

"What are you doing?" she cried.

"The dratted stuff was in the way," said Amy. "And Christmas has come and gone so it's time it was down."

"Time it was down. Don't you know nothing, Amy Clint? Why, it's not to come down till Twelfth Night. Don't you know it brings terrible bad luck to take it down afore?"

Amy had turned white. I looked from one to the other. Mrs. Couch had lost her fat comfortable look; she was like a prophet of evil. Her eyes, never very big, had almost disappeared into her pudding of a face.

"Put it back quick," she said. "It may not have been noticed."

"Who might have noticed it?" I asked.

But she was too shaken to tell me.

Later when she was rocking in her chair I asked her why decorations must not come down before Twelfth Night. She said it was knowledge that was passed down from generation to generation except among the ignorant like that Amy Clint. Witches looked on it as an insult.

"Why? What have they got to do with Christmas?"

"There's things that can't be explained," said Mrs. Couch mysteriously. "My brother's sister-in-law was a scoffer. She took down her decorations on New Year's Day and look what happened to her."

"What?"

"She was a corpse within the year. So if that don't show, what does?"

I was not entirely convinced that Mrs. Couch's brother's sister-in-law's untimely death was connected with the taking down of Christmas decorations but it seemed unwise to express doubts.

That memorable holiday came to an end with a climax which seemed dramatic at the time.

On the 20th January I was to return to school and my mother was busily sewing name tapes on my things and preparing my trunk. She and Mr. Jeffers would drive me to the station. Mr. Jeffers said it was like old times having a young lady to be driven to school—and Cluntons' too. It was clear that he doubted the propriety of this particular young lady's going to that exclusive establishment since she was only the housekeeper's daughter, but like Mrs. Couch he was prepared to accept the fact that times had changed.

I was sorry my stay at Roland's Croft was coming to an end. Already I seemed like a part of the household. There were two things I regretted and I had hoped that there would be a miracle to bring these about: That I might look inside the Treasure Room to assure myself that it was only precious ornaments which were there, and that I should have an opportunity of seeing Mr. Sylvester Milner.

One of my mother's theories was that if you wanted something very badly and you believed you would get it, you would, providing you did everything in your power to achieve that end. "Faith and determination," she used to say. "And one is as important as the other."

It would be summer holidays before I saw Roland's Croft again, for it was too far to come home for the few days at Easter. And I had not seen Mr. Sylvester Milner nor the inside of his Treasure Room.

About five days before I was due to leave for school, there was an intimation that Mr. Sylvester Milner would soon return. Ling Fu would precede him. It seemed the most incredible bad luck that Mr. Milner should be coming back two days after I had left for school. However I should at least see his mysterious servant.

I watched from a window and was rather disappointed to see a small man alight from the trap. He looked up at the house as though he knew he was being watched and I jumped back. He could not have seen me of course but I had that guilty feeling eavesdroppers get. I just caught a glimpse of his Oriental features. I was disappointed that he should be in European dress and did not have a pig-tail.

He changed his costume in the house though; there he wore shiny alpaca trousers and a loose kind of tunic; his slippers had silver markings on them and turned up slightly at the toes. He looked more Oriental thus.

"Creep creep creep about the house," complained Mrs.

Couch. "You never know where he is. What's wrong with a good English valet? Tell me that?"

He interested me although he rarely looked my way; and two days before I left for school I saw from my window that the curtains of the Treasure Room had been drawn right back so I knew he was in there.

The urge was irresistible. I could go up to the third floor. I would have to make up some excuse for being there if I were discovered. I wanted to see the view from the upper windows? Would that do? I was too impatient to waste time thinking of a better excuse.

Stealthily I mounted the staircase. The house had that quietness which was so noticeable beyond the first floor. Up I went to Mr. Sylvester Milner's apartments. My mother had had them all specially cleaned so that they would be ready for his return and there was a smell of the polish she herself made and which she insisted was the best and should always be used—a mixture of beeswax and turpentine. And there was the Treasure Room—and the door was open.

My heart began to beat very fast. I paused on the threshold and peeped in. There was no one there. I took a step into the room. It was true there were beautiful figures everywhere. Some were large, some small. There were vases beautifully colored and several Buddhas in what I supposed to be jade. I gazed in fascination at their strange faces, some benign, some sinister. I took a few paces into the room. I was actually inside Mr. Sylvester Milner's Treasure Room!

There was a small room leading from this one in which was a sink and some cleaning materials. Just as I was peeping into it I heard footsteps. Someone was coming along the corridor! If I tried to get out I should inevitably be seen, so I stepped into the little room and waited.

To my horror I heard the door of the room shut and a gentle grating sound as though a key was being turned in a lock.

I came out into the Treasure Room and went immediately to the door. I was locked in.

I stared at the door in dismay as the implication of what this meant swept over me. I was sure it would result in dire consequences. This was the room full of precious objects. No one was allowed to go into it except Ling Fu. I, who was here under sufferance one might say, had dared break the rule, and for my sins was locked in.

I went to the window. There were bars across it. To protect the treasure I supposed. Perhaps I could attract someone's attention. I desperately hoped it would be my mother's. There was no one in the grounds. I went to the door and was about to rap on it when I hesitated. The only person I wanted to open that door was my mother. I felt it would be very embarrassing indeed to face Ling Fu and tell him that I had pried into the room when he was not there. I imagined that he had slipped away for a few seconds into one of the rooms on this floor and by a quirk of fate I had come along precisely at that time.

I looked round the room. It was true then that Mr. Sylvester Milner was a merchant and this was his merchandise. There was no great mystery such as I had imagined. I knew nothing of these things but ignorant as I was I could not help but be impressed by their beauty. They were very valuable I was sure, but I was a little disappointed because I had hoped this room contained some dark secret which would give me a clue to the character of Mr. Sylvester Milner. But it was just as they had said —it was his storeroom of treasures and because they were so valuable he did not want the room left open to the servants, and so entrusted them to the care of Ling Fu who perhaps because he was Chinese understood something of their value.

It was an anticlimax and my curiosity had merely placed me in a difficult position. How could I get out of this room without betraying my indiscretion? If my mother discovered me she would be horrified but she understood how I had always found it impossible to curb my curiosity. I should be hustled out and warned never to do such a thing again. But how could I attract her attention? I went to the window. Those bars made me feel like a prisoner; I tried the door again. Then I looked round the room for inspiration, and I almost forgot my dilemma in the contemplation of those beautiful things. There was the figure of a woman carved in ivory; she was so tall and graceful, so beautiful that I felt overawed. I went to examine her more intently. Her features were finely etched and the expression so lifelike that I felt she was watching me. I did not greatly care for the obese Buddhas with their baleful eyes. There was one huge one in what might have been bronze. He was not fat, he was seated on a lotus flower; his eyes were malevolent and wherever I looked I felt they followed me.

I would have to get out of here. They might be only valuable pieces of stone, bronze, and ivory but there was a certain alien quality about them which fitted in with everything I had ever felt about the house.

I should not like to be in this room when darkness fell. I had a silly notion that then all these seemingly inanimate objects would come to life; it was these—and their master Mr. Sylvester Milner—who had brought that strangeness into the house.

How to get out? I was again at the window. Someone might come into the garden. Oh let it be my mother, I prayed. But even if it were one of the maids I could attract her attention. It was hardly likely to be Mrs. Couch who rarely stirred from the house. Whoever it was I would be grateful and humbly confess my curiosity.

I went to the door, passing the bronze Buddha with the evil eyes. They seemed to sneer as they followed me. I turned the handle. I shook the door. I beat on it and called out in sudden panic: "I'm locked in."

There was no answer.

Memories of my childhood came back to me. How

many times had I been told "Curiosity killed the cat."
And I could hear my mother's recounting the fate of
Meddlesome Matty who lifted the teapot lid to see what
was within.

I had been wrong to come in here. I knew it was forbidden. It was, as my mother would tell me, abusing hos-
pitality. I had been graciously allowed to stay here and I
had behaved with ill grace. I was as bad as Meddlesome
Matty and the Curious Cat. Both had suffered for their
curiosity and so should I.

I tried to be calm. I looked once more at the beautiful
objects. My attention was momentarily caught by a collection of sticks in a jade container. I supposed them to
be made of ivory. I counted them. There were forty-nine
of them. I wondered what they were.

I went into the small adjoining room and examined it. I
opened a cupboard door and saw brushes, dusters, and a
long coat which presumably Ling Fu wore for cleaning.
There was a chair and I sat down on this and stared de-
spondently at my feet.

From below I heard the sound of horse's hoofs and I
ran to the window. That was the carriage coming round
from the coach house and Jeffers was taking it down the
drive.

I went back to the chair and asked myself how I could
get out of this place.

I didn't care that I should be caught. I only wanted to
get out. I called at the top of my voice. No one answered.
The walls were thick and people rarely came to the third
floor.

I was beginning to get frightened particularly as twilight, which came early on these winter afternoons, would
soon descend. It must have been just after three when I
tiptoed into this room. It would now be past four.

My mother would not miss me yet but later she
would . . .

I started to imagine what would happen to me. How

often did Ling Fu come to the room? Not every day.
Then I should be locked away like the bride in the Mistletoe Bough. They would find nothing but my skeleton.
But before that I would have to face a night alone with
that leering bronze Buddha. Some of the other pieces
made me feel uncomfortable too. Even now when the
shadows were beginning to fall they seemed to be changing subtly. And when it was dark . . . The idea of being in
the darkness with such objects sent me to hammer on the
door.

I tried to think what was the best thing to do. From the
window I could see the wintry sun low in the sky. In half
an hour it would have disappeared.

I hammered on the door again. There was no response.
They would miss me soon, I consoled myself. My mother
would be anxious. Mrs. Couch would sit in her rocking
chair and talk of the terrible things that could happen to
lost girls.

The room was filling with shadows; I was very much
aware of the silence. The shapes of the ornaments seemed
to change and I tried in vain to divert my eyes from the
bronze Buddha. For a moment those eyes seemed to
flicker. It was almost as though the lids came down over
them. Before it had seemed merely mocking; now it was
malevolent.

My imagination grew wilder. Mr. Sylvester Milner was
a wizard. He was a Pygmalion who breathed life into
these objects. They were not what they seemed—pieces of
stone and bronze. There was a living spirit within each
one of them—an evil spirit.

The light was getting more and more dim. Some impulse made me pick up the ivory sticks. I stared at them
in concentration trying to think how I could get out of
this room before it was completely dark.

Then I heard a sound. For the first time in my life I felt
the hair lift from my scalp. I stood very still, the ivory
sticks in my hand.

The door was slowly opening. I saw a flickering light. On the threshold of the room stood a figure. For the moment I thought the bronze Buddha had materialized, then I saw that it was only a man standing there.

In his hand he carried a candlestick in which was a lighted candle. He held it high so that the light flickered on his face—a strange face, blank of expression. On his head was a round velvet cap the same mulberry shade as his jacket.

He was staring straight at me.

"Who are you?" he asked imperiously.

"I'm Jane Lindsay," I answered and my voice sounded high pitched. "I was locked in."

He shut the door behind him, advanced into the room and came close to me.

"Why are you holding the yarrow sticks?" he asked.

I looked down at the ivory pieces in my hand. "I . . . I don't know." A terrible horror had come to me because I knew that my second wish had been granted; I was face to face with Mr. Sylvester Milner.

He took the sticks from me and to my amazement set them out on a small table which was inlaid with what I learned was ivory. He seemed absorbed by this—more interested in the sticks than in me. Then he looked at me intently.

"H'm," he murmured.

I stammered: "I'm sorry. The door was open and I looked in . . . and then before I knew what had happened someone came and locked it."

"This room is kept locked," he said. "Why did you think that was?"

"Because these things are valuable, I suppose."

"And you appreciate fine objects of art?"

I hesitated. I felt I could not tell him an untruth for he would know immediately.

"I'm sure I should if I knew about them."

He nodded. "But you are inquisitive."

"Yes, I suppose I am."

"You must not come in here without permission. That is forbidden. Go now."

As I walked past I glanced sideways at the ivory sticks laid on the table. I had a terrible fear that he would seize me by the hair as I passed and turn me into one of the figures. I would disappear strangely and no one would know what had become of me.

But nothing of the sort happened. I was out in the corridor. I ran to my room and shut the door. I looked at myself in the mirror. My cheeks were scarlet, my hair more untidy than usual and my eyes brilliant. I felt as though I had had an uncanny adventure.

My mother came into my room.

"Wherever have you been, Jane? I've been looking for you everywhere. Your trunk is almost ready."

I hesitated. Then I thought I had better confess the truth.

"I think, Mother," I said, "that I have met Mr. Sylvester Milner."

"He came back a short while ago. Did you see him from your window?"

"I saw him in the Treasure Room."

"What!" she cried.

As I told her what had happened she grew pale. "Oh Jane," she said, "how could you! When everything was going so well. This will be the end. I shall be asked to leave."

I was very contrite. She had worked so hard and my curiosity had destroyed our chances even as the cat's had killed it.

"I didn't mean anything wrong."

How often in the past had I said those words. "I just thought . . . a quick look and out again. You see, the way they talked about the Treasure Room I didn't think it could just be things, ordinary things. I thought there must be something mysterious . . ."

My mother wasn't listening. She was, I knew, thinking of packing and leaving in a month's time and the weary business of finding a post would begin again. And where could she ever find anything as suitable as that which she had held at Roland's Croft?

It was a melancholy drive to the station two days later with Jeffers and my mother. She was hourly expecting a summons from Mr. Sylvester Milner. I looked back at the portico and the Chinese dogs and thought: I shall never see those again. My summer holidays would be spent somewhere else.

I shared my mother's melancholy and mine was even greater than hers for it was heavy with guilt.

She embraced me warmly. "Never mind, Janey," she said. "It's over and done with. I daresay your father will find something else for us . . . perhaps even better."

I nodded gloomily. There could not be for me a more fascinating place than Roland's Croft, with its cosy kitchen and servants' hall and its eerie Treasure Room and most of all perhaps its strange owner.

With every post I waited to hear that we had received our congé.

Nothing happened.

Then my mother wrote and said: "Mr. Sylvester Milner never mentioned finding you in the Treasure Room. It seems to have slipped his memory. That's something to be grateful for and if I hear nothing of it from him by the summer when you'll be coming for your holidays it must be all right."

We did hear nothing, and I prepared to go to Roland's Croft for the summer holidays.

The three wishes I had made with the silver sixpence had all come true.

II

Those summer holidays were spent at Roland's Croft and the next too so that I had come to regard it as my home. They were my family—Mrs. Couch in her rocking chair, Mr. Catterwick king of the pantry and stiff with dignity, Amy and Jess who began to confide in me about their love affairs. The excitement when holidays approached never diminished and I loved it all—the forest which I insisted was haunted, the garden with its beautiful laid-out lawns, well-kept paths and flower beds and copse of firs on the forest's edge; the meals round the big table, the chatter, the gossip and the recounting of the grandeur of other houses and the old days in Roland's Croft when the Family was there.

For me there was in addition the third floor of the house where the treasures were and where Mr. Sylvester Milner and his servant Ling Fu had their quarters.

There was a change in the house when Mr. Sylvester Milner was there and it was far more exciting. Then there were dinner parties and bustle in the kitchen. People stayed in the guests' rooms—merchants who consumed large quantities of food and drank a good deal of wine. Mrs. Couch and Mr. Catterwick enjoyed these occasions. It was what a house should be. Mrs. Couch liked to work herself up into a state of excitement over the dinner and Mr. Catterwick enjoyed letting us know how great was his knowledge of wines.

After a dinner party we would all sit round the big table and hear from Jess and Mr. Catterwick what the guests were like. Mr. Catterwick often reported that there was a lot of high-flown talk and he couldn't understand half of it and Jess said that in some houses you'd get some exciting scandal. It was more interesting than talk about a lot of vases and figures and what was happening in outlandish places.

I wished that I could hide myself under the table and listen. For there was no doubt in my mind that the most interesting person in the house was Mr. Sylvester Milner.

Sometimes when I was in the gardens I would look up to the barred window and I often fancied I saw a shadow there. Once I saw him quite clearly. He stood still looking down and I stood looking up. I began to get the impression that he was watching *me*.

This thought began to obsess me. He had never mentioned to my mother that he had discovered me in his Treasure Room. She had said that she thought it very understanding of him, though she did wish he had put her mind at rest at that time. She began to feel confident that we were safe here. But in a year or so I should be leaving school and the problem would then arise as to what I should do.

The girls at Cluntons' were destined to have London seasons, when they would attend balls and no doubt in due course find husbands. My circumstances were very different. My mother said that perhaps my father's family would after all realize their duty and come forward to launch me, but she said it halfheartedly, and although her outlook was optimistic she always believed in making provisions.

"You will be an extremely well-educated girl," she said. "There are few schools to compare with Cluntons' and if we can keep you there until your eighteenth birthday you will have had as good an education as any young lady could have." I was nearly seventeen years old; we had a year to consider.

"We owe a lot to the grace of Mr. Sylvester Milner," I said.

My mother agreed that it had been a good day for us when she had answered that advertisement. It was true that nothing could have happened to change our lives so

completely and since we must live without my father, this
was the best possible way to do it. It was as though we
lived within a large family and there was always something of interest going on.

It was when I came home for the summer holidays
during which I would be seventeen that my mother appeared to be excited about something. She met me at the
station in the jingle, she herself driving Pan the pony.

I was always thrilled when the train drew into the little
station with the name Rolandsmere colorfully displayed in
geraniums, pansies, lobelias, and yellow alyssum. There
was lavender and mignonette bordering the bed in which
the name had been planted and their delicious perfume
filled the air.

I noticed that my mother was suppressing some excitement and that what had happened was good. She embraced me with the usual warmth and we settled into the
jingle. As she took the reins I asked how everyone was at
Roland's Croft and she told me that Mrs. Couch had
baked a welcome home cake for me and had talked of little else but my return for days and that even Mr. Catterwick had said that he hoped the weather would be fine for
me. Amy and Jess were well but Jess was far too friendly
with Jeffers and Mrs. Jeffers did not like that at all. Amy
was being courted by the unmarried gardener and it
looked as if they might make a match of it which would
be good, for they wouldn't lose Amy then.

"And Mr. Sylvester Milner?"

"He's home."

She was silent. So her excitement had something to do
with him.

"He is well?" I asked.

She did not answer and I cried in sudden fear: "Mother, everything's all right, isn't it? He's not sending us
away."

It was a long time since he had discovered me in his
Treasure Room, but perhaps he liked to keep people in

suspense for a long time. I had thought he must be a kind man, but I had always felt him to be inscrutable. Perhaps he had only pretended to be kind.

"No," she said. "Far from it. He has been talking to me."

"What about?"

"About you."

"Because I went into the Treasure Room . . ."

"He is interested in you. He is a very kind gentleman, Jane. He asked me how long you would stay at school. I said that the young ladies of your father's family had left Cluntons' when they were eighteen and that I hoped you would do the same. He said: 'And then?' "

"What did you tell him?"

"I said we should have to wait and see. He asked me if your father's family had provided for you in any way. I told him they ignored this duty and he said that he thought that you must be considering taking a post of some sort when you left school. He said: 'Your daughter will have the education to teach others. Perhaps this is what you have in mind for her.' "

I shuddered. "I don't want to think of that," I said. "I want to go on like this forever . . . going to school and coming home to Roland's Croft."

"You've taken to this place, Janey."

"I was excited by it the moment I saw it. There's the forest and the Treasure Room and Mrs. Couch and all of them, and of course Mr. Sylvester Milner."

"He wants to talk to you, Jane."

"Why?"

"He didn't tell me."

"How . . . strange! What does it mean?"

"I don't know. But I believe your father knows how anxious I am about the future. I believe he is doing something about it."

"Do you think he forgave me for trespassing?"

"You were young. I think he forgave that."

"But he is so . . . strange."

"Yes," said my mother slowly, "he is a strange man. You never know what he's thinking. It could be quite different from what he's saying. But I think he's a kind man."

"When am I to see him?"

"He wants you to take tea with him tomorrow."

"Do you think he's going to tell me he doesn't want inquisitive people in his house?"

"It couldn't be that after all this time."

"I'm not so sure. He might like to keep people on tenterhooks. It's a kind of torture."

"We haven't been on tenterhooks. I never gave the matter a thought after those Christmas holidays."

"I'm not sure. I often thought he was watching me."

"Janey. You're imagining again."

"No. I saw him twice at his window when I was in the garden."

"Now don't start working up one of your fantasies. Be patient and wait till you see him tomorrow."

"It's hard because tomorrow seems a long way off."

Young Ted Jeffers came out and took the jingle round to the stables. I went into the kitchen. Mrs. Couch wiped her floury arms on a towel and embraced me. "Amy," she called. "Jess. She's here." And there they were, so pleased to see me and telling me I'd grown and would have to get more color in my cheeks and was quite the young lady.

"Now she's here we'll have the tea so don't stand gaping," said Mrs. Couch.

It was certainly coming home. There was Mrs. Couch's pride with WELCOME HOME, JANE pink icing letters on white icing, and her special potato cakes and Chelsea buns, all my favorites well remembered.

"They say it's going to be a hot summer," said Mrs. Couch. "All the signs. Not too much sun, I hope. It's bad for the fruit. Then I shan't be able to get my plums the right flavor. Last year's sloe gin has come up better than ever and the elderberry's ready for tasting."

There was a slight change in everyone—Amy was flushed with a kind of radiance because the gardener was planning as she told me later "to make her his own"; Jess had a glitter in her eyes and she and Jeffers flashed secret messages to each other. Mr. Catterwick unbent for a moment to say it was like the old days to have someone home to the house from Cluntons', and I felt happy to be there.

After tea I went to the stables to look at Grundel the pony which Mr. Sylvester Milner had allowed me to ride the last time I was here.

"She's been waiting for you, Miss Jane," said the young boy whom Mr. Jeffers was training as a groom. And as she nuzzled up against me, I believed she had.

Then I took my usual walk through the copse to the enchanted forest and I thought how wonderful it all was and that I had come to love this place. And all the time at the back of my mind was the thought: Tomorrow I shall see him. Perhaps he will tell me what he really thinks of me, why he did not forbid me the house after I had behaved so badly as to trespass in his secret room; why he watched me—as I was sure he did—from the windows of his apartments.

The next day I was ready about an hour before I was due to go to his sitting room. I had combed my hair and tied it back with a red ribbon. I put on the best gown I possessed. My father had chosen it for me a few months before he died. It had been my birthday present and I recalled the September day when we had gone to buy it. It was light navy in color with small scarlet silk-covered buttons down the front. It was my favorite dress, and my father had said it became me well.

My mother came into my room, a slight frown between her eyes.

"Oh, you're ready, Jane. Yes, that's right. You look neat."

"What should he want to say to me, Mother?"

"You will know soon enough, Jane. Be careful."

"What do you mean?"

"Don't forget that we owe all this to him."

"You work hard here. I daresay he is glad to have you."

"He could find another housekeeper easily. Don't forget he has allowed you to come here, to live here, almost as a member of the family. Not many would have done that and I can't imagine what *we* should have done but for that."

"I'll remember," I said.

"Are you ready?" I nodded and together we mounted the stairs to his apartment.

My mother rapped on the door. His rather high-pitched voice bade us enter.

He was seated in a chair wearing his mulberry velvet coat and smoking cap. He rose as we entered. "Come in, Mrs. Lindsay," he said.

"Here is my daughter," she said unnecessarily, for his eyes were already on me.

He nodded.

"Thank you, Mrs. Lindsay." Then to me, "Pray sit down, Miss Lindsay."

My mother stood hesitantly for a moment and then left us. I took the chair that he indicated and he sat down in the one he was occupying as we entered.

"I have been aware of you since you came to my house," he said.

"Yes," I answered.

"So you knew."

"I thought I saw you looking at me from your windows."

He smiled. My frankness seemed to amuse him.

"How old are you, Miss Lindsay?"

"I shall be seventeen in September."

"It's not a very great age is it?"

"In a year I shall be eighteen."

"Ah, that is what we are coming to. Now we will have some tea." He clapped his hands and as if by magic Ling Fu appeared.

Mr. Sylvester Milner said something to him in what I later learned was Cantonese. Ling Fu bowed and was gone.

"You think it strange that I should have a Chinese servant, Miss Lindsay, because you have never known anyone to have a Chinese servant before. Is that so?" He did not wait for an answer. "The fact is it is not strange at all. It is very natural. I spend a great deal of my life in China —in Hong Kong chiefly and there it is normal to be Chinese. I have a house there. You will have heard that I am away from this house for months at a time. Well then I am in my other house. What do you know of Hong Kong, Miss Lindsay?"

I racked my brains. I did not want to appear to be an ignoramus. I desperately wanted to seem intelligent in his eyes. I felt this was very necessary to my future. "I believe it is an island off the coast of China. It is a British protectorate I think."

He nodded. "The British flag," he said, "was first hoisted at Possession Point in January 1841. The island was merely a barren point then. There was hardly a house on it. That has changed in forty-five years. It is very different now. The end of the Opium War put us in possession as it were. What do you know of the Opium War, Miss Lindsay?"

I said I knew nothing.

"You will have to learn. I think you will find it interesting. We are a great trading nation. How do you think we have become great? We became great through trade. Never despise it. It brings the good life to so many. I doubt not you have noble ideas of the flag, eh. It floats

over Canada, India, Hong Kong . . . and that makes you
proud. But who put the flag there? The traders, Miss
Lindsay. That is something you must never lose sight of.
China went to war with us in 1840, forty-six years ago,
because we supplied opium which we brought from India
to China. We were wrong you would say. We introduced
many to the drug. Yes, it was wrong. It was bad trade but
even that brought work and wealth to some. One of the
things you will have to learn is that there is never only
one side to any question. There are always many. Life
would be very simple if there were but one. We should all
know exactly what to do because there would be the right
and the wrong. But nothing is wholly right nothing wholly
wrong. That is why we make our blunders. Here is the
tea."

The teapot was blue with a gold dragon engraved on it,
the cups were of the same design. Silently Ling Fu disappeared. Mr. Sylvester Milner poured out the tea.

"China tea, Miss Lindsay. So much in this house has a
Chinese flavor as I am sure with your desire for knowledge you have already discovered."

He handed me a cup of tea and from a barrel with the
same blue and gold dragon design a finger of a biscuit
which tasted of honey and nuts. I did not believe it was
Mrs. Couch's making.

"I trust the tea is to your liking."

I said it was, although it was very different from the
thick brew which was served in Mrs. Couch's kitchen.

"I have been going back and forth to China since I was
fifteen years old, Miss Lindsay, a little younger than you
are now. That is thirty years ago. A lifetime . . . when one
is seventeen, eh?"

"It seems a very long time."

"One can learn a great deal in thirty years. I am a
merchant. My father was a merchant before me. I in due
course inherited his business. I have never married so I
have no son to follow me. Every man hopes for a son.

Every king wants an heir. The King is dead, Long live the King, eh Miss Lindsay."

"That is certainly so."

"I know that you will have deduced by now that I am forty-five years of age." There was a slight twinkle in his eyes. "A young lady as eager for knowledge as yourself would immediately have seen that. Pray do not feel uncomfortable. I have no patience with the incurious. What can they learn about life and what can anyone know without learning? I am going to confide in you because you are interested in everything around you. You could not resist looking into the forbidden room. Well, Miss Lindsay, you are Eve. You have eaten of the tree of knowledge and now must take the consequences."

For a moment I thought he was going to tell me we were dismissed, and this was after all a kind of slow torture. I had read somewhere that the Chinese practiced this and as he had talked so much about China, this could be his way of telling me.

His next words dispersed that fear. "You and I, I believe, could be very useful to each other."

"How, Mr. Milner?" I asked.

"I am coming to that. I am a merchant whose business is to buy and sell. During my visits to China and my travels throughout the world and in this country I discover rare and valuable objects. I sell them all over the world. I have many collectors who are waiting to see what I have discovered. You have peeped into my little museum. Some of these pieces are worth a great deal of money. Some I sell at a large profit, others for a small profit, and some I cannot bear to part with. My collection necessarily changes. Sometimes it is more valuable than at others, but it is always worth a great deal of money. But at all times it represents business. What pleasure there is in handling these beautiful objects it may well be that you will one day understand. Allow me to refill your cup."

He did so and I ate more of the honey and nut fingers. He smiled at me with what I felt to be approval.

"I see that you are . . . adaptable," he said. "That is good.

"Now I come to the purpose of this meeting. I need a secretary. Now when I say a secretary I do not mean someone who will merely write at my dictation. It is more than that I need. I need someone who is prepared to learn something about the goods I handle. You see, the person I am looking for would have to have very special qualities. Do you begin to understand me?" he asked.

"I think so."

"And what do you think of this proposition?"

I could not hide my excitement. "I could learn, you mean, about these precious things, I could really be of use to you?"

He nodded. "I have been talking to your mother about your future. When I found you in my showroom you were holding the yarrow sticks. Do you know what yarrow sticks are?"

"No. But I remember the sticks."

"They fascinated you, I expect. They tell the future to those who can understand their message. They told me that your life was in some way linked with mine."

"These sticks told you that. But how . . . ?"

"When you have learned more of the ways of the East you will not be skeptical. The power of yarrow sticks has been known for thousands of years. I laid out the sticks after you had gone and I was looking to see how significant your presence was going to be in this house. Was it to be of importance? The answer was Yes."

"A sort of fortune telling," I said.

He smiled at me. "I think you will be an apt pupil."

"When shall I start?"

"When you have finished with your education. That will be in a year or so. In the meantime I wish you to study the books I will give you. They will teach you how to recognize great works of art."

"I shall come home for my holidays as I've been doing, shall I? And learn here?"

"In this house," he said. "You shall have a key to my showroom. You will study the objects there and learn how to recognize value. You will learn too something of how my business is conducted. Your mother has told me that there is no provision for you from your father's family and it will be necessary for you to earn a living. As what? A governess? A companion? What else is there for a young lady of our times? This will be different. I offer you a chance to learn, a look into the fascinating world of Art. What do you say?"

"I say I want to do this, I want to do it very much indeed. Couldn't I leave school and start now?"

He laughed. "Now that would not be possible. First you must finish your education. Then you have an apprenticeship to serve. Fortunately that apprenticeship can be served while you are still at school. In your holidays you can study the books I give you to read and you can see some of the most wonderful treasures to come out of China."

"I knew it was a lucky day when we came here. It is going to be wonderful."

"You cannot look too far into the future," he said. "I must tell you that I am the head of a very successful and profitable business. You know the nature of it. I buy and sell. Because of my knowledge of Art and of the country from which it comes I know how to buy at the right prices. And those who are interested in building up valuable collections know they can trust me. My father was a great trader; he ranged the world but was more often in China. He left the business to his sons of whom I was the eldest. We should have worked amicably together but there were differences and we split up. We became to a certain extent rivals, which was inevitable. I was the more successful. It was a somewhat uneasy situation. I don't think my brother Redmond ever got over his disappointment that I was the one to whom my father bequeathed The House of a Thousand Lanterns."

"The House of a Thousand Lanterns!" I echoed.

He smiled. "Ah, I see the name arouses your interest. It is intriguing, is it not? It is the name of my house in Hong Kong."

"Does it really contain a thousand lanterns?"

"There are lanterns in each room. There must have been a thousand there at some time for it to have been so named."

"That is a great many lanterns. It must be a big house."

"It is. It was presented to my grandfather for some great service he did to a highly placed mandarin."

"It sounds like something out of the Arabian Nights," I said.

"Except," he answered, "that this is Chinese."

I knew that my eyes were shining with excitement. I felt that he had opened a door to me and that I was looking into a strange exotic world.

I said: "I long to begin learning."

That pleased him. "I like your impatience, and your curiosity. They are what I need. But you have to learn, of course. It may well be that when you have seen how much there is to learn you will not wish to continue. You have a year before you need decide."

"I have decided," I answered firmly.

He was pleased. "If you have finished tea I will take you to my showroom. As I have said, you shall have a key and go there when you will. Study what you see there. Compare these things with replicas and pictures you will see in the books I give you. Note their grace, learn how to discover the period in which a piece was created. Some of the objects are not merely hundreds of years old but thousands. Come with me now and we will go to the showroom."

I followed him and he unlocked the door and once more I was in that room.

My eyes immediately went to the bronze Buddha which had struck me as being malevolent and which had frightened me so much when I was locked in this room.

His gaze followed mine. "You noticed that?" he said. "It's a fine piece. I could never bring myself to part with it. It dates back to the third or the fourth century A.D. At that time Buddhist missionaries from India came to China. You will read about this in your history. They came traveling in caravans and sometimes on foot. They traveled for years and as they passed across Asia they rested for a while and carved shrines where they could worship during their brief sojourns. It was during the T'ang Dynasty that Buddhism reached its highest influence in China and it was at this time that this image was made."

"How very old it must be."

He smiled at me. "Old by English standards. By Chinese . . ." He shrugged his shoulders.

"There is something evil about it," I said. "The eyes follow you."

"Oh, that is the skill of the artist."

"It seems to have some living quality."

"All great Art has. Look at this. This is a figure of Kuan Yin, the goddess of mercy and compassion. Do you not think that is a beautiful piece?"

It was the figure of a woman sitting on a rock; she was carved in wood and painted with exquisite colors and gold leaf.

"It is said that she hears all cries for help," he said. "Now she would be of the Yuan Dynasty which was the thirteenth and fourteenth century."

"How valuable these things must be!"

He laid a hand momentarily on my arm. "That is so. That is why I will not sell some of them. You will have to learn about the various dynasties and what art was produced during them. A good deal of study will be necessary and then when you leave school at the appropriate time you will be ready to take over your duties."

He showed me some scrolls with delicate landscapes painted on them.

"That is an art to be absorbed over many years," he said. "You must not take too big a bite at first. I will send a book for you to read and we will have tea again together very soon. Then I shall tell you more."

I said very earnestly: "I want so much to learn."

I went straight to my mother who was waiting in my bedroom for me to come.

She looked at me anxiously and I flung myself into her arms.

"The most wonderful thing has happened," I told her. "I am going to learn about Chinese Art and his collection. I am going to work with him. He is going to train me."

My mother withdrew herself and held me at arm's length. "What's all this?"

"That's why he wanted to see me. He liked my curiosity. I'm going to learn, I'm going to be his secretary . . . no, his assistant! I shall learn until I leave school and then I shall know a great deal and I shall work with him."

"Tell me properly Jane, please. No imagination now."

"It's true. I'm going to learn. The future is assured. No governessing. I shall not be a companion to some horrid old woman. I am going to learn about China and I'm going to work with Mr. Sylvester Milner."

When my mother realized that this was indeed so, she said: "Your father has arranged this. I knew he was looking after us."

I brought all my enthusiasm to the new project. During those summer holidays I read voraciously. I spent a great deal of time in what I ceased to call the Treasure Room. It was now the showroom. I was very proud to be the only one in the house apart from Ling Fu and Mr. Milner who had a key. I occasionally took tea with Mr. Milner; we were becoming good friends.

The household regarded me with a kind of awe. Although I had been accepted with affection in the servants' hall they now conceded that I was not quite one of them. It was true I had all the time been attending Cluntons' but now Mr. Sylvester Milner himself had selected me for special attention.

My mother blossomed in her gratification. She would watch me, her head a little on one side, her lips pursed and sometimes they moved as though she were talking to my father. I knew she did when she was alone. I heard her say once when I came upon her unexpectedly, "Well, we didn't do so badly without the high and mighty Lindsays." She was sure that she shared her pleasure and pride with my father. Mr. Sylvester Milner was the fairy godfather who had swept away our anxiety with a wave of his magic wand.

What golden days they were! I spent hours lying in the fir copse, a book propped up before me while I was conveyed right back into the past. "Begin as early as you can," Mr. Sylvester Milner advised me.

I read of the Shang and Chou Dynasties and the coming of Confucius who with his disciples compiled books which related the traditions and customs of his times. I skimmed through the Tsin and Han Dynasties to the Yuen and the Ming and learned of a civilization far more ancient than our own.

Knowing a little I was able to assess the vases and ornaments more easily and to understand what they expressed, and the more I learned the more fascinated I became. By the end of that summer I was dedicated and it was with great regret that I went back to school for the winter term.

If I was interested in a subject I could always excel at it and now what I wanted most of all was to leave school and to start my new work. I applied myself to lessons but I was remote from the world of schoolgirls. Their little comedies and dramas seemed childish to me; I was not exactly unpopular but I was aloof and my yearning to leave became intense.

I decided that when I went home—as I began to think of Roland's Croft—I would ask if I might not leave at once and not wait until my eighteenth year.

That Christmas, to my great disappointment, Mr. Milner was away. It was spent much as it had been the previous year, but I was no longer so excited by the decorating of the tree and the hall, and tasting of the pudding.

I spent a good deal of the time in the showroom and I fancied that the expression on the face of the bronze Buddha had changed and that there was a veiled approval in the long sly eyes.

I was reading more than ever and had Mr. Milner's permission to borrow any of the books in what he called his Chinese Library. This was a very small room leading from his study. I made good use of this.

Something unpleasant did happen that Christmas. So immersed was I in my own affairs, that I did not attach much significance to it at the time. My mother and I were walking in the forest and she was speaking of her very favorite topic, how glad she was that Mr. Sylvester Milner had taken such a fancy to me. Suddenly she said, "One moment, Janey. You go too fast for me." She sat down on a tree trunk and as I looked at her I noticed how flushed her cheeks seemed. She had always been highly colored but never quite so as then and I fancied she had grown thinner.

It occurred to me then that she looked different. I sat down beside her and said: "Are you all right?"

"Just a bit of a cold," she said. "It'll pass."

I gave the matter no further thought but on Christmas morning when I went in to give her her Christmas present she was not yet up. That was unusual for she was usually astir early.

"Happy Christmas," I said. She woke up suddenly and smiled at me and then she put her hand on her pillow. It was as though she were trying to hide something.

I was puzzled but soon she was smiling and I was so excited because it was Christmas morning that I forgot the incident.

Later when we talked about my future she thought it was an excellent idea for me to speed up my schooling.

"The sooner you begin with Mr. Sylvester Milner the better," she said.

But Mr. Sylvester Milner thought I should complete my education and it was not until I came home for the summer term in July that I left school forever. I was still only seventeen and would be eighteen in the following September. My duties with Mr. Sylvester Milner had begun.

I was completely absorbed. Each morning I would spend an hour with him when he would dictate letters which I would write out for him. I had developed a good copperplate style for this purpose. I took a great pride in being able to spell the names of the various dynasties without asking him, and as my knowledge increased the more interesting everything became.

Once he showed me a beautiful vase he had acquired and asked me to place it. I was about three hundred years out but he was pleased with me. "You have much to learn, Miss Jane," he said, "but you are overcoming that obstacle of ignorance."

I began to learn something not only of the Art of the Chinese and their history but of Mr. Sylvester Milner too. He had been the eldest of three brothers; they had all been involved in their father's business, although the youngest of them, Magnus, had had little inclination for it.

"It's not a profession one can follow with success unless there is complete dedication," explained Mr. Milner. "I and my brother Redmond had that dedication, but we found it difficult to work together. There was so much that we could not agree on and after my father died, we separated. Redmond died of a heart attack quite recently, but he has a son, Adam, who continues with his business. In a way we are business rivals." Mr. Milner looked regretful. "Adam is a good worker and quite an authority on many aspects of the business—a serious young man, very different in temperament from his father. I have two nephews, Miss Lindsay—Adam and Joliffe."

"Are they brothers?"

"No. Joliffe is the son of my youngest brother, Magnus. Magnus married a young actress. He tried to join in her profession but without much success. Nothing Magnus did was ever very successful. He and his wife were killed together when the horses drawing a carriage which he was driving ran amuck. Joliffe was only eight years old at the time. Now he is another of my business rivals." He sighed. "Ah, Joliffe!" he went on. I waited to hear more but he seemed to have decided that he had told me enough.

Mrs. Couch mentioned Joliffe one day. She sat in her rocking chair and said: "Oh, that Joliffe. There's a one for you."

Her eyes sparkled and she became almost coy. " 'My goodness Master Joliffe,' I said to him, 'you don't think you're going to get round me like you do the young ladies, do you?' And he came back at me, 'Well, you are a young lady at heart, Mrs. Couch.' Saucy! Never without his answer!"

"He comes here then?"

"Yes, now and then. Unannounced. Mr. Sylvester Milner don't like it. He's what you'd call a precise gentleman. Of course, being his brother's son, like, he looks on this as his home . . . one of them anyway."

Jess dimpled when she spoke of Mr. Joliffe. "You'd go a long way for him," she confided. And when his name was mentioned Mr. Jeffers looked a little scornful and muttered something about women who didn't know a rake when they saw one.

Amy said that Mr. Joliffe was not quite what you'd call handsome but when he was there you hardly ever looked at anyone else—not even them that had spoken for you. It was something in him, but you had to be careful.

Even my mother's face softened when she spoke of him. Yes, he had visited the house. He was a very charming young man and she had enjoyed looking after him on the occasions when he had come. He never stayed long though. He was restless. He rode a lot and was always on the go. She thought that since Mr. Milner had no children of his own he might be thinking of making his nephew his heir.

Mr. Sylvester Milner did mention Joliffe once or twice to me after that first time and I sensed that he did not share the opinion of the ladies.

Joliffe it seemed had a natural instinct for detecting works of Art. All the same Mr. Milner shook his head so that I knew Joliffe did not have his entire approval.

"It was my father's desire that I and my brothers should work together. Then we should have controlled a very large part of the market. And now there are three of us, rival firms, instead of working in unison. It must be that I am not an easy person to work with."

"I have not found that so."

He smiled at me well pleased. "Ah, but you, my dear Miss Jane, are in a different capacity. Both Adam and Joliffe wanted to hold the reins. That was something I couldn't allow."

There was a great deal I should have liked to know about Mr. Milner's family, but once he had told me of the existence of these relatives he became rather secretive and I realized that he had told me what he had because it was in a sense connected with the business. He talked far more about Chinese Art and what had been produced in the various dynasties.

Often he would hear of some precious object which someone wished to sell and he would travel to wherever it was. He went all over the country to see such things.

Once he came back in a state of great excitement because he believed he had made a great discovery.

He sent for tea and I presided over the dragon teapot while he told me why he was so excited.

"I have found another Kuan Yin. You remember the goddess of mercy and compassion. It is a beautiful piece, not large. It may well be that for which my father was searching. Though I believe that particular one was never allowed to go out of China. Yet . . . I cannot be sure."

"You have one already, in the showroom."

He nodded. "A beautiful piece but alas not *the* Kuan Yin. This is an image of the goddess which was made by a great artist during the Sung Dynasty. This began about nine hundred years ago. It was created at that time of great strife when civil war and bloodshed were the curse of China. Emperor Sung-kaou-tsoo was a man of many gifts; but he used these to subdue the vassal Tartars and in the battles which followed millions died. Because this was a time of great suffering the people appealed to the goddess Kuan Yin who was said to hear every cry of sorrow and distress. There is a legend that the goddess inspired the creator of this image and that she herself lives in it. Not only is it the most beautiful piece ever seen but it has a mystical quality. It is every collector's dream to find the Sung Kuan Yin."

"You think you have found it?"

He smiled at my enthusiasm. "My dear Miss Jane, four times I have hoped I found her. I have discovered the most beautiful Kuan Yins and when I have handled them I have said to myself: 'This is she. There could not be another so beautiful.' But each time I have been proved wrong. That piece you have seen is indeed a fine specimen. That is why I have kept it. But it is, alas, not *the* Kuan Yin for which we all search."

"How shall you know her when you find her?"

"When I find her! I should be the most fortunate man in my profession if I ever did so."

"And this new one . . . ?"

"I dare not hope too much, for my disappointment would be so great. So I try to calm myself."

"How will anyone recognize this image if you who are so knowledgeable cannot be sure?"

"The creator engraved somewhere on the wood of the image the word Sung, but that could be copied and was. First we must ascertain that the piece is truly of the Sung Dynasty. Then we are halfway there. But there were several copies even at that time. The artist when he had engraved the letters painted them with a paint which he alone could mix. There is a subtle difference in this paint —a faint luminosity which never fades. Many tests are necessary to ascertain whether this is the true piece. And those of course which date back to the Sung period are very valuable in themselves. But it is this particular one which every collector seeks."

"When the others are as beautiful why should one be so much more valuable?"

"You could say it is due to the legend which attaches to it. The man who finds this piece and treasures it has given refuge to the goddess—so the story goes. She will listen to his cries of distress; she will never fail to pay heed to his pleas and as she has unlimited power she will look after him for as long as she is his. You see that man will have good fortune and he will know contentment all the days of his life."

"It seems to me that it is the legend that made it valuable."

"It's true, but it is a work of great artistry as well."

"Do you really think that you have this piece?"

He smiled at me and shook his head. "Deep down in my heart no, for I have an idea that it would never be allowed to leave China. I found this in a sale in a country mansion here. No one there seemed to realize what it was. It was listed as 'Chinese Figure.' There was other *chinoiserie* there—mostly of the eighteenth and nineteenth centuries. It's an acquisition though and I shall test it."

Soon after Mr. Sylvester Milner had brought home the Kuan Yin which now stood in the showroom, he heard of two important sales somewhere in the Midlands and he decided to visit them both. He would be away for about a week he told me, and smilingly he added, "This is one of the occasions when I am pleased to have an assistant to take care of my affairs while I am away."

Ling Fu traveled with him as he often did and I had heard from some of the merchants who came to the house that Mr. Sylvester Milner's Chinese servant was becoming well known in Art circles.

I was delighted to be in charge and several times a day looked into the little sandalwood box, which I kept at the back of one of my drawers, for in this box was the key of the showroom, so fearful was I of losing it.

My greatest recreation was riding and walking, and the forest never failed to delight me. I had always loved trees —the rustle of their leaves in summer, the shifting shapes their shadows threw on the ground when the sun was shining, their arms stretching up to the sky in winter making a lacy pattern against the cold blue. But I think what fascinated me most was the history of this forest which had been made by William the Conqueror in the eleventh century and I liked to sit under a tree or on a fallen log and let myself imagine that I saw the hunters of centuries ago with their bows and arrows hunting the deer and wild boar. There was one favorite spot of mine. It was an old ruin and it must have stood thus for hundreds of years; ivy now grew over the ancient stones. The whole of one wall was still standing and part of a parapet jutted out from it. I had often used it as a shelter when I was caught in sudden rain.

This was what happened to me on this day. I had gone for my afternoon walk in the forest. The trees were thick with leaves, and it was pleasant to walk in their shade for it was a hot and sultry day. I was struck by the stillness; all the usual murmurs of the forest were silent on this day —there was a hushed heavy atmosphere. I wondered if on such a day as this William Rufus had ridden out to the hunt and had he had any premonition that he would never ride back? One account said that his body had been found inside the crumbling walls of a building from which no doubt his father had turned out the owners that it might be part of his forest, though others believed that the body of the King was found under an oak tree and that this was a ritual killing. There he had lain with the arrow in his chest—and that was the mysterious end of the man known as the Red King.

What fancies I had in the forest! I used to wonder how much of life was predestined. I remembered that even Mr. Sylvester Milner had studied the yarrow sticks. Had what he saw there made him decide to offer me the position which I had accepted? If I had not picked up those sticks at precisely the right moment would my mother and I now be asking ourselves what sort of way of earning a living I should find? Could a man such as Mr. Sylvester Milner really believe in such things?

I was thinking today about the Sung Kuan Yin and how wonderful it would be if I could be the one to discover this much sought after piece.

The stillness of the forest was unearthly. The sky was rapidly darkening. Then the forest was suddenly illuminated and away in the distance I heard the clap of thunder.

A heavy storm was about to break. Mrs. Couch was always terrified of thunder. She used to hide herself in the cupboard under the stairs which led from the servants' hall to the ground floor. She used to say: "My old granny told me it was God's anger. It was His way of showing us we'd done wrong." I tried to give her the scientific explanation but she scorned it. "That's come out of books," she said. "All very well but I prefer to believe my granny. 'Never shelter under trees,' she told me once. 'Trees is terrible things for getting struck.' "

My mother joined her voice to that. "Get wet," she would say, "but never stand under trees when there's thunder and lightning about."

The darkness made it eerie. I was aware that the storm was coming closer and I knew that it would break overhead in a few minutes and I should not have time to get out of the forest. I was, however, close to my ruin and the jutting parapet would provide some shelter until the storm was over.

I ran to it and was just in time, for the deluge had begun. While I was congratulating myself on having got to shelter in time, a man came running towards me.

A voice said: "What a storm! May I share your shelter?" His jacket was soaked and when he took off his hat a stream of water fell from it.

I noticed at once how pleasant he was to look at. As he looked up at the sky and laughed, I saw strong-looking white teeth but his most startling feature was his eyes because they were a dark blue—and his brows and short thick lashes were as black as his hair. But it was not the contrast of blue and black which was arresting, it was something in his expression. I could not analyze it in a few moments but I was definitely aware of it. For the rest he was tall and rather lean.

"It seems as though I came just in time." His eyes were

on me and I flinched a little under his gaze, which had the effect of making me wonder whether my hair was tousled and reminding me that the morning dress of sprigged cotton which I was wearing was not my most becoming.

"May I come under the parapet?"

"You will get very wet if you don't."

He came and stood beside me. I withdrew as far as I could, for he disturbed me.

"Were you taking a walk too?" he asked.

"Yes," I answered. "I often do. I love the forest. It's so beautiful."

"It's also very wet at the moment. Do you often walk here . . . alone?"

"I like to be alone."

"But a young lady on her own! Might she not meet with . . . dangers?"

"I had never thought of that."

His blue eyes seemed to be alight with laughter. "Then you should without delay."

"Should I?"

"How can you know what you will meet here?"

"I am not far from the house."

"Your home, you mean?"

"Yes, my home. In fact when the storm started I debated whether to make a dash for it or come to this place."

"I'm still surprised that you are allowed to roam here alone."

"Oh, I am well able to take care of myself."

I moved a step or two away from him.

"I didn't doubt it for a moment. So your home is near here?"

"Yes . . . it's Roland's Croft."

He nodded.

"You know it?"

"Owned by an eccentric old gentleman. Is that right?"

"Mr. Sylvester Milner is not eccentric, nor is he old. He is a very interesting man."

"But of course. You are a relative of his?"

"I work for him. My mother is the housekeeper there."

"I see."

"Do you think the storm is abating?"

"Perhaps, but it would be a mistake to leave this shelter yet. Storms have a habit of returning. One should make absolutely sure that they really are over before venturing out into them."

"And you live in this neighborhood?" I asked.

He shook his head. "I am taking a short holiday here. I was just out walking when the storm arose. I saw you through the trees making off with such resolution that I was certain you were going to a shelter. So I followed." His eyes crinkled with a kind of secret amusement. "I wonder what this place was," he went on. "Look at these walls. They must be hundreds of years old."

"I'm sure they are."

"What was here, do you think? Some sort of dwelling?"

"I think so. I believe it could have been here for nine hundred years."

"You could well be right."

"Perhaps it was some house which was partially razed to the ground to make way for forest that kings might hunt to their pleasure. Can't you imagine it? The King gives the order: lands to be made forest land and the devil take anyone whose home is on it. No wonder those kings were hated. You can feel the hatred sometimes in this forest."

I stopped. Why was I talking to him in this way? I could see that he was amused. The manner in which he looked at me showed it.

"I can see that as well as being a young lady bold enough to roam the forest alone you are a highly imaginative one. Now I think that that is a very interesting combination—boldness and imagination. That should take you far."

"What do you mean, take me far?"

He leaned towards me slightly. "As far as you want to go. I can see too that you are very determined."

"Are you a fortune teller?"

Again he laughed. "At moments," he said, "I have clairvoyant powers. Shall I tell you something? I'm a descendant of Merlin, the magician. Can you sense *his* presence in the forest?"

"I can't and he could not have been here—had he existed at all. The forest was made by the Norman kings long after Merlin died."

"Oh, Merlin fluttered from century to century. He had no sense of time."

"I can see you are amused. I'm sorry if I seemed foolish."

"Far from it. Foolish is the last word I would apply to you and if I am amused it is in the nicest possible way. One of the greatest pleasures of life is to be amused."

"I love this forest," I said. "I've read a great deal about it. I suppose that's what makes me imagine things." And I thought what an extraordinary conversation to be holding with a stranger. I said quickly: "The sky is a little lighter. The storm is beginning to fade away."

"I hope not. It is so much more interesting sheltering from the storm than walking through the forest alone."

"I am sure it is abating." I stepped out from the parapet. He took my arm and drew me back.

I was very much aware of him.

"It's unsafe to venture yet," he said.

"I've such a little distance to go."

"Stay and make sure. Besides, we don't want to cut short this absorbing conversation. You're interested in the past, are you?"

"I am."

"That's wise. The past is such an excellent warning to

the present and future. And you feel that there is something significant about this ruin?"

"Any ruin interests me. It must at some time have been someone's home. People must have lived within its walls. I can't help wondering about them, how they lived, loved, suffered, rejoiced . . ."

He watched me closely. "You're right," he said. "There is something here. I sense it too. This is a historic spot. One day we shall look back and say, 'Ah, that was the place where we sheltered from the storm.' "

He put out a hand as though to grasp mine and drawing back I said: "Look. It is lighter. I'm going to chance it now. Goodbye."

I left him standing there and ran out into the forest.

The rain was teeming down, the wet foliage wrapped itself round me as my feet squelched through the sodden ground. I had to get away though. I was uncertain of what he would do. There was something about him— some vitality which I felt would submerge me if I stayed. He had been laughing at me, I was well aware of that, and I was not sure of him. I was very excited though. I had half wanted to stay and had been half eager to get away.

What an extraordinary encounter and yet it had merely been two people sheltering from the rain.

When I arrived at the house my mother was in the hall.

"Good gracious, Jane," she said, "wherever have you been?" She came to me and felt my dress. "You're soaked to the skin."

"I was caught in the storm."

"How breathless you are! Come along upstairs. You must get those things off and Amy shall bring hot water. You must have a hot bath at once and put on dry things."

She poured the hot water into the hip bath in her bedroom and I was immersed in it. She put a little mustard in—her own special remedy—and then made me dry myself and put on the clothes she had got out for me.

When I was dressed I was aware of the bustle in the servants' quarters and I could not resist going down.

Mrs. Couch was puffing a kind of contentment. Jess and Amy were pink in the cheeks.

"My goodness me," said Mrs. Couch, "if this is not a day and a half. First my buns catch in the oven and then Mr. Joliffe comes."

Sprawling on a chair, his legs slightly apart, his heels touching the floor, was the man I had met in the forest.

He smiled at me in a way with which I was to become familiar—half teasing, half tender.

"We're old friends," he commented.

There was silence in the kitchen. Then I said as coolly as I could, addressing myself to Mrs. Couch who was gaping at me: "We sheltered from the rain . . . in the forest."

"Did you now," said Mrs. Couch looking from one of us to the other.

"For about ten minutes," I added.

"It was long enough for us to become friends," he replied, still giving me that smile which touched me in a way I could not then understand.

"Mr. Joliffe is quick to make friends," said Mrs. Couch.

"It saves so much time in life," he retorted.

"Why didn't you tell me that you were Mr. Milner's nephew?"

"I thought I would give you a big surprise. But you might have guessed, you know."

"You said you were a visitor."

"So I am."

"Taking a walk in the forest."

"So I was, on my way to my uncle's house. Jess, ask Jeffers to send to the station for my bag."

"Why yes, Mr. Joliffe," said Jess blushing.

I felt disconcerted. They were all behaving as though he were some sort of prince. It made me a little impatient.

Mrs. Couch was saying fondly: "Just like you, Mr. Joliffe, to come without a word! We drank the last of the sloe gin last week. Now if I'd have known I'd have kept some back. I know how partial you are to my sloe gin."

"Nowhere in the world is there sloe gin to compare with that of my dear Mrs. Couch."

She wriggled in her rocking chair and said: "Go on with you. But I'll see there's black-currant tart for your dinner."

I said I had work to do and went out. I felt his eyes following me as I went.

The house changed because he was in it. I was caught up in the excitement. Everything was different now. All the solemnity which the presence of Mr. Sylvester Milner brought with it had disappeared. Instead of being a house of certain secrets, somewhat mysterious and now and then a trifle sinister, it was a gay house. He had a habit of whistling rather tunefully. He could imitate the songs of birds and he could produce some of the gayer Sullivan tunes from the Savoy operas with great verve. There was something joyous about him. He appeared to love life and everyone about him was caught up in his enthusiasm for it. He never lost an opportunity of charming everyone and I soon came to the conclusion that he was making a special effort as far as I was concerned.

When I rode out he was beside me; if I went for a walk in the forest I would not have gone far without hearing his whistle behind me. We talked a great deal about ourselves; I told him of my father and his untimely death in the mountains and he told me of his parents' accident and how he had been brought up between his uncles Sylvester and Redmond.

"In an atmosphere rather like that of Roland's Croft," he explained. "Everything seems to be submerged beneath Chinese Art. Do you feel that here?"

"It is Mr. Milner's business, of course."

"But everywhere you go there is the influence of China. The vases on the stairs; bits and pieces here and there, and that fellow of my uncle's shuffling round. Do you feel it?"

"Yes. It fascinates me."

"That's because you haven't been brought up with it. Mind you, I'm in it too . . . up to my neck."

"You mean in the business?"

"Yes. Well, why not? I learned how to recognize a Ming vase at my uncle's knees, you might say. I'm an independent fellow, though, Miss Lindsay. When my uncle Sylvester sent me out to China I got the feeling that I wanted to use my skill, my powers of detection, for myself. Do you understand?"

"Yes. You are yet another branch of the same business."

"You put it succinctly. We are all in the same lake as it were but we are all pulling our own craft."

He talked a great deal about Hong Kong—a place which evidently fascinated him. Mr. Sylvester Milner had talked to me too, but differently. With Mr. Sylvester I heard of the various dynasties, how they flourished and passed away. Joliffe made me see a different scene. The green hills running down to sandy beaches on Hong Kong Island; the ladder streets up which people climbed the steep inclines; the letter writers who translated for those who could not read, and wrote to their dictation; the Chinese fortune tellers in the streets, shaking the containers which held the sticks which would be selected and laid out that they might foretell the future; the sampans which made up the floating villages. He talked in a manner which fascinated me and although I had been very interested in what Mr. Sylvester had taught me, this was colorful and alive and it imbued me with a desire to see it for myself.

On the second day of his visit he had asked me where I took my meals.

"Sometimes with my mother in her sitting room, sometimes in the servants' hall."

"While I dine in solitary state. It won't do. You shall dine with me . . . tête-á-tête, how's that?"

His word was law. He lightly assumed the place of head of the house while Mr. Sylvester was away. Mrs. Couch without hesitation laid a place for me in the dining room where Mr. Sylvester entertained his guests. I sat at one end of the long table, Joliffe at the other. This amused him, but I felt uneasy wondering what Mr. Sylvester would say if he returned and found me here.

I soon forgot my apprehension though in the intoxicating company of Joliffe Milner.

I remember on the third day after his arrival my mother came to my room.

She said: "Joliffe is very interested in you, Jane."

"Oh yes," I said, "it's the work. He's in the same business as his uncle."

My mother looked at me strangely. If feeling exultation in a certain person's presence, and when he was not there being completely deflated, was being in love, then I was in love with Joliffe Milner. It was clear, I supposed. Even I looking in the mirror could see the change in myself.

"Do you think he is a *serious* young man?" she asked.

"Serious? I hadn't thought of that. He laughs about most things so one could hardly call him serious."

I was halted then by the look on my mother's face and the fleeting thought struck me that she had changed in the last year. Her color was as vivid as ever but her face had fined down a little; her eyes seemed brighter than usual. There was about her a rather secretive look. This was scarcely perceptible but I who knew her so well might be one of the few who noticed. There was a change. Why? I asked myself. What is it? Then I forgot it because my thoughts at this time were dominated by Joliffe Milner.

"He is a very charming man," said my mother. "Your father was a charming man, but . . ."

She shrugged her shoulders and my thoughts were too far away to ask her to continue what she was about to say.

I put on my riding kit—my mother's gift to me—and went out riding. I was joined, as I had hoped I would be, by Joliffe.

And there passed another of those enchanted mornings.

I had my duties and in spite of this new excitement in life I must not ignore them. There was some post to be dealt with. I had always enjoyed working in the little study adjoining Mr. Sylvester's Chinese Library; I had felt a certain sense of responsibility which was gratifying.

But since Joliffe was at the house, I longed to be out with him.

I had made a habit of going two or three times a week into what I still called the showroom. I had always been thrilled to unlock the door and cross the threshold and to be entirely alone with those precious objects which by now were becoming familiar to me.

But because of Joliffe's presence in the house I had neglected to go there and when I realized this decided to do so at once.

I went in, shut the door and stood looking round. My eyes always went immediately to the bronze Buddha which had struck me the first time I had entered this room, and from the Buddha to the Kuan Yin. Then I thought it would be a good exercise to compare her with the new one which had so excited Mr. Sylvester when he had brought it home.

I went to the glass showcase in which he had placed it. I stared. The figure was not there.

It could not be so, for she had been there when I was last in this room.

But that was before Mr. Sylvester had gone away.

There was only one explanation. He had taken the figure with him. He had not told me, which was strange. He might have been sure that I would miss it. How odd that he should take it and say nothing.

I was so disturbed by this that I could not concentrate on anything else. I carefully locked the door and went back to my room. I was a little shaken. I could not understand why, having talked so earnestly about the importance and value of the statue, he should have taken it and said nothing.

I went to my window and looked out at the barred windows of the showroom.

No one could have got in. I was the only one in the house who had a key. The answer was simple, Mr. Sylvester must have taken the image with him. Perhaps he was going to have some test made on it.

I went out riding with Joliffe and that was enough to make me forget everything else. It was wonderful to pick our way through the forest and canter across the glades. We stopped at an old inn for cider and farmhouse sandwiches, and sitting in that inn parlor with its stone floor and hams and sides of bacon hanging on the rafters, the brass gleaming in the open fireplace, I was happier than I had ever been in my life and I knew that the reason was Joliffe.

As we sipped our cider which was a little potent and ate the homemade bread and freshly baked ham, I asked him how often he came to Roland's Croft.

"Not often."

"They behave as though you are there every day. You enjoy your visits there I believe."

"Never one as much as this one."

He turned his blue eyes on me and they undoubtedly implied that this was the best of visits because I was there.

We were quiet as we rode back. I thought he was on the verge of saying something that would be very impor-

tant to us both so I was in a state of great expectancy. It
was strange for him to be silent. It was like discovering a
side to his nature which I had not suspected existed.

We returned in the middle of the afternoon and I did
not see him for the rest of the day. He left word that he
had an appointment and would not be in to dinner. My
mother and I dined alone in her sitting room. She was in
a strange mood. She talked a great deal about the days
when my father had courted her.

"Do you know, Janey," she said, "I used to have
qualms. You see if he hadn't married me they wouldn't
have cast him off, would they? He would have had a
comfortable income, instead of that meager annuity,
wouldn't he?"

"He would rather have had us," I assured her.

"He must have told me so a thousand times. I'd like to
see you settled, Janey. Of course you have this post here
with Mr. Sylvester and he's a very kind gentleman
but . . ."

She looked at me as though asking me to tell her
something. I knew that she was hoping that Joliffe would
ask me to marry him. She wanted me to know the happiness she had enjoyed with my father.

"Mind you," she went on as I remained silent. "You're
young yet. Only eighteen, but I was eighteen when I married your father. We met and we knew at once. It was as
quick as that."

She was hoping for confidences. But I had none to give
her.

I couldn't sleep that night. I lay awake thinking of the
inn parlor and the manner in which Joliffe had looked at
me. I went over our conversation and in the middle of it
all I remembered that the Kuan Yin was not in the
showroom and the strangeness of this struck me afresh.

I dozed and dreamed I was in the room and the eyes of
the bronze Buddha suddenly moved and they were accus-
ing me.

After an hour of this I got up and went to the window. I looked across at the barred window as I used to when I first came to the house. How different the place looked in moonlight—mysterious, eerie—the sort of place in which anything could happen.

I was getting cold but I knew I would not sleep so I sat there and quite suddenly I saw the flickering light. I could not believe it. That light was behind those barred windows. There was no mistaking it. Someone—something—was in the showroom.

I had begun to tremble and the match shook as I lighted my candle. I went back to the window. It was dark and . . . there it was . . . that flickering will-o'-the-wisp.

Thieves! I thought. And Mr. Sylvester away and I am responsible!

I put on my dressing gown and thrust my feet into slippers. I had to go and see.

Swiftly I mounted the stairs. I was standing outside the door. I took the handle and slowly turned it. The door was locked. It was then that the goose pimples rose on my skin and a feeling of sheer terror came over me. Burglars did not seem half as terrifying as that *something* which had clearly been—and perhaps still was—in the room.

I sped back to my room. I took the key from the sandalwood box and came back. I tried the door again. It was still locked. I turned the key and went in.

How eerie the room looked. I lifted my candle and because my hand was shaking my shadow danced on the walls. The candlelight fell on the now familiar objects. There was the Buddha. He was terrifying in candlelight. His eyes half closed, his expression malevolent, his effortless lotus pose making him aloof and disdainful.

My heart was racing, my throat was parched, I was prepared for anything to happen. Yet I advanced into the room. I must not dismiss the idea that that light had been brought in by a human being who had entered the room by some means and may have stolen something.

There was the valuable Ming vase. The jade cabinet was intact.

Then I stared. For in the glass case smiling benignly at me was the Kuan Yin which this morning had not been there.

I was imagining it. I opened the case. I touched her. In truth she was there. Yet this morning she had been missing.

Something very strange was happening here. I looked about the room. It was uncanny. These objects had been in the world for centuries; they would have passed through so many hands. Was it true that seemingly inanimate objects became imbued with the tragedies and comedies of the lives of those to whom they had belonged?

Then to my horror I heard a noise. Surely it was a stealthy footstep. I had the feeling that I was about to be trapped.

I moved forward so that I was sheltering behind the bronze Buddha. I saw the flickering light at the door. A dark figure was there.

I caught my breath audibly. A voice said: "Who's there?"

Floods of relief swept over me for it was Joliffe's voice.

"It's you, Joliffe," I said.

"Jane!"

I came out into the room and we stood facing each other, our candles in our hands.

"What are you doing here?" I whispered.

"What are you?"

"I thought I saw a light in here. I came to see what was happening."

"I heard someone moving about. I came to investigate."

"Who could it have been?"

"You were the one I heard."

"But I saw a light here."

"Do you think there's a burglar in the house?"

"The door was locked. How could he have got in?"

"He wouldn't have come in and carefully locked the door after him. It was a trick of light you saw."

"It couldn't have been."

"It was. How lovely you are, Jane, with your hair loose like that."

His presence always intoxicated me. I could only think that we were alone together and although in incongruous circumstances it didn't matter.

He came closer to me. "What good fortune to meet like this."

"How ridiculous. We can meet during the day."

"This is exciting." He put his candle down and took mine from me. Then he put his arms about me and held me tightly.

"I love you, Jane," he said.

I just wanted to lie against him, for I loved him too and I was happy as I never had been before.

He took my face in his hands and said: "Jane, there has never been anyone like you."

"There was never anyone like you, I'm sure."

"This was inevitable. Did you sense from the first day we sheltered beneath the parapet?"

"I think I did."

"Oh Jane! Life will be good, won't it? You'll let it be, won't you?"

"I only want to be with you," I answered.

We kissed and I had never dreamed that there were such kisses. I was in a state of euphoria and the transition from terror to bliss was too sudden. Everything seemed unreal. I was in love with a man I had so briefly known and we were here together half clad in this room which for me had always seemed like part of a fantasy.

I expected to wake at any moment to find that I had dreamed of that flickering light and I would find myself seated at my window where I had dozed off.

But no, I was here, and Joliffe's arms were about me

and he was telling me that he loved me and he was urging me to love him completely and utterly.

I was very young and inexperienced; love to me was a romantic and beautiful thing as my mother had always presented it to be. She and my father had met and loved romantically; they had married within three weeks of their meeting and he had sacrificed a life of comfort for her. That was love.

The bronze Buddha seemed to be looking at me with cold disdainful eyes.

"What a strange place for a lover's meeting," said Joliffe. "Let's get out of here."

"I must go back to my room," I said.

"Not yet," he whispered.

He took me in his arms again but I couldn't shut out the thought of the Buddha's watching eyes. It was foolish. What was it but a piece of bronze and yet . . .

"I must get out of this room," I said.

Resolutely I picked up my candle. He took his and we went out of the room together. I locked the door.

We faced each other in the corridor.

He was holding my hand firmly. "I can't let you go," he said.

"We may wake someone."

"Come to my room . . . or I'll come to yours . . ."

I drew back. "No, we couldn't do that."

He said: "Forgive me, Jane. I'm carried away by . . . all this."

"We will talk about everything tomorrow," I answered.

He held me in his arms again and I withdrew myself hastily and turning fled back to my room.

I set down the candle on the dressing table and looked at my reflection in the mirror. I could hardly recognize myself. My hair hung round my shoulders, my eyes looked brilliant and there was a faint color in my usually pale cheeks. I was looking at a new person. I was looking at Jane in love.

What a strange night! I had made two startling discoveries, but one had almost driven the other from my mind. Joliffe loved me. That was all important. The fact that the Kuan Yin was back in its place when it had been missing and no one but myself had a key seemed of minor importance beside the overwhelming discovery that I loved and was loved. I could easily convince myself that I had been mistaken about the Kuan Yin. It was back in its place. That was all that mattered. One phrase kept echoing in my mind: Joliffe loves me.

I sat by the window looking across the courtyard. I looked at the darkened window with the bars across it, and I went over every detail of the scene in that room, starting from the moment when I had seen the light of his candle.

I could feel his arms about me.

In the morning we would make plans for our wedding for I knew that Joliffe would be a very impatient man.

It was four o'clock in the morning before I went to bed and then I did not sleep. I drifted into doze after doze in all of which Joliffe was there.

I slept late and I awoke to find my mother standing by my bedside.

She was saying: "Wake up, Jane. What ever's come over you? You are a sleepyhead this morning."

I sat up and memories of last night came back to me.

"Oh Mother," I said, "I'm so happy."

She sat down by the bed. "It's Joliffe, isn't it?"

"How did you guess?"

She laughed at me.

"We're in love, Mother."

"I daresay it'll be an early wedding."

"Yes, it will, of course."

"When did he ask you?"

"Last night." I did not tell her where and in what circumstances. I knew she would not like to think of our wandering round the house at night in our dressing gowns.

"So I expect you were awake until the early hours and then slept on."

"That's about it."

I could see that she was delighted. "There's nothing I could have wished for more," she declared. "I longed to see you settled. A post with Mr. Sylvester is very nice but I want to see you with a husband to care for you."

That indefinable change in her seemed to have disappeared. She was her old self; excited, rosy cheeked, bursting with energy.

She held me against her. "It's what I wanted. I saw how you felt the moment you set eyes on him. He's charming. He's full of life. The exact opposite of your father who was always so serious, but I don't hold that against him! I can't tell you what this means to me. I feel your father is watching over us as he has done from the moment he passed on. It's what I've prayed for. Get dressed, Janey love. I'll see you in a while."

I did not know then that she went to Joliffe. I did not know what she said to him.

I think at that time she and I were both rather innocent.

When I was dressed and went downstairs my mother and Joliffe were talking together.

He rose and took my hands when I came in; he kissed me tenderly.

"Joliffe and I think there's no sense in waiting," said my mother.

"So you have made arrangements between you," I said.

She laughed and Joliffe's eyes were ardent.

This is the complete happiness, I thought.

Joliffe went away and said that he would be back very soon. There were one or two matters to be settled.

Mr. Sylvester Milner returned.

I debated whether to tell him about the disappearance and return of the Kuan Yin but I had almost convinced myself that I must have imagined its disappearance. I did not want him to think I was frivolous.

He showed me a few purchases that he had made. "They are not very spectacular," he said, "but useful additions. I doubt though that I shall have much difficulty in placing them."

I then blurted out that I was engaged to be married.

I was unprepared for the effect on him. I had known that he would not be pleased since he had taken such trouble to train me, but, I consoled myself, it was a contingency that he must certainly have been prepared for.

"Married!" he said. "But you are far too young."

"I shall be nineteen in September."

"You are just beginning to know something of Chinese Art."

"I'm sorry. It seems ungrateful, but Joliffe and I . . ."

"Joliffe. My nephew!" His face had darkened. "That is impossible," he added.

"He came here while you were away."

His eyes narrowed. His benevolent smile had disappeared. He looked rather like the bronze Buddha.

"You scarcely know him."

"It seemed enough time . . ."

"Joliffe!" he repeated. "Joliffe! No good will come of this."

"I'm sorry, Mr. Milner . . ."

"Not as sorry as you will be if you go on with this. I'll send for Joliffe. I'll talk to him."

There was silence. I said: "Do you want me to do the letters now?"

"No, no," he said. "This is far too upsetting. Leave me now."

Disconcerted, bewildered, and unhappy, I went to my mother's sitting room. She was making herself a cup of tea.

"Why, whatever's the matter, Jane?"

"I've told Mr. Milner about Joliffe and me. He doesn't like it."

"Well," said my mother emphatically, "he'll have to lump it."

"I see his point. He's trained me."

"Stuff and nonsense! What's training when a girl's future's at stake! I expect he wanted someone with money or something for his precious nephew."

"He never struck me as being like that."

"But he strikes me now."

"I'm so sorry he's upset. I like him. He's been so good to us."

"Well, he's had a good housekeeper though I say it myself, and you were a good secretary to him. But times have got to change and there's always the possibility of a girl's getting married."

"What if he dismisses you when I marry Joliffe?"

"Then he dismisses me."

"But you thought it was so good here, and so it has been. Think how kind he's been letting me stay here."

"Well, so he has, but he doesn't own us for all that. No, he's been good to us but you've got your future to think of. I want to see you settled, Jane, with a good home and a good husband and in time babies. There's nothing like it. I always wanted to see you settled before I went."

"Went . . . went where?"

"To join your father."

"What a silly thing to say! You're here with me and you'll stay here for years and years . . ."

"Of course, but I want to see you settled. I'm sorry Mr. High-and-Mighty Milner doesn't think you're good enough for his nephew, but I happen to think otherwise and so, bless him, does Joliffe."

Mr. Sylvester Milner sent for my mother. I sat in her room waiting for her to return. When she came her color

was high and she was in true fighting spirit. She had
looked like that when she had talked of the Lindsays, my
father's family.

"What did he say?"

"Oh, he was very polite and gentle but he's against it."

"So he really doesn't think I'm good enough to marry
his nephew."

"That's what it amounts to, but he puts it the other
way round. He says Joliffe's not good enough for you."

"Whatever does he mean?"

"He says he's a ne'er-do-well. He's never settled down
and won't be a good husband."

"What nonsense! Is he going to turn you out when I
marry?"

"He didn't say that. He was very dignified. He said at
the end: 'I can't stop your daughter marrying my nephew,
Mrs. Lindsay, but I hope with all my heart that she will
not. I have a high regard for your daughter, and if she is
to marry I would rather she made a more suitable match.'
I stood my ground very firmly and I said: 'My daughter
will marry where her heart is, Mr. Milner, as her father
did before her. We're determined once we make up our
minds. And perhaps we know best what's good for us.'
We left it at that."

"Is he very angry?"

"More sad I'd say. At least that's what he wants us to
think. He shakes his head and looks like some old prophet when he does it. But we're taking no notice of him."

It was all very well to say that, but my joy was damp-
ened a little.

The excitement in the servants' hall was great. Mrs.
Couch rocked on her chair and her eyes were soft. "So
you're the one he's chosen! I always knew you'd been
born lucky. A housekeeper's daughter going to Cluntons'
like a lady . . . and now along comes Mr. Joliffe. What a
man! Mind you, you'll have to watch him. Charmers like

that don't grow on every tree and there'll always be them looking to pluck what don't belong to them. Men like that Mr. Joliffe can need a lot of looking after."

"I'll look after him, Mrs. Couch."

"I don't doubt you will. As soon as I clapped eyes on you I said to Jess: 'There's a little Madam for you. She knows what she wants and she'll get it.' So I was right. You got Mr. Joliffe, and I reckon there's been a lot of competition for that one."

Amy said that she reckoned I'd got a handful there but what a handful! Her Jake whom she was marrying at Christmas was a good steady sort and right for her but Mr. Joliffe was a man any girl would fall for given half a beckon; Jess said he was a man and a half and I was lucky.

I went about during those days in a kind of haze of delight. Things looked different; the grass was more luscious, the flowers in the garden more colorful; the world had taken on a new beauty because Joliffe was part of it.

Mr. Sylvester was of course the only one who cast a gloom. He watched me covertly when I thought he did not notice. I supposed he was regretting all the time he had wasted on me.

One day he said to me: "I know it is no use trying to dissuade you. I can only hope that you will be less unhappy than I fear. My nephew has always been irresponsible. He is wild and adventurous. Some people might find these characteristics attractive. I have never found them so. I can only hope that you will never regret your decision. When we first met we tried the yarrow sticks. We will try them again before you go."

On his table was the container with the sticks in it. He held it out to me and asked me to take some. I did so. As I handed them back to him he said, "The first question we will ask is, 'Will this marriage be a happy one?' "

He proceeded to lay out the sticks. He looked at them,

his eyes glowing beneath his skull cap. "Look at this broken line here. This means an emphatic No."

"I'm sorry," I said, "but I don't believe in this fortune
telling."

"It's a pity," he answered sadly, and began to study the
sticks he had laid out.

In November, Joliffe and I were married in a registrar's
office. It was a quiet wedding. Joliffe had got a special license for he said we didn't want a fuss.

My mother was in a state of exultation. She looked like
a bride herself.

After the ceremony she kissed me fondly.

"This is the happiest day of my life since my husband
died," she told Joliffe and me. She turned to him earnestly: "You will take care of her."

He swore he would and we went away for our honeymoon.

My mother returned to Roland's Croft.

The Woman in the Park

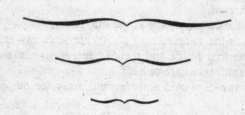

It was like being born into a new world of discovery. I began to realize how young I had been, how inexperienced. It was an intoxicating existence. I had been so unworldly before. Life was not all that I had believed it to be. I suppose my parents had lived an ideal married life; they were serene in their happiness, simple one might say. Joliffe was never that.

He was the most exciting person I had ever known and if he had been as easy to understand as my parents, could he have fascinated me so? As I emerged from the ecstatic dream which our honeymoon was I began to see how little I knew of the world, what a simpleton I had been. Everything before had been so clear cut—the good, the bad, the right, the wrong. Now they were merging into each other. Something which I might have condemned before, I discovered was a little risky, but amusing. The greatest quality seemed to be an ability to amuse.

Joliffe was passionate and tender, delighted to initiate me into a way of life which I had never known existed before. My innocence he found delightful, "amusing" in fact. But at the same time I knew that it would not continue to amuse. It was something I had to grow out of.

We spent the first night of our honeymoon in a country hotel, with Tudor architecture—oak beams, and floors which sloped, of the Queen-Elizabeth-Slept-Here variety. There were old tennis courts—the Tudor kind where Henry VIII was said to have played; and in the evening after dinner we strolled into the old Tudor garden with its winter heath, jasmine and yellow chrysanthemums.

I was living in a dream then; there was Joliffe my new husband at whom I had already noticed women turned to look, and he had eyes for me only, which made me feel proud and humble all at once.

So that first night together was spent in the ancient bedroom with the tiny leaded paned windows through which shafts of moonlight touched the room with a dreamlike radiance, and it was Joliffe's delight to lead me to understanding. When he slept, for I could not, I watched his sleeping face while the moonlight threw shadows over it and it seemed then that it changed and put lines where there were none and it was as though I saw Joliffe as he would be twenty years hence and I told myself passionately I will love him then even as I do now.

He awoke and I told him this and we were solemn talking of our love. And strangely enough—as though some premonition of disaster had cast a sudden shadow— I assured myself that whatever happened in the future nothing could spoil the magic of this night.

That was only the beginning of our honeymoon. It must be spent in style, as I discovered everything must be with Joliffe. We were to go to Paris, a city he dearly loved. "All honeymoons," he declared, "should be spent in Paris."

We went by train to Dover and crossed the Channel in a mild swell and took the boat train from Calais to the French capital.

"The first thing we must do is get you some clothes," said Joliffe. "I have friends in Paris. I can't introduce my little country mouse to them."

Little country mouse! I was indignant. He laughed at me. He took off my hat—one which I had thought greatly daring with its little emerald green feather on black satin and its green velvet ribbons tied under my chin. He grimaced at it. "All very well for walks in the forest but hardly suited to the Champs-Élysées, my darling."

And my gown of dark green merino with the velvet collar which mother and I had thought the height of good taste was just a little too homely, he said.

I was hurt but my spirits rose as we went to the little shops and new clothes were bought for me. I had a gown with a little cape of black and white and a black hat which was scarcely a hat for it was just a twist of black net with a huge white bow in it.

"It won't be of the least use," I declared.

"My darling Jane will learn that the last thing that is expected of a hat is that it should be useful. Piquant, elegant, decorative, yes. Useful never."

"How can you know so much about women's clothes?" I demanded.

"Only one woman's. And I know about hers because she is my wife and I adore her."

I had a gown for evening which was daring, I thought. Joliffe said it was just right. It was white satin and he gave me a jade brooch set in diamonds to wear with it. When I put it on I was startled by my reflection. I was indeed a different person.

During those two weeks in Paris I was in turn deliriously happy and vaguely apprehensive. I was enchanted by this magic city. I loved it best in the morning when there was a smell of freshly baked bread in the streets and an excitement in the air which means that a big city is coming to life. Blissfully I wandered through the flower markets on either side of the Madeleine, Joliffe at my side; I bought armfuls of blossoms to decorate our bedroom and their haunting scent stayed with me forever. We strolled along the boulevards, climbed to Sacré Coeur and explored Montmartre; I shivered over the cruel leering faces of the gargoyles of historic Notre Dame; I laughed at the traders in Les Halles. I reveled in the treasures of the Louvre and I mingled with the artists and students seated outside the cafés of the Left Bank. It was the most wonderful experience I had ever known. It was all that a honeymoon should be. And whatever new and wonderful sights I saw, whatever thrilling experiences were mine, it all came back to one thing: Joliffe was with me.

He was the best possible companion; he knew this city so well. But I began to notice that the Joliffe of our morning rambles and tours of exploration was different from the man he became in the evenings. I was learning that people were more complicated than I in my innocence had believed them to be—some people at least, and Joliffe for one. There were many facets to the natures of some. I could not at that time understand why my husband could revel in the simple pleasures by day and in the evening subtly change to the sophisticate. This alarmed me faintly. I felt at a disadvantage.

In the afternoon we used to draw the blinds and lie on our bed talking idly or making love. "It's an old French custom," said Joliffe; and these were the happiest times.

Then in the evening we must join his friends of whom there seemed to be many. We must go to Marguery's to sample his special *filet de sole* in its sauce of Marguery's creating which could not be found anywhere in the world; we must dine at the Moulin Rouge and see the dancing at the Bal Tabarin; we must join Joliffe's friends at the Café de la Paix. I used to hope that we would dine alone but we rarely did. There were always friends to join us. They talked volubly in French which I did not always find easy to follow; they drank what seemed to me a great deal and shared jokes of which I sometimes did not grasp the point. At such times I seemed to lose touch with Joliffe and it was then so hard to believe that he was the same man with whom I shared those interesting mornings and ecstatic afternoons.

I saw the artists Monet and Toulouse-Lautrec; we mingled with the literati and people from the theatrical world; they were colorful, larger than life—women with exquisite complexions which I innocently thought were their own, their gowns of breathtaking elegance made me feel gauche and out of place and I longed for the peace of our hotel room.

But Joliffe loved this society. He could not have enough of it. I felt angry and in a way humiliated by the manner in which some of the women regarded Joliffe. It was even more disconcerting because he appeared to enjoy it.

One night as we jolted back to the hotel in our cab I said: "I've come to the conclusion that I shall have to grow accustomed to the way women look at you."

He answered: "How do they look?" But of course he knew.

"I have heard it said that women like men who like them. Is that true?"

"Don't we always like those who like us?"

"I mean women collectively. They don't have time to find out whether you like them personally. It's something they know by instinct. Women like you, Joliffe."

"Oh that's because I'm so good-looking," he said jocularly. He turned to me. "In any case I'm indifferent to what they think of me. There's only one whose opinion is of importance."

Joliffe could say things like that. He could sweep away hours of doubting fears in a second, and although I began to feel that there was much I did not know of him and of life, I loved him more every day.

Many of the people we met were his business associates.

"In a business like mine," he said, "I travel a great deal. I have to. When I hear of treasures here in Paris, in London, in Rome . . . I come to see them. I'm always looking for treasure."

"Does one look here for Chinese treasure?"

"It's everywhere. There was a time when it was fashionable to collect *chinoiserie*. People did it all over Europe. Thus many of the art treasures of China found their way here."

He took me along to a dealer on the Left Bank one day. That was one of my happiest days.

There in a dark little room were some beautiful objects. I cried out in delight, and I realized how I had missed the showroom at Roland's Croft and working with Mr. Sylvester.

How delighted I was to surprise both Joliffe and the dealer with my knowledge when I recognized some exquisite scrolls of the T'ang Dynasty and placed them somewhere round the tenth century.

I was grateful for the tuition I had received.

I was drawn into a new intimacy. We drank wine in a little room at the back of the showroom—myself, Joliffe, and Monsieur Ferrand the dealer. I felt that I entered a magic circle. I was very happy. The color engendered by wine and happiness touched my cheeks. My eyes were shining. It will always be like this, I told myself.

Monsieur Ferrand wanted to show us some rings he had had brought to him. Someone had come back from Peking with them. The jade was beautiful—some in the delicious apple green, some a translucent emerald color. I liked the apple green better though I knew the darker ones to be more valuable.

There was one of this lightish green shade most exquisitely carved and in the front was an eye the pupil of which was a diamond. It was most unusual.

"Said to be the eye of Kuan Yin," explained Monsieur Ferrand. "I had to give a good price for it because of the legend you know. The owner of this ring will always be able to look into the eye of the goddess. That should be very useful."

"I haven't seen a piece like this before."

"I hope not. This one should be unique."

I took it up and slipped it on my finger. Joliffe took my hand and across the table his eyes met mine. They were alight with love and I thought—strangely enough at that time—anything that happens is worth while for this moment.

"It looks well on your finger, Jane."

"Just imagine, madame," put in Monsieur Ferrand, "the goddess of good fortune would always be on hand as it were."

Joliffe laughed.

"You must have it, Jane. Married to me, you may need it."

"Married to you I am the last person to need it."

A shadow passed momentarily over his face. I had never seen him look like that before—sad, almost apprehensive. But he was almost immediately gay again.

"Nevertheless you must have it. Although I shouldn't say so in front of Monsieur Ferrand because I must strike a bargain with him."

They talked over the ring and I tried it on again. At last they decided on a price and I put it back on my finger. Joliffe took my hand and kissed the ring.

"May good fortune always be yours, my darling," he said.

I sat in the cab leaning against Joliffe, turning the ring round and round on my finger.

"I have reached the very peak of happiness now," I said. "There can't be anything more."

Joliffe assured me that there was.

How the days flew—happy days except for the evenings when we entertained or were entertained by his friends and business associates. Then my eyes would ache with the smoke and the lights and my ears would be weary with the music and I would strain to translate what I was sure were the risqué jokes of some people who came and sat at our table and drank champagne with us.

Many of the women seemed to know Joliffe. Like all others these had their special look for him.

There was one happy day when we dined quietly in the hotel—tête-à-tête at a table secluded by palms. I remember I was wearing a dress of green and white striped taffeta which Joliffe had chosen for me. I had grown accustomed now to the clothes I was wearing. I wondered whether my personality was changing. I knew when I saw my mother again she would recognize a change at once.

As we sat over dinner I said: "Joliffe, I don't know you very well."

He raised his eyebrows pretending to be shocked.

"So you have been living with a man whom you don't know?"

"I know that I love you."

"Well that's good enough for me."

"Joliffe, I want to talk seriously."

"I am always serious with you, Jane."

"I want to talk about practical things. Are you rich?"

He laughed. "I have to confess, Jane, that you are not married to a millionaire. Would you like the marriage annulled on the spot?"

He had said he was always serious but he was not. I could see that evasive look creeping into his face now.

"We have been living rather extravagantly here."

"Every man is entitled to live extravagantly on his honeymoon."

"So we shall economize when we go home?"

"Economize! What a dreary word. It won't be so costly living in our house in London as it is here in this hotel in Paris, if that's what you mean."

"What will it be like in London? We haven't made any plans."

"There have been so many more exciting things to do."

"Yes, but it's time we settled down."

"First you want to economize then settle down. What a practical woman I've married."

"Perhaps you should be glad of that. We have to consider the future."

His eyes glowed as they looked into mine. "I find the present so entrancing. I'm letting the future take care of itself."

"Joliffe, I think you're a little feckless."

"Guilty perhaps, but it has to be proved."

"I think you're evading the future."

"What, when you're in it!"

"Do you love me very much, Joliffe?"

"Infinitely."

"Then everything will be all right. Have you a house in London?"

"I have a house in Kensington. Opposite the Park—the gardens you know, Kensington Gardens. It is very pleasant. A tall, somewhat narrow house and it is looked after by an excellent man and his wife."

"And we shall live there?"

"When we are in London. I travel around a great deal in the course of my business."

"Where?"

"All over the world. Europe and the East and to a place called Roland's Croft. It was there that I made my truly great find. There I found my fortune."

There was no way of making him talk very seriously. He wanted to avoid it. This was a night for love and how could I put any obstacle in its path?

Later he explained to me that he had inherited the London house from his parents and he had used it ever since as a *pied-à-terre*. Albert and Annie had been servants of his family for years. Annie had in fact been his nurse. They kept the house in order when he was away and looked after him when he was in London.

He had prepared them for the coming of his wife.

As for his business, I knew already what that was. He had been brought up in the tradition. If anything else had been chosen for him he would not have been able to do it.

"This hunting for articles which have such significance in beauty, history, legend, whatever it is . . . it's irresistible, Jane. Some men want to hunt the fox or the deer or the wild boar because the hunting instinct is inborn. I never wanted to hunt animals to the death. That seems to me a worthless object, but to unearth treasures which lay hidden from the world, that fascinated me, ever since I lived with my uncle and heard him and my cousin Adam talk of these things. Then when my uncle Sylvester was with them—they all worked together in those days—I would listen. I learned a good deal, and I promised myself that I would be the greatest collector of them all one day."

"I understand perfectly," I said. "I feel that too. Joliffe, I am going to help you. How glad I am that I have started to learn something. Not much I know for it's a lifetime's study. But you were pleased with me, weren't you, when I recognized that scroll?"

"I was proud of you."

"I owe all that to your uncle and when I think of that I am a little ashamed. He did so much for my mother and me—and then I left him."

"Didn't you know that a woman should forsake all others and cleave to her husband?"

"Yes, yes, but I think your uncle Sylvester was hurt."

"Good God, Jane. Did he think you were some sort of slave?"

"He has never shown me or my mother anything but the greatest kindness, but he did teach me, train me . . . and before I could be of any real use to him I went away."

"Don't worry about old Uncle Sylvester. He'll get over it. Did he ever talk to you about The House of a Thousand Lanterns?"

"Yes, he did mention it."

"What did he tell you?"

"That it was his and that it was in Hong Kong. What a strange name for a house. A thousand lanterns is a great many. Have you seen it?"

"Yes."

"Is it as romantic as it sounds?"

He hesitated. "It's a strange house. Rather repelling in a way, yet fascinating. I saw it first when I was about fourteen. Uncle Redmond, who was alive then, had taken me out with him and Adam. At that time he thought I would work with them. Places make an impression on you which you often never forget. A house with a name like that . . ."

"I'd like to see it. I can imagine it. Are there really a thousand lanterns?"

"There are a great many. Lanterns on the porch, and wind bells which made a strange tinkling noise. I was impressed because it was my first visit to Hong Kong. Everything seemed so strange then. It seemed dark in the house and the servants with their pigtails and silent way of moving about impressed me deeply. I thought it the most foreign place I'd ever seen. When my uncle lives there he conforms somewhat to the Chinese fashion. I remember he told me that one must always respect other people's customs. When in Rome do as the Romans do and the same applies to China."

"Is it true that the house was presented to some ancestor of yours?"

"To my great-grandfather. He was a doctor. He went out to China and worked there among the people. One rich and influential mandarin was very grateful to him because he saved his wife in childbirth and not only the wife but child too. It was a boy and boys are important to the Chinese. Girls they often put out into the streets to starve to death—not so boys. They are very unkind to members of your sex whom they consider of little importance."

"And so the mandarin gave your great-grandfather this House of a Thousand Lanterns."

"Yes. When he died some years after the birth of his son. There is a letter which he wrote and which is in the family's possession. Translated it says that the house is a miserable gift for the birth of a son, but among the thousand lanterns lies his greatest treasure, and he was putting this into the care of the man to whom he would be grateful forever."

"How mysterious."

"There may have been some discrepancy in the translation but it seems that the house is a gift and it is a sort of container for something of greater value. It's a puzzle. You know the Chinese love puzzles."

"And what was this treasure?"

"It was never discovered."

"Do you mean that people looked for it?"

"People have looked for it since the house was given to my great-grandfather. Nothing has been found. It seems that the old mandarin was anxious to prove his gratitude and the house was indeed far more than my great-grandfather would have thought possible for something he did often in the course of his profession. But the legend persisted and The House of a Thousand Lanterns is regarded with some sort of awe."

"You mean by the people who live near it?"

"By the servants too. It is always kept in readiness, for

my uncle is the sort of man who doesn't give warning of his coming. He wishes to come and go without fuss."

"I wonder if I shall ever see The House of a Thousand Lanterns?"

"I shall take you. We'll go together."

"One thousand lanterns. How many rooms are there to accommodate so many?"

"There may not be a thousand. It's a poet's phrase, isn't it? The Chinese would like that. It sounds better than eight hundred and ninety-five. I've never counted them. But the lanterns are a feature of the place. They are in every room and on the porch, in the garden . . . everywhere. Inside them are oil lamps. They look effective when lighted. If ever it comes to me I shall have a thorough search made to find out whether the old mandarin was romancing when he talked of the treasure."

"Will it go to you?"

"My uncle has no family. As you know, he never married. It would naturally have gone to Uncle Redmond had he lived. There is Adam of course—Adam is two years older than I. But as Uncle Redmond didn't get on with Uncle Sylvester and Adam is his son . . . well, you see my reasoning. It's not an impossibility."

"Do you want this house, Joliffe?"

"I want it very much. Something tells me that mandarins don't lie when they are about to join their ancestors. Yes, I want that house . . . very much. There's only one thing I want more, and that's my Jane."

It was hard to get that conversation out of my mind. The House of a Thousand Lanterns had caught my imagination. I could picture all those lanterns hanging from ceilings, fixed to walls, all with their little lamps inside them. And one day I should see them. I longed to do so. It was exciting and yet there was a deep feeling of regret to remember that to come to my present bliss I had been obliged to desert Mr. Sylvester Milner.

As we strolled along the Left Bank we talked a great deal and I was building up a picture of Joliffe's life and planning how mine should fit into it.

That he was enthusiastic about his business was obvious and again and again I was thankful that I could share in this enthusiasm. Once more thanks to Mr. Sylvester. He talked easily to me and my happiness deepened. It was going to be a wonderful life.

Then I made a discovery which put a curb on my happiness. It was like the first real sign of cloud on the blue horizon.

We had dined with friends of Joliffe's and had returned to our hotel. We made love and lay drowsily side by side. I was wearing the jade ring with carved eye of Kuan Yin and I said: "I think I believe in it. Ever since you gave it to me life has been especially wonderful."

"What's that?" said Joliffe half asleep.

"The Kuan Yin," I answered.

"If I could find the original . . ."

"We'll look for it, Joliffe. What would you do if you found it?"

"There's a problem. Keep it and have the goddess listen to my cries of despair and come to my aid, or sell it and make a fortune. Which shall it be, Jane?"

"It would depend on how much you believed in the legend."

"Fortunes are more tangible than legends."

"I wonder whether the one your uncle found is after all the true one and if it is what he would do."

"That one . . . that's one of hundreds."

"How do you know?"

"I had it tested."

"What!" I was wide awake.

Joliffe opened one eye and pulled me closer to him.

"Who saw a light in the room? Who came up in her dressing gown and found instead of a burglar . . . love?"

"What are you saying, Joliffe?"

"You're in the family now, my Jane. It was my light you saw in the room. What sharp eyes you have and what were you doing awake at that hour when the whole household was supposed to be fast asleep?"

"Joliffe, I don't understand."

"Then you are not applying your usual perspicacity. Why do you think I chose that time to pay a visit? Because I knew Uncle Sylvester had the Kuan Yin."

"How did you get into the room? I was the only one in the house with a key."

He laughed. "That wasn't quite true, Jane dear. I had a key."

"But how? There are three. Uncle Sylvester's, Ling Fu's, and mine."

"There are four as far as I know. Maybe more. I have one too, you see."

"But . . . how?"

"My dear Jane I have known Roland's Croft for years. I have stayed with my uncle. At one time he was training me to work with him."

"He gave you a key?"

"Let us say I acquired one."

"How?"

"By seizing my opportunity, taking it from its secret place and getting another cut. Now I have access to his room whenever I wish as long as I choose the opportunity."

"Oh Joliffe!"

"Now you're shocked. You have to grow up, Jane, if you are going to be in this business. We are rivals . . . we must know what goes on in the enemy's camp; all's fair in love and war. This is a kind of war."

"Oh no."

He drew me to him and kissed me but I did not respond.

"I'm tired of Kuan Yin, Jane."

"I want to know what happened."

"Oh darling, haven't you got it? I came down when my uncle was away. I went by stealth in the dead of night to that room, removed the Kuan Yin, took her to be tested and then brought her back. In the act of replacing her my very inquisitive wife-to-be discovered me and we met by moonlight—no there wasn't a moon. Pity, it would have been so fitting. Never mind, the starlight had to do and there took place that enchanting, tender interlude which must have made all the gods jealous of me. Jane, I love you."

"But it was wrong," I said.

"What do you mean . . . *wrong?*"

"To go to that room, like that. It was like stealing."

"Nonsense. Nothing was removed which was not returned."

"Why didn't you come when your uncle was there? Why didn't you ask him . . . ?"

"There are trade secrets. You have to understand this. For all we know some rival may have the original Kuan Yin. He may be holding it, biding the moment to sell. This is business, Jane."

"To come there, and go into his private room, and take it away . . ."

"I knew it was safe. He was away and I knew where he'd gone. I knew there was time to get it out and back again. Oh, enough of this. I'm tired of the subject."

But I could not get it out of my mind. I felt cheated in some way although it was Mr. Sylvester Milner who had been cheated.

I did not like these methods of business.

It made me see Joliffe differently. I loved him as deeply as ever but it was not the same. Apprehension had crept into my beautiful existence. It was the fear of what I might discover next.

II

A few days later we crossed the Channel.

I was delighted with Joliffe's house in Kensington. It was tall, rather slender in a terrace of such houses which all displayed the graceful elegance of the period. There were four stories, on each of which were two large rooms, and Annie and Albert, who were waiting to greet us, lived over the stables in the mews which was situated at the back of the terrace. Annie was the typical ex-nanny who doted on Joliffe and now and then forgot that he was a grown man. She called him Master Jo and scolded him in a manner which he loved, for quite clearly she adored him, and Joliffe, I was discovering, looked upon feminine adulation as his due. Albert, pale and wiry, was a handy man who looked after the carriage and horses and had very little to say.

I took to the establishment immediately. Our room was on the third floor. Its windows opened onto a balcony with a view of the tiny garden and the stables. The garden could hardly be called such by Roland's Croft standards. It was a square of crazy paving with a border of earth in which grew a few evergreen shrubs. There was a solitary pear tree though which gave fruit rather reluctantly—little green hard pears which Annie said were only good for stewing.

From the drawing room on the first floor I could watch the horse cabs clopping by and look across the road to the trees of Kensington Gardens. I was soon delighting in those gardens and often took a morning walk there.

Now that we were in London and our honeymoon was over I saw less of Joliffe. He had an office in the city and he was often there. This left me to my own devices. I

would stroll down the flower walk where the nannies sat
with their charges and sometimes I sat with them and listened to their discussions about their children's characteristics and those of their employers. I wandered along
by the Serpentine and explored the Orangerie of the Palace with its William and Mary façade; I walked past the
windows behind which our Queen had once played with
her dolls though it was hard to imagine as a little girl the
black-clad widow she had become. I saw the summer
flowers replaced by the hardier blooms of autumn in the
pond garden and the thick leaves of summer gradually
turn russet and drop. I liked to sit by the Round Pond
and watch the children with their boats and I would take
bread with which to feed the swans and the birds.

It was at the Round Pond that I first noticed the
woman. She was in a way not the sort of person one
would miss. She was tall—buxom almost and she had
abundant red hair which escaped from her hat in ringlets.
With her hourglass figure she was beautiful in an over-
ripe rather coarse way.

I made a habit of going straight to the pond to feed the
swans and I saw her again. It was the third time I saw her
that I noticed she was aware of me. I had bent forward to
throw a piece of bread to a swan and when I turned my
head I saw that she was standing quite close to me. Her
eyes were large, very light blue; and there could be no
doubt whatever that they were fixed upon me.

I walked quickly towards the palace and went to the
pond garden. This was a replica of the one made by
Henry VIII at Hampton Court; it was shut in by railings
and the path round it was the pleached alley where the
trees had been trained to meet overhead—thick and
heavy in summer, bare branches in winter. There were
gaps in the trees on each side of the garden to enable
people to look over the low railings at the flowers and
pond.

I went into the alley and after walking a little way, I paused to look at the garden through one of the gaps. At the opening opposite was the red-haired woman.

I stepped backwards and made as though to turn to my left; and when she could no longer see me because of the trees in the alley I made a sharp right turn and walked swiftly out round the alley and out to the avenue of elms. Then I went home.

I told myself I had imagined she had followed me. Why I should have felt so uncomfortable I could not imagine; except that it gives one an uneasy feeling to think oneself followed.

When I arrived home there was a letter from my mother. She was coming up to London to see me. She was longing for a glimpse of me in my home.

I was delighted and when Joliffe came in he shared my pleasure.

"I'll have to show her what a good husband you have," he said.

I filled the house with flowers—chrysanthemums, asters, dahlias, and starry Michaelmas daisies. I had consulted with Annie. I wanted a very special luncheon on this day and Annie was determined that this should be a meal my mother would never forget.

Joliffe would make sure that he was home that day.

Soon after twelve the cab came jingling up and I was at the door to greet her.

We flew into each other's arms and then she withdrew that she might have a look at me. I could see she was pleased with what she saw.

"Come in, Mother," I said. "Come and see the house. It's rather nice."

She said, "It's you I've come to see, Janey love. So you're happy, eh?"

"Blissfully," I answered.

"Thank God."

I took her into our bedroom and myself removed her bonnet and cloak. "You're getting thinner," I said.

"Oh, I'm all right, dear. There's no harm in that. There was a bit too much of me before."

Her cheeks were reddish, her eyes brilliant. I put this down to her pleasure in seeing me.

She brought out a bottle of sloe gin. Mrs. Couch had sent it, believing that it was Joliffe's favorite beverage.

"She'll want to hear all about you both when I get back," said my mother. "I am so happy to see you settled."

Joliffe came in and warmly greeted her, and soon Annie was announcing that luncheon was served.

It was a happy meal, though my mother ate very little. I was amazed because in the old days my father had laughed at the size of her appetite.

I told her about our honeymoon in Paris and asked how everyone was at Roland's Croft. Mr. Sylvester was away at the moment. All the servants were well. Amy and the under gardener were making plans for their wedding and would be married at Christmas. She was worried about Jess because she was still far too friendly with Jeffers and Mrs. Jeffers was getting really militant.

"Of course," said my mother, "Jeffers is like that and if it wasn't Jess it would be someone else."

"Poor Mrs. Jeffers!" I sighed. "I'd hate it if Joliffe paid attention to someone else."

"You're safe," said Joliffe, "for two reasons. First, who could possibly compare with you? Secondly I'm far too virtuous to indulge in such folly."

My mother's eyes filled with tears. I knew she was thinking of my father.

We talked long over the meal and then we went back to the drawing room and there was more talk.

At four o'clock she had to leave to catch her train, for she must return to Roland's Croft that day. Albert brought the carriage round and we went to the station to put my mother on her train; we embraced fondly and she wept a little.

"I'm so happy that you are settled," she whispered. "It is what I've always wanted. Bless you, Janey. Be happy always as you are now."

We waved goodbye to her and then came home.

It was a happy enough evening. Joliffe said we must have a quiet one just ourselves and we sat by the fire and saw pictures in it and his arm was about me as the twilight settled in the room.

"How peaceful it is," I said. "Joliffe, life's wonderful, isn't it?"

He stroked my hair and said: "Yes, Jane, while we have each other."

A few days after my mother's visit I went to the Round Pond and there was the red-haired woman. She was sitting on a seat as though waiting for someone.

When I saw her I felt an odd tingling in my spine and the thought entered my head: She is waiting for me.

I felt a ridiculous impulse then to turn and run. It was absurd. Why should I? What had I to fear from a stranger on a seat in a park?

It is only that she seems to be following me, I thought.

I went straight past her and took a turn into the pleached alley. I paused and sure enough on the other side of the garden looking straight at me through the gap on that side was the red-haired woman. She must have risen from her seat when she saw me and followed me.

I wondered whether to wait there for her and if she came round ask her if she wanted something of me. My heart began to beat fast. How could I accuse her of such a thing when I was not sure? But I *was* sure that she was following me.

She had moved from the gap now. I knew that she was coming round towards me. If I turned she would follow me.

What could she want of me?

I steeled myself to speak to her. We were almost level now and as she looked straight at me, I felt hideously repelled and my great desire was to get away from her as soon as possible.

No words came. I was walking past her, subconsciously quickening my pace. I came out of the alley. Unless she had turned and followed me it would be some minutes before she made the journey round.

I started to hurry out into the open, towards the pond. When I was there I paused and saw her. She was walking slowly in the direction I had taken.

I crossed the road and let myself into the house with my latchkey.

As I turned to shut the door I saw the red-haired woman crossing the road.

I was in the drawing room when Annie came in. She said there was a "person" below asking to see me.

"What sort of a person, Annie?"

Annie repeated, "A person," with a little sniff, which meant that she did not entirely approve of our visitor.

"What does she want?"

"She said she wanted to speak to you."

"A lady then."

"A *person*," insisted Annie emphatically.

"What name did she say?"

"She said you'd know her when you saw her."

"That's odd," I said. "Perhaps you'd better show her up."

I heard them coming up the stairs. Then Annie tapped at the door and threw it open.

I stood up in astonishment for the red-haired woman was coming into the room.

"We've met before," I said. Annie who had looked very suspiciously at the visitor seemed then to think all was well. She shut the door on us.

"In the Gardens," she answered with a slow smile.

"I . . . I saw you several times."

"Yes, I was never far behind, was I?"

"Did you want something?"

"I think we'd better sit down," she said, as though I were the visitor.

"Who are you?" I asked.

She smiled wryly as she said: "I might be saying the same to you."

"This is rather mysterious," I said coldly. "I am Mrs. Joliffe Milner. If you have come here to see me . . ."

She interrupted: "You are not Mrs. Joliffe Milner," she said slowly. "There is only one of those. It'll surprise you to learn that one is not you. *I* am Mrs. Joliffe Milner."

"I don't understand you."

"You will fast enough. You can call yourself Mrs. Joliffe Milner if you like, but the fact remains you're not. How can you be when Joliffe was married to me six years ago?"

"I don't believe it."

"I thought you wouldn't. I'd have spoken to you before, but I thought you'd want proof. And what better proof than the marriage lines, eh?"

I felt faint.

"You are lying. It isn't possible," I said.

"I knew you'd say that. But there's no denying what's down in black and white, is there? Just look at this. We were married six years ago in Oxford."

I looked at the paper she thrust into my hand and read what was written there.

If this document was a true one she had indeed been married to a Joliffe Milner six years ago.

It was like a nightmare. She crossed her legs, lifting up skirts beneath which were flounces of pink petticoat; her black stockings had openwork decorations up the sides.

"You look as if you'd had a shock," she said and she gave a little giggle. "Well, you have, haven't you? It's not every day you hear the man you thought was your husband is someone else's."

I began rather shakily: "I don't know who you are or what your motive is . . ."

"My motive," she interrupted, "is to tell you what you ought to know. You're a lady, I can see that. You're well educated and I've no doubt you were very pleased with yourself . . . till now. I've watched you in the Gardens. I wondered whether to speak to you then. I had to do a bit of detective work to find him. Then I thought this is better. I'd call and tell you. I'll wait here and see him if you like. That's going to be a nice surprise for him! What about some refreshments? I could do with a glass of wine."

I said to her: "I don't believe a word you're saying."

"Not when you've seen the lines?"

"It's not possible. If he were married to you how could he marry me?"

"He couldn't. That's the point. He's not married to you, he's married to me."

"He would never do such a thing."

"He thought I was dead. I was traveling down from Oxford to London by train. That was a year ago. There was a disaster on the line outside Reading. You must have heard of it. It was one of the biggest crashes ever. Many people were killed. I almost was. Unlucky for him not quite. I was in hospital for three months and nobody knew who I was for some time. I had no papers on me and I couldn't remember much myself. As for my devoted husband, he made no effort to claim me. Jolly good riddance, he said. He'd realized long before that what a mistake he had made. It goes to show that young gentlemen up at Oxford for their education shouldn't get caught up with barmaids, leastways they shouldn't go so far as to marry them. Joliffe was a hot-head. No sooner do I say 'Unhand me, sir. Nothing of that till I get my marriage lines' and there are my marriage lines as you see them now! But marriage is for good. That's what he forgot. So there you have the story of my life in a few sentences. It's not uncommon. He's not the first young gentleman who's acted rash and lived to regret it."

"If this had been so he would have told me . . ."

"Joliffe tell you! You don't know half what goes on behind that handsome mug of his. I used to say to him, 'All that charm of yours will be your downfall.' There were lots of fellows after me, I can tell you, but it had to be him and there he was caught. He couldn't let me meet his family, could he? He saw that. What ructions there'd be! So he got me rooms in Oxford and we were there for close on a year. Married bliss! It didn't last very long. He saw his mistake. He was always making excuses and going away. Then I was coming to meet him in London and there was this train. He always used to say he was lucky. I reckon he thought the day that train went off its rails was the luckiest in his life. But he didn't look far enough, did he?"

"This is such a fantastic story," I said.

"Life with Joliffe Milner would always be like that. Fantastic, that's the word for it."

"You had better come back when my . . . Mr. Milner is here."

She shook her head.

"No, I'm staying. I want to come face to face with him. I want you to be there when I do. Because if you're not he'll cook up some story for you. He's a great cooker-up, our Joliffe. No, I want to catch him, just like that before he's had the time to work something out."

"This is going to be proved a great mistake. There must be some other Joliffe Milner who is your husband."

She shook her head.

"Oh no, I've made sure of that."

I did not know what to do. From the moment I had first set eyes on her I had felt a sense of terrible foreboding. There had been something about the manner in which she had shadowed me which had filled me with apprehension.

I could not bear to sit in this room with her. I said: "You will excuse me . . ."

She inclined her head with a smirk as though she were the mistress of the house, giving me leave to go.

I ran up to our bedroom. It was like a nightmare. It simply wasn't possible. It was some horrible joke in the bad taste to be expected of such a person. I was thinking of her in Annie's terms. A person!

What a wretched half hour I spent. I wondered what she was doing in the drawing room. I imagined those big calculating eyes assessing everything. If Joliffe had married surely he would have told me. But would he? There was so much I did not know about him and the more I discovered the more I realized there was to learn.

It seemed an age before I heard his key in the lock. I sped to the top of the stairs. He was in the hall and smiled when he saw me.

"Hello, my darling."

"Joliffe," I cried. "There's a woman . . . She's here."

He came up the stairs two at a time. I did not wait for him to reach me. I started to walk towards the drawing room and threw the door open.

She was seated on the sofa, her legs crossed, showing the flounces of petticoats, a sly smile on her face.

The next seconds I knew would be the most important through which I had ever lived.

In that short time I promised myself that he would look at her, prove her to have made false accusations, show me and her that he was not the Joliffe Milner whose name appeared with hers on those marriage lines.

I advanced into the room. He followed me. He stopped short. She smiled at him insolently. And in that moment I felt my world collapsing about me.

"Good God," he said. "Bella!"

She answered, "Your own loving little wife, no less."

"Bella . . . *no!*"

"A ghost returned from the grave. Not quite. Because I was never in the grave. A little shock for such a devoted husband."

"Bella," he repeated. "What . . . does this mean?"

"It means I'm here. Mrs. Joliffe Milner herself come to claim her conjugal rights and all that goes with it."

He said nothing. I could see that he was completely stunned.

"It was quite a job to find you," she said.

"But I understood . . ."

"You understood what you wanted to understand."

"You were killed. There was proof. Your coat had your name on it."

She laughed with exaggerated heartiness. "That was Fanny. Remember Fanny? She had a sealskin hat and I lent her my sealskin coat. Oh that was a lovely coat, one of your presents to me. Remember? I was so fond of it I had my name worked on the lining. We went up to London together—she in my sealskin I in her beaver. She was killed, poor Fanny, and they thought she was me of course. I was nearly done for. I didn't know who I was for three months . . . then it came back slowly. It took me a long time to find you, Joey, but here I am."

I said: "It's true . . . what this woman says . . ."

He looked at me blankly.

I turned and went from the room.

I stumbled up to our bedroom and I asked myself what I could do next. I was bewildered; my happiness had disintegrated so rapidly that I could not think clearly. The only thought which kept hammering in my head was: Joliffe is that woman's husband. Not yours. You have no place in this house. It belongs to her.

What could I do? I should have to go away, leave them together.

I must do something. I took a case and started to put a few things into it. Then I sat down and covered my face with my hands. I wanted to shut out the sight of this room where I had been so happy for I knew that that happiness was built on no firm foundation. It had collapsed as quickly as the houses of cards my mother used to build with me when I was a child.

Joliffe came into the room. He looked stricken—all the assurance drained from him. I would never have believed he could have looked like that.

He took a step towards me and held me in his arms.

I lay against him for a few moments trying to shut out that hideous scene in the room below. But I had to face the truth, I knew it.

I withdrew myself and said: "Joliffe, it's not true. It can't be."

He nodded miserably.

"Why didn't you tell me?"

"I thought she was dead. It was all past and done with, I thought. It was something I wanted to forget had ever happened."

"But you married her! That woman is your wife! Oh Joliffe, I can't bear it."

"I thought she was dead. Her name was given as one of those who died in the disaster. I was out of the country at the time and when I came back I heard the news and accepted it as true. How should I know that someone else was wearing her coat?"

"So she is your wife."

"I'll have to take steps, Jane. We'll find a way."

"She's here, Joliffe. She's in this house. She's down there now. She said she had come to stay."

"She'll have to go."

"But she's your *wife!*"

"That doesn't force me to live with her."

"There's only one thing I can do," I said.

He looked at me wretchedly.

"I must go away," I went on. "I'll go to Roland's Croft. I'll be with my mother. We'll have to see what I should do."

"You're my wife," he said.

"I'm not. She is your wife."

"Don't go, Jane. We'll leave here. We'll go away, we'll go abroad."

"But *she* is your wife, Joliffe. She will never let you forget that. I can't stay here. Let me go to my mother. I'll stay with her for a while until . . . we work something out."

"I can't let you go, Jane."

"You have no alternative. I must go now, quickly. It will be easier this way."

He pleaded with me. I had never seen him like this before. His marriage to Bella had been an act of youthful folly. He would find a way out, he promised me. *I* was his wife, not that woman down there.

But I knew that this was not so. I knew that I had to get away.

Reality seemed to have receded. It was hard to believe that I was not in the midst of a nightmare. I packed two bags and this helped to calm me. It occurred to me then that this was how life with Joliffe would have been. I would never have known what or who would arise from the past. Joliffe was the most exciting person in the world and this was partly because he was unpredictable. I had lived a quiet and sheltered life. I had been unprepared for what could happen to the adventurous like Joliffe. The knowledge came to me then that I had never really known Joliffe. I loved him, yes—his appearance, his personality, his gaiety, the spirit of adventure that was innate in him —but I did not know the true man. He had gradually begun to emerge. It was as though a mask was slowly shifting and showing me what I had not known existed.

I had been innocent, unworldly, but on that day I began to grow up.

Albert drove me to the station. He said nothing, but his expression was mournful. A porter carried my bags and put me in a first-class compartment and so I traveled down to Roland's Croft.

It was dusk when I arrived at the little station. There was no one to meet me this time, but the stationmaster, who knew me, said that the station fly would be back in fifteen minutes if I'd wait for that.

"An unexpected visit, Mrs. Milner," he said. "They don't seem to know up at the house that you're coming."

I said: "No, they don't."

"Well, 'twill be a matter of fifteen minutes most likely."

I guessed fifteen minutes meant thirty and I was right but in due course I was driving along to the house.

Jeffers came hurrying out at the sound of wheels. He looked blankly at me.

"Why," he said, "if it isn't young Mrs. Milner! Was you expected? I had no orders to meet you."

"I was not expected," I assured him. "Will you have my bags brought in please?"

He looked a little disconcerted.

Amy was at the door. Her astonishment was apparent.

I said: "Hello, Amy. Would you please tell my mother I'm here."

"Why, Miss Jane, she's not here."

"Not here! But where is she?"

"You'd better come in," she said.

There was something mysterious happening. This was not the greeting I had expected. Amy had turned and run to the servants' hall calling Mrs. Couch.

When the cook appeared I ran to her. She took me into her arms and kissed me.

"Why Jane," she said. "You could have knocked me down with a feather."

I said: "Where's my mother, Mrs. Couch? Amy said she was not here."

"It's true. She was took away three days since."

"Where to?"

"To the hospital."

"Has she had an accident?"

"Well not exactly, dear. It's her complaint."

"Her complaint?"

"It was that cough and all that. It's been coming on some time."

"I wasn't told."

"No, she didn't want you worried."

"What is the matter with her?"

Mrs. Couch looked uneasy. "The master's home," she said. "I think it would be a good thing if you was to see him. I'll go along myself and tell him you're here, shall I? Where's Mr. Joliffe? Hasn't he come with you?"

"No. He's in London."

"I'll tell the master. You go up to your old room and I'll tell him."

In a haze of apprehension I went up to my old room. It seemed that something terrible was happening to everyone I loved. What was this mystery about my mother? There was no mystery about Joliffe. The truth was horribly clear. He was married and I was not his wife. But my mother . . . in the hospital! Why had I not been told?

There was the familiar room. I went to the window and looked across to the barred windows of the showroom, and poignant memories of the night when I had been there with Joliffe came back to me. Joliffe who had cheated then, and who was married all the time so that I was not his wife!

What is happening? I asked myself. Everything is collapsing about me.

Mrs. Couch was at the door.

"The master will see you now," she said.

I followed her to the room where we had often sat together and drunk tea from the dragon teapot.

He rose as I entered and took my hand.

"Sit down," he said.

I did so.

"I'm afraid I have bad news for you," he went on, "and it is useless to keep it from you any longer. Your mother has been very ill for some time. She was suffering from consumption. She did not wish you to know. That is why you were not told. She was anxious that you should not be upset during your first months of marriage. At length she became so ill that it was necessary for her to go into a hospital that she might have the best of attention. That is where she is now."

"But . . ." I began.

He silenced me. "It is a great shock for you, I know. Perhaps it would have been better if you had been warned. She had been suffering from this complaint for a few years now. In the last months it has intensified. I think you have to prepare yourself for the fact that she cannot live much longer."

I could not speak. My grief welled up within me. He regarded me with a compassion which was very real and comforting.

"I can't believe this," I said.

"It is hard, I know. We thought that one sharp blow would be better for you than a long-drawn-out anxiety. Her only thought was for you."

"I know it. Can I see her?"

"Yes," he answered.

"Now?"

"You must wait till tomorrow. Then Jeffers can drive you to the hospital."

"But I want to see her at once."

"You could not see her at this time of day. She is very ill. She may not know you. Give yourself time to grow accustomed to this grief."

He looked so wise sitting there in his mulberry smoking jacket and little velvet cap, that I felt a certain comfort in looking at him.

"It is too much," I said suddenly. "This . . . and Joliffe . . ."

"Joliffe?" he said quickly.

I knew I would have to tell him, so I did so.

He was silent.

"Did you know that he already had a wife?" I asked.

"If I had I should have spoken up. But it does not surprise me. What shall you do?"

"I don't know. I was going to talk it over with my mother."

"She must not know. It gave her great gratification to believe you had someone to look after you."

"No, she must not know."

"You will have to decide what you are going to do."

"I know."

"You could, of course, stay here. You could resume your post with me. It would be a solution."

For the first time since Joliffe's wife had told me the truth I felt a faint gleam of comfort.

Mr. Sylvester Milner drove with me to the hospital. He waited in the carriage while I went in.

When they took me to the room in which my mother lay I scarcely recognized her, so thin had she become. She had not the strength to sit up, nor to move very much, but she knew me and a great joy came into her eyes. I knelt by the bed and I could not bear to look at her so I took her hand and held it against my cheek.

Her lips moved faintly: "Janey . . ."

"I am here, dearest," I said.

Her lips moved but her voice was so faint that I had to bend my head to hear it. "Be happy, Janey. I am . . . because it's turned out so well for you. You have Joliffe . . ."

She could not say more. I sat by the bed, her hand in mine.

I must have sat for almost an hour until the sister came and told me I must go.

Mr. Sylvester Milner and I drove back to Roland's Croft in silence.

Before the week was out she was dead. In less than twelve days I had been struck two terrible blows. I think one took my mind off the other. Such a short while ago I would not have believed either possible. I had come to my mother to tell her of my troubles and she was no longer there. That seemed even more difficult to grasp than that I was no longer Joliffe's wife. Deep in my heart ever since I learned of his taking the Kuan Yin from the showcase I had been ready for anything Joliffe might have done. Somewhere at the back of my mind had been the uneasy thought that there was something not quite real about our romantic meeting and our hasty marriage. But that my mother who had always been with me should be dead was hard to accept. And the thought that she had been dying while I was being so carelessly gay in Paris wounded me deeply.

Mr. Sylvester was a great comfort. He arranged for my mother's funeral and she was buried quietly in the little village churchyard. Everyone from the house attended and Mr. Sylvester walked beside me to the grave.

Mrs. Couch had pulled all the blinds down when my mother died. She said it indicated death in the house. When we returned after the funeral she served ham sandwiches which was the right thing, she told me, and showed a proper respect for the dead. Then she drew up the blinds which was the right time to do it. She could be relied on to know of these things, she whispered comfortingly to me, because her own mother had had fourteen children and buried eight.

I sat with them in the servants' hall and Mrs. Couch and Mr. Jeffers vied with each other in telling stories of past funerals they had attended. I could have seen the humor at any other time, but I couldn't see anything but my bright gay little mother and to think of her silent in her grave was more than I could endure.

I went to my room and I had not been there very long when there was a knock on my door. It was Sylvester Milner.

In his hand he held an envelope.

"Your mother left this for you. She asked me to give it to you on the day she was buried." His kind eyes smiled gently. "You have reached the lowest depths," he went on. "Now you will begin to rise. Such tragedies are all part of the business of living but remember this: 'Adversity strengthens the character.' There is nothing on Earth that is all evil, nothing that is all good."

Then he pressed the envelope into my hands.

When he had gone I opened it, and the sight of my mother's rather untidy sprawling handwriting brought tears to my eyes.

My dearest Janey, (she had written)
    I am very ill. I have been for a long time. It's this cursed illness, the bane of my family. It took my father when he was about my age. I didn't want you to know, Janey love, because I knew how sad it would make you. The two of us had always been close, hadn't we, especially since your father died? I hid it from you. Sometimes I'd cough so badly there'd be blood on my pillow and I was afraid you'd see it when you came suddenly into my room. I didn't want you to guess and I did well, didn't I? You never knew. I used to worry about you. You were my one concern. But what luck we had. That was your father looking after us. Good kind Mr. Sylvester Milner was like the fairy godfather. First he gave me the post (mind you I was very good at it) and then he let me have you there (not that I'd have taken it if he hadn't) and there were Mrs. Couch

and the rest of them who were like a family to us. So it all came out well. And then he said you were to work for him. I was pleased then but it wasn't quite what I wanted. I wanted you to be settled. I wanted you to be happy as I'd been with your father and when Joliffe came along and fell in love with you at first sight—and you with him—I was overjoyed. You now have a husband who will care for you as your father cared for me. I came up to see the specialist the day I visited you. He told me I hadn't got long and that I'd have to go into a hospital. I said to myself then "Lord now lettest Thou thy servant depart in peace." Because I knew I could go happily. You and Joliffe are so much in love. He'll be with you now. He'll take care of you and there was something your father used to say. It was almost as though he knew he'd go first and leave me. It was something in Shakespeare, something like this.

"No longer mourn for me when I am dead" . . . and it goes on:

"I in your sweet thoughts would be forgot
If thinking of me then should make you woe."

It would grieve me, Janey love, if I was to look down and see you sad. That's something I couldn't bear. So I want you to say this: "She had a good life. She had a husband and a child and they were all the world to her. She's now going to join one and she's left the other in the hands of one who loves her."

Goodbye my precious child. One thing I ask of you: Be happy.

Your Mother.

I folded the letter, put it into the sandalwood box where I kept those things which were precious to me, and then I could no longer contain my grief.

The day after the funeral I received a letter from Joliffe.

My dearest Jane, (he wrote)

My uncle has written to tell me of your mother's death. I long to be with you to comfort you. My uncle has more or less threatened me if I come to see you. He means I think that he will cut me out of his will. As if that would keep me away! He says that you need time to recover from these two tragic blows and that the best way is in your work with him.

Jane, I must see you. We have to talk. I was a mad young fool to marry Bella and I honestly thought she had been killed. She swears she won't let me go. She has installed herself in the house. I'm consulting lawyers. It's an unusual case. I don't know what they can make of it.

Send me word and I'll be wherever you will come to me.

I love you, Joliffe.

I read and reread that letter. Then I folded it and put it with my mother's in the sandalwood box.

Over tea in Mr. Sylvester Milner's sitting room he showed me some pottery he had acquired.

"Look at this delicate tracery," he said. "The forest and hills shrouded in mist. Is it not delicate and beautiful? Would you say it is the Sung period?"

I said that as far as I could say it would seem to be.

He nodded. "There's no doubt. What a fascinating ghostly quality there is about this work." He looked at me closely. "Your interest in it is returning a little, I think."

"I never lost my interest."

"That is how it works. The attraction is always there. You are growing away from your sorrow. That is the way. Has Joliffe communicated with you?"

"He has written."

"And asked you to join him?"

I did not answer and he shook his head. "It is not the way," he said. "He is like his father. He could be irresistible and charming. Different from his brothers. Redmond and I were the businessmen, and Joliffe's father was the charmer. He lived in a world of his own making. He believed what he wanted to believe. It worked up to a point and then there comes the reckoning. You will not go to him."

"How could I? He has a wife."

"Yes, he has a wife, but he has asked you to return to him. That is like his father. Everything must come right for him—that is what he believes. Why? Because he is Joliffe who fascinates everyone—or almost everyone. He cannot believe that he cannot fascinate Fate. But Fate will not be lured by charm.

> " 'The Moving Finger writes; and, having writ,
>   Moves on; nor all thy piety nor wit,
>   Shall lure it back to cancel half a line,
>   Nor all they charm (if I may paraphrase)
>   wash out a word of it.'

"There are the plain facts. You thought yourself to be a wife and you are not. It was a tragic experience for you. Put it behind you. Start from here. In time the wound will cease to ache."

"I shall try to do that."

"If you truly try you will succeed. Now I am going to work you very hard, for work is the best healer. I have no housekeeper. I want you to take over in some measure the work your mother did. Mrs. Couch will help. She has intimated that she wants no strangers here. You will decide on meals when I have guests; you will join us often as there will be talk of business and you are learning that. You will continue to read the books I give you and perhaps accompany me to sales. Your life will be so busy that you will have little time for grief. This would be what your mother would want. Do not see Joliffe. I have written to him telling him I will not receive him here. He must get his affairs in order. Will you try to take my advice?"

"I am sure," I told him, "that your advice is good, and I will do my best."

"Then we have made a bargain."

The Convenient Marriage

I tried to keep the bargain. Joliffe did not write again. Often I walked in the forest and my footsteps invariably took me to that ruin where we had sheltered and first met. I used to hope that I would find him there, that I would hear his voice calling me. If he had come to me I am sure I should have forgotten everything but my love for him. I looked for letters every day; when I was near the station if a train came in I would watch the people coming out hoping that one of them would be Joliffe.

But he did not come or write. I wondered what was happening in Kensington and if Bella was with him. At one moment I upbraided him to myself. He had not come because his uncle had threatened to disinherit him if he did. At another I feared that he would return and that I would throw all convention aside and go to him.

I worked hard. I studied books and the objects of art which were brought to the showroom. I learned as quickly as I could. I looked for and won Mr. Sylvester's approval. I thought: He is right. This is the crutch on which I can lean until I grow stronger.

He entertained more often than before and our guests were not all those concerned in his profession. He had become more neighborly and he visited and was visited by people who lived round about. Our immediate neighbor was Squire Merrit who owned a large estate. He was a great favorite of Mrs. Couch's for he was a good trencherman and never failed to show his appreciation of her dishes. During the season he would send a brace or two of pheasants over to her by one of his servants and he used to say that no one could cook a pheasant as she could and he hoped he'd be invited to share these.

Mrs. Couch would purr and murmur as she rocked back and forth in her chair and said that it was like the old days when gentlemen *were* gentlemen. She much preferred him to some of the men and women who came to talk about Art. I didn't agree, although Squire Merrit was a jolly enough man. I found much more gratification when I was asked to attend a dinner party—as I often was—and could join intelligently in the conversation. Sometimes out walking I would catch a glimpse of the beautiful birds in Squire Merrit's woods and I was sorry to think that they were being carefully nurtured only to be shot.

When the season started, we often heard the sound of guns. I would be glad when it was over. Mrs. Couch, however, rocked back and forth and expounded on the ways of cooking pheasant.

She had done a great deal to help me since I had been back. Her affection was warm and genuine. She would shake her head often over "that Mr. Joliffe." But I could

see that she was fond of him and she did not adopt that
censorious attitude towards him which Mr. Sylvester did,
and I liked her for it.

She had always been interested in what was in the future and often at tea she would make us all turn our cups
upside down and then she would read the future in the
leaves. Sometimes she used the cards as well and would
lay them out on the kitchen table and clucking over the
spades and hearts.

Dear Mrs. Couch, she had been fond of my mother and
had taken on herself the duty to look after me as best she
could.

I began to feel that in spite of my dire misfortune I was
lucky in having such a household to return to where I
might lick my wounds and prepare myself for whatever
was to come.

It was a weekend, Squire Merrit was entertaining a
shooting party to which Mr. Sylvester had been invited
but he had declined the invitation. He confided to me that
he preferred to see the picture of a beautiful bird on a
vase or a scroll rather than lying dead on the grass for a
dog to retrieve.

I was in the kitchen with Mrs. Couch and we were discussing the next day's dinner as friends of Mr. Sylvester
were expected.

"If it's that Mr. Lavers," Mrs. Couch was saying, "he's
fond of a good roast. Nothing fancy mind. He likes his
food plain. A good bit of roast ribs of beef would suit him
I reckon and I'll make some of my own horse radish. I'll
have to give that Amy a talking to. She's getting that
absent-minded. It wouldn't surprise me to hear she was expecting . . ."

Amy had married the gardener and Mr. Jeffers now
had his eye on one of the village girls. "He's got the wandering eye, if you ask me," said Mrs. Couch, "and wandering eyes never rest long in one place." She glanced out
of the window. "My patience me! What's this?"

Her red face was a shade paler and her chins shook a little as her mouth dropped open.

I sprang up and looked through the window.

Two of the gardeners were carrying what looked like an improvised stretcher and on it was Mr. Sylvester Milner.

It was a silent house. It seemed as though fate was determined to deal one blow after another. Life was becoming like a nightmare. It seemed as though everywhere the life I had known was slipping away from me.

They had carried Mr. Sylvester in and the doctor had come immediately. He had said that an operation would have to be performed without delay and they had taken him away.

There was nothing we could do but sit around and talk. All we did know was that a bullet had lodged in his spine and would have to be removed.

Mrs. Couch made pot after pot of tea in the big brown kitchen earthenware teapot and we all assembled at the big table and talked of what had happened. Amy, protruberant enough under her apron to confirm Mrs. Couch's conjectures, was the center of attraction for once because Jacob, her husband, had been one of those who had helped carry the stretcher into the house.

"There was all this shooting going on," she said, "so nobody noticed. How long he'd been lying there is anybody's guess. The shooting started after their lunch and it was four when he was found. Could have been half an hour or more. One of the guns, they say it was, don't they, Jake?"

Jacob nodded. "One of the guns," he repeated.

"You could have knocked Jake down with a feather couldn't you, Jake?"

Jacob said: "Yes, you could have."

"There he was coming back with some of the weed killer he was getting for the weeds."

"The weeds is something shocking," said Jacob, and looked embarrassed to have contributed to the conversation.

"When he suddenly stumbles and there's Mr. Milner lying there . . . bleeding, wasn't he, Jake?"

"Something shocking," Jacob confirmed.

"So he gave the alarm and then they made this stretcher and brought him in."

Mrs. Couch stirred resolutely. "I don't know," she said, "it's like fate. Death don't walk single. Death begets death, like they say in the Bible. When I was pulling the blinds down for poor dear Mrs. Lindsay I said to myself: 'And who'll be the next?' "

"Mr. Milner isn't dead," I reminded her.

"As near to it as makes no odds," said Mrs. Couch. "There's change coming in this house. I've felt it in my bones these last weeks, I wonder who the next owner will be, and who they'll want to keep. Might be more like a house should be. There's that about it. But Mr. Milner, he was a kind man in his way."

I cried out: "Please don't talk of him as though he's dead. He's not."

"Yet," added Mrs. Couch prophetically.

I couldn't stand it any longer. I turned and ran out of the room. As I did so I heard Mrs. Couch say: "Poor Jane. It's her mother going off like that. Enough to upset any of us."

Mr. Sylvester did not die. The operation was a success in that his life was saved, but he would not recover the full use of his limbs and was semi-paralyzed. The doctors called it a miracle as they had performed the tricky operation of removing a bullet from his spine. This was proved to have been fired from a gun which had come from Squire Merrit's gun room though it was uncertain which member of the party had fired the actual shot. The obvious explanation was that Mr. Sylvester had ventured too near the shooting party and a shot intended for one of the birds had accidentally caught him.

Three weeks after the accident he was recovered enough to receive visitors and I went to see him.

He looked smaller and younger, I thought, without his smoking cap; his light brown hair was plentiful and only faintly touched with grey.

He was very pleased to see me.

"Well, Jane," he said, "this will put an end to my wanderings for a while."

"It may not be so."

"They have explained to me rather fully what has happened. I have to be prepared for the existence of a semi-invalid."

"Even if that were so you have many interests."

"There you are right. I can still buy and sell, but sellers will have to come to me. It is a good thing I have trained you well."

I said: "If I can be of the least service to you I shall be glad."

"You will be. You are looking sorry for me. That shows you have a kind heart and that is a good thing to have. Sympathy for the troubles of others and courage in our own. That is one of the greatest gifts any human being can have. The fates are being good to you, Jane. They are giving you a chance to learn this lesson."

"I'd rather fate had been a little less good."

"Never rail against fate, Jane. What is to be will be. That is how the Chinese see it. Accept your fate meekly, submit to it, look upon it as experience. Never rail against it. Then you will come through."

"I shall try."

"You will come to see me again. Bring any letters, any papers. We will work on them together."

"Would your doctors allow that?"

"My doctors know that fate has decided to immobilize me to a certain extent. I must learn to adjust myself and

any time I spend in mourning for what I have lost can
bring me no good. That is something we must remember.
Like a good general I must re-form my forces and go on
with the battle. You will help me, Jane."

"I will do everything I can."

"Come then tomorrow and we will talk business. You
will see how quickly I will recover then."

So I went each day to the hospital while he was there
and I took with me any letters that came; there were also
books and catalogues which we looked over together.

Those sessions were salvation to us both.

And then the suspicions which had been with me for
some time were confirmed.

I was pregnant.

In due course Mr. Sylvester came back to the house.
He had already regained a little use in his legs and could
manage to hobble very slowly on a crutch. This was great
progress. Enquiries were still going on as to how he had
come to be shot and from whose gun the fatal bullet had
been fired, but there was no satisfaction in this. The in-
ference seemed to be that it was a case of accidental
shooting, not the first of its kind by any means.

The household settled back into a slightly new routine
which soon became normal. Instead of Mr. Sylvester's
going away, guests came to see him. They often came for
dinner and sometimes stayed for a night or two. I was
housekeeper, hostess, and secretary, which kept me busy.
I was grateful for that.

Joliffe wrote twice more. The first of these letters implored me to come to him. In the second which came two
weeks later I sensed his desire for me to do so was less
urgent. He was going to "move heaven and earth" he
wrote to free himself; then all would be well.

He was constantly in my thoughts yet I felt that I was
seeing him differently. In my unworldly eyes when I had
been blindly in love with him I saw a perfect being, but

now I saw a new Joliffe, a young adventurer, not always sure of himself, taking chances, not always strictly honorable . . . I saw Joliffe the sinner. It was as though I had been looking at a painting through a veil which made it mystic but wonderful and when the veil was removed the flaws began to show themselves. I did not, I think, love him less. I knew that I could still be charmed, but I saw him differently and I wanted to look more and more deeply into what was there.

Strange as it seems I was glad of the respite. It may have been that my body was changing and I must needs change with it. A new life was growing in me and this in itself will always be a miracle to the woman to whom it happens, commonplace occurrence though it may seem to the rest of the world.

In the first few days when I became certain, the wonder of what was to happen obscured all else. I was glad therefore to be by myself, to think of what this meant. I could not at this stage look at the practical side. I could only think of the wonder of having a child of my own.

Then I began to ask myself how my child would be born. I was not a wife so how could I with decorum become a mother?

There was something uncanny about Mr. Sylvester Milner. It had always seemed so. He would sit in his chair with that inscrutable smile on his face and I often thought when he turned his eyes on me that he was looking straight into my mind.

It seemed this was so because he said to me one day: "Am I right in thinking that you are with child?"

The blood crept up from my neck to the roots of my hair.

"Is it . . . obvious?" I asked.

He shook his head. "But I guessed."

"I was not sure myself until a few days ago. I should not have thought . . ."

He lifted a hand. "It was a certain serenity in your demeanor, a certain peace, a kind of contentment . . . I cannot describe it. You see it in the women's faces in some of the later Chinese pictures. An indefinable quality but these artists caught it. Perhaps it is due to the fact that I have looked so much at these portrayals that I recognize it."

"Yes," I said, "I am going to have a child."

He nodded.

It was a few days later. I had dined in the servants' hall because there were no guests and on these occasions Mr. Sylvester took his meals in his own room.

Mrs. Couch was talking about the way things had changed. She knew now about Joliffe's marriage. It was impossible to keep that secret from them and it had been the great topic of conversation in the hall, although when I was present the matter was not discussed. I had grown used to the sudden embarrassed pause when I entered a room.

Mrs. Couch shook her head and occasionally referred to Joliffe as though he were dead. Then her eyes would sparkle at the memory of him. "He was a one," she would say, "and my word, didn't he like my sloe gin!"

She would sit at the table with her hands folded and purr over the cards, her face assuming innumerable expressions as she read out the warnings.

"Hearts, ah, I always did like them. Good fortune and wedding bells. A handsome dark man . . . ha, here he is . . . looking straight at you." But when the spades turned up a shudder would reverberate throughout the kitchen. She prided herself on seeing things coming. She had seen my mother's death. "It was there in the cards as much as a year before she died." She had seen, but then she hadn't liked to say it, that my relationship with Joliffe meant tears. "There they were as real as you are sitting there. I could have told you that." And now Mr. Sylvester's accident. "Plain as a pikestaff. I saw it as death . . . well, he did come near it and it was that heart card that saved him."

I could smile at her always and wondered what she would say she had seen in the cards when she knew of my condition.

She was just preparing to lay the cards, as she called it, for me, when Ling Fu slipped quietly into the kitchen.

Mr. Sylvester was asking if I would go to his room.

I went up at once.

"Ah Jane," he said, "there is something I want to say to you. I have been thinking this over for some time and I'm now going to put a suggestion to you. Of course you may think it ridiculous, absurd, but at least I think that, in your circumstances, you should consider it."

I waited curiously.

"You have, I am sure, thought carefully of your position. You are to have a child but you are an unmarried woman. I know that you were deceived and this is no fault of yours, but the fact remains. This as the years go on could create an embarrassing situation not only for you but for the child. It is for this reason that I have decided to put this plan before you."

There was a pause and he looked at me as though he was considering how best to put this suggestion which I might think ridiculous.

"When your child is born you cannot be known as Miss Lindsay. That would create an impossible position for you. You can of course call yourself Mrs. Milner, but you will in fact have no right to this name. You are in a difficult position. But for the child you could have put this experience behind you and started a fresh life. With a child it will not be possible."

He seemed as though he were talking round the subject. It was not like him. He showed no outward embarrassment but I sensed it was there.

He paused for a moment while he regarded me gravely.

"You could, of course, become Mrs. Milner in truth by . . . marrying me."

I was astounded. It was the last thing I had expected. I really could not believe that I had heard him correctly.

I was silent and he said ruefully: "I see the idea is repugnant to you."

Still I could not speak.

He went on: "It seemed to be a . . . solution."

My voice sounded unnaturally high as I replied: "Would you consider marrying to provide a solution for someone else's difficulties?"

"It is not entirely so. You have been wronged by a member of my family. You believed yourself to be married and there is to be a child. If you married me that child would be called Milner. I would see that he or she was brought up as my son or daughter. You would have no financial anxieties. That is your side of the case. Mine is that I have always wanted a son or daughter of my own. I never married. Perhaps I sometimes felt I might . . . but somehow it never happened. Now my accident has made it impossible for me to beget a child. The doctors have told me that. If we married I would regard your child as mine. I should have your companionship . . . your help in my work. You see the advantages are not all on one side. What do you think?"

"I . . . I'm afraid I can't think very clearly just now. I want you to know that I appreciate your goodness to me . . . and to my mother. From the moment we came here we found security. She was very grateful to you."

He nodded. "You have qualms. You do not see me as a husband. Do understand that I should not be a husband in every sense of the word. You know my disabilities. It would be a marriage of friendship, companionship, you understand?"

"Yes, I understand."

"Think about it. You would be mistress of this house,

your child's future would be secure. He or she would have the best of educations and a comfortable home. For myself I should have someone to look after my house, and be a companion to me, someone who shares my interests and could help carry on my business. I need that help now, Jane. You are the only one who could give it. You see it would indeed be a convenient marriage for us both."

"Yes," I said, "I do see that."

"And your answer?"

"I was unprepared for this."

"I understand. You would like a little time to consider it. But of course. There is no hurry . . . except of course . . . the child."

I went to my room. The last months had been so eventful that I wondered what would happen to me next.

Oh Joliffe, I thought, where are you now?

Could I wait for him? Could I go to him? What of my child? I must think first of the child. Indeed the child filled my thoughts, excluding Joliffe. It was so painful to think of him. Would he ever come back to me? What if he did and I was married to his uncle? I pictured his reproaches and Sylvester's standing by and explaining that it had seemed so convenient.

I had begun to picture what my life would be if I married him. It was an indication that I was actually considering such a possibility.

A marriage of convenience! Why did people talk about them with a faint touch of pity. Why should not a marriage of convenience be a happier union than one of sudden passion which was no marriage at all?

I wanted to forget Joliffe. Somewhere deep down in my mind born of my newly acquired knowledge of life, was the conviction that I must forget Joliffe. I knew Joliffe was not free; I did not believe Bella would ever release him; nor could I ever be quite sure of what I must expect from him. He was too charming; life had given him too much; he expected fortune's gifts to be showered on him and he took them without asking himself what right he had to them.

Joliffe was a wonderful companion for a romantic-minded young girl, but was he for a serious-minded woman with a child to care for?

Moreover, I was not the same girl who had sheltered under the parapet in an enchanted forest with one of the gods come down from Olympus. Oh no. I was a woman in a difficult situation. I would be an unmarried mother and I had a child to plan for.

In this house I could look after my child as my mother had looked after me. Sylvester Milner had been a fairy godfather to us. He was still, for he was putting a proposition to me which could solve my troubles.

What if I did not marry him? Could I stay here? Perhaps. But my child would have no father. Sylvester had offered to become that. With such a father the child's future would be assured.

I was not a romantic girl. I was about to be a mother. My child must be my first consideration.

I knew then that I was going to accept Sylvester's proposal.

II

Mrs. Couch was delighted and Mr. Jeffers said you could have knocked him down with a feather. Mrs. Couch could never be knocked down by such flimsy objects while she had her cards and teacups to warn her. This she had seen in the teacups.

"A new mistress to the house," she had said. "I saw it clear as daylight."

"Clear as mud," scoffed Mr. Jeffers.

There was a feud between them because of his "goings on" with young females.

"There it was—one little grout beside a big one. I said to myself 'That's a woman beside the master' and there in the corner was the marriage sign."

She was delighted nevertheless. They all were.

"Though who'd have thought it of him," said Amy.

"Men," added Jess, who was quite knowledgeable on that subject, "you never can tell with them."

"My word," said Mrs. Couch. "We do see life with you about, young Jane. I suppose we've got to call you Madam now. The mistress, eh?"

"I daresay the master would appreciate that," I replied.

Mrs. Couch nodded. Later she said: "In front of the servants just to make it right and proper. But to me you'll always be young Jane."

She was pleased. "It'll be like a proper house. The Hall is very pleased. And a little baby too. It's a good thing you got that before. Poor Mr. Sylvester Milner could never accommodate . . . if you know what I mean. But with a little one on the way I reckon the wedding will be prompt. It has to be when there's a nipper on the way."

And so I prepared for my convenient wedding.

Sometimes I was almost on the point of calling it all off.

What was I doing? It was a year since I had joyously gone to Joliffe as his bride. I had no doubts then, no qualms.

And what had I known of Joliffe? What did I know of Sylvester?

I tried to think of him dispassionately. I liked him; I could say I was fond of him. He had interested me from the moment he had discovered me in the Treasure Room. I was never bored in his company; we had this great interest between us. I was stimulated to learn as I was sure he was to teach me. It can be a success, this marriage, I thought.

He had implied very clearly that ours would be no intimate relationship. We should have our own rooms; there would be little difference in the life I was leading now and what would follow. I should look after the house and help with his business as I did at this time; the difference would be that I should be his wife and my child would be born in comfort, to security. I should not have to scheme for mine as my mother had for hers.

I could almost hear her voice saying: "We arranged this for you, Janey, seeing how things went. Your father and I arranged it."

The marriage ceremony would be in the little church a quarter of a mile from the house. It would naturally be a quiet wedding.

A week before it was to take place I was going through the post with Sylvester as I did every morning. He would read through his letters and if they were business ones he would pass them to me. In due course I would be traveling to sales as he used to, but I was not quite knowledgeable enough for that just yet. Later I should be able to buy and sell, but my apprenticeship was not yet completely served.

Sylvester suddenly paused and looked up at me.

"Here is a letter from my nephew. He proposes to come to the wedding."

"Joliffe," I began, my heart leaping uncomfortably.

"No, no. This is Adam, my brother Redmond's son. He is home in England after two years in Hong Kong."

"So he is coming here."

"I did not expect any of my family to come," he said.

My heart leaped, turned over and seemed to stop for a second when I saw Adam. The reason was of course that he was standing with his back to me in the sitting room, holding a figure in his hands, and from the back he looked just like Joliffe.

When he turned the resemblance was scarcely perceptible. This man was an inch or so shorter than Joliffe, but
still tall; his broader shoulders made him look less tall
still. His features were like Joliffe's but his eyes were different; where Joliffe's were blue, this man's were grey, a
rather cold color as the sea is on a dull day. He lacked
those black lashes which were such a startling feature in
Joliffe's face. And of course he lacked the charm.

The illusion did not last long. It was just a faint family
resemblance.

Sylvester was seated in his chair.

He said, "Jane, this is my nephew, Adam Milner.
Adam, the lady who is to be my wife."

He bowed rather stiffly. Every minute he was growing
less like Joliffe.

"It is fortunate that I shall be in England at the time of
the wedding," he said.

He was studying me intently and I thought I detected
a faint hostility in his glance.

"Come and sit down, Jane," said Sylvester. "I have
asked Ling Fu to bring us tea. What did you think of the
figurine, Adam?"

"Very pleasant," he answered.

Sylvester raised his eyebrows and grimaced at me.
"That is all he can say of our beautiful piece, Jane. It's
genuine Sung."

"I doubt that," said Adam. "It's later than that."

"I could swear it's Sung," said Sylvester. "Jane, take a
look at it."

As I took the figure from Adam I felt the eyes of this
man on me and they were cynical. I said: "I'm afraid I'm
not sufficiently competent to make a judgment."

"Jane is very cautious," said Sylvester, "and over-
modest I think. She has learned a good deal since she came
here."

"You came here with your mother, did you not, when
she started to keep house?" said Adam.

"Yes," I answered.

"And now you are becoming a connoisseur."

His voice was pleasant enough but his eyes mocked me. I fancied he was implying that he thought me an adventuress. I felt angry towards him. I disliked him not for his attitude but for being enough like Joliffe as to remind me of him and to bring back poignant memories of the days when I was innocent enough to believe I would live happily ever after.

"I am certainly not a connoisseur. Sylvester"—I said his name with difficulty and always with a faint touch of embarrassment—"has been kind enough to teach me all I know."

"I've no doubt that you have learned a great deal," he said and there was insinuation behind his words. I was reading his mind. He thought that I and my mother were adventuresses. We had come here in the first place, made a cosy spot for ourselves, then I had married Joliffe and come to grief so I had returned and brought Sylvester into my net.

I began to dislike this Adam.

Ling Fu brought in the tea. I presided over the tray and was silent while the men talked.

Adam seemed to direct the conversation into channels which could exclude me.

He wanted to hear all about the accident. He "had been very anxious," he said.

"I'm flattered," replied Sylvester.

"Oh these rivalries, they are friendly enough," said Adam Milner. "The family feeling is apart from business."

I sat listening to him, and sensing his hostility to me, I believed he had come to try to dissuade his uncle from marrying.

Later I asked Sylvester if this was his intention.

Sylvester laughed. "He's astonished at the thought of my marrying," he admitted. "Clearly Adam was of the opinion that I'm in my dotage. It's amusing that he should suddenly become so interested. However I assured him that I'm perfectly sane and that I believe my marriage to be one of the wisest steps I ever took."

"He seems rather a dour young man."

"He's serious minded and I believe already has a name in the trade for a keen eye. His knowledge of the Second Great Chinese Empire is said to be greatly respected. He's an expert on the T'ang and Sung Dynasties. Redmond used to be very proud of him. He's really dedicated and determined to succeed, I think. He was always so much more serious than er . . ."

"Than Joliffe," I said quickly. "He seems to resent me."

Sylvester smiled. "Not you personally. I have an idea that Adam might now like me to join up with him. Clever as he is he may find the going a little difficult on his own. I have an idea that he thought that because of my accident I should be glad to have him . . . on his terms. But I have you to help me and I have always wanted to keep the reins firmly in my own hands. Neither of my nephews is of the kind who likes to take a back seat. I shall not amalgamate. And now that I have you to help me there is absolutely no reason from my point of view why I should. That is what he resents."

"It seems rather an unpleasant outlook."

"It's business," answered Sylvester. "As a matter of fact Adam is a very worthy young man. Serious minded, alert, knowledgeable. But since his father and I parted company I prefer to be on my own."

"I suppose he came to see what I was like."

"He must have found you interesting. I'm sure he did. I could tell by his manner."

"I don't think he altogether liked what he found."

Sylvester laughed.

I was married to Sylvester on a typical April day——the

sun shone one moment and there was a downpour the next. The church was decorated with daffodils and narcissi and little bunches of violets. There was a freshness in the air.

Sylvester walked on his crutch to the altar. It must have seemed a very unconventional wedding. I was in a blue gown cut full to hide my pregnancy and a hat of the same blue with a curling ostrich feather.

Squire Merrit, who regarded himself in some measure as responsible for Sylvester's accident and was constantly displaying a desire to make amends, gave me away. I had a strange feeling in that church as the question was asked if anyone knew of any just cause or impediment why the ceremony should not be performed; I held my breath almost expecting a voice from the church to say: "Yes, you are my wife. You know you are . . . and always will be."

Joliffe, I thought in panic. Oh, where are you?

But there was no Joliffe to interrupt the ceremony.

In the pews sat the servants, headed by Mrs. Couch who wiped her eyes and declared later that it had been beautiful and she felt as though the bride was her very own daughter. "It's so dramatic," she had said, "when you think of Mr. Joliffe and it's his baby and Mr. Sylvester coming in and marrying you. It's a true romance it is really."

Adam Milner was there, aloof, cold, and disapproving. And so I became Mrs. Sylvester Milner.

After my marriage, life went on just as it had before and in a few weeks I ceased to marvel at it.

The very ceremony of marriage had somehow created a new intimacy between us. I began to think of him as Sylvester and that made it easier for me to call him by that name.

As for him he changed a little. He seemed contented, reconciled to his disability.

I was now looking forward to the birth of my child and

that tended to make me forget all else. Sylvester was very concerned about my health; I had the impression that he wanted the child almost as much as I did. I knew his philosophy of life was that of the Chinese. One accepted what the fates offered and was thankful for it and it was one's own fault if one did not distil some goodness from it.

I must be aware of his kindness and the comfort that was given me in that house.

Often I thought of Joliffe, but the child was beginning to take up my entire thoughts. I was now very much aware of its physical existence and I was content to lie and think of it while I longed for the day of its birth. Mrs. Couch was delighted.

"Children in the house. It's what I've always wanted. No house is right without 'em, little minxes . . . into this and into that. But they make a *home*."

Amy who had given birth to a daughter assumed great importance. She regarded herself as an oracle. She greatly enjoyed advising me as to what I should and should not do.

Jess said it made her feel like settling down.

And there was Sylvester. He behaved as though the child were his and there was no doubt that when my baby was born that was how it would be regarded. He had plans for it and he became much more human than he ever had been when he talked of it.

"He will be brought up here in this house. He will learn to love beautiful things. We will teach him together."

"What if it should be a girl?"

"I do not think sex is a barrier. If the baby should be a girl she shall have all the advantages that a boy would have had."

I was touched that he should want to help plan the nursery. We had turned a room next to mine into this. I had it papered in pale blue with a frieze of animals as a kind of dado, and the entire household was excited when the white wood cot arrived with its blue coverlet.

I used to go into the room and look at it with wonder. The others did too. We were constantly finding someone there, as though in silent worship of the infant who soon was to make its longed-for arrival.

We talked of it constantly. Sylvester and I grew closer to each other. I tried to thank him for his goodness to my mother and me, but he only shook his head and said he had derived nothing but comfort and pleasure from our coming to his house.

I was fond of him. I had always respected him. I used to try to tell myself that I had been fortunate. And then memories of Joliffe would come to me and I would be transported to the house in Kensington and I thought of Joliffe and myself together there—then life seemed hard to bear until my longing for my baby overcame all other emotions.

Sylvester insisted on my seeing a London gynecologist and Mrs. Couch traveled up to London with me. I was deeply touched by his joy when the report came that all was normal. However he insisted on the midwife's staying at the house for more than a week before she was needed.

And in due course my child was born. To my great joy he was perfect in every way. I called him Jason after my father.

He dominated the household—a lively little boy with the lustiest pair of lungs imaginable.

Sometimes I used to think he would be horribly spoiled for there was not a member of that household who did not dote on him.

Mrs. Couch wanted to make special dishes for him, and I had to watch that she didn't overfeed him. Amy and she quarreled over this, Amy for once standing out against the formidable cook.

"Poor mite," cried Mrs. Couch. "Some people would like to starve him. But I'm not having that."

"Babies' digestions are not like ours," Amy declared pontifically.

And they were off.

"Just because you've had a baby . . ."

"Which is more than you have."

"The impertinence! You take care, Madam Amy."

I had difficulty in making the peace.

Even Jeffers who had hitherto rarely expressed his appreciation of any but young women, put his head on one side and said, "Didums."

Of course my son was the most intelligent baby that ever had been born. When he had his first tooth Mrs. Couch wanted to make a cake to celebrate the occasion; when he gurgled something that sounded like "Brrh" we all declared he had said "Mama." "Chattering away he was," said Mrs. Couch and I must confess we thought it only the slightest exaggeration. I used to take him into the sitting room when we had tea and display him in all his glory to Sylvester's admiring gaze.

On his first birthday we had a party in the servants' hall. A cake with one candle. His bright eyes regarded the cake with appreciation and a chubby hand had to be restrained from seizing the flame.

"Well, I never did," said Mrs. Couch. "He knows what it's all about, don't you, Master Sly Boots."

Amy's little daughter who was present picked a piece of icing from the cake when she thought no one was looking and was pounced on by Mrs. Couch which meant further trouble with Amy.

Jess rocked Jason in her arms with a faraway look in her eyes which meant she was thinking that having a good time here and there was all very well but it was babies that counted.

And when I carried him up to his nursery and bathed him, for I would not have a nurse to look after my baby, and laid him in his blue-and-white cot I gave way to my favorite daydream which was that Joliffe stood beside me as we looked down on our son. I felt that bitter loneliness then, that longing which was sometimes so great that I felt that nothing—not even Jason—could quite make up for the loss of Joliffe.

When the baby was asleep and I was in my lonely bed I used to go over every minute of that honeymoon with Joliffe.

I used to say to myself then that if I had never experienced love and passion I should not have known what I had missed. Yet without them how could I have had my precious Jason.

The child had become my whole life. He brought me comfort; he filled the emptiness I must feel without Joliffe, though even he could not do this completely.

I wanted Joliffe. I could not disguise the fact. And I was growing more and more aware of the barrenness of my life.

I thought of the years ahead, those years which Sylvester had so carefully planned for Jason—they would be sterile years, because to make life secure for Jason I had married a man of whom I was fond in a way in which one could be fond of a respected teacher. But I was young; I had known deep passion; I had loved. I had to be truthful with myself—I still loved—a man who was another woman's husband.

When I look back I think of Sylvester's great understanding and humility. He was, I know, far more considerate of my feelings than I was of his.

He understood that I loved Joliffe and that Joliffe had betrayed me—although perhaps he was not to blame for this. Yet I was sure Sylvester believed he was. Sylvester thought Joliffe irresponsible; he had not wanted me to marry him because he had thought he would not make a suitable husband. He had known Joliffe from his boyhood. Of course they were such entirely different people. How could they be in sympathy with each other?

Sylvester did everything he could to make my life interesting—and interesting it was. It was merely that the vital force was lacking. I was young and by no means of a frigid nature. I had tasted the sweets of a union with a lover and I could never forget it.

The great interest between us was of course Jason, but in addition he took me more and more into his confidence. I read a great deal after Jason was in bed and I was becoming moderately knowledgeable in Chinese matters. I learned of the religion and customs of that country. I went up to London once or twice to Sylvester's offices in Cheapside. I met his staff there and transacted some business for him. I was delighted with my success and so was he.

"It is wonderful," he said. "You are indeed becoming my right hand."

Which was small repayment for what he had done for me.

I thought then that it might be that Jason would one day take over his business and I would want to be beside him to advise and help. I had an added incentive.

Sylvester sensed this and encouraged me. He told me about the London office which was small compared with their premises in Kowloon. "There the bulk of the business is done. There we have our warehouse and offices. One day, Jane, you will go there."

"I shall have to wait until Jason is older."

He nodded. "I should like to go with you. I want very much to see again my House of a Thousand Lanterns."

Whenever that name was mentioned for some strange reason I felt a tingling in my blood.

He used to talk of it quite a lot. He tried to describe it to me but it eluded my imagination and I could not visualize it. A house built years ago on the site of a temple.

I could feel excited at the prospect of seeing it.

"Perhaps I could make the journey," he said.

"That would surely be impossible?"

"Don't the philosophers say nothing is impossible?"

"How could you go?"

"I can walk across the room with a stick. I walk a little in the gardens. Perhaps if I made up my mind I could overcome my disability sufficiently to make the journey."

His eyes glowed at the thought and although I believed it was impossible, I let him go on imagining it.

Whenever he spoke of The House of a Thousand Lanterns a change came over him; he seemed younger, more vital than he did at any other time. Then I could almost believe in the possibility of making the journey there.

One day when Jason was eighteen months old I took one of my trips to London. I looked forward to these days. I liked to feel myself growing more and more knowledgeable about the business, and the excitement of seeing Jason when I returned made a happy ending to my day.

Jeffers would drive me to the station and at the end of the train journey I would take a cab to the office in Cheapside. When I had finished what I came to do I would have a cab back to the station and Jeffers would meet me at the other end. It had become a routine. I was no longer a young girl. I was a matron.

On this occasion all went according to plan.

I arrived at the office where they were expecting me. I met John Heyland, Sylvester's head clerk, his two assistants and the young man in charge of the storeroom. There I saw the jade ornaments which would be delivered to buyers. Luncheon was brought in from a nearby restaurant and I took this with Mr. Heyland who talked of the old days before the family had split up. He thought it was a pity. Now there were three firms where there had been one—with Mr. Sylvester, Mr. Adam, and young Mr. Joliffe all working on their own. He had been in the Hong

Kong office with Sylvester's father who would, he assured me, turn in his grave if he knew there was all this division in the family.

I decided that I would do some shopping before I caught my train, so I arranged to leave the office early, and as I came out into the street there was Joliffe.

"Why, Jane!" he cried, his eyes alight with excitement so that poignant memories flooded my mind and for a few seconds I was happy simply because he was there.

Then I stammered: "How did you know I was here?"

All the old charm was in his smile and there was a hint of mischief in it too. He used to say "Didn't you know I was the omniscient one?"

"Simple detection," he said now. "A nod, a wink, a word in the right direction."

"Someone in there told you," I said aghast. "Oh Joliffe, you had no right . . ."

He took my arm and held it firmly. "I had every right."

"I have to catch a train."

"Not just yet," he said.

My heart leaped in a joyous expectation as I reminded myself that I had left two hours for shopping.

"I must talk to you, Jane."

"What is there to be said? It's all clear, isn't it?"

"There is so much to be said. So much to be made clear."

"I must not miss my train. Jeffers will be waiting."

"Let him wait. In any case your train won't leave for two hours. We'll get a cab. I know a place where we can have tea. We can be quite alone . . ."

"No, Joliffe," I said firmly.

"All right then. We'll go to the station. I'll be with you till the train leaves. That will give us a little time to talk."

Before I could answer he had hailed a cab. We sat side by side and when he took my hand and looked into my face, I turned away, afraid of the emotions he could arouse in me.

"So we have a son," he said.

"Please, Joliffe . . ."

"He is my son," he went on. "I should see him."

"You can't take him from me," I said fearfully.

"As if I would. I want him and you . . . but mostly you, Jane."

"It's no use."

"Why? Because you made that foolish marriage?"

"It was not foolish. It was the right thing to do. The baby has a wonderful home. He will grow up in the security he needs."

"And which he couldn't have with me?"

"How could he when you have a wife living?"

"Jane, I swear to you I thought she was dead. You must believe me."

"Whatever I believe the fact is that she exists. She would be there always in our lives. How could a child be brought up happily in such circumstances?"

"You left me before you knew there was to be a child. You didn't love me, Jane."

The cab stopped at the station. We alighted and he gripped my arm firmly as though he feared I would run away. We went into the station buffet. It was noisy as such places are. Every now and then we heard the shunting of the trains, the shrill whistles, and the shouts of porters. It was not the ideal surroundings in which to discuss such a highly emotional problem.

We had two cups of tea which neither of us wanted, for all we desired then was to be in each other's arms and leave explanations until later.

"What are we going to do?" he asked desperately.

"I shall go back to Roland's Croft. You will go to your wife."

"You can't do this."

"What do you suggest I should do?"

He stretched across the table and took my hand.

"Don't go back," he said earnestly. "Don't catch that train. You and I will go away together."

"You must be mad, Joliffe. What about my son?"

"You could bring our son with you. Go back now then and get the boy. You, I and he will go away together. We'll go right out of the country. I'll take you to Hong Kong. We'll start a new life . . ."

For a moment I gave myself the luxury of believing that it was possible. Then I withdrew my hands.

"No, Joliffe," I said. "It may sound possible to you but not to me. In the first place you have a wife. She is with you now, isn't she?"

He was silent and I felt a sick pain in my heart because I knew she was. I pictured her in the house where I had been so happy. So it was a fact that they were together. Annie and Albert would look after her as they had looked after me. It was more than I could bear.

"You know how it happened," he said. "I was young and reckless. And again I swear to you that I believed her to be dead."

"It seems to me that you accepted this solution rather gladly."

"I'll be frank with you," said Joliffe earnestly. "I was relieved. You wouldn't understand this, Jane. You are not as impulsive as I am. I was caught . . . as many young men are. I married Bella and then almost immediately regretted it. When I thought she was killed I admit I was relieved. It was like fate wiping out a mistake so that there was a clean slate to go on with."

"Poor Bella! So you thought of her death as an act of a benign fate which brought relief to you! What of her?"

"Oh come, Jane, I'm telling you the truth. I'm no saint. I made about the biggest mistake a young man can make. I had tied myself for life to Bella. Naturally it seemed a relief when I thought that episode was wiped out forever."

"What a shock for you when she came back!"

"The biggest in my life."

"It would have been better if you had never had your temporary relief . . . for you . . . for Bella perhaps and certainly for me."

"You've changed. You've become hard."

"I've learned something of the world. I'm less easily deceived perhaps. I have a child to fight for now."

"Who is mine too."

"Yes, Joliffe. But he regards Sylvester as his father now."

Joliffe brought his fist down on the table. "How could you, Jane! How could you marry him . . . an old man, my own uncle!"

"He is a good man and has brought me nothing but good. He loves the child. He will give him all that a child needs."

"And his true father?"

"You have a wife. I can see endless trouble. I would not allow my son to be brought up in circumstances where there could be trouble at every turn. He now has a good home, a secure and peaceful home. How could he ever have had that when you had a wife who could appear at any moment? He is Jason Milner, and he has every right to that name. I think I have done the best thing possible in the circumstances for my child and that is my main concern."

"What of me?"

"It is over, Joliffe. Let us try not to remember."

"You might as well ask the sun not to shine or the wind not to blow. How could I ever forget? How could you?"

I stirred the tea which had grown cold.

Then I said: "Joliffe, what are you doing now? Tell me."

He shrugged his shoulders. "Wanting you all the time," he said. "I had to see you. I have a friend in your husband's office. He told me when you were coming . . . so I waited."

"He had no right to do that. It was disloyal to Sylvester. Who was he?"

He smiled and shook his head. "He took pity on me," he said.

"So Bella has moved into the house?" I asked.

He nodded. "At first I went away to a hotel. She would not leave. She threatened all sorts of things if I left her."

"So you went back to her."

"Not back to her. We live in the same house. There it ends. I am planning to go away in a few weeks' time. I have business in China. I shall go to Canton for a while and then to Kowloon. I shall stay away. I can manage things very well from over there where the main business of buying is done."

"She will go with you."

"It is to escape from her that I go."

"So you will leave her in your house . . ." I thought of it as our house. I pictured her going across into the Gardens to feed the swans on the Round Pond, and I longed for those days when I had been so blissfully happy.

The clock which hung in the refreshment hall had a malicious face I decided; its hands were turning far too quickly. The precious time was romping away.

He followed my gaze. "So little time left," he said. "Jane, come away with me."

"How could I?"

"You are really my wife."

"No, I am Sylvester's wife."

"That marriage is a mockery of a marriage. What is marriage? Is it loving? Is it sharing? Is it living in that intimacy which makes you part of each other? Or is it signing your name on a contract? You are my wife, Jane. You are part of me and my life and when you take yourself from me, when you attempt to sever that intimacy which is between us . . . you have broken our marriage. We belong together. Don't you know that?"

I said: "You are married to Bella and I to Sylvester. And it must remain so."

"What do you know of love? It is clear that you know nothing."

I retorted angrily: "If you knew how I suffered . . . if you could understand . . ."

He took my hand.

"Jane, Jane, come away. Bring the child and come."

I looked at the clock.

"I must go."

He rose with me, his hand gripping my elbow.

I shook my head. I must get away from him. I was afraid that at any moment I would say what he wanted me to. I felt a wild impulse to throw everything away except my life with Joliffe. That was what I wanted more than anything: Joliffe and my son. The three of us belonged together.

But even in that moment common sense was telling me that what I wanted was impossible.

The train was coming into the station—and only a few more moments were left to us.

He took my hands; his eyes were pleading.

"Come, Jane."

I shook my head; my lips were trembling and I could not trust myself to speak.

"I shall go away soon," he said. "It will be for a long time."

Still I could not speak.

"We belong together, Jane . . . the three of us," he said.

The train was in the station. I withdrew my hands. He opened the door for me. I went into the compartment and stood at the window. He was on the platform, all the longing which I felt myself, clear in his eyes.

The train started to move. I stood at the window after I

could no longer see him and I said to myself: This is what they mean when they say one's heart is broken.

I did not go to London for some time after that. I made excuses and cut off my visits. When I finally did go I believed Joliffe had already left for China.

My child was my consolation. No boy ever had a happier home. He was completely secure and this made him contented. He was an inquisitive little boy as Mrs. Couch used to say fondly "into everything." No child was ever more greatly loved. To me he was everything in the world. Sylvester, I knew, doted on him. I don't think he had ever visualized such contentment—even incapacitated as he was. I was glad that his marriage had not been a failure for him. As for Mrs. Couch her greatest pleasure was to have Jason in the kitchen and she was overcome with delight when he sat on the floor and played with the saucepan lids. Nothing we could give him attracted him so much up to the time he was two as those saucepan lids and it delighted Mrs. Couch that these desirable objects came from her domain.

His second birthday was celebrated by a cake with two candles and I don't think Mrs. Couch put as much loving care into anything she had ever cooked before. To her he was "Master Sly Boots" or "Sir Know It All" or "Me Lord into This and That." "Under my feet morning noon and night," she would say with a cluck of the tongue. Of course he loved her. He would take currants and nuts from the table when she wasn't looking; she would pretend to chase him with her rolling pin and when he was tired she would gather him up on her ample lap and sing him to sleep.

His coming had changed the house, but perhaps most of all it had affected Sylvester.

I learned a great deal about him. He had always been overshadowed by his brothers—Joliffe's father and Redmond. He had been aloof and never able to shine in company. He had made up for it by a certain business ability which the others could not rival. I wondered why he had not married until he had married me—and I often thought that ours was such an unusual marriage that it could scarcely be called one at all.

Once he told me that years ago he had thought of marriage. She was a young actress, beautiful, lively, charming —he ought to have known she would never seriously have considered him. She had married Joliffe's father.

Yes, I was learning.

And his feelings for me. I had interested him from the moment I came into his house. I had a vitality, a curiosity, a desire to learn which won his respect.

My mother had brought a homely atmosphere to Roland's Croft; when I came home from school for holidays the place was like a home. He had always wanted a home. Then of course his accident had happened and his whole life was changed.

Marriage between us had offered a smoothing out of our problems. I was to have a home for a child, a name, security, as for him he acquired that family which he had always wanted and as soon as Jason was born he regarded him as his son.

He said on more than one occasion: "It worked out well, did it not?"

And I assured him that it did.

Jason's third and fourth birthdays were celebrated as the main events of the year. Christmases were now important occasions. There was a great tree in the kitchen and I was surprised when Sylvester wanted one in his sitting room. I decorated them with the help of Jason. And in the kitchen he helped Mrs. Couch hang sugar mice and bags of humbugs on the tree. "And no taking the eyes off mice when my back's turned. Nor popping humbugs into your mouth," admonished Mrs. Couch. "The place for eyes is on the mice and humbugs in their bags."

But she would be the first one to pop a sweet into his

mouth and if she occasionally overindulged him in such matters the love she bestowed on him made up for that.

Sometimes I wondered what Sylvester was thinking when he listened to the whoops of delight and the blasts from tin trumpets, for Jason greatly loved noise of any sort.

I did not have to ask myself. He loved it as we all did for the pivot of our existence was this son of mine—mine and Joliffe's.

It was during Jason's fourth Christmas that the idea became a certainty.

We had decorated the rooms and among the paper fripperies were some small Chinese lanterns. They had stumps of candles inside them and looked very pretty when they were lighted.

Sylvester stared at them when we put them up.

After Jason had gone to bed he said to me: "They remind me of my house in Hong Kong."

"The House of a Thousand Lanterns," I said. "Are they like these then?"

"No, quite different. I *must* go there, Jane. I *am* going there."

"Do you really think you could make that journey?"

"If you came with me."

"Leave Jason!"

"I wouldn't ask such a thing."

"Then you mean take him with us?"

"I want him to learn the business as he grows up. You can't begin too early. If you are steeped in these things from childhood they become part of your life."

"But to take a child all that way!"

"He will not be the first. You teach him yourself. So he will go on learning his lessons as he travels and later in Hong Kong. It is six years since I was there. I get reports of what is happening but it is not enough. I must go. And Jane, I want you to come with me."

The more I thought of the idea the less impossible it

seemed. I asked him to tell me more about this house of
the lanterns. He tried to explain it but it defeated my
imagination.

I knew that it was an old house, that it had been built
on the site of an ancient temple, that it was in the center
of several walled courtyards which extended all round it.
"It is rather like a Chinese puzzle," said Sylvester. "You
go through one gate into the first, then through another
and another. There are four of these walled courtyards
and in the center the house itself."

I longed to see it. I had fought hard over the last few
years to forget Joliffe but I had not succeeded. I often
thought of Bella and pictured her living in the house
which had so briefly been my home. Was it true that they
had lived their separate lives? How much had Joliffe
withheld from me? I did not entirely know Joliffe. No, I
told myself fiercely, that was why he excited me. There
would always be so much to discover.

My absorption with my child had saved me perhaps
from running away with Joliffe, for I did not believe I
could have endured the barren years if I had not had my
beloved child.

Now the thought of going to a new land, to see that
house which had deluded my imagination filled me with
excitement.

Jason's fifth birthday was celebrated and, soon after,
the decision was made. Sylvester's doctors thought that
the journey was possible and no harm could come
through it; in fact one of them thought the stimulation
would be good for him.

Mrs. Couch was horrified. The thought of taking little
children among heathens was something beyond her com-
prehension. She was indignantly tearful and I knew it was
because, as she said, her kitchen wouldn't be her kitchen
without Master Sly Boots in and out of everything.

She was sullen for some time. I said I did not think the
visit would be prolonged but she continued to shake her

head. She brought out the cards and saw disaster there. There was even the ace of spades which kept turning up. The teacups gave due warning. There was a journey over water and no good would come of it.

In spite of these prognostications of evil we made our plans.

And on an autumn day when Jason was nearing his sixth birthday we sailed from Southampton for the Far East.

Lotus Blossom

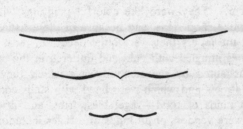

The impact of the Hong Kong scene upon me was tremendous. I was expecting something exotic, entirely different from what I had ever known, and having steeped myself in Chinese history, manners, customs, and art, I had believed myself to be in some measure prepared. But I could never have pictured anything so varied, so colorful, and so mysterious.

The center of life was the harbor, one of the finest known to man, I believe. Ships came in from all over the world and there was constant activity along the waterfront. A strip of sea about a mile long separated Hong Kong Island from the mainland and ferries constantly plied back and forth. From Kowloon one could look across to the steep mountain ridge and the island's capital city of Victoria. The junks and the sampans crowded the waters; these were the homes of thousands of families, many of whom rarely came ashore. These people fascinated me. I would see women sitting on the little boats, babies in slings on their backs while they prepared the men's fishing nets; it seemed incredible that these little boats with their wicker mat sails were the only homes they had.

Perhaps more even than the harbor life the streets intrigued me. They were like colorful paintings with their banner-like shop signs, and because of the artistic formation of the letters they were quite beautiful; reds, greens, and blues mingled with gold and fluttered in the breeze. I was enchanted by the steep byways which they called ladder streets and which were lined with stalls containing various kinds of food—vegetables, fruit, and dried fish. There were vendors of all kinds of articles including birds in cages and exquisitely painted paper kites.

The letter writers interested me. They were usually seated at a table with writing material on it. I often looked with pity on those who had brought a letter to be read to them after which they would dictate the answer. They struck me as so pathetic as they watched the lips of the reader as he read, and his pen as he wrote the characters on the paper.

The fortune tellers were always in demand with their containers of sticks which were shaken before the sticks were selected and the future told. I was amused by the one who used a trained bird to select a card from the pack which would be closely studied by the seer who would then proceed to tell the future.

Everywhere there was teeming life and dire contrast. Here were the beggars with their begging bowls and the lost hopeless look in their eyes which haunted me long after I had dropped my coin in the bowl. I was astounded by my first glimpse of an imperious mandarin being carried in his sedan chair by six bearers while his train of attendants walked in two files on either side of him. Two of the members of his party carried gongs which were struck at intervals as the procession passed in order that all might know what majesty was in their midst. A placard was carried on high and on this was inscribed all the titles of the mandarin. It was interesting to see the awe with which shoppers and passers-by regarded this procession. Humble in the presence of such glory they stood eyes downcast, and when one boy stared in frank amazement and forgot to bow his head he received a cut from one of the canes carried by two men in the party whose sole duty appeared to be to chastise those who failed to show the required respect.

In contrast to this proud spectacle were the rickshaw men—usually painfully thin and wizened, standing hopefully by their vehicles or running breathlessly through the streets with their burdens.

Each day I found something new to absorb my interest. But more than anything I was fascinated by The House of a Thousand Lanterns.

Since we had left home, each day had been filled with new experiences. There had been the sea voyage which had taken so many weeks and brought us halfway round the world. Other travelers found us an unusual party—myself, my older husband, our small child, and Sylvester's servant Ling Fu. Jason was of an age to find everything that happened an adventure and yet at the same time to take it all for granted. We suffered the usual discomforts of such travel but I was delighted to find that we were moderately good sailors. Sylvester had made the journey many times and was well known to the captain and crew. It was convenient that this was so, for with his disability the voyage could have been an ordeal but so delighted was he to be on his way to Hong Kong that he seemed to gain new strength.

We dined often with the captain who regaled us with

stories of adventure at sea; I was continually watchful of Jason for I was terrified that his adventurous spirit would lead him to some disaster. The voyage might be long but with so much to concern myself I could not call it tedious.

We called at various ports on the way round and to one like myself who had never been out of England except for my Paris honeymoon this was an exciting experience. Sylvester could not easily get ashore but he was determined that my pleasure should not be spoiled and often Jason and I would take a drive round some foreign city in the company of the captain or some of his officers.

By the time we reached Hong Kong the ship had become a home to me and I felt a curious sense of regret to be leaving her. This was soon submerged beneath the new experiences which crowded in on me.

When we landed it was to find Adam Milner waiting to meet us and with him was a rather thick-set pleasant man whom I imagined to be in his mid-thirties. He had a frank pleasant face and I took to him immediately. I guessed him to be Tobias Grantham, the manager of Sylvester's Hong Kong branch, for Sylvester had told me a good deal about him. "He's a canny Scot," he had said. "He was in our Scottish office. His sister Elspeth keeps house for him. She thought she had to come out to protect him from the dangers of the East. A good upright woman, but as so many of her kind, sometimes a bit uncomfortable."

Sylvester's pleasure in being in Hong Kong and in seeing Tobias Grantham was obvious. He was delighted too that Adam had come to meet us. He had, I knew, always deplored the rift in the family and was pleased at any sign of bridging it.

Adam was cool to me but Tobias Grantham was most deferential. He remarked that Sylvester would find everything in order at The House. This I was to discover was the manner in which The House of a Thousand Lanterns was always referred to.

Two men in black trousers and tunics, their hair in pigtails with conical straw hats on their heads waited at a respectful distance. When Tobias gave a sign they collected the baggage which was available—most of it was in the hold and would be brought to us later—and put it into a rickshaw.

Jason clutching my hand watched everything with wondering eyes.

It was Tobias Grantham who spoke first to him. He said: "Is this young sir then?"

Jason replied: "I'm not a young sir. I'm a boy. I'm Jason."

"Could be a young sir too," replied Tobias.

The idea seemed to please Jason. Tobias knelt down so that their eyes were on a level. "Welcome to Hong Kong, young sir."

"Are you a Chinaman?" asked Jason.

"No. As English as yourself."

"Why aren't you a Chinaman?"

"Because I'm not Chinese."

Tobias stood up and smiled at me. "I hope you'll be happy here, Mrs. Milner."

"You'll find it very different from England," said Adam.

"I'm prepared for that," I replied.

Adam handed me into the waiting rickshaw, then Sylvester was helped in and Jason sat between us.

"We'll follow you when we've seen to the luggage," said Tobias Grantham.

The rickshaw man took the shafts and we were off. Jason was round-eyed with wonder; I was more or less the same.

Sylvester smiled at me. "So we're here, Jane."

"It's fantastic," I said.

It was indeed. Everywhere there seemed to be rickshaws pulled by fragile-looking men, barefooted in the thin cotton trousers and tunics, their pigtails flapping as they ran.

We skirted the teeming streets with their beautiful signs rippling in the slight breeze; the air was full of strange smells the main ingredient of which seemed to be fish. It was like a series of colorful images flashing before the eyes but when I think back to that first day in Hong Kong the picture which dominates all others is that of The House of a Thousand Lanterns.

It was on the outskirts of Kowloon and surrounded by gardens so that it appeared to be more isolated than it was. We first came to a wall with a gate on either side of which was a stone dragon. An old man in the inevitable cotton trousers and tunic squatted at the side of this gate and as we drew up he stood up sharply, opened the gate and bowed low.

Sylvester called a greeting. There was almost a lilt in his voice. I could tell how excited he was to be here.

Our rickshaw man took us through the gate and we were in what appeared to be a courtyard; a path in delicately colored stones led to another wall and a door. We passed through this and were in a similar courtyard. I later discovered that the grounds were like a series of boxes without lids which fitted into each other. At the center of these was the house.

We had reached that center square and there it was: The House of a Thousand Lanterns. Before it was a lawn on which grew miniature shrubs and there was a small stream over which a little bridge had been set. It was like a doll's garden. At the side of the house scattering petals from its purple blosssoms stood a fully grown tree. It looked enormous in comparison with the miniatures. I had never seen such a tree before and later discovered it to be the Bauhinia.

I took all this in during a few seconds for I was aware of little else but the house. It was imposing and bore a resemblance to the houses I had seen on painted scrolls. It stood on a sort of platform paved with marble slabs of pink and white. There were four stories, each one protruding over the others; and it was made of some kind of golden stone which glittered when the sun caught it. It was built in the Chinese style with gilding and carving and there was a pergola over which myrtle was growing.

Lanterns had been set up at intervals along this pergola; there was one on either side of the porch and a big one hanging down over the center. I immediately thought: There must be a thousand such lanterns in this house.

"Mama, look," screeched Jason. He had discovered the dragons on either side of the porch. "They're like the ones at Roland's Croft only bigger."

I told him that he would probably see a great many dragons now. He put his finger into the mouth of one of the dragons and looked up at me to see if I were watching. He shivered with pleasure.

We mounted three steps and were on the marble platform where a Chinese servant appeared to materialize like the genii of the lamp; he opened the door.

We were in a hall which was paved with marble. Two wooden columns supported the roof it seemed for they disappeared through the ceiling on which a delicate design had been traced. The wooden pillars were painted red and there was a delicate tracery of gold. I looked closer and saw that the tracing represented the ubiquitous dragon.

The alien quality of the place enveloped me. I was not sure whether there really was an atmosphere of unfriendliness or whether it was merely the strangeness of everything that made me imagine this.

About the hall hung six lanterns. I found myself counting them. A thousand is a great many, I told myself. Where will they put them all?

A strange smell of something like incense was in the air and as we stood in the hall silent figures appeared. There were twelve of them—Sylvester's servants who took care of this house when he was away.

They arranged themselves in a neat line and one by one they bowed first to Sylvester and then to me. Then they all knelt and bowed their heads so low that they touched the floor.

Sylvester stood for a moment surveying them; then he clapped his hands and they rose. He said: *"Haou? Tsing, tsing!"* which meant: "Are you well? Hail and Hail." It was the conventional Chinese greeting. Then he said in English: "I am glad to be here. Peace be with you." He took my hand and it was as though he were presenting me to them.

They bowed and inclined their heads acknowledging me.

Then they bowed to Jason.

"You shall be taken to the rooms which have been prepared for us," said Sylvester. "You will get to know the servants in time."

I thought I never would for they all looked alike to me.

Sylvester's rooms were on the ground floor owing to his disability which prevented his mounting stairs easily. Leaving him and gripping Jason's hand I followed a servant up the stairs. We came to a corridor. Lanterns hung from the ceiling. There were still more stairs to climb before we reached the apartment which had been allotted to me. I was pleased to find a small room leading from it which was to be Jason's temporarily.

These rooms had been furnished in the European style, but there were one or two touches to remind me that I was far from home. The draperies were of blue satin embroidered in white silk. The bed was European with silk cushions and a coverlet to match. There were low stools instead of chairs, and a few delicately etched scrolls on the wall. There was a very fine mirror in a gilded wooden frame on a dressing table but it looked alien in this room. In fact the touches which I learned had been put there for my comfort seemed out of place. The carpet was rich

Chinese depicting a fire-breathing dragon. Jason noticed it first of all and was on his knees studying it.

The room which led from mine and which was to be his for a time at least was a kind of dressing room. It was very simply furnished and I learned afterwards that Tobias had had these quarters prepared for us when he knew we were coming.

"I hope you will not be too tired to join me for dinner," Sylvester had said.

Indeed I was not tired. My mind was stimulated by my new surroundings and I wanted to absorb as much as I could as quickly as possible.

Some of my bags arrived and I started to unpack as I faced a barrage of questions from Jason. This was a funny house, he said. He liked Roland's Croft better. He wondered what Mrs. Couch was doing. Would she come here? He was momentarily sad when I told him this was unlikely but his mood soon passed. Like me he had too much that was new to interest him.

Some food was brought for him by one of the servants. He frowned at it; it wasn't like the food he had had at Roland's Croft nor on the ship, but he must have been hungry for he ate it. It was some kind of fish cooked with rice and there was fruit.

I wondered how he would feel about being left alone in his room while I dined with Sylvester. He was intrigued by the lantern which hung from the ceiling and which could be pulled down on a chain and then went up again on its own accord when released. I said it should be left burning all night. He would be perfectly safe with the communicating door left open.

This knowledge comforted him and he was asleep almost before he was undressed.

I left the door open, unpacked a few things, changed my dress and went down to find Sylvester.

When I shut my bedroom door the alien quality seemed to close round me.

I looked along the corridor at the rows of lanterns and was not sure which way to turn. There must have been about ten lanterns suspended from the ceiling. Every other one was alight. As I stood there a figure seemed to materialize at the end of the corridor.

A cold feeling of horror gripped me, and for a second I knew what people meant when they said they were paralyzed by fear, for if I had tried to move I should for a few seconds have been unable to. The light shed by the lanterns was sparse but that was a face looking at me out of the gloom. As the use of my limbs came back to me my first impulse was to run in the opposite direction. The figure had not moved. It appeared to be just standing there. I forced myself to take a step forward. Still it remained motionless. As I advanced it had taken on shape and I could see now that it was a statue of life-size proportions.

A figure of wood and stone. Nothing more. How could I have been so foolish? Because this house had lived in my imagination for so long I had built fantasies about it and now that I saw it, I had the feeling that it was even more mysterious, more strange, more menacing perhaps than I had imagined it.

I went close to the figure. It was Kuan Yin—the benevolent goddess. This one looked slightly less kindly than others I had seen. Her eyes seemed to look straight into mine . . . veiled eyes. I could almost imagine she was telling me to go away, which was what a benevolent goddess would do to someone who was in danger.

In danger! Why should that have come into my mind? I thought of my son alone in his room while I was away.

That was absurd. *I* should be in the house.

I ran back to my room. Quietly I opened the door. I looked into Jason's room. He was lying on his back, his eyes closed, his fingers gripping the edge of the sheet, a happy smile on his face. His dreams were evidently pleasant. I wanted to pick him up and hug him but I dared not for fear of awakening him. So I tiptoed out of the room, turned my back on the figure of Kuan Yin and found the staircase which I had ascended.

Sylvester had come out into the hall. He stood leaning on his stick watching me descend.

"Oh there you are, Jane," he said. "Dinner is about to be served."

He took my arm and leaned rather heavily on me as we went into the dining room. It was dim because the draperies had been drawn across the window and there was only the light from the lantern which hung from the ceiling.

There was something alien about the room, and I was discovering what it was. It was this mingling of East and West. The table and the chairs looked as though they had come out of a French château—so did the marble console table with the gilded legs. It was as though one culture had been overlaid with another.

Sylvester read my thoughts. He had an uncanny way of doing this which often disturbed me. I felt either he had special powers of discernment or I was too easy to read.

"Yes," he said, as though continuing a conversation, "it's not in keeping, is it? You'll find that throughout the house. Western furniture has been brought in for greater comfort. But these rooms on the ground floor are all paneled which makes them more unusual still."

We took our places at the table.

Immediately a servant brought in bowls of soup; the soup was appetizing and I must have been more hungry than I thought. We ate in silence while the servants padded in and out. The soup was followed by salted meat and fish served with rice and tea. There was also some kind of drink which was not unlike whisky and which Sylvester told me was made with rice.

The meal was something of a ceremony. I felt the servants were watching me intently and I was sure Sylvester, like myself, was relieved when it was over. We retired to a small room which was furnished like a study. It was dimly lighted by the lantern which hung from the ceiling.

"So, Jane," said Sylvester, "we are here."

"It's hard to believe."

He had seated himself in a carved chair and I sat on a pouf of embossed leather.

"What do you think of it?"

"I don't know yet."

"Too soon to decide," he said. "But you'll be fascinated. Everyone is. They undergo a change when they come into this house. The servants . . . everyone. Even my imperturbable nephew Adam is not as immune from its influence as he pretends to be."

"He is a very taciturn young man."

"Oh, he's very serious. He's more like me than any other member of the family. And that he should be Redmond's son is extraordinary. He certainly doesn't take after his father. Tobias would have liked to stay to dine with us, but I think this is not the time. Tomorrow we'll talk business."

"He must have a lot to tell you."

"He intimated that. I want you to be present, Jane. I want you to learn as much as you can about the business. You'll get to understand how things work out here much more than you could in London. We'll get Tobias to show you over the warehouses down by the harbor. They're called 'Go-Downs' here. You've a great deal to see."

There was an excitement about him. He was delighted not only to be here but to have me with him. That he liked my company I knew but it was more than that even. He wanted me to learn his business; and I knew that he was thinking that one day Jason would control it and that I should be there to help him.

"And the house?" he said. "What do *you* think of the house?"

I looked over my shoulders for I had the eerie feeling that the house itself was listening.

"I have hardly seen it. It was almost dark when we arrived."

"It is the strangest house I ever knew," he said slowly. "There are some who say that it should never have been built."

"Who says that?"

"The superstitious. It is built on the site of an old temple, you see. And there's evidence of that. The pagoda was actually part of the temple."

"What pagoda?"

"You haven't seen it. It's in the garden just beyond the outer wall. You'll see it from your window in the morning. It's rather fine. It's built of stone and imbedded in the walls are colored stones which glisten in the sunshine . . . There are some amethysts and topaz. It's a wonderful sight. The servants regard it as a holy place. They're in awe of it."

"Wasn't the temple dedicated to Kuan Yin and wasn't she supposed to be benevolent?"

"Yes, the Goddess of Mercy," he said. "But even she, so they think, might not be pleased to find a house built where once her temple stood, and that house in the possession of a barbarian! Oh yes, we are all barbarians. They call us *Fân-kuei*, which means foreign ghost. We're spirits or devils. Foreign devils they call us."

"Not very complimentary."

"I'm sorry to say that it implies a certain respect, for they respect what they fear."

"Yet one of them gave this house to your grandfather."

"Perhaps it was not a very suitable gift . . . but I'm glad he gave it to him. My father loved the place. He used to talk a great deal about it, and he left it to me not only because I was the eldest son but because he knew I had more feeling for the house itself than the others had. You will see for yourself in time, Jane. You feel the spell of the place. Now I think you must be tired for I am."

He picked up a bell. It rang loudly through the room and Ling Fu appeared.

He did not need to be told that his master wished to be taken to his room.

I went to mine. I was tired yet I was not at ease. I undressed and went to bed, first having looked in at Jason who was sleeping.

I was undoubtedly tired but I could not sleep. I was actually in The House of a Thousand Lanterns. I kept thinking of my first sight of the house, the walls, the courtyards and the golden-colored building with the dragons on either side of the porch, the almost stealthy servants, the quiet of the house, the rugs so many of them depicting the fire-breathing dragon, the atmosphere of East and West uneasily mingling. And the lanterns.

I longed for morning. I wanted to see the place in daylight. I wanted to go to the harbor with Sylvester and learn about the business that was conducted there. There was so much that I wanted to know and I was not sure what the discovery would bring.

I dozed and dreamed that I went from my room onto the landing and that the goddess there beckoned me in some strange way without moving at all and I could not stop myself from advancing towards her. When I was close a voice issued from her. "Go home, foreign ghost. There is nothing good for you here. For you do not belong, foreign devil, go away while there is time."

"I can't go," I said. "I can't. I must stay here . . ."

Her eyes changed. They were no longer benevolent; I felt myself caught in a cold vise.

"Let me go!" I cried and I was awake . . . but the nightmare was in the room. My hand was gripped . . . someone was there.

"Mama, Mama. I'm frightened." It was Jason's hand that was gripping me. "You were shouting."

The relief was great. I drew him into my bed.

He was cold and he clung to me.

"There's a dragon in my room," he said.

"It was a nightmare," I told him.

"He's not there when I open my eyes. Fire comes out of his mouth."

I said: "It was a dream."

"Did you dream about him too?"

"I dreamed about something."

"Shall I stay with you in case you have another dream?"

"Yes," I said, "tonight we'll stay together."

I felt him relax.

"It was only a dream," he said, soothing me.

"That's all, Jason, only a dream."

In a few minutes he was asleep. I was not long after. The warm body of my child gave me comfort in that strange house.

In the morning the house had lost much of its sinister aspect. It was fascinating and I wanted to explore it.

Sylvester spent the morning in bed for he was exhausted. He had arranged that in the afternoon we should go down to the warehouse and could look round while he had a conference with Tobias Grantham and his staff. I thought I would go on a tour of exploration and I decided that I would take Jason with me for I did not wish him to be left alone just yet in the house with servants whom he could not understand. When he had settled in and grown accustomed to the place it would be different.

There must have been some twenty rooms in the house. They were similar to each other, and all had the one feature—the hanging lantern from the center of the ceiling. These were in wrought iron and were beautifully engraved with figures of men and women. I wondered again if there could possibly be a thousand lanterns. One day I promised myself I would count them. In my tour of the

house I encountered servants who bowed low and yet
averted their eyes as I passed.

We went out into the courtyards and through the three
gates into the grounds beyond. Jason loved the miniature
gardens and I had to explain to him how the trees were
stunted. His face puckered for he was a little sorry for
them. "I think they're unhappy," he said. "They want to
be big like other trees."

And then we found the pagoda. Of course it was magnificent with its glittering walls and the wind bells which
tinkled quietly when the breeze caught them.

"Oh look, Mama!" cried Jason. "It's a castle . . . No
it's not. It's a tower."

"It's a pagoda," I said. And I knew it was the one of
which Sylvester had spoken.

"What's a pagoda?"

"That," I answered.

"Who lives there?"

"No one now. It's part of a temple."

Jason was awestruck. We went through an arch where
once there may have been a door. Inside was a strange
smell of something like incense. And dominating the circular space was the well-known figure of the goddess. On
either side of her burned a joss stick and it was this which
had given out that pungent odor.

"What are they for?" whispered Jason.

"Someone has put them there for the goddess. They
hope she will pray for them."

"Will she?"

"She's supposed to pray for everyone who asks."

"But if she's a goddess why does she have to pray for
them? Why can't she give them what they ask for?"

"Hush."

"Is it like church?" whispered Jason.

"Yes, it's like church."

I looked up at the tall walls. I could see the sky

through the roof. This pagoda must have stood for hundreds of years. It was here when there had been a temple where the house now stood. But the crumbling statue of the goddess still remained carved out of stone and there were those (they must be some of our servants) who still burned joss sticks to her.

We came out into the sunshine and I led Jason back to the miniature garden. He knelt and examined the tiny trees and the little bridge over the imitation stream. He was so enchanted with the garden that he forgot the temple.

I told him he might stay there for a while if he promised not to go beyond the wall. Then I left him and went into the house. Ling Fu appeared suddenly and told me that a visitor had arrived and Sylvester wished me to join him.

He led me to a room next to Sylvester's bedroom which was furnished as a sitting room. Adam was there.

"I came to see if there was anything I could do," he told me.

"That was thoughtful of you."

"I was anxious, of course, about my uncle." He turned to Sylvester. "I never thought you would make the journey."

"Oh come, I'm not so incapacitated as all that."

Adam sat down, crossing long legs. He looked elegant and there was no denying that he had a certain dignity. He wore a dark blue waistcoat and tightly fitting jacket; his shirt was very white with a frilly front and his cravat was of a blue to match his coat. The blue made his eyes seem less steely. On a table was his top hat and an ebony-topped walking stick.

"I suppose you will go to the Go-Down this afternoon," he said.

"I hope to go this afternoon." Sylvester turned to me. "That's the warehouse. Did I tell you that they call them

Go-Downs here? I couldn't discuss anything of importance with Toby last night so I am eager to get down there at the earliest possible moment."

"You rely very much on Tobias," said Adam.

"I have never found any reason not to."

"Do you ever think that one day he might like to strike out on his own?"

"Not everyone thinks along those lines." Sylvester's smile was quizzical. "It can be a hazardous undertaking," he added.

I thought Adam's expression hardened. He changed the subject abruptly by turning to me.

"You'll find everything different here from at home," he said. "The people most of all. Their outlook is not ours. Sometimes that makes communication difficult."

"I have read a certain amount," I told him. "Sylvester always kept me well supplied with books, so I don't feel it's as alien as it would otherwise have seemed. I think I shall adjust myself quickly."

"You have a child to look after and I know you do a great deal for my uncle."

"Jane knows a good deal about the business, too. I want her to come down to the Go-Down and hear what's going on."

Adam was silent for a few moments and I thought I detected a slightly scornful look about his mouth. Clearly he didn't think I was capable of being much help. Then he said thoughtfully: "You need a companion . . . a kind of go-between, a maid perhaps."

"There are plenty of servants," said Sylvester. "She can take her pick."

Adam shook his head. "That's not quite what I meant. These people speak little English. She needs someone to help look after the child, someone who can go with her to the shops. She can hardly go alone."

Sylvester looked uneasy.

"I could suggest someone," went on Adam. "In fact I

know the very one." He turned to me. "You need someone who can be with you . . . someone who is more than
a servant . . . someone who has enough English to talk to
you about China and who will help you to understand the
Chinese. I have the answer. She is a young girl—half
Chinese, half English. She speaks English after a fashion.
She has been brought up in a less closed household than
most. I think Lotus Blossom is the girl for you."

"What a beautiful name!"

"It's the English version. It is pretty, and she is very
. . . presentable. She is fifteen years old or so but that is
not immature in China. I shall send her to you and if you
like her . . . then you can keep her."

"Who is this girl?" asked Sylvester.

"I've had dealings with her family. They'll be glad to
find a place for her. Yes, Jane, you must meet little Lotus
Blossom and if you take a fancy to her you will find her a
very useful companion. When you go shopping you will
need her with you. She will bargain for you and in a
manner be a kind of chaperone. She will help look after
the child. You will find her useful in all manner of ways.
That's settled that point then."

Sylvester said: "I realize that Jane will need someone.
We may as well try this girl."

"She shall be sent along to you," replied Adam.

When he left Sylvester was thoughtful.

"Adam is determined to be agreeable," he commented.

"You sound surprised that he should be," I replied.

"Well, there was a rift and I saw little of him during
the years preceding his father's death. I have a notion that
he would now like to join forces with me."

"Would you want that?"

"No, not now. I have other plans." He smiled at me
warmly and I thought I understood. At one time Adam
and Joliffe would have been his natural heirs. It was different now that Jason had appeared.

He changed the subject and talked to me about the

district in the days when his father had been alive. Then
the traders used to come out; they anchored in the harbor
and the chief commodity they carried was opium. Fifty
years had passed since the Opium War between Britain
and China at the end of which the British flag had been
hoisted over Hong Kong Island.

"It was nothing but a barren rock then. Now of course
it's thriving, flourishing. People are being ferried back and
forth between the island and Kowloon hundreds of times
a day. The whole place now is teeming with life. Tea is
one of the most profitable exports. The climate's suitable
for it. It provides work for the people and revenue for the
government. The Chinese are a hard-working race, Jane.
It must have been a great day when the British flag was
hoisted at Possession Point, and we've been prospering
ever since. But you'll get to understand something of the
country although it will often leave you baffled."

Sylvester lay back in his chair looking tired.

"The idea of Tobias's striking out on his own!" He
laughed. "Yes, I think Adam might well be hinting that
he would like to come back. I wonder how things are
going with him. Not so well, I imagine. No doubt we shall
see. Of course it is very easy in our business to make a
mistake."

"Could that really be so? He seemed so contented."

"I know Adam well, Jane. He always puts on a good
face. We could sink a great deal of capital into something
which even though it's intrinsically good has little sales
value. Sometimes so much capital is locked up in our
pieces that we could find it difficult without borrowing
extensively to meet our creditors. My father and I were of
a more cautious nature than Redmond and my brother
Magnus. They could be led astray by their enthusiasms. I
was never like that. Tobias has been trained by me. I can
trust Tobias."

"It is good of Adam to send this girl to us."

"Oh yes, it's a good idea. Well, this afternoon we shall go to the Go-Down."

"Do you feel equal to it?"

"I have you to lean on. You can help me into the rickshaw and Tobias will be at the other end."

I left my son in the care of Ling Fu, for on our journey out a friendship had sprung up between them. They said little but found a quiet contentment in each other's company, and I knew Jason was safe with him.

The rickshaw took us down to the waterfront where the warehouse was and now I saw more distinctly than I had the day before the teeming life of the place. The rickshaw men running with their burdens, their feet bare, their conical hats tied under their chins with string and their pigtails flying aroused my pity because they appeared to be too fragile to pull the carriages and their occupants. There was noise and clamor and everywhere the ever persistent odor of fish. On the sea was the floating village —sampan after sampan side by side, the homes of families who had never known any other. In these little boats —some gaily painted, others dark and shabby, families had lived for generations. Lines of washing fluttered in the breeze and I saw a woman bathing a baby on the deck of one. Cooking smells filled the air. From one a boy was diving for coins which a European traveler was throwing into the water. He stood poised on the edge of his boat— like an etching against the sunlight—naked but for a loin-cloth. I saw people buying from a vegetable boat and Sylvester told me that these people who had lived in their boats all their lives had been born in them, bred in them, and rarely came ashore.

"If you could go inside one," he went on, "doubtless you would see that an altar had been set up, and joss sticks were burning. You'd see a red lucky paper strip to drive away devils. Look at that lorcha there." He indicated a boat which was bobbing on the water. "You can see the eyes painted on it. That is so that it can see its way. It would be very unlucky to go on the water in such a boat without eyes."

"They seem to be very superstitious."

"They are poor," said Sylvester. "It is so important for them to have what they call good 'joss.' That is good fortune. So they burn their joss sticks in the temples or in their houseboats and they are careful not to arouse the wrath of dragons."

People scurried about—mostly dressed in similar fashion—men and women alike in black trousers and jacket and often the conical hat to keep off the sun.

I saw a woman carrying such a heavy load that she could scarcely stagger; she was in black, her clothes dusty and shabby and she wore a hat with a black silk fringe.

Sylvester followed my gaze and told me that she was one of the Hakka women.

"They came from South China during the Yuen Dynasty and settled northwest of Hong Kong. They work hard, especially the women, and it's mostly manual labor. You'll see many of them in the fields."

"They look as if they have a hard life."

"Life is often hard for Chinese women."

I commented on the overpowering smell of fish and Sylvester said: "Odd that it should have been called Heung Kong which means Fragrant Harbor."

"A lovely name," I said, "but hardly fitting at the moment."

"No doubt before there was all this activity it was fragrant."

The rickshaw had pulled up and we were at the Go-Down. Tobias was waiting for us and he helped me to alight first and then Sylvester.

Leaning on my arm on one side and his stick on the other, Sylvester entered the building with Tobias.

We went into a rather elaborately furnished office. There was a showcase in it and in this case were some very fine pieces of jade and rose quartz.

A chair was found for Sylvester who was glad to sit down after his exertion and when we were seated Tobias told us what had been happening during the years when he had managed the business with only postal communications to and from Sylvester.

Sylvester would see that trading had been good. He would know of course what had been bought of any interest and he himself had found some fine pieces in England. In spite of the fact that the last years had been difficult for some traders, Tobias had made out very well.

"What do you know of my nephew Adam's affairs?" asked Sylvester. "You can speak before my wife. She shares my confidences."

Tobias shrugged his shoulders. "I believe him to have had some difficulties."

"You don't know the extent of these?"

"He would hardly confide in me, I'm afraid, but one hears rumors."

"He is being very helpful to me and I wondered. Well, you can take my wife round the offices, Tobias. I will wait here and look through the books."

So Toby, as I soon came to think of him, took me on a tour of the business premises. I was impressed. I had had no idea of the size of them. He explained so much to me, how goods were bought and shipped to various places all over the world, and what kind of works of art found the readier market.

"When a client is looking for one particular thing," went on Toby, "the request would doubtless go out to several dealers like ourselves. So we would all be looking for the priceless piece for this one customer. The competition is keen. That's what makes it so exciting. I understand, Mrs. Milner, that you will come here now and then to see how things are going."

"I should like that. I did go occasionally to the London offices."

"They're a sort of clearinghouse. It is here that the main business is done." He explained everything lucidly and I found myself liking him more every minute. There was a frankness about him which was appealing.

Before we rejoined Sylvester he said: "If you need anything at any time, Mrs. Milner, please send for me and I'll always come and do what I can."

I felt that I had found a friend.

It had been a very interesting session and I enjoyed discussing it with Sylvester all the way back to The House of a Thousand Lanterns.

II

I shall never forget the first time I saw Lotus Blossom. Adam himself brought her and I saw them standing together in Sylvester's study, the tall Adam and this fragile girl.

Her name suited her for she was beautiful. She was tiny and dainty; her hair which she wore loose was jet black and glossy; it was only married ladies, she told me later, who made it into a bun. Her eyes were not slanted as much as most Chinese; her skin was lighter too; it was matte and clear and the more the shade of certain magnolia petals. She wore the traditional cheongsam, and hers was made of silk, pale blue in color with a delicate white pattern traced on it. The little stand-up collar, the simple lines which fitted her slight figure to perfection, the slit in the side of the skirt made her look like a doll.

As I went forward to greet them Adam said: "Oh, Jane, I have brought Lotus Blossom. Lotus, this is the mistress of the house, Mrs. Sylvester Milner."

The girl bowed so low that I thought she was going down to the floor.

"Joy fills me to greet Great Lady," she said in a quaint voice which was as charming as everything else about her.

"I'm glad you have come," I answered.

"Very good news," she said. "I hope I serve you well."

"My husband will wish to see you," I told her.

Lotus Blossom's eyes opened wide. She looked fearful.

Adam laid his hand on her shoulder reassuringly. "All will be well, never fear. You will serve this lady well and in turn for that she will care for you."

"I hope I serve her well," said Lotus Blossom in a faintly apprehensive voice.

"I am sure we shall get along together," I said.

In the study Sylvester sat dozing in his chair.

"Sylvester," I cried, "your nephew has arrived with the little Chinese girl."

"Bring them, Jane. Ah, here is the child."

Lotus went forward and this time knelt and placed her forehead on the carpet.

"My dear child, there is no need to do that. Come here. I understand you speak English."

"I have learn," she answered. "I very bad speaker."

"You will improve here," said Sylvester, and I smiled affectionately remembering how he was always eager that people about him should learn. "Sit down and Ling Fu will bring tea."

I placed myself opposite the girl for I was fascinated by the delicate fluttering of her hands, the graceful manner in which she moved, and those bright slanting eyes which were smiling, humble yet proud, candid yet inscrutable. I noticed that she was intent on every movement of what Sylvester called the tea ceremony. And when the tray was placed before me she rose and took the cups from me as I poured out and presented one first to Sylvester then to Adam.

"And this is yours," I said.

She looked dismayed. "But you first, Great Lady. I should not take."

I assured her that she could and I compromised by serving myself first and then pouring one for her. She took the cup gravely. I noticed that Adam watched her intently. I was not surprised for she was lovely to behold. He seemed very eager for us to like her and he clearly thought her charming.

"Lotus Blossom will do all sorts of things for you," he said. "You will soon be wondering how you managed without her. She will help with the child. You are a good nurse, are you not, Lotus? And you will teach Mrs. Milner something of the customs that prevail here."

Lotus Blossom sat very still, her hands folded, her eyes downcast, her pose one of extreme humility. She looked as though she had stepped out of one of the Chinese scrolls.

In a few days she had become part of the household. I was delighted with her. She was so gentle, so eager to please, and I was enchanted by her exotic beauty.

Jason had taken a great fancy to her. He confided to me that she was funny but nice. She called him Little Master, a term which he relished. In return he called her Lottie, and somehow the name began to be used by us all. Perhaps it was a pity; she was like a flower but Lottie seemed better for everyday use.

She was amused by it.

"Very good," she said. "I have family name. It makes me a family."

Her English was quaint and I was not so eager as Sylvester was to change it, for the manner in which she spoke suited her.

It was through Lottie that I began to understand something of the land in which I was living. What to me was quite extraordinary was to her quite natural, and once she had overcome her awe of me and I had broken her of the habit of bowing low every time she saw me, she began to chatter freely.

"Perhaps I never come to serve Great Lady," she said, "but for the big Tai Pan." I discovered that she was referring to Adam's father.

"One day he find me in the street. I am left there. Perhaps I will die of cold for it was winter. Perhaps the wild dogs will come along and eat me. Instead comes the Tai Pan."

"In the street. What were you doing there?"

"Little girl child." She shook her head. "Girl child are no good. They not wanted. Boy child is treasure. He will grow up and work for his father, he will look after him in old age. Girl child . . ." She made a gesture of disdain and shook her head. "No good. Perhaps marry but too long to keep. So girl child is put into street. She will die of cold or starve or the dogs will have her . . . and if by morning none of these have happen she is swept up and put in the pit with the dead ones and buried there."

"This is not possible!"

"Is possible," she replied firmly. "Girl child no good. There I would die but big Tai Pan find me and he take me to Chan Cho Lan to live in her house; I have English father. Not good. Not Chinese . . . not English . . . not good."

A pitiful story I thought, the liaison between East and West and the result was that this exquisite child had been put out into the streets to die.

I asked Sylvester if this could be true.

"Oh yes," he replied, "it is a shameful custom. I have heard that four thousand female babies perish during a year in Peking alone. These poor innocent creatures whose only fault is to be born female are abandoned, and starving dogs and swine are let loose to devour them."

"It's monstrous!"

Sylvester shrugged his shoulders. "They must be judged against their times, their customs and beliefs. The poverty of these people is hard to conceive. They cannot afford to feed their girls from whom they gain little. The women of China are little more than slaves."

"And she was really found?"

"Yes, by my brother Redmond. I remember now hearing of it. He brought the child in from the streets and found a home for her."

"Why did he choose her amongst all the girl babies which must have been exposed on that night?"

"It was luck for Lotus Blossom that he came across her. 'Good Joss' she would call it. It would seem to her that the gods had some special reason for preserving her."

Her coming into the house had had a great effect on me. So fragile, so dependent she seemed at times, at others she would assume the role of protectress. The rickshaw would take us into the center of the town and we would shop together. She would bargain with the traders while I stood by, marveling at the manner in which her gentle humility changed to shrewdness. The soft accents would become indignantly shrill as she and the salesman berated each other. I feared they would come to blows, but she assured me that it was all part of the business of buying and selling and expected.

With her, I felt completely at home in those alien streets, and because she was with me I attracted less attention than I would with someone of my own race. She would chatter away in her own tongue and then turn to me and make some acid comment such as "He very dishonest man. He ask too much. He think he get from you because you not Chinese." Her voice would become strident, her flower-like hands would express contempt and outrage. I never ceased to find pleasure in watching her. Together we would explore the alleys known as Thieves' Market. There would be displayed antiques of all description, among them Buddhas, some in ivory, jade, and rose quartz. They fascinated me and whenever we had an hour to spare I would want to go there. There were also

vases, ornaments, and scrolls. I delighted in assessing
their age. Once I bought a Buddha in rose quartz and de-
lightedly took it back to the house for Sylvester's inspec-
tion. I had found a bargain he assured me; and I remember now how when I told Lottie she took the figure
and hugged it ecstatically to her little breast; then she
knelt and took my hand and said: "I will serve you as
long as I live."

She charmed me in a hundred ways and soon I couldn't
imagine the household without her.

I gave lessons to Jason every day and Lottie came to
join them. They would sit at the table and Jason would
labor over his copperplate writing, his tongue peeping out
from one side of his mouth as though to inspect what his
hands were doing. Lottie was learning to write too and we
all read together in English. I had brought books with me,
some old annuals which I had had as a child and which
contained colored pictures and stories with a moral.

Both of them would listen gravely to these stories and
then they would read them aloud. I was very happy with
them and there was no doubt that Jason was growing
fond of Lottie. She had become nurse to him; they would
play in the gardens together. Often I would see them from
my window walking hand in hand.

I was beginning to love the little half-Chinese girl. She
was very accomplished and could embroider and paint
exquisitely on silk. I liked to watch the beautiful Chinese
characters flow from her hand when she wrote.

"You teach me to speak better English," she said. "I
teach you Chinese."

Sylvester was delighted at the thought of so much
learning going on.

"You will find it a difficult language," he warned me.
"But if you could master even the rudiments it would be
of great use to you. The original Chinese characters were
simply hieroglyphics like the ancient Egyptian ones. It's
important of course that you should understand the mod-

ern language. The Sung-te is the form used in printing. It's very beautiful as you've noticed."

I smiled inwardly but affectionately. Sylvester always made me feel like a student and I had never lost my desire to shine in his eyes. It was a strange relationship for husband and wife but then ours was no ordinary marriage.

"It was an excellent plan of Adam's to send the girl to us," he said. "It's good for Jason. He'll get to understand something of the Chinese way of life and she'll be a help in that. I've plans for Jason."

I guessed what those plans were. He wanted my son to learn, from him and me, the joy of buying and selling works of art, the eternal quest for the masterpiece which never flags. And how could he better be inspired than by living here where these particular treasures might be found?

I had discovered that Sylvester was a very rich man—the house in England, this one here, the warehouses on the waterfront, the offices in London, meant that his interests stretched far and wide. Since he had been in sole control his business had extended considerably. I wondered often how much Adam's attentions to us were due to a desire to join forces with him again.

Sylvester talked of his nephew now and then. He was undoubtedly pleased that they were friendly. I gathered that at the time his father Redmond had broken away the relationship between them had been very cool indeed. Sylvester had a high opinion of Adam, and I was sure that had things not turned out in the way they had he would very likely have made Adam his heir. He was quite obviously the favorite of the two nephews. Sylvester's opinion of Joliffe was not very good. I imagined that he had always thought him irresponsible, but in view of what had happened he had no time for Joliffe now.

I understood the way in which Sylvester's mind was working. He looked on Jason as his own son and wanted to make him his heir. Everything had changed since the birth of my boy. I wondered how much Adam guessed of this.

I found Adam somewhat taciturn and I had the impression that he disliked me. I was not really surprised, for if he had an inkling of what was in Sylvester's mind he would naturally be displeased that my son might displace him and that would be very galling, especially if his own business was not flourishing.

I was growing more and more friendly with Tobias Grantham. It was a great pleasure to go down to the warehouse when Sylvester was not feeling well enough as I used to go to the London office. There I would work a while with Toby. We would have tea together sometimes in his office and once he took me to his home where I met his sister. She was a stern-faced woman several years his senior and to enter her neat little house was like being transported to Edinburgh. Her accent was more pronounced than Toby's and she was inclined to be censorious of anything alien to the Scottish way of life, a rather uncomfortable woman, as Sylvester had said; but her devotion to her brother was obvious and I found myself liking her in spite of a rather prim and unrelenting manner.

I enjoyed those occasions very much and with this and the change Lottie had brought into the house I began to feel a kind of quiet contentment. Sometimes I recalled the ecstasy I had known with Joliffe and he would refuse to be dismissed from my thoughts. He would be back in England now and I often wondered what was happening between him and Bella. I knew that I would never again feel the ecstasy I had shared with him and sometimes in the loneliness of the night the bitter sorrow would envelop me and I would long to see him again.

But in the morning when Jason stood by my bedside and climbed in with me I would be assuaged. He would read to me as I lay dozing, for now that he was able to read he read everything that came within his reach. Then Lottie would come in—demure in blue trousers and tunic, her long hair tied back with a turquoise blue ribbon and she would bow and wish a happy day to Great Lady and Little Master.

One day she had taken Jason out to the pagoda—it was a favorite place of theirs; they used to sit inside it while she told him stories of dragons. He could never hear enough of the beasts. They had fascinated him from the moment he had discovered one outside the gates.

The rain had fallen in torrents and when they came in they were soaked to the skin. I made Jason take off all his wet clothes and rubbed him dry with a towel. Then I made him put on dry clothes.

I turned to Lottie and noticed that she was still wearing her wet shoes.

"Take them off at once, Lottie. Here are some slippers."

She looked at me in dismay and puzzled, I pushed her into a chair and pulled off her shoes before she could answer.

Then she did a strange thing. She picked up her wet shoes and ran out of the room.

When Jason was dressed I went to find her. She was lying on her bed on her back and the tears ran slowly down her cheeks.

"Whatever's the matter, Lottie?" I demanded.

But she would only shake her head.

"Lottie," I said, "if anything is wrong you must tell me."

Still she only shook her head.

"You know I am fond of you, Lottie. I want to help you. Do tell me what is wrong."

"You will hate me. You will find me ugly."

"Hate you! Find you ugly. Nothing could be farther from the truth. You know that. Tell me. Perhaps I can put right whatever is wrong."

She shook her head. "It can never be right. It is forever and you have seen . . ."

I was puzzled, not having the faintest notion of what she was talking about. "Lottie," I said, "if you don't tell me what is wrong I will think you are not fond of me after all."

"No, no," she cried in distress. "It is because I have reverence for Great Lady that I so ashamed."

"Is it something you have done which makes you ashamed?"

"It was done to me," she said tragically.

"Now Lottie I am going to insist that you tell me."

"You have seen my feet," she said.

"Why Lottie," I said, "what do you mean?" I took her little foot in my hand and kissed it.

"Peasant's feet," she said. "Coolie's feet. No one cared for them when I was little."

I was horrified. I knew that she was referring to the fact that unlike so many Chinese girls her feet were perfect because they had not been bandaged in such a way as to distort them when she was a child.

This seemed to me very pathetic. I tried to comfort her. I told her how fortunate she was to have a pair of perfect feet.

I could not convince her though.

She only shook her head and silently wept.

I was gradually and almost imperceptibly becoming accustomed to the social life of Hong Kong.

I met Adam now and then; my feelings for him changed a little when I saw him handling a beautiful Ming vase and forgetting his animosity to me—of which I had been conscious since I met him—he explained its quality to me. The coldness disappeared then; he seemed vital and so earnest that in spite of myself I found I was warming towards him. He still lived in a tall narrow house near the waterfront, which he had shared with his father until the latter's death. Like the House of a Thousand Lanterns it was half European half Chinese, and many Chinese servants moved silently about the place.

Jason seemed to have forgotten already that he had known any other life. Only rarely now did he talk of Mrs. Couch with regret. Lottie was ample compensation. At times it seemed that they were two children playing together; at others she assumed great wisdom and a quaint air of authority which he recognized. It was a comfort and pleasure to observe how fond they were of each other and as I knew he was safe with her I allowed him when he was with her to go beyond the four walls which enclosed the house. Lottie had procured for him a kite made of silk and split bamboo. This kite was Jason's most cherished possession. It was beautifully made and on it was a delicate painting of a dragon. Lottie had done this herself knowing his interest in such animals. From the dragon's mouth issued fire. In the kite were little round holes supplied with vibrant cords, so that when the kite was flying there came from it a humming sound similar to that which would be made by a swarm of bees. Jason rarely went anywhere without his kite; he kept it near his bed so that it was the last thing he saw before closing his eyes and the first on opening them. He called it his Fire Dragon.

Lottie was delighted that a gift of hers should give such pleasure, and I told Adam how grateful I was to him for having brought her to me.

He replied that he believed he had earned double gratitude from me and from Lottie.

There was no doubt that she was forming a bridge for me. The more I knew Lottie, the more I began to understand the Chinese. I could even speak a little of their language; I learned a great deal of their customs; and I was completely absorbed by everything around me.

There was one thing that continued to be sadly missing in my life. I still longed for Joliffe. While I had been ex-

pecting Jason and in the first year or so of his life he had
absorbed it, but now that he was growing up and acquir-
ing a little independence I began to be more and more
aware of that aching emptiness. I was a normal woman; I
had known a period of happy marriage and I wanted Joliffe.

How sensitive Sylvester was, how discerning. He understood me far more than I ever understood him. From
the moment I had entered his house, he once told me, he
had been aware of a strong affinity. He had known that I
was to be important in his life.

"Things changed," he said, "when you came. I think it
started at the moment I saw you in that room with the
yarrow sticks in your hand. When you went off with Joliffe I was desolate. It seemed as though the pattern had
gone wrong. I was unhappy not only because of my loss
but for you. I knew you had made a mistake. That you
and I should marry seemed incongruous at that time. I
knew that in normal circumstances you would not think
of me as a husband. but you see how fate worked . . . and
here we are together . . . as I know we were intended to
be."

This mingling of mysticism and shrewd business instincts was surprising and yet I suppose Sylvester was no
more complex than other people, for I was learning that
we are all a mass of contradictions.

In any case he was very kind and considerate to me.
He understood, even more than I, the meaning for my
restlessness. He knew that I longed for Joliffe.

"You should ride now and then," he said. "Adam has
stables. I'll ask him to find a good mount for you. Tobias
can accompany you."

Then I began to see more of the country. I saw the
paddy fields where the rice—the staple food of China—
grew. I saw the manner in which the land was irrigated
and watched the working of the water wheel. I saw the
ploughs which were sometimes drawn by asses or mules

oxen and water buffalo or even men and women; I saw the tea plants which was one of the main sources of China's wealth and learned the difference between sou-chong, hyson, and imperial bohea. I watched the fisher-men with their nets and wicker traps and I believed Toby when he told me that China gets more from one acre of land than any other country.

I would enjoy my rides with Toby. We had become the greatest friends; we shared jokes and our minds were in tune. He knew a great deal about the Chinese and we would discuss the mysticism of the East and then go to his house for tea and a douche of Scottish common sense from his sister Elspeth. I looked forward to these occa-sions so much that I began to think that if I had never met Joliffe and was not now married to Sylvester I could have quietly fallen in love with Toby. Well, perhaps that is not the way to describe it. Having once fallen in love the term had a special meaning for me and I knew that I could never recapture the ecstasy I had known with Jo-liffe. The fact was that I was beginning to feel a deep af-fection for Toby.

Adam noticed my growing friendship with Toby. Typi-cally he took action and when I went to the stables for my horse, I found him there too.

"I shall accompany you and Tobias," he said.

I raised my eyebrows. He certainly had a rather irritat-ing didactic manner.

"Oh," I said, "did Toby invite you to join us?"

"I invited myself," he said.

I was silent and he went on: "It's better so. The two of you are so much together."

"So you are here as a sort of chaperon?"

"You could call it that."

"I'm sure that is unnecessary."

"In some respects, yes, but there is a certain amount of comment."

"Comment?"

"People have noticed. They talk, you know. It's not good . . . for the family."

"What nonsense. It was Sylvester who suggested Toby should accompany me."

"Even so, I will come."

When Toby arrived he showed no great surprise to see Adam. We rode off together. Adam was interesting and informative but his presence had a sobering effect on us.

After that I became accustomed to these threesome rides and in time Adam seemed to unbend a little and the three of us would talk about Chinese Art and treasures so enthusiastically that the rides became as enjoyable as ever.

One day when we came near to the waterfront we saw a big blaze in the sky.

We spurred up our horses to see where the fire was and to our horror it was discovered that it was Adam's home. I shall never forget the change in him.

He leaped from his horse and ran. I heard afterwards that he had gone into the house and rescued one of the Chinese servants—the only one who was trapped in that blazing furnace.

Everyone else was safe but it did mean that Adam was without a home.

It was only natural that he should come to The House of a Thousand Lanterns. Sylvester insisted on it.

"There's plenty of room here," he said. "I should be offended if you did not come."

"Thank you," replied Adam stiffly. "But I promise you I shall do my best to find somewhere to live as quickly as possible."

"My dear nephew," protested Sylvester, "you know very well there is no need to hurry. You have had a great shock. Don't think about hurrying. We shall be delighted to have you. Isn't that so, Jane?"

I said of course we should.

Adam looked at me ruefully, and I was reminded of

the first time we had met when I had had the impression he had thought me something of an adventuress.

I was almost certain that he regarded me as an interloper.

The fire had gutted the house. It was nothing but a shell. Adam ruefully told us that although it was insured he had lost some valuable pieces which were irreplaceable. He was very disconsolate. He told me in detail what had been lost and I commiserated with him. "We might never again find such pieces," he mourned.

"There's a kind of challenge in the search though," I reminded him. "You won't find the same pieces, of course, but might there not be something equally rewarding?"

He looked at me quizzically and with a sudden intuition I realized he was comparing my tragedy with his. I had lost Joliffe; he had lost his treasured collection. Might we not both find something equally compensating?

From that moment my relationship with Adam changed. It was as though he cast off a mask which revealed new phases of his character. I came to the conclusion that he was a man who armed himself against life because of something he feared from it; now it was as though he had laid aside some of his defensive weapons.

We entertained now and then. There was quite a social life in the colony.

"The English community sticks together here," Sylvester explained to me. "Naturally we visit each other's houses."

We gave the occasional dinner party and sometimes visited friends who had known Sylvester and his family for years. I enjoyed these parties and once or twice when Sylvester was not well enough to attend them, he insisted that I go with Adam. The conversation was usually lively and although it was not always about Chinese Art, manners, and customs, which Sylvester so much enjoyed, it often revolved round the affairs of the place.

I was beginning to settle into this way of life.

One day Lottie came to my bedroom. She looked enchantingly secretive, her dark eyes sparkling.

"Great Lady, I have big favor to ask," she said.

"What is it, Lottie?"

"Very great lady begs you visit."

"Begs me visit her? Who is this great lady?"

Lottie bowed as though in reverence to some absent deity. "Chan Cho Lan asks you come."

"Why does she ask me? I don't know her."

Lottie's face puckered. "Great Lady must come. If not Chan Cho Lan lose face."

I knew that the last thing any Chinese wished to do was to lose face. So I said: "Tell me more about this lady."

"Very great lady," said Lottie in awestruck tones. "Daughter of mandarin. I was in her house when I am little girl. I serve her."

"And now she wishes to see me."

"She asks if honorable great lady will visit her miserable house. You not come she lose bad face."

"Then I must go," I said.

Lottie smiled happily. "I serve her . . . I serve you. So she see you and she say 'How does that miserable one who once serve me and now serve you?' "

"I shall say that I am fond of her and she is certainly not miserable."

Lottie lifted her shoulders and giggled—a habit which some might have found irritating because it could indicate embarrassment, sorrow or pleasure so that one could never quite be sure of her feelings. I found it rather charming.

And so I went to the house of Chan Cho Lan.

I was surprised that we had no need of a rickshaw. The house was quite close to ours. I had been unaware of it because it was surrounded by a high wall. So Chan Cho Lan was our nearest neighbor.

I left Jason with Ling Fu, and Lottie and I walked the short distance. A Chinese servant opened the gate for us and we went into the courtyard. The lawn was very similar to our own. There were the miniature trees and shrubs and a bamboo bridge. These were dwarfed by the great banyan tree which spread itself over the grass.

I was astonished at the sight of the house which was almost an exact replica of The House of a Thousand Lanterns with one exception—the lanterns were missing.

The tinkle of wind bells sounded like a gentle warning as we approached. A man in black trousers and frogged tunic appeared suddenly. Pigtailed and conical-hatted, he bowed. Then he clapped his hands. Lottie walked past him and we mounted two steps to the marble platform on which the house was built. A door opened and we stepped inside.

A gong sounded and two more Chinese who seemed identical to those I had seen before came towards us bowing.

They signed us to follow them.

It was gloomy in the house and I was immediately aware of the silence. The same uneasiness struck me as that which I had experienced when I had first entered The House of a Thousand Lanterns.

In what appeared to be a hall, two Chinese dragons stood side by side at the foot of a staircase; the walls were hung with embroidered silk and I knew enough to realize that they depicted the rise and the fall of one of the dynasties. I couldn't help attempting to assess their value, such a collector had I become. I should like to have examined them more closely and I immediately thought of bringing Adam here and asking his opinion.

Lottie was signing to me that we must follow the servant.

He pushed aside a curtain and we were in another room. Here again the walls were hung with similar exquisitely embroidered silk. Beautifully colored Chinese rugs were on the floor. There was no furniture but a low table and a number of tall cushions—rather like the articles we called poufs at home.

We stood waiting and then Chan Cho Lan came into the room.

I was startled at the sight of her. Beautiful she undoubtedly was, but hers was a different beauty from the fresh and natural kind I so admired in Lottie. This was the cultivated beauty—the orchid from the hothouse rather than the lily of the field.

I could not take my eyes from her. She could have stepped right out of a painting of the T'ang period.

She did not so much walk as sway towards us. I later heard the movement described as the waving of a willow stirred by a faint breeze and this described it aptly. Everything about Chan Cho Lan was graceful and completely feminine. Her gown was of silk of the palest blue very delicately embroidered in pink, white and green; she wore trousers of the same silk material; her abundant black hair was dressed high on her head and two bodkins stuck in crosswise held it in place. Jewels sparkled in her hair in the form of a Chinese phoenix (the foong-hâng, Lottie afterwards told me, for she talked of Chan Cho Lan ecstatically when we returned to The House of a Thousand Lanterns). The face of this exquisite creature had been delicately painted and her eyebrows curved to what Lottie called the young leaflet of the willow but which reminded me of a new moon.

A delicate aroma clung to her. She was a creature made to adorn any place in which she happened to be. I was very curious as to who she was and what her life had been.

She bowed to me and I was indeed reminded of the willow tree as she swayed on her tiny slippered feet. I thought immediately of Lottie's distress about her own feet and I guessed that Chan Cho Lan had not escaped the torture. I felt awkward and I wondered what she thought of me.

"It was gracious of you to come," she said slowly as though she had learned the phrase off by heart and was repeating a lesson.

I replied that it was even more gracious of her to invite me.

She fluttered her hands. They were beautiful hands and she wore nail shields of jade. Her nails must have been about three inches long. Lottie indicated to me that I should be seated so I sat on one of the cushions; Lottie remained standing until Chan Cho Lan gracefully sat.

Agan there was a flutter of the hands and Lottie sat down. Chan Cho Lan clapped her hands. I heard the sound of a gong from without and a servant came into the room.

I could not understand what was said but the servant disappeared and almost immediately a round japanned tray was carried in and there began the tea ceremony with which I was now very familiar.

Lottie performed it with grace and I could see that she was nervous because the eyes of her one-time mistress were upon her.

She carried the porcelain cup to me first and then to Chan Cho Lan and sat waiting permission to take tea herself. This was graciously granted. The dried fruits and sweetmeats were brought in and with them the little forks with which we selected them. I showed my appreciation of these with smiles.

"You have taken this miserable girl into your noble house," she said. Lottie hung her head.

I replied that our house was enriched by Lottie's presence. I then began to extoll her virtues. I told her that I

was a stranger and that Lottie was teaching me to understand her country.

Chan Cho Lan sat nodding. I told her how Lottie
looked after my son, and how fond he had become of her.

"You happy lady," she said. "You have fine man
child."

"Yes," I said, "I have a fine boy. Lottie will tell you
that."

Lottie nodded and smiled.

"Miserable girl must serve you well. If not you use
bastinado."

I laughed. "There's no question of that. Lottie is like a
daughter to me."

There was an imperceptible silence and I realized I had
startled them, but Chan Cho Lan was too well mannered
to express surprise.

Lottie brought more sweetmeats and I took one with
the little two-pronged fork.

Chan Cho Lan then spoke to Lottie. Her voice was low
and musical and she moved her hands beautifully as she
spoke. I could not understand her but Lottie translated.

"Chan Cho Lan say that you must take care. She
happy I am there to look out for you. She say The House
of a Thousand Lanterns is a house where there can be
much bad. It is built where once was temple, she says. It
may be goddess not pleased that people live where once
she was worshipped. Chan Cho Lan wish you to take
care."

I asked her to tell Chan Cho Lan that I was grateful to
her for her concern, but I did not think any harm would
come to us as I believed the temple had been Kuan Yin's
and she was the good and benevolent goddess.

Chan Cho Lan spoke again and Lottie translated: "It
might be that Kuan Yin lose face because people live
where once there was her temple."

My answer was that the house had stood for more than

a hundred years and was still standing and it seemed no harm had come to anyone.

I caught the words fân-kuei in Chan Cho Lan's reply and I knew that meant a foreign ghost, spirit or devil, the term used to describe those not Chinese. And I knew she meant that although the goddess might not object to Chinese living on the site of her old temple she might object to foreigners.

But the house had been in the possession of Sylvester's grandfather and no ill fortune had come to him. I told Lottie this, but whether she explained it or not I don't know.

A look from Lottie told me that it was time to take my leave.

I rose and Chan Cho Lan immediately rose too. The perfume which came from her as she moved was strange and exotic—like a mixture of frangipani and roses, as exquisite as herself.

She bowed and said that she was gratified that a noble lady had honored her miserable abode.

She clapped her hands and the servant came to take us out.

It had been a strange encounter. I couldn't understand why Chan Cho Lan had wanted to see me. Perhaps, I thought, she was anxious for Lottie's welfare and wanted to make sure that her one-time maid had a good home. On the other hand she might have been curious to see the mistress of The House of a Thousand Lanterns.

I was beginning to understand a little of these people and I knew that one could never be sure what they meant. What appeared to be the obvious reason for a certain line of conduct would scarcely ever prove to be the true one.

Lottie behaved as though she were in a trance. She was a little sad too. I believed it was due to the fact that she would never be able to totter along like a willow in the wind because she had two perfectly normal feet that would comfortably carry her wherever she wanted to go.

That beautiful creature was a woman and therefore probably interested in other women. I wondered whether Lottie saw her now and then and talked of me. Perhaps this was it and she had wanted to see what I really looked like.

And she had thrown in the warning about the house for good measure.

III

I had been to the Go-Down to see Toby on some special business which Sylvester had wished to be cleared up. I was often able to do this for him. The rickshaw would take me to the warehouse and wait for me and bring me back. Toby was always delighted to see me. He was a very good businessman and entirely loyal to Sylvester and I sensed that he was often uneasy as to his growing feelings for me. He told me once that Sylvester had given him his big chance. He had at one time worked in the Cheapside office and when he was about sixteen his father had remarried. Toby had been devoted to his mother who had died a year before the second marriage. His sister Elspeth left home when their father remarried and went away to teach in Edinburgh. The position had become intolerable to Toby; his stepmother, he realized, was a worthy woman but he could not endure to see anyone in his mother's place. Sylvester had understood his feelings and his remedy had been to send him out to the Hong Kong branch. There Toby said he had been able to see things clearly and how wrong he had been to grudge his father his happiness.

He was constantly harping on his gratitude to Sylvester. I understood perfectly. As for myself I knew I would never feel strongly about anyone again. All I could hope for was to drift along in comparative peace and accept the way of life which was left to me.

On this occasion I came back to the house and I heard voices in Sylvester's sitting room.

Adam was with him. I thought he looked rather grim but when I came in they stopped talking abruptly.

After Adam had gone, Sylvester said to me: "Adam almost suggested that he join up with me."

"You mean in business?"

Sylvester nodded. "He was saying that I should rest more, that I needed someone to take the burden from my shoulders and so on. I told him that Tobias was a fine manager and that with you here and everyone at the Go-Down, I manage very nicely."

"Perhaps, after all, it would be a good idea if he were to join you. You have a high opinion of his skill."

"No," said Sylvester very firmly. "I know my nephews, both of them. It's a sort of arrogance they have. All of us have it. Redmond and Magnus did too. We all think we know best. That's why we couldn't work together. We all want to be the Tai Pan. Adam was very complimentary to you, Jane."

"Oh?"

"But he said that it was difficult for a woman to deal with sly traders."

"Did he indeed."

Sylvester laughed. "You'll show him that you can do as well as he can. That's the spirit, Jane." He looked at me intently. "You've got a rare business instinct," he went on. "I have no qualms about the future."

The days were passing quickly. Christmas came. It was not, of course, celebrated in China and we kept it very quietly in The House of a Thousand Lanterns. There was no Christmas tree which was a pity for Jason remembered the previous Christmas when Mrs. Couch had presided over the table in the servants' hall and the pudding had been brought in surrounded by brandy flames. I did fill his stocking though and one for Lottie which amused and delighted her.

We were, however, approaching the Feast of Lanterns. There were often festivals and it sometimes seemed to me that the people were either placating, adoring, or abusing the dragon. They appeared to be obsessed by the creature, so magnificently portrayed in their art, but this particular feast had nothing to do with that mythical monster. The Feast of the Lanterns seemed particularly our feast for we lived in the house which was said to contain a thousand.

This feast took place on the night of the first full moon of the new year.

Sylvester had seen it many times, and he delighted in informing me about it.

"It's really one of the most tasteful of the entertainments," he said. "The object seems to be for people to show each other what beautiful lanterns they can contrive. It is a delightful spectacle and you will see lanterns of all shades and colors and of all kinds of designs in the processions. Then there will be fireworks across the harbor and you can be sure there will be a dragon or two."

I looked forward to it. "It is I suppose of special significance to us," I said.

"Oh you mean because of the house." He laughed. "I suppose so."

Lottie told me that the servants were saying that we should have a special celebration to placate the goddess because this was the house of the lanterns and perhaps if she were shown that we appreciated living in a house built on her temple she would not lose face with the other gods and goddesses.

I told Sylvester this and we agreed that we would make a very special occasion of the Feast of Lanterns. We would have a dinner for the family and a few friends and Chinese food should be served in the Chinese manner. A lantern should be lighted in each room and over the porch we would set up one which should be made with moving figures inside it. Adam designed the lantern which would be in the best Chinese tradition.

It was magnificent and made of silk, horn, and glass. Inside was a horizontal wheel which was turned by the draft of air created by the warmth of the lamp. There were figures of beautiful women who reminded me of Chan Cho Lan and there were brightly plumaged birds. Fine threads were attached to the figures and as the wheel turned, they moved. The effect was beautiful. This enormous lantern was fixed above the outer gate. When darkness fell it would be like a beautiful beacon.

The servants were delighted and Lottie told me that this would bring great good joss to the house. The goddess would undoubtedly be pleased.

For several days there had been preparations in the kitchen. The guests arrived in the later afternoon and we should dine before dusk so that we could see the procession as soon as it began.

This was a very special occasion indeed. We sat on our cushions and were served first with basins of soup. It was the first time I had tasted birds' nest soup and it was Lottie who told me afterwards what it contained. "It is good for you," she told me. It was made from the nests of small swallows who were said to collect a glutinous substance from the sea with which to make their nests. These were the size of tea saucers and they were collected before the eggs were laid. She showed me some which were brought to the kitchen; they were of a lightish red and transparent. To make the soup they were dissolved in water. I found the concoction rather insipid. But it was served as a great delicacy so we had to make a show of enjoying it.

Following the soup were salted meats and rice served in small porcelain dishes; there followed sharks' fins and deers' sinews, all of which we ate with chopsticks—at which I had by this time become adept—though we used little china spoons when necessary. We drank heated sweet wine with it and cups of tea.

Although most of us were well acquainted with Chinese food this was the first time I had had it served and eaten in the completely Chinese manner. It was very impressive, particularly when as we were finishing the servants began lighting the lanterns.

After the meal I went up to Jason's room where he had been eating under the supervision of Lottie. She had been telling him about the feast downstairs and how the goddess would be pleased with us because although each of us was a fân-kuei we had acted as good Chinese.

Jason was excited at the prospect of seeing the procession and by now the big lantern which was to hang over our porch had been lighted and shone like a beacon.

We all went down to the waterfront which was the best place to see the revelry. And what a sight it was. From every sampan there rose a lantern. There were greens, blues, mauves—every conceivable color was represented with red predominating. There were simple lanterns and ornate lanterns. There were silk lanterns and paper lanterns. Many of them sported revolving scenery which was contrived in the same manner as the one which adorned our porch. There were revolving ships, idols, butterflies, and birds. It was as though everyone had vied to make a more glorious lantern than his neighbor. I shall always associate these occasions with the sound of the gong. One heard it constantly and it never failed to arouse a certain apprehension in me. It always sounded like a warning.

Adam held Jason in his arms so that he could see everything. Jason was shouting to us all to look at this and that. Lottie stood beside me, quietly proud of the display. On the sea were ships dressed up as dragons. Lights shone through the paper and some of them breathed fire. It was a colorful display and even more interesting than the lanterns were the crowds who had assembled to take part in or watch the revelry. Men in the magnificent robes of mandarins mingled with the coolies. Hakka women in their wide black-fringed hats stood side by side with other workers from the paddy fields, and servants from rich families, as the procession of lanterns wound its way along the waterfront. Beneath the lanterns a row of men bore a massive dragon; the men writhed and gyrated as they went to represent the movements of the great beast. Within the framework were lights so that it presented quite a terrifying appearance, jaws open with fire coming through and lights showing in its great eyes.

Jason was beside himself with a delighted fear.

Then the fireworks started.

Jason and Lottie seemed of an age in their excitement, and watching them I was more reconciled to my fate than I had ever been. It was to be but a brief satisfaction.

In due course we were rickshawed back to the house. We went into the room we had made our drawing room and Lottie took Jason off to bed. Sylvester was talking in the animated way he had when he was discussing Chinese customs.

He was saying: "There must always be a dragon. The dragon dominates the lives of the Chinese. He is the bogyman of China. They fear him, they seek to placate him, and sometimes to destroy him. He is supposed to be all powerful. I was here once at the time of an eclipse. It was then believed that the dragon, suffering from an insatiable hunger, was trying to swallow the sun. The beating of the gongs was terrific. They were supposed to be frightening the dragon. Yet I have seen a feast to honor him many a time."

Toby, who had not come back to the house with us, arrived at that moment. He was clearly excited.

He said: "A ship is in the harbor. It comes from home."

I was awakened in the night by Jason who had had a dream of a fire-breathing dragon. He was sure he was outside the window trying to get in. I took him into my bed as I had on the first night and explained that the dragons were made of paper and it was men inside them who made them move.

"It's true here in your bed," he whispered. "But it changes in mine."

So I kept him with me and as he slept I was overwhelmed by my love for him and I thought that as long as I had him to plan for, to live for, I could be content. I thought again of Sylvester and how good he had been to me and I vowed to myself that I would look after him and always share his interests. I would be at the Go-Down tomorrow and with Toby I would learn what goods had arrived for us and I would take an account of these to Sylvester for I would insist on his resting after the previous night's feast and procession.

I was up early and when I was dressed Lottie came to tell me that, early as it was, there was a visitor.

Lottie looked a little secretive and did not meet my gaze, but perhaps I thought this afterwards. However I went down through the quiet house to the drawing room where Lottie told me the visitor waited.

I opened the door. Then I thought I was going to faint, for rising from a chair and coming towards me was Joliffe.

He stood before me gazing at me, and my feelings were such as I could not describe so overwhelming were they. Such joy it was to see him again, yet that joy was tinged with fear as to what his coming would mean.

He said "Jane!" That was all, but it said so much. There was longing and the pain of separation, the joy of reunion, and there was hope.

I clung to my composure and kept my distance. I thought: If he doesn't touch me I can be calm. I can stand outside this scene. I can make it seem as though some other person is taking the part of Jane and I am but a looker-on. But if he were to put his hands on my shoulders; if he were to draw me to him . . .

That must not happen.

I said: "What are you doing here, Joliffe?"

He must have realized that we had to talk of rational things, for he answered: "I came in on the ship."

"You will stay . . . ?"

"For a while," he said.

"But . . ."

I was becoming involved. I thought: We can't both stay here. There's not room for us. We shall see each other often and how can we do that?

He said: "How are you, Jane?"

"I am well."

He laughed. "And . . . happy?"

"We have an interesting life here."

"Oh Jane!" he said reproachfully, "why did you do it?"

"I don't understand."

"Don't pretend. You understand perfectly. Why did you marry my uncle?"

"I have told you before."

"You should have waited."

I turned away. It was fatal, for he had laid his hand on my arm and in a second I was held against him and all the magic was there again; and I knew that I had been living in a false contentment. I knew I would never be happy without Joliffe.

"No, no," I said breaking away. "This must not be."

"I'm free now, Jane," he said.

"And Bella?"

"Bella is dead."

"That was convenient . . . for you, wasn't it?"

"Poor Bella! She never recovered from the accident."

"She seemed very strong and healthy when we met."

"She was badly injured in the accident. How badly was not realized. It was only much later that this became apparent. The accident had started up something . . . an internal growth. She had only a few years to live."

"And now, you're free as you say."

"The pity is . . . you're not."

I walked to the window.

I said: "Listen, Joliffe, there must be no more of this."

He was beside me. "What do you mean? No more of what? How can there be no more of something that exists?"

"I am settled here. I want no complications. What was between us is over."

"What a monstrous thing to say. You know it will never be over . . . as long as either of us lives."

"You shouldn't have come here. Why did you?"

"I have my work. It brings me here. But most of all I came to tell you I was free."

"Of what interest should that be to me?"

"I wanted you to realize how wrong you were. You should never have married my uncle. If you had not the way would be clear for us now."

"And my son?"

"*Our* son! I would have cared for him . . . and for you."

"I believe I did the right thing. And having done it . . . I hope I shall continue to do what is right. Go away, Joliffe. I don't want us to meet."

"I must see you. I've sworn I won't go on as before. I want to see my son."

"No, Joliffe."

"He is my son, you know."

"He is happy here. He looks on Sylvester as his father. I don't want him disturbed. Joliffe, how can you come here . . . to this house . . . of all places."

"It used to be one of my homes. Where else should I go?"

"You can't stay here."

"You're afraid. You shouldn't be afraid of life, Jane."

"We should all be afraid of doing what is not right."

"My poor Jane!"

"Poor Jane! Poor Bella! Perhaps we are both to be pitied for becoming involved with you."

"You will never be sorry for that."

"I want you to go away, Joliffe."

He looked intently at me and shook his head, and at that moment the door opened and Jason ran in.

He stood for a moment looking from me to Joliffe.

Joliffe grinned at him and a slow smile broke over Jason's face.

"This is Uncle Adam's cousin," I said. I saw Joliffe grimace slightly in my direction.

"Have you got a kite?" asked Jason.

"No, but I had one when I was a boy."

"What sort?"

"Made with bamboo horn and varnish. It had a dragon on it."

"Breathing fire?"

"Breathing fire," said Joliffe. "Nobody ever flew a kite higher than I did."

"I did," said Jason.

Joliffe put his head on one side and shook it slowly.

"We'll have a race," said Jason excitedly.

"Yes, one day we'll have a race."

Lottie had come in. "I'm here, Lottie," said Jason. "Where's my kite?"

Joliffe and Lottie looked at each other. She knelt and put her forehead on the floor. Jason solemnly imitated her.

Joliffe took her hand and helped her to her feet.

She answered: "Great master is gracious."

To see her standing there, her hand in his, for he retained it for a second or so, looking so young and beautiful sent a pang of jealousy through me.

I said: "Jason, will you go with Lottie. It's time you had your breakfast."

"Is Uncle Adam's cousin going to have breakfast?"

"I expect he will somewhere."

Jason stood looking at Joliffe and I could see the admiration in his eyes. I wondered what his reaction would have been if I had said: This is your father.

"You come and have breakfast with me," said Jason.

"That is not possible," I said sharply. "Go now."

"We shall see each other later," added Joliffe.

"Bring your kite," said Jason.

"I will," said Joliffe.

They went out.

"My God, Jane," he said, "that's a fine boy."

"Please, Joliffe, this is a difficult state of affairs. Don't complicate it."

"You helped to complicate it."

"In innocence," I said. "But don't let's go into that now. I shall ask Sylvester what's to be done. I shall tell him that you have been here."

"Good and obedient wife," he said bitterly. And I knew that the sight of me and of Jason and the thought that we were lost to him filled him with grief and anger.

I also knew enough of him to understand that he was not like myself. He would not accept a situation and try to make the best of it.

Joliffe wouldn't compromise.

I left him and went to Sylvester's room. He had not risen but Ling Fu had brought him breakfast and he was sitting up in bed having it.

"You're up early, Jane," he said. "The ship . . ." He paused. "Is something wrong?"

I said: "Joliffe came in on the ship. He is here."

"In this house?"

I nodded.

"He must go away," said Sylvester.

"He says his work has brought him here."

"I can't send him back to England but at least he shall not stay in this house."

The Feast of the Dead

Now everything was changed. It must be so because Joliffe was in Hong Kong. I could no longer accept my fate; I must rebel against it. There was only one way to peace of mind and that was in forgetting Joliffe, which was something I could never do.

He had had an interview with Sylvester. I don't know what was actually said but the gist of it was that although Adam was staying in the house there was no place there for Joliffe. In view of his one-time relationship with me that was quite impossible.

Joliffe had no alternative but to accept this while at the same time he made it clear that he wished to see his son. I knew him well enough to understand that he would use Jason as an excuse.

Sylvester was very shaken. He understood me so well that he must have been fully aware of the effect Joliffe's return had had on me in spite of my efforts to hide it. He was apprehensive. Sometimes I was amazed at the depth of the feelings I had aroused in this quiet, restrained man. I knew that it was not only his relationship with me which he felt might be in jeopardy but he feared for Jason. There was something aloof in his nature which made an intimate relationship difficult for him to achieve. It had occurred to me that our marriage may have seemed to him the perfect one . . . a marriage without a physical relationship which had yet miraculously brought him a son who had the blood of his family in him.

He seemed to shrink from physical contact. Or did I think that because I was so much aware of Joliffe's overwhelming masculinity? He looked pale and shaken and I knew he was suffering from one of his headaches, but he had been firm enough when he had forbidden Joliffe the house.

When I went down to the Go-Down Toby looked very serious.

He was angry with Joliffe.

"He should never have come here," he said. "He knew the complications his return would give rise to."

"He has his business," I said, hearing myself actually defending Joliffe.

"He has managed all this time with his agents. It is only now that you are here . . ." He looked at me earnestly, trying to assess what effect Joliffe's return had had on me.

I hoped I preserved my calmness.

"Whatever existed between us is over now," I said. "It has been for a long time."

Toby frowned. "It's difficult in a place like this not to see people."

"Perhaps he won't stay," I said.

Toby sighed. I knew that was what he hoped for.

Adam mentioned his cousin to me. "I hear his wife is now dead," he said, studying me closely.

"I believe that is so."

"He shouldn't have come here. He could have left any business to his agent."

"Why should everyone be so concerned?"

Adam frowned. "It's nonsense to pretend. We know that you went through a form of marriage with him. We know that Jason is his son. This creates a difficult situation. Joliffe has always been sublimely indifferent to the embarrassment—or feelings—of others. He's like his father. You have settled down with Sylvester now. He should have had more sense than to come back."

"There is no need for anyone to make this fuss. Until this week it was years since I'd seen him."

Adam nodded. "He's got the famous Eddy charm which was said to come down through our grandmother. She ran away with a lover. It's a certain feckless streak in the character and it comes out in some of us."

"It didn't come out in you, Adam."

"You seem to pity me for that."

I shook my head. "Oh no, I'm congratulating you."

"Yet everyone finds these irresponsible people so attractive. You must have done. Or why did you marry Joliffe—or think you married him?"

I wanted to say: Because I loved him. Because I thought then—and it seemed I was right—that he was the only one in the world for me. How could one say such things to prosaic Adam? I said: "For the same reason that most people marry."

"People marry for varying reasons. Some because it seems expedient to do so."

"You are cynical."

"But realistic. Didn't you marry my uncle Sylvester for that reason?"

I said angrily: "You always resented my marrying him, didn't you?"

He shrugged his shoulders and turned away. I was angry with him, but whenever Joliffe was mentioned I could never trust myself far and I wanted now to escape from him.

He looked over his shoulder and said: "Don't forget you married my uncle . . . and whatever happens you are still married to him."

"Am I likely to forget it?"

"Some people forget their marriage vows," he said, and was gone.

He was a most uncomfortable person. All my old resentment of him returned.

There was a note from Joliffe. He wanted me to see him. I ignored the note. There came another. Jason was his son, he wrote. If I would not see him, he was determined that he would see his son. That was his right.

I was determined to enter into no negotiation with him that Sylvester did not know about, so I went to him and told him what Joliffe was asking.

He looked pale and wan; his stick was propped up by his chair and I felt a deep pity for him.

"He has some right to see the boy," he conceded.

"He has not bothered with him for more than five years," I said.

"Yet he is his father."

"I wish he would go away," I said, but even as I spoke I felt false for I meant no such thing. I couldn't bear him to go away, and I knew by the manner in which Sylvester looked at me that he was aware of my feelings.

He was just, and I think, too, that he knew that I must not turn my back on life. He was aware of the emptiness of my existence; he knew of my secret longings. There was something of the fatalist about Sylvester. It was almost as though he were saying: Here is Joliffe; he can offer you ardor, youthful passion and enchantment which you and he may call love; he can offer all that with insecurity. On the other hand I can give you affection, calm, quiet, faithful companionship, a serene home for your child, a future which is assured. Fate is offering you a choice. It is for you to decide.

I knew that he feared that one day I would go away with Joliffe because it was quite clear that that was what Joliffe intended, and that I would take Jason with me and he, Sylvester, would be alone again. His fatalist attitude may have come to him through his study of Chinese philosophy, but it was there. He feared and yet he made no attempts to put temptation from me.

I told myself I was not going to be tempted. I knew where my duty lay to my husband and my precious child. That was what I told myself, and it was the reason I must not see Joliffe. It had been enough to see him once to know that I could easily forget everything but my need of him. And that was something I was determined should not happen.

I would contrive never to see him alone. But he should see Jason.

Sylvester said: "In due course the child will know who his father is. He might hold it against us if we did not allow them to meet. Joliffe should not tell him of their relationship but he should see him."

It was arranged that Lottie should take Jason to the hotel where Joliffe stayed. She was not to let Jason out of her care and the meeting should be only of an hour's duration.

In return for this concession, which was arranged by Adam, Joliffe should give his word that the child would be returned to The House of a Thousand Lanterns at the end of the hour.

I wondered at the wisdom of this after that first meeting. Jason returned starry-eyed. Adam's cousin was the most wonderful man. He had a kite and they flew them together because he had taken his to show him. In the gardens of the hotel they had watched them soar up into the sky.

"His went highest," said Jason ruefully. "He's going to give me a new one."

"But you've got the one Lottie gave you," I reminded him.

He was reflective. "But the one he'll give me will be a bigger and better one. *He* said so."

"Lottie might be hurt."

"Oh I'll fly the one she gave me sometimes. Mama, when am I going to see Adam's cousin again?"

What an uneasy state of affairs it was! Once I saw him when I was riding in a rickshaw and my heart turned over. On another occasion when I came out of the Go-Down he was waiting for me as once he had waited in Cheapside.

His eyes were pleading; he looked a little haggard and I thought: He's as unhappy as I am.

He stood before me almost abjectly. "Jane, this is absurd. We must talk."

"There's nothing to say," I replied.

"We've got to work out something."

"It's all been worked out. Go home, Joliffe. Go back to England. It's better that way."

"You don't know what it's been like."

"*I* don't know!" I was angry. "I knew when I discovered that I was not in truth your wife."

"I'm free now, Jane."

"You forget I'm not."

I turned to the rickshaw which was waiting for me.

"There's the boy," he said. "Think what it would mean to him."

"It's just for this reason that you should go away," I retorted.

I stepped into the rickshaw. The man picked up the shafts, his face impassive.

Lottie knew how uneasy I was.

She said the goddess had lost face because a house had been built on her temple, and there was no good joss for those who lived in it.

"It's nothing to do with the goddess, Lottie."

"Serenity has gone," she said.

How right she was! I suppose I had been serene in a way before—quietly pursuing my life, trying to pretend that I was content.

I often found Lottie's eyes on me. They were mournful, watching. She knew that the coming of Joliffe had changed me.

She it was who took Jason on his visits to Joliffe. Adam accompanied them; it was all very ceremonious. Adam told me that he waited in the hotel while Jason went to the gardens with Joliffe and he sent Lottie out to sit in the gardens too.

There had been three meetings between Jason and Joliffe and already Jason adored him. He would ask every day: "How many days to Adam's cousin, Mama?" And he would mark them off on a calendar.

I said to Sylvester: "It's a mistake to let them meet. He is charming the boy. I don't like it."

I knew Sylvester was very much afraid but that fatalistic attitude seemed to take possession of him; it was as though he wanted not only me to choose between him and Joliffe, but for Jason to do so also.

One day I received a fright because Jason was not in his room. He had said he was going there to read his book as he often did in the afternoon and when I went for him it was to find him gone.

I called for Lottie but I couldn't find her either. As they were both missing I was not as disturbed as I might have been.

I went down into the courtyard and as I did so I looked up in the sky and saw the two kites flying—the well-known one which was Jason's and the big flamboyant one which I guessed Joliffe had acquired.

They are together, I thought.

I went out through the gates and made my way to the pagoda.

As I came close I could hear voices.

"Look at mine. Look at mine!" cried Jason.

"It'll fly higher yet," answered Joliffe.

They had their backs to me so they did not see me, but I had seen not only them but Lottie seated on the grass, her back to me as she regarded them.

I sent for Lottie.

She looked fearful and shame-faced. She had brought Jason home an hour ago.

I did not ask him where he had been. I waited for him to tell me. I was shocked that he did not mention he had been with Joliffe.

That was why I wanted to talk to Lottie.

I shut the door and bade her be seated. I saw that her hands were trembling.

"You look guilty, Lottie," I said.

She hung her head and I went on: "So you took Jason out to meet someone?"

She nodded wretchedly.

"You know that those meetings should take place at the hotel and not in the pagoda. Don't you, Lottie?"

She nodded again.

"And yet you deceived me. You teach my son to deceive me."

"You must whip this miserable wicked one," she said, kneeling and laying her forehead on the floor.

"Lottie, get up and don't be silly. Why did you do this?"

"Jason loves so much to meet Mr. Joliffe."

"Jason meets him once a week. That has been arranged. But you have taken it upon yourself to change this."

She lifted her face to me; her eyes were wide, awe-struck. She looked over her shoulder as though she expected to see someone there.

"Mr. Joliffe is Jason's father," she said.

"Who told you this?" I demanded.

She lifted her shoulders helplessly. "It is so. I know this."

Of course she had heard it. Adam had talked of it: So had Sylvester and I. When were families able to keep secrets from their servants. And Lottie understood English.

"It bring great bad luck to disobey the father," she said.

I took her by the shoulders.

"Yes, Lottie," I said, "Mr. Joliffe is Jason's father but you have not told him this?"

"No, I have not told. I would not tell."

I believed her. For one thing it was something Jason would never have been able to keep to himself.

"You must never tell," I said. "If you do . . ." I hesitated. Then I went on: "If you do, you shall go away. You will go back to where you came from."

A look of intense horror came over her face. She began to tremble.

"I will not tell. It is not good to tell. He but child. But it is bad luck to disobey father."

"And Mr. Joliffe asked you to take him out to the pagoda, did he?"

She hung her head.

"Never do it again," I warned. "If you deceive me again in this way I shall send you from here."

She nodded wretchedly. She wanted to kneel again. The kowtow meant that she was abject in her misery and her desire to expiate her sins was all that mattered.

I said: "It's all right, Lottie. You are forgiven. But don't dare do it again."

She nodded, and I was satisfied that I had made my point.

But I was very anxious because I knew that Joliffe was capable of doing anything to get his way. I remembered vividly the occasion when I had found him in Sylvester's showroom in the middle of the night; and even then when I should have been warned of someone who employed such devious methods, I had refused to heed the warning; now while I wondered what he would do next I was afraid every day I would hear that he had decided to go home.

There was undoubtedly change in the house. It had started soon after Joliffe's return. I had become aware of the shadows when darkness fell; and the lanterns seemed to cast an eerie light over everything.

When the house was quiet I would fancy it was listening, brooding, waiting, which was absurd. I visualized what must have stood on this very spot in those days before the house had been erected. There would have been priests passing to and fro through the courtyards of the temple; I could imagine their chanting and the striking of gongs and their performing the kowtow before the image of the goddess. So vividly did I picture them in their yellow robes with their shaved heads that I almost expected to see the ghosts of some of them flitting up and down our stairs.

It was as though a new mood had crept into the house. Sylvester sensed it too. I knew it although we never mentioned it.

It might have begun in our minds. Fear was there. Sylvester clearly feared what might happen . . . and so did I.

He seemed to shrink; he looked older. There were days when he did not leave his bedroom.

Adam noticed this. He asked me if I did not think we

should call in Dr. Phillips, the European doctor, to look at him.

To my surprise I was relieved that Adam was in the house. Now that Joliffe had come to Hong Kong he seemed to provide a certain safeguard. I felt that if I had given in to Joliffe, as Joliffe rather obviously was hoping I would, Adam would have displayed a certain smug satisfaction. There was a very practical side to his nature too. If I went away with Jason, would not Sylvester have to take him into partnership? I imagined I could see the thoughts behind Adam's inscrutable expression.

He had looked at several houses but had found nothing really suitable and Sylvester had shown quite clearly that he was pleased for him to stay. I was aware that since Joliffe's return Sylvester's attitude towards Adam had changed. Sylvester had a great affection for his nephew and an admiration for his knowledge and dedication. I imagined at one time he had felt the same towards Joliffe. Sylvester and Adam had so much in common. I was constantly coming upon them in deep and excited discussion over some piece one of them had found.

I agreed that the doctor should see Sylvester and because Sylvester was against this, Adam decided to ask Dr. Phillips to dine with us and then he proposed to bring up the subject of Sylvester's health in a casual manner.

Sylvester was a little annoyed, but at length decided to submit to an examination.

The doctor's verdict was that he could find nothing wrong. He talked to Adam and me for some time and pointed out that a life of inactivity was bound to have its effects. There was a weakness, a tiredness, but that might be the inevitable result of his accident.

"Just keep him cheerful and don't let him risk getting chilled."

Adam said he was relieved but he still thought he had done the right thing in getting the doctor's opinion.

Later Sylvester asked me for the truth of what the doctor had said.

I told him.

"I'd like to know, Jane," he said. "There's a theory that invalids shouldn't be told how bad they are. It's good in some cases, I suppose. But I'd like to know my fate ... my joss as they say. If I hadn't long to live I'd like to know it."

"Whatever gave you such an idea? He merely said that you were probably feeling the effects of your sedentary life, and you should take care to keep interested in what's going on and not get chilled."

"I'm glad that Adam is here. Of course I believe that he is finding business a little difficult and would like to come back. I don't want that, Jane. Oh, I have the greatest respect for his talent. He's quite an authority in several ways. But I have my reasons for not wanting him back with me. He has been talking about the house. He believes the legend that somewhere here there is a secret to be discovered."

"Have you searched for this mystery, Sylvester?"

"I have been through the house, tested each room as my grandfather, father, and others have before me."

"There must be a hidden door somewhere."

"If so it has never been found."

"Tell me about your brother Magnus."

"Joliffe is so like his father that sometimes I could almost believe Magnus is back with us. Magnus was our father's well-beloved son. We used to say he was like Joseph and that if our father had had a coat of many colors, Magnus would have been the one to inherit it."

"Yet he left this house to you."

"Magnus died before he did. Even so, he would have left the house to me. There are some who say that this house might be a burden." He looked about him. "I am sure many of the servants believe it to be haunted in some way. I have always thought that my father left it to me because I was more serious than Redmond who was alive at that time and he thought I would be the one to overcome the difficulties of living here."

"You surprise me."

"Oh there is an aura here. You sense it, Jane. My grandfather's wife ran away soon after he came here. She was always frivolous, it was true, but it was actually when this house came into my grandfather's possession that she left him. He never got over it. My father was not a happy man. He lost his beloved son. You see misfortune befell all those who owned the house. My father believed I would ride any storm more successfully than Redmond."

"But he divided the business between you."

"Yes, equally. And there was a share for Joliffe. My father apologized to me a few months before he died. 'In a few years time,' he said, 'this equality will have vanished. You, my eldest son, will be in command and the others will fall far behind you.' It was true I had the biggest instinct for business."

"And then you divided."

"Our personalities clashed. They were held in check while our father lived, but afterwards we wanted our own way. My father was right. I was soon more successful than Redmond and Joliffe too. They had more . . . outside interests. Perhaps I was more dedicated. It was not long after we split up that Redmond had a sudden heart attack and died. Adam took over. He did not want to join up with me then; he was sure he could succeed on his own and he has done well, to a certain extent. So there we are—three rival firms one might say—the uncle and his two nephews." He hesitated. "I've told you before that when I was young I admired an actress. We became great friends. My brother Magnus saw her. He married her. Joliffe was their son."

I wondered then whether Sylvester felt a certain animosity towards Joliffe because he was the son of a woman he had loved. But that was not really Sylvester's nature. Rather would he have loved Joliffe the more because of this. It was due to Joliffe himself that he had lost Sylvester's regard.

"It wasn't really a happy marriage although she was devoted to Magnus. He had that fascination for women. He was exuberant, adventurous, good-looking, gallant, and charming . . . all that women look for. He liked all women too much though to care deeply for one. I had none of these gifts. I was the serious one dedicated to my business."

"Well, it provided some consolation."

"That's what we learn, Jane. There are always compensations in life."

"Did she regret her choice?"

"Oh no, no. If she could have had her time over again it would always have been Magnus. She was often hurt but she never wavered in her adherence to him. They died together. She wouldn't have wanted to go on without him."

"And Joliffe was their only son?"

He nodded. "I made plans to adopt him. I decided he would be like my own son. I tried to mold him to my ways. That was like trying to hold back the tide. He was Magnus's son."

He was silent for a while. Then he went on: "Well, then you appeared, Jane. Right from the beginning, you know I was aware that you would play an important part in my life. When Joliffe came and I thought you were truly married to him, it seemed like some sort of terrible pattern repeating itself."

"Yes," I said, "I see that. And now he is back."

"Yes," he said, "and I wonder."

"That pattern is changed," I assured him. "I think I am not unlike you. I am serious. I acted rashly once. I don't think I would do so again."

"No, you will not. And this is part of *my* pattern. It is going to be as I planned."

He looked tired and I could see that he did not want to talk any more.

I suggested he sleep a little. But he said he would like to play mah-jongg.

When I came back with the board his eyes were closed and I saw that he was asleep.

He looked so tired and there was a new parchment-like tinge to his face. I felt a great pity and tenderness for him.

I was spending more time with Sylvester. I could see that he was growing weaker every day. I could not say exactly what was wrong with him; nor could he. He was just tired and listless. Sometimes he would spend a whole day in bed; at others he would get up in the afternoon and sit in his chair. There was a kind of meek resignation about him. I had the impression that he had made up his mind that his life was drawing to an end and had resigned himself to this.

It was an attitude which I found exasperating. I wanted him to make an effort. He smiled at me gently when I suggested that he try to dress for dinner.

"There comes a time in life," he said, "when one must let it flow over one. The tide is coming in, the waves gently touch one and one knows that it is only a matter of time before one will be submerged."

I said with vehemence that I did not accept such a philosophy.

"No, Jane," he said, "you are one of the fighters of the world."

I would bring Jason to him and my son would read aloud to show how he was progressing. He would chatter freely and tell Sylvester stories which he made up himself. There was almost always a dragon in them. Sylvester taught him to play his beloved mah-jongg and I was clearly happy in a quiet satisfied way.

Toby came often to see him and they would be closeted together; the English lawyer came too and I knew that Sylvester was setting his house in order.

II

Up to this time I had made an effort to ignore the utter strangeness of The House of a Thousand Lanterns. Now it could no longer be ignored. It was like a living thing, a presence, a personality; it thrust itself upon me. I refused to believe that any misfortune which had befallen previous owners had been due to an evil influence which emanated from the house, and yet it was there . . . this vague indefinable sensation.

Sylvester talked to me about the house. "I shall never know the secret now, Jane," he said sadly.

"Is there a secret? You and others have searched the house. If there was anything to be discovered it would have come to light by now, I feel sure."

"Do you sense something here?"

I hesitated. "I think that it is possible to build up this . . . what is it you called it? An aura? It is something in the mind. It is nothing tangible."

"You are a sensible woman, Jane. And you are right. Fear is often in the minds of those who suffer it. You could be the one to discover the secret of the house which could be that there *is* no secret. That the mystery exists only in the minds of those who created it. Read to me now."

I read from the works of Dickens which he always enjoyed. I think that took him far away from the moment to another world, for nothing could have been farther from his room with its swinging lanterns than the English scene.

He kept a book of quotations from the great Chinese writers by his bedside and he used to study them before he slept.

I remember some of them. Two seemed particularly to apply to me. One was "The gem cannot be polished without friction, nor man perfected without trials." And I thought then what a different person I had become since those days with Joliffe. I was more understanding now of others, more mellow. I wondered whether the girl I had been in those days—in love with my own life and without much thought to spare for others—would have been able to offer the comfort to Sylvester which I did at this time. Another of these quotations was "The error of a moment becomes the sorrow of a lifetime."

I used to think of this quite a lot.

That was a strange time for in Sylvester's room was this sense of acceptance, of a brooding watchfulness. The house seemed quiet, waiting. Yet there was a subtle expectancy. Although I might assure myself that it did not exist outside my imagination I sensed it. It was in the quiet rooms each with its center lantern and other small ones placed about; it was in the soft swish of a curtain and the breeze which gently ruffled the miniature trees and the wind bells. It was in the pagoda, that place which had been a tryst for Joliffe and Jason. I went there often because I wondered whether Lottie had disobeyed me and had brought Jason to see Joliffe there. I half hoped I would find Joliffe and I half feared to.

I felt that I was living in a strange half world—between two lives, for the house would have told me, if Sylvester had not, that he was going to die.

I wondered what would happen then, but I forced myself to shut my eyes to one dazzling prospect. Joliffe was free . . . as I would be. I felt guilty and ashamed that I could contemplate a possible outcome of this.

I was very conscious of the presence of Adam in the house. Often I resented his didactic manner; he had a disconcerting way of announcing something of which he was sure. I always wanted to contradict but I discovered that he was almost always right.

He had adopted a kind of pose of protection; as though he were there to defend me even against my will. I was irritated by this and wanted to tell him that I was not in the least feeble. Sylvester had schooled me and I had learned my lessons well. And the first of these was the capability of standing on my own feet.

But I said nothing and we drifted on.

Lottie said: "The Master is tranquil. He is waiting for Yen-wang."

I knew that Yen-wang was to the Chinese what Pluto was to the Greeks. Yet there were times when I rebelled at this calm acceptance. I tried to shake Sylvester out of it.

"One of your theories used to be that anyone could do anything. If a man wants to get well and determines to, why should he not?"

"We have self-will up to a point," he said. "But when the hour is approaching there is no turning back the clock."

That night I awakened startled. I sat up in bed and it was as though horror crawled over my skin. There was a faint light in the room which came from a crescent moon and the lantern was like a black creature hanging from the ceiling.

Then I knew what had awakened me. It was a movement at my door. The creak of a handle being slowly turned. I leaped from my bed and as I did so the door slowly opened.

In the gloom I made out a figure standing there. For a few seconds I thought that one of the ghosts of The House of a Thousand Lanterns had materialized.

Then to my astonishment I saw that it was Sylvester.

I was dreaming. It couldn't be Sylvester. He could only mount the stairs with the greatest difficulty.

I whispered: "Sylvester." There was no response. He had held up both hands before him and was advancing into the room.

I stared. I must be dreaming. Then the realization came to me: Sylvester is walking in his sleep.

Stealthily I went towards him. I took his hand. A slow smile seemed to touch his lips yet I could see that he was asleep.

I marveled that he should have been able to get up the stairs. I felt he had been impelled to come to me and that although he was sleeping he seemed to be aware that he had found me.

I had heard that if people walked in their sleep it was unwise to awaken them and that they should be led quietly back to their beds. I therefore gently turned Sylvester and drew him from my room and to the stairs. I went ahead of him and slowly led him down.

I took him back to his bed and covered him up. But I was loath to leave him lest he get up again.

I sat there for some time watching him. He looked like a man who is already dead. The flesh seemed to have fallen away and exposed the bone structure of his face. I thought of all the comfort he had brought into my life and what his loss would mean to me, for I knew, as certainly as he did, that his end was near.

I was growing cold and there was nothing I could do for him by sitting there so I rose but as I did so he opened his eyes.

"Jane," he said.

"It's all right, Sylvester."

"What time is it? Why are you here?"

"It's all right." I knew I had to tell him the truth, so I said: "You were walking in your sleep. I brought you back."

He half rose and I said: "Lie back. We'll talk about it in the morning. You will sleep peacefully now."

"Jane," he whispered.

I bent over him and kissed his forehead.

"Try to sleep," I said.

In the morning we talked about it. He was puzzled. "I don't think I ever did it before," he said.

"Perhaps many people do," I replied soothingly, "and it is never found out."

"And I was in your room. How did I manage that?"

"It was amazing."

"It must have been some compulsion . . . in my dream . . . something which gave me the strength to mount the stairs."

"Is that possible?"

"I think it might be. I have been anxious about you, Jane. Perhaps that was how it manifested itself in the dream. I must have been dreaming I had to get you . . . to tell you something perhaps. It may have been that I dreamed you were in danger. I must have been forcibly impelled to see you if I could mount the stairs. Jane, I *am* anxious about you. When I am no longer here . . ."

"Please, it distresses me."

"My dear Jane, how good you are to me and always have been. You know I owe most of the happiness I have ever known to you."

"That gives me a lot of comfort but I want you to stop talking as though you are going to die. Perhaps this dream is a sign of what you can do if you want to. Let's concentrate on your getting well."

"No, no, Jane. We must face the truth. Death is in the house."

I shivered. "Oh no. That's wrong. We must not even think such a thing."

"But it's true. I sense it. And so do you. We are sensitive people, Jane. And here there is an affinity with the occult, don't you feel it?"

"I always thought you were a shrewd and practical businessman."

"I am so because I recognize that there is much in life that is a mystery to me and to us all. I have seen death, Jane. Yes, really seen death in a material form."

"What do you mean?"

"It was late afternoon. The door of my room opened and there was a shape there. A dragon shape with the mask of death. I've seen it in processions and there it was . . . looking straight at me. It was there and it was gone."

"It was a bad dream, for how could there be such a thing?"

"No, I was awake. And although it might seem impossible at home in Roland's Croft, here it could happen."

"You can't believe such things."

"I knew it for Death, Jane. This is no ordinary house. You sense that even as I do. Things could happen here which never would elsewhere. Don't you sense the secrets, the mystery, the presence of the past?"

"I am going to ask the doctor to give you something to make you sleep soundly. I intend to watch over you, Sylvester."

He smiled and taking my hand kissed it.

I felt very tender towards him.

The month of April had come and I thought with nostalgia of spring in England. The daffodils would be blooming in the London parks and I imagined the children with their boats on the Round Pond. Then I was transported straight back to the brief ecstatic period with Joliffe and quite clearly I saw Bella's face smiling, with the sinister look in her eyes—the messenger of Fate who had come to destroy my happiness at one stroke.

Excitement invaded the house; the servants whispered together. A great occasion was approaching.

Sylvester said to me: "You know what is coming, Jane. It is the Feast of the Dead."

I felt sick with horror. I remembered this custom from my reading and had forgotten that this was the time of the year it took place.

"It occurs twice yearly," said Sylvester, "in the spring and in the autumn, but the great occasion is the springtime . . . now."

"It's a morbid custom," I said.

"Oh no, they don't make a morbid thing of it. They honor their ancestors. As you know the main force in Chinese life is ancestor worship. Any sin is forgivable in the pursuit of it. Confucius laid down the law that burial and mourning rites are the most important of all duties. The Chinese adore with a kind of idolatry those who have died. This is the most important occasion of the year therefore—the honoring of the dead."

The preparations had begun. Throughout the day we would see parties making for the hillside where the burial grounds were situated. Sylvester had told me that such spots were chosen throughout China because the land could not be used for cultivation and there were buried the grandest mandarins and the lowliest peasants.

For days men, women, and children went there to wash the tombs in readiness for the great day. When I rode out with Toby we saw the red and white streamers of paper flying out in the wind. These had been attached to the tombs that all might know they had been cleaned and made ready and that no dead person had been forgotten.

Lottie was among those who made the pilgrimage to the hill. She took food and candles and wrapped herself in coarse cloth.

I shall never forget that day. The house was deserted. All the servants had gone to the hills.

Tobias had taken Jason out on a small pony, for Jason was learning to ride, and Sylvester and I were alone in the house.

How quiet it was apart from the occasional sound of the gongs which came from the mourning processions as they wound their way up to the hillside.

I would be glad when this day was over.

Sylvester had been dressed and sat in his chair. He had become very thin and in the dim light he resembled a skeleton.

How I wished they would not keep sounding those gongs. They reminded me of the knell of the funeral bell. And I was reminded of my bright mother who had been dying and keeping that terrible knowledge from me.

"This is a horrid ceremony," I said aloud.

"The sadness is brief," Sylvester replied. "Very soon now the feasting will begin."

"The feasting!"

"You don't imagine they will waste all that food they've taken up there, do you? They are too practical for that. They have paid honor to the dead, now they will have a banquet of the food they have brought. Up at the hills they will light the lanterns and the wailing will cease. All will sit down for the food will be spread on the tombs and they will eat, as they would tell you, with their ancestors."

"And tomorrow they will have forgotten?"

"Some forget their dead . . . others never do."

We were silent for a while.

Then he said. "Very soon now, Jane, I shall not be here."

I said vehemently: "Please stop. For so long now you have been almost courting death."

"I knew He had entered the house, Jane, and I knew for whom He had come."

"That's nonsense. You have just seemed to lose the will to live."

"I lost it because it was taken from me."

"By whom?"

Then he said a strange thing. "I am not sure."

"Sylvester, what do you mean?"

He shrugged his shoulders. "In any case, my time has come. It is part of the pattern. I knew what I must do. This house will be yours, Jane, when I am gone."

"I don't want to talk about it."

He laughed gently. "Don't say that. The house is listening. No one likes to be unwanted. It makes for a loss of face. Yes, I know this is what I must do. This house and this business will be yours, Jane. I have trained you for this. You have the dedication . . . the serious mind. You are the one and you will train the boy and in time he will be there to take it from you. As for the house . . . with its secret, I believe that you have found the truth. Fear is in the mind, Jane. That is the answer to the riddle. You will live here in peace."

I said: "You cannot have left all this to me . . . a woman."

"I have always had a great respect for women, you know. And you are my wife. These years with you have been the happiest I have known since I lost Martha to Magnus. You changed everything when you came. And you learned . . . you learned so quickly. Your pleasure, your enthusiasm, your dedication were my delight."

I said: "I should not be fit . . ."

"Nonsense. Who was it who reminded me that anyone could do anything if that one made up his or her mind."

"You believe that?"

"I do."

"Then believe that you will get well. You *will* get well. I will nurse you. I will cook everything for you myself . . ."

I stopped short, horrified by what I had said. It was as though the house had held its breath and was waiting, it was as though some unknown voice had whispered those words to me.

"It's too late, Jane," he said. "The time has come. You will know how to carry on. You will find Toby a good man. A reliable man. Trust Toby. I care for these treasures of mine. I have been a successful businessman with my skillful buying and shrewd selling, but I have loved my merchandise. As you know some things I have kept because I could not bear to part with them. I have covered everything, I believe, taken care of every contingency. It has occurred to me that you may not wish to be alone."

"What do you mean, Sylvester?" I asked sharply.

"I know you well, Jane. I do not think you are a woman to want to live alone. You may decide to marry."

"Oh, do not talk of such things. I have a husband who has been good to me."

"Bless you, Jane. But let us look facts straight in the face. When I am no longer here, you will be lonely. You may need someone. Choose wisely, Jane. Once . . ." He stopped for I had winced. I knew he was thinking of Joliffe. He went on quickly: "I have, as I said, taken care of possibilities which may occur. Jason is very young. So are you, but if anything should befall you I have appointed Adam as Jason's guardian until such time as he comes of age. But you, Jane, shall be in command for as long as is possible."

He was hinting that if I married he would like Adam to be my husband—Adam or perhaps Toby. He trusted Toby absolutely but Adam was his own family. What he was most anxious to do was to keep Joliffe out.

"I want you to be well," I cried. "I want *you* in command."

"You are good to me, Jane," he said. "You have always been good to me. It has been a good life . . . on the whole. There was sorrow but I learned to control it and the Chinese say that the more talents are exercised the more they will develop."

He fell silent and I believed him to be asleep.

I sat beside him and thought back over the past, of the first time we had met and how I had feared that my mother and I would be turned away.

Then the enormity of what he had said swept over me and I would not think of it. I wanted to sit still and listen to the quiet of the house, the sudden distant sound of the gongs from the hillside.

That night Sylvester died in his sleep . . . the night of the day of the Feast of the Dead. He would have said it was an appropriate time to die.

I had become not only a widow but a rich woman.

The Widow

It was a time of great activity for me. I had so much to learn; I had to assume a new dignity; I had to convince not only those with whom I did business that I was capable, but myself as well.

Whenever I felt inadequate I would assure myself: Sylvester believed in you. He was certain you could do it.

There were many formalities to be gone through; I spent hours with the lawyers. I was astounded by the extent of Sylvester's business which I had inherited in a kind of trust for Jason. I was determined to keep that business flourishing not only to convince myself that I could, but for him.

I seemed to grow in stature; I learned to make firm decisions; I understood how to deal with people and preserve a friendly formality. I even began to look forward to new difficulties because I found such satisfaction in overcoming them.

I sensed that Adam would have liked to take over. "You must let me deal with these things," he said. "It's too much for a woman."

"That was not Sylvester's idea," I told him.

"Well, if there is anything I can do . . ."

"Thank you, Adam."

He moved out of The House of a Thousand Lanterns. He couldn't very well stay there now that Sylvester was dead. He rented a small place near us.

"You'll know I'm not far if you want anything," he told me.

Deeply I mourned Sylvester. I had not realized how much he had meant to me until I lost him. Sometimes I would awake in the night with a horrible sense of desolation and I would lie sleepless thinking of the many kindnesses he had shown me. I was determined to try to do everything he would have wished me to.

We had buried him in the English cemetery. The Chinese of the household were disappointed that we did not observe their rites. They would have liked to have seen a funeral procession to the hillside with incense and offerings and the family taking money and garments to the tomb so that Sylvester might make use of them in the world of spirits. I did, however, bow to their conventions in one respect. I dressed myself and Jason in white.

Lottie was thoughtful. "Great Lady will marry again," she said.

"Marry!" I said. "What put that into your head?"

She spread her hands and looked at me wisely.

I said: "An English widow does not think of marriage until she has been a widow for a year."

"So?" she said, her head on one side, birdlike. "Then in a year you marry."

She seemed content with that.

A year, I repeated to myself.

Joliffe had come to the house for the funeral. I was aware of his smoldering eyes on me.

The will was read after the funeral according to the English custom. I was not surprised, having been warned by Sylvester of its contents; I was only astonished that there was so much. It was left to me but as he had told me there was a proviso. Sylvester could be trusted to cover all contingencies. In the event of my death before Jason reached the age of twenty-one, Adam was to control affairs.

I wondered whether he had been afraid that I would marry Joliffe and wished to exclude him.

It was the day after the funeral when Joliffe came to the house. He was shown into the drawing room and when I went down to see him he approached me with outstretched hands.

I avoided them. I was afraid of his touch. That was how vulnerable I was.

He said: "I must talk to you, Jane. There is much we have to discuss. We are free now, Jane . . . both of us."

I turned away. I could almost see Sylvester there in his chair, covering his eyes with his hands in dismay.

"Please, Joliffe," I said, "I am a widow of a week. Have you forgotten that?"

"It is because of this, that we have so much to say."

"Not here," I said. "Not now . . ."

He hesitated for a moment and then he said: "Later then, but soon."

I escaped to my room and thought of Joliffe and those days when we had been in Paris together. I remembered well the reckless joy of meeting Joliffe, of falling in love with him; then there came pictures of that dreadful day when Bella had arrived. If one reaches the pinnacle of ecstasy, the descent is very great indeed.

One thing I had often said to myself during the years

after I had lost Joliffe was: Never again if I could help it would I put myself in a position to suffer like that. I recalled some wise words of Sylvester: "To be involved is to suffer. One should make sure that one does not too lightly become involved."

Another thing he had advised me: "Never make hasty decisions. Look at your problem from all angles, weigh up carefully each aspect."

Sometimes I felt that Sylvester was very near to me, watching over me, so often did I remember his words of wisdom.

It was a few days later when Lottie came to tell me that Joliffe was in the pagoda and was asking if I would go to him there.

I went and as I entered he came up from behind me and put his arms about me.

"No, Joliffe," I protested.

"But yes," he answered, turning me round and kissing me in such a way that I was transported back to the days of our passion.

"Please, Joliffe," I said. "Let me go."

"Not yet. When shall we be married?"

"I would not dream of marrying for a year."

"That old convention! It is not as though you were ever anybody's wife but mine."

I drew myself away from him. "I was never your wife. You had a wife when you went through a form of marriage with me."

"Forms!" he said. "Names signed on dotted lines. Do they make a marriage?"

"It is generally believed to be so," I said.

"No," he said. "You were my wife, Jane. You and I were meant for one another. If you know what it was like when you went away . . ."

"I did know, Joliffe," I said quietly.

"Then why do you hesitate?"

"I was young and reckless, inexperienced of the world. I shall never be that again. I have become serious."

"The businesswoman!" he said. "All Hong Kong is talking of you. They wonder how long it will be before you have a husband to take the burden from your shoulders."

"If burden it is, it is one I am determined to relinquish to no one. Sylvester has trained me well over many years. He believed me capable. I have a son to work for. Perhaps I have enough in life."

"What nonsense! You will have many sons. You are not a woman to put love out of your life forever."

"I have to discover what sort of a woman I am, Joliffe. I'm constantly surprising myself."

"You were hurt, weren't you? I love you, Jane. I didn't want to tell you about Bella. Not then. I would have told you later when you were older and more tolerant of youthful follies. Besides I thought it was an incident closed forever. And then she came back from the dead as it were—and you left me! Oh Jane, how could you have done that!"

"It seemed to me the only way."

"Conventional Jane, she couldn't love without the marriage lines and she can't go to her true husband now because she must wait a year after the death of a husband who was no husband."

"Joliffe, please don't talk about Sylvester. He was good to me. He meant a great deal to me. Perhaps our relationship was something you couldn't understand."

"I understand it perfectly."

"No, Joliffe, you don't. He was my best friend for years. I owe everything to him . . . even meeting you."

"How like you, Conventional Jane, to put an aura round the dead. They immediately become sanctified in the minds of some people. Sylvester was a man of genius in business. He also had his eyes to the main chance. He married you because he wanted a nurse, a pupil and a son, and you could provide all those needs. Let's be practical. Here in this place we can talk freely. That house stifles me."

"That was why you wished to see me here?"

He nodded. "Part of the house and yet not it. There's something about the pagoda. I always thought so." He looked at the crumbling figure of the goddess, at the shaft of sunlight penetrating the roof. "I used to come here as a boy. And I thought: In the pagoda I can talk to Jane."

"There is nothing we have to say as yet," I answered. "I need time to think. I am unsure of many things."

"You need your specified year," he said.

"Yes, I need my year."

"And you will not marry within that year?"

"I will not."

"And how am I to live a year without you?"

"I suggest in the same way that you have been living so far."

"You ask a lot, Jane."

"When we truly love we are prepared to give a lot."

He regarded me steadily. "I have never felt towards anyone else as I do towards you. I shall live for the time when we are together. One year to the day I shall be back for you. Then we shall go through that ceremony the second time, only the next time it will be binding." Then he came to me again and took me into his arms and he kissed me and there was the same magic in his embrace that I remembered so well.

A few days later Adam told me that Joliffe had left Hong Kong.

There was not a great deal of time for riding. I wondered whether I should engage a governess for Jason but it would have probably meant bringing someone out from England and I enjoyed those lessons so much. Jason was so bright and it was not merely maternal pride which made me think so; and Lottie's quaintness amused me and her eagerness to learn delighted me. I could not give up my little schoolroom which I had set up in one of the top rooms. I had put up a big wooden table and there was a cupboard in which books could be kept. Over the table hung the center lantern. Jason loved to be allowed to light the oil lamp inside it. From the window we could see the pagoda, which dominated the view from all windows on that side of the house.

I was confiding a great deal in Toby. I made a point of going to the Go-Down every day after the first few weeks. I was learning more and more from Toby and he was delighted to teach me. Our friendship grew warmer. I knew he was a man whom I could trust. I told him I would not stay in Hong Kong forever. There would come a time when I could no longer teach Jason and he would have to go away to school. That would be in a few years' time and I would not consider the idea of his being in England while I was here.

"There's time to work that out," said Toby.

"Plenty of time," I answered. "Sylvester was delighted to be able to leave everything in your good hands. That was the only reason he could stay in England as long as he did."

"You can rely on me as he did," he answered earnestly and when he looked into my face I did not want to meet his gaze. That he hoped for a deeper relationship I knew. I had been aware of this before even though Toby was too honorable a man to have willingly given me an inkling of this while Sylvester lived—but I had sensed it.

Sometimes I used to think what an admirable solution that would be . . . as far as the business was concerned. I could never have had a better manager. He could be firm and certainly his opinions and ideas of how things should be done were unwaveringly honorable, and he was almost always right. I knew that he was completely trustworthy.

As for my feelings for him they went deep. I respected him; I admired him; I liked his company for he had a light wit which was the best sort since it did not depend on hurting others to achieve its point. I could have seen marriage with him as a happy ending . . . if I had never known Joliffe. I could have had a life of peaceful contentment.

Strangely enough my relationship with Adam had begun to change. I was stimulated by his company where at one time I had been irritated. I found his serious, aloof, and rather critical approach amusing.

One day we went independently to a mandarin's palace where certain objects of art were being offered for sale. I had taken to going to such places alone more and more often, which had caused some surprise in the beginning but now was being accepted. It was recognized that I was an unusual woman. I was known as Madam Milner, the wife of the great Sylvester Milner, one of the richest traders in the Far East. And he had left everything to me. At first it was believed that this was the action of a man in his dotage who was enamored of a wife so much younger than himself. But I had done well, it seemed. Perhaps it was due to Toby's influence that I was accepted. I was different because I was a woman. I had a woman's intuition. My knowledge of Chinese Art was becoming formidable. And I kept a good manager in Toby Grantham who, everyone knew, was of the best. He remained loyal to me although it was rumored that he had had attractive offers from other companies. It seemed that I was not to be lightly dismissed.

My rickshaw man was a familiar sight in the town and I noticed passers-by watch me with lowered eyes. They would murmur something about Madam and the strangeness of foreign devils who set up their women as though they were goddesses.

On this particular occasion as the house was some miles away in the country I rode there on horseback. At first on these expeditions I had taken Toby with me but later formed the habit of going alone.

The mandarin's house looked like an ivory carving as I approached; it was gilded and ornate like The House of a Thousand Lanterns and stood upon a platform paved with beautiful mosaics.

My horse was taken by a servant and I went into the house. The door opened onto a large square hall which again reminded me of our own at The House of a Thousand Lanterns. The beams of the roof were supported by columns which were painted in bright colors. I made out the form of the ubiquitous dragon.

In this room were several objects for display and these were what I and several others had come to see. Most of the people assembled were Europeans and many of them known to me. I was greeted on all sides and I felt a little glow of satisfaction by their manner which told me clearly that I was accepted as one of them.

There was one beautiful leaping figure which I admired very much. I was standing looking at it when I felt some-one close behind me, and turning, saw Adam.

"I see we have one thought in mind," he said.

"It's beautiful," I said. "I can't quite place the period."

"Chou Dynasty, I think."

"As far back?"

"It's probably copied by someone in a later century but the Chou influence is there." His face glowed a little. "There's such movement in it. Definitely Chou influence. It betrays the kind of people they were—lively and barbaric."

I said admiringly: "I wish I were as knowledgeable as you."

"I've had a little longer to learn. Besides with me it's a full-time occupation . . . or dedication if you like. You have had other things to absorb you."

"I'm still eager to learn all I can."

"Good, but you'll never catch up."

"Why shouldn't I?"

"You have a child who is more to you than Art of any kind."

"Perhaps that makes me appreciate beauty all the more."

He shook his head. "Emotional entanglements take the mind off Art."

"It's not borne out. Great artists have often been great lovers."

"Yet the one great love of their lives is their Art. The gods and goddesses of the Arts would not tolerate rivalry. But I'm not an artist, I'm only an appreciator. To learn of these things is entirely absorbing, so much reading, so much research. There isn't time for anything else."

"I don't agree with you. Artists and appreciators of Art would know nothing of life if they didn't experience it."

"This is not the sort of conversation to carry on here. Let's continue it later. I shall try for the Chou figure. What of you?"

"I want it," I said.

"May the best man . . . or woman . . . win."

We looked at other things. There were some beautiful ivory pieces. I bid for some of these and got them and I found a beautiful Ming vase which delighted me.

These would be collected later by someone whom Toby would send from the Go-Down. Then I went back to the Chou piece intending to bid for it.

To my dismay it had gone.

Adam was smiling at me sardonically.

"A little negotiating," he said.

"But . . ."

"It sometimes happens. You see, there are certain things you have yet to learn."

I was put out not only to have lost my chance of getting the piece but to have been proved wanting . . . and by Adam.

"Never mind," he said. "Next time perhaps we could go together and I could give you a little advice. I shall accompany you back for I do not think it is wise for you to ride through the country alone."

I was about to protest but having been shown my lack of experience in one matter I was a little subdued.

As we rode back, he talked about the various dynasties and he glowed with a kind of inner radiance. I could have listened entranced for hours.

"This Woman Supreme idea at the moment is absorbing," he said. "You are doing very well, but you'll grow tired of it."

"If you mean carrying on as my husband intended me to I can assure you I won't."

"You could always have a say in how everything was run. But won't there be times when family matters take over?"

"My son's education, you mean?"

"That, of course, but if you were to marry again . . ."

I was silent.

"You are young and attractive. There will be offers. After all you yourself have a good deal to offer. You are a woman of substance."

"Quite a good catch, in fact," I said.

"There must be some who are aware of it."

"So I am bait for the fortune hunters?"

"I'll swear there are one or two who would be delighted to take charge of your interests."

"Perhaps, and they will find that I intend to keep charge of these myself."

"You should marry," he said gently. "But be careful, be wary before you take a hasty step in that direction."

"I promise you I shall be very wary."

He leaned towards me suddenly and laid his hand on mine.

Then he withdrew it sharply.

"If at any time you need my help on any matter," he said, "I shall be glad to give it."

"Thank you."

When he helped me from my horse I fancied he held me a little longer than was necessary; our eyes met briefly; his gaze had lost its coldness.

Later the Chou piece arrived at the house. It was addressed to me and when I saw what it was I went to Adam and told him that there had been a mistake. The piece he had ordered to be sent to him had come to me.

He smiled at me. "It's no mistake. It was for you."

"But you bought it."

"True and now it's yours. A gift from me."

"Adam!" I cried. "But it's so beautiful!"

"I should not want to give you something you did not think desirable."

I turned away. I felt a new emotion.

He said quietly: "I'm glad it pleases you."

And I knew suddenly that there were three men who wished to marry me.

Joliffe who had said so vehemently, Toby who had shown me through his devotion, and now Adam who had told me so with a Chou figure.

I had the hazy impression that the house was laughing at me. Three men indeed! The answer is not hard to find. You are by no means old. You are moderately attractive and you are very rich.

With all the practical matters which had had to be settled since Sylvester's death I had not at first thought so much about the house; then suddenly the realization that I was the owner of The House of a Thousand Lanterns began to obsess me.

I went from room to room. I liked to be alone, to shut myself in, to brood, to ask myself if it was true that these strange emotions which the place aroused in me had grown out of my imagination. How easy it was to believe that a house such as this was a living thing, that it was saying something to me.

I longed for Sylvester to be there, to talk to me as we

used to. I missed him so much and found it impossible to stop grieving for him. I had relied on him. I was constantly wanting to ask his advice about some new discovery and longed to be able to talk to him about so many things. Sometimes I would wake from a hazy dream in which I was touching some article which had delighted me. I would be saying: "I must show this to Sylvester." Then would come the sad realization that I could never show him anything again. Not my gratitude, my respect, my love . . . yes, I had loved him deeply.

Lottie talked about the house as though it were alive. She feared it had lost face because it now belonged to a woman.

I retorted that the very goddess on whose temple it was said to have been erected had been a female. Wouldn't she therefore be pleased rather than dismayed?

Lottie was certain this was not so. "Women," she would say and shake her head grimacing, "of no account. Men . . . that is different."

Lottie herself would have had evidence of the lack of importance of her sex. She would remember that at the time of her birth she had been put out into the streets to die; every day in the floating city of sampans one would see baby boys tied to the boats so that they could not fall over into the water and drown, while no such precaution was taken with baby girls. I felt indignant on behalf of Chinese women. Their feet were mutilated if they were of the upper classes and their only education was how to embroider and paint on silk and serve the men who would be chosen as their husbands. Even then when they were given in marriage they must suffer their husband's concubines under the same roof.

When I considered all this I saw Lottie's point that the house which was essentially Chinese might be affronted to be in the possession of a woman.

"In a year you marry," said Lottie confidently. "Then master in the house. No more lost face."

I said: "It would still be *my* house."

Lottie lifted her shoulders and laughed. She didn't believe that.

Since he had given me the Chou figure my relationship with Adam had changed.

We had taken to going to sales together and we often met at dealers. I think Toby was a little piqued at our growing friendship although he was too discreet to mention it.

Adam was like a man with a purpose; there was about him a quiet determination. I knew that when my year of widowhood was over he was going to ask me to marry him.

And so was Toby.

I pondered about them a great deal but Joliffe was always in my thoughts for he would be back. It was impossible to consider Joliffe dispassionately as I could the others. When I thought of his breaking into Sylvester's Treasure Room and taking away the goddess to have it valued, I reminded myself that Toby would say that was unethical for Toby was a man of honor. And Joliffe? Joliffe was an adventurer; in the old days he would have been a buccaneer. I could imagine him on the high seas storming ships and carrying off their treasure . . . and perhaps their women. I had loved Joliffe; but I did have an affection for both Adam and Toby. Yet I think I was not *involved* with them. Was that being in love? I could stand outside my relationship with Adam and Toby, but I could not as far as Joliffe was concerned. I might make up my mind to take one course of action with him and when he was there he could completely change it. There was one other with whom I was deeply involved—my son Jason. But he must come first. I had married Sylvester for his sake, and now if I married again, Jason should once more be a major consideration.

Both Toby and Adam seemed to realize what an important part Jason would make in my choice.

Of the two Toby was Jason's favorite. Jason was perfectly happy in his company. Both Adam and Toby had given him riding lessons and at that time riding was his passion. Toby knew how to handle him; he had the right amount of firmness and friendship; he never talked down to him; they were man to man and at the same time Jason looked up to him. Adam was more aloof. He was not a boy's man at all but I noticed that Jason had a great respect for him.

Once I asked my son whether he liked Adam.

Oh yes, he answered, he liked him. "Joliffe's his cousin," he added, as though that were the reason.

I should marry in time. I was not a woman to want to live my life alone. Jason was growing up; he needed a father. So as the weeks passed I thought often of marriage and living out my life—perhaps between England and Hong Kong as Sylvester had done. I wanted more children; I wanted a full life. I wanted the comfort of a large family and a man beside me to be my companion, and at the same time I wanted the satisfaction of increasing my knowledge and the thrill of the hunt for treasures. Strangely enough all the three men who were constantly in my thoughts could share my interests.

I wanted someone to share this house with me, and as these thoughts refused to be banished from my mind I was trying not to think too much of Joliffe. Oh Sylvester, I would think, if you were here I would not be in this dilemma.

One day when Adam and I were returning after a visit to a sale we talked of the house. I said: "I expect you will laugh at me, but since it passed into my hands I feel it is different."

"Different in what way?" he asked.

"I can't explain. It's a subtle difference. When I'm in a room alone I feel that there's a presence there . . . that something is being conveyed to me."

He smiled. "That was at dusk I'm sure."

"It might have been."

"Shadows set the imagination working and in a place like The House of a Thousand Lanterns the imagination would be on the alert."

"What is it about the house that makes me feel this aura of mystery . . . and that there is something rather sinister about it."

"It is the house of an Oriental. Despite your knowledge of things Chinese, it is alien to all you were brought up to expect in life. It's a strange house, too, I grant you that. All those rooms . . . every alcove fitted with lanterns."

"And you think this is the only reason why I feel this strangeness?"

"I think it very likely."

"Sylvester said that it contained some treasure."

"That's the legend."

"Where could it be?"

"Who can say?"

"If there is something, there must be a secret hiding place in the house."

"If there is it has eluded all the previous owners. They have searched in every room."

"Do you think it is just a legend that has grown up?"

"I think that may well be."

"I am the first woman to own this house. It seems a challenge in a way."

"What will you do?"

"I shall try to find the solution."

"Where will you begin?"

"I shall have to wait for some inspiration. Where would the treasure be likely to be?"

"It depends what the treasure is."

"Sylvester did not think it was gold or silver or precious gems. He believed it was something more subtle. Do you know it has occurred to me that it could be the statue of Kuan Yin. You know *the* statue. The one every dealer seeks to find."

"Whatever gave you that idea!"

"This house was built on the site of a temple. There is a statue of her in the pagoda and one in the house."

Adam was looking at me intently. His eyes had darkened with an excitement he sought to suppress. To find the Sung Kuan Yin was the dream of every dealer.

"Do you think that if the mandarin who gave my great-grandfather the house had possessed Kuan Yin he would have given her away?"

"It might have been the ultimate sacrifice. His wife and son had been saved."

"Your imagination runs away with you, Jane."

"That's what my mother used to tell me. It may be a wild idea, but I am going to find that piece if it is in this house."

"How?"

"I shall search every room."

"That's been done a hundred times."

"Yet the secret must be there."

"If there is one, no one has discovered it in over eighty years."

"Perhaps I shall be the one."

Adam gave me one of his rare smiles.

"I am going to join forces with you. Where shall we begin?"

"That is what I shall have to discover. Perhaps the house will tell me." I smiled at him, for I saw the curl of his lips.

He was the most practical of men. He would never be given to flights of fancy. Perhaps he was the man I needed in my life. I asked myself: Was I right in thinking Sylvester meant this? He must have trusted Adam since he had named him Jason's guardian.

And Jason? Jason liked him. He felt the confidence children feel in a strong man—besides he was Joliffe's cousin.

II

We were going to visit Chan Cho Lan. Adam, Lottie, and myself.

Adam explained to me.

"The lady is quite a power in the district. The family has known her for some years. At one time she acted as a kind of liaison between us and some of the wealthy mandarins. She is of a good family and there is no one quite like her in Hong Kong for like you she is mistress of her house and has no husband now. She keeps a large establishment in which she trains girls in the graces of social life."

I told him that Lottie had taken me to her and we had already met.

"Lottie holds her in great awe," I said. "I think she was afraid when she took me that I should not observe the correct etiquette. Lottie, being brought up in her house for a time, was well aware of it. I found it all fascinating. Why does she invite us again?"

"She invites members of our family now and then. It is to show she maintains good will towards us."

I remembered last time I had been there and the strange grace of this woman. I dressed myself in white silk chiffon, as I was still in mourning for Sylvester. It was a color becoming to me and I was glad. Not that I would attempt to rival the beauty and grace of Chan Cho Lan but I did feel that I should look as well as possible.

Lottie was delightful in a light green silk cheongsam; her hair was loose and she wore a frangipani flower in it.

We walked the short distance and as we went through the gates I heard the sound of a gong and the strains of that peculiar tinkly off-key Chinese music. When we were ushered in, Chan Cho Lan rose from a cushion to greet us.

I recognized the fragrance of jasmine and frangipani as she swayed before us—beauty in person. Her robe was of pale lilac color embroidered with gold; her lovely hair was held up by jeweled pins and the delicate coloring of her face was exquisite.

Adam towered above her and she bowed low to him. Then they closed their hands and lifted them two or three times towards their heads.

Adam said: "*Haou? Tsing. Tsing.*"

"*Tsing. Tsing,*" murmured Chan Cho Lan.

Then she greeted me in the same way.

With Adam walking beside her she led the way from the reception room into a dining room where a round table was laid with china bowls, china spoons, and ivory chopsticks.

Chan Cho Lan and Adam talked together in Cantonese in which Adam seemed very fluent. He sat beside our hostess; and Lottie and I took the places allotted to us. I was surprised that Lottie was included, and I wondered whether Adam had asked for this. He had shown more than once his interest in her, and he had made it very clear how pleased he was that she fitted into my household.

A servant came with hot damp cloths on a tray. We picked them up with tongs and wiped our hands; they were fragrant, smelling of rose water.

Jasmine-scented tea was then brought to us and this was clearly the prelude to the meal. Chan Cho Lan said how much we honored her miserable table and with what happiness she welcomed us. Adam replied on our behalf. He gave the impression that he knew exactly what was expected and that dining in such circumstances was an everyday occurrence with him.

Our hostess studied me with interest. I did great honor to Hong Kong, she said. I was a lady of great importance.

Very illustrious. Adam lifted his small cup of tea and gave a toast to two illustrious ladies while Chan Cho Lan lifted her hands and shook her beautiful head from side to side, obviously denying her claim to the description.

"We live close," said Chan Cho Lan.

"Neighbors," replied Adam. "Therefore it is good to be neighborly."

She clearly did not understand and Adam explained to her in Cantonese.

Lottie, silent and awestruck, looked on with a kind of wonder. Adam seemed to have abandoned his usual rather taciturn manner and was quite capable of keeping the conversation going either in Cantonese or the sort of basic English he used with Chan Cho Lan.

When the great bowl came in which was filled with fragments of chicken and duck and we were expected to help ourselves from it, Adam picked out pieces which he fed to Chan Cho Lan implying that he sought the best pieces for her. This was the custom and Lottie did the same for me.

It was very ceremonious and it was fortunate that I was aware of the procedure for there are few places where it is easier to commit a breach of good manners than at a Chinese dinner table. Through the meal from the *deem sum,* or hors d'oeuvres, through the meat dishes—flavored with lotus seeds and wrapped in the finest dough—to the soup which was made from birds' nests and the dessert, fruit dipped in a sweet substance that was like toffee, I contrived to do what was expected of me. Toasts were intermittently drunk in *shau-shing,* a wine distilled from rice. It was sweet and cloying.

"*Yam seng,*" said Adam and Chan Cho Lan bowed her beautiful head and repeated with him "*Yam seng,*" as they drained their small porcelain cups.

The rose-scented damp cloths were brought round several times and we wiped our hands; then Chan Cho Lan rose to her feet. Adam took her hand and we fell in behind them while she tottered to another room. Here we sat on pouf-like cushions. There was a dais at one end of the room where musicians were seated.

A gong sounded and dancers came in. I have rarely seen dancers so graceful as those I saw in Chan Cho Lan's house that day.

The costumes of the dancers were colorful and gay and I quickly realized that there was something symbolic in the dances. They were about lovers and one of the dancers before the dance began would tell us what these movements were meant to portray.

First of all there was the meeting of lovers. Eight young and lovely girls performed this, going through coquettish motions as they approached and retreated. Courtship was portrayed by the girls playing in the fields chasing butterflies. They carried ribbons in their hands and as they danced they released them to form symmetrical shapes; they laughed joyously as they circled and were joined by girls dressed as young men in gay costumes. This was falling in love and the expressions of the dancers ranged from frivolity to seriousness.

Then there was the bridal dance with one graceful girl representing the bride, the other the groom. More dancers —guests at the wedding—performed with joyous abandon.

It stopped when the bridegroom led off his bride and the other dancers fell in behind them.

"Now they live happy ever more," said Chan Cho Lan.

We clapped our hands and Chan Cho Lan nodded gravely.

"Before you go," she said, "I wish you see the shrines."

She was looking at me so I said that I should be delighted.

She bowed and with Adam beside her again led the way along a passage which was lit by lanterns rather similar to those in my house. We came to a door which was covered by brocade. As she opened it, an odor of incense enveloped us. It came from joss sticks burning in the room. An aged man with a long beard, wearing a silk robe which reached to his ankles and with a round hat on his head, bowed to us and stood aside.

There was a hushed air in the room. Then I saw the shrine. It was dazzling; and there dominating it was a statue of Kuan Yin. The goddess was carved in wood and seated on what appeared to be a rocky island. Her beautiful benevolent face smiled at us. Joss sticks burned on the shrine.

"The Goddess of Mercy," murmured Chan Cho Lan.

"She presides over the shrine," whispered Adam to me. "And on the walls you see Chan Cho Lan's ancestors."

I looked at the paintings of men who all looked alike in their mandarins' robes with their long beards and hands clasped before them.

I was more interested in the shrine, for around it were etchings portraying the story of the goddess' life on earth. There she was as a princess being beaten by her father because she refused to marry. In the second picture she was in a nunnery working as a scullery maid. She was seen in various stages of persecution by her wicked father and finally going to paradise. When her father was sick she descended to earth to nurse him. Deified, glorified, she was the goddess to whom all turned in their need.

It was clear that this room with its shrine dedicated to her and Chan Cho Lan's ancestors was a sacred place and I was surprised that she had allowed us as barbarians to enter it.

We took a ceremonious farewell with much bowing and talk on her side of how miserable the entertainment had been and on ours how unworthy we had been to have been given it, which I must say I found a little irritating. I wanted to thank her and tell her what a wonderful experience it had been and I did so.

As we walked across to The House of a Thousand Lanterns I thought Lottie looked as if she had paid a visit to the paradise of Fō. Yet she was a little sad. I guessed it was because she herself had been brought up in that establishment, yet Chan Cho Lan had never trained her as a dancing girl to entertain her guests, nor had she prepared her for a grand alliance by crippling her feet.

I wondered why. In due course, I promised myself, I would find out.

I talked about it afterwards with Adam.

"Chan Cho Lan seems to be very friendly with you," I said.

"Our family has been friends with hers for many years and she regards me as the head of ours since Sylvester died. She has quite a history. When she was a child she was chosen to be one of the Emperor's concubines. He had a great many and some of these were never even seen by the Emperor. To qualify for a concubine a lady must be of noble family. She is sent to the palace and selected for her beauty, grace, and accomplishments. The Emperor does not do the selecting. His mother or his major domo does that. The girls go to the palace at an early age but some of them never have a chance of catching the Emperor's eyes; they remain in seclusion guarded by eunuchs, always hoping, I suppose, that the summons will come. It never came for Chan Cho Lan. If it had I am sure the Emperor would have been pleased. It is influence and relations at court who draw their lord's attention to a girl. In the meantime they live as girls do in a school, and paint on silk and embroider and talk of themselves and what they know of the world—which is precious little—and when they are past their first flush of youth, which is about eighteen years old, they may leave the Emperor's court and husbands are found for them. Chan Cho Lan was passed to an old mandarin who lived but a year or so after the wedding. Since then she has become a lady of distinction in her own right. Because she was trained in all the graces to charm an Emperor she decided not to waste her gifts but to bestow them on girls of her choosing. So she took under her wing the selected girls and some she trains to be dancers, as those we have seen today. Others, if they are young enough when they come to her, have their feet bound and are brought up to make good alliances. She assesses the girls and trains them for what she thinks will suit them best. She is a kind of matchmaker or marriage broker, a very profitable business, and it is said that she is one of the richest women in Hong Kong."

"She seemed interested in me," I said. "Or did I imagine that?"

"She is—it is because you have a reputation for being an astute businesswoman—very different from her profession of course, but she would wish to know someone who could be as successful as she is. Life has dealt similarly with you, as she would see it, although you are a world apart. Moreover you are a member of our family, and for that alone she would be interested."

"I have rarely seen you so eager to please," I could not resist saying.

"I must return politeness with politeness. Moreover in the past she has introduced many a mandarin to my father and me, someone who is looking for some rare statue or painting. She would let us know if someone of her acquaintance had something to dispose of. I want her to continue to do so."

"Oh," I said with a smile, "so it's business after all."

I could not forget the exquisite grace of the dancers. As for Lottie, she continued to appear bemused.

"You have like dance?" she asked.

"Yes, I liked that."

"And all leading to the marriage."

"I suppose it is a common theme," I said.

Lottie did not understand that. "It was for you," she said. "It is a sign. You marry soon."

"It had nothing to do with me personally. It was just the theme of the dance."

"Was for you," she said wisely. "One year nearly up."

"Why, Lottie," I said, "are you not content with things as they are?"

She shook her head vehemently. "Not good for house. The house ask for Master," she said.

"Well, I am the one who must decide that, Lottie," I reminded her.

"You decide," she said confidently. "One year from end of Master you decide."

Lottie seemed to have made up her mind that I would marry. I was not sure.

As I lay in bed I looked up at the lantern swinging from the ceiling.

A thousand lanterns, I thought. Was the secret of this house in the lanterns?

It must be. In what way was this house different from any other? By the fact that it was said to contain a thousand lanterns. I looked round the room. It was not one of the largest in the house. There was the huge lantern hanging from the center and smaller ones placed at intervals round the walls. I counted twenty. Then there was the room in which Jason slept. There must have been about fifteen there.

I said to myself: The secret must be in the lanterns.

There was a pressure of business that day and I forgot about the lanterns, but I remembered that evening.

I had dined and was having coffee when Adam called. I was surprised to see him at this hour but his visit was explained by his excitement over an interesting piece he had bought that day.

"I couldn't wait to show you," he said, "I'm sure it's a discovery. What do you think of it?"

He unwrapped it from a calico bag and held it reverently in his hands.

"It's an incense burner," I said.

"That's so. What dynasty would you say?

"I should imagine it's about the second or the first century B.C. If so, I should say the Han Dynasty."

He smiled at me warmly. He always seemed to be a different person at such times and it was on these occasions that I found myself liking him more and more.

"Where did you find it?" I asked.

"A mandarin friend of Chan Cho Lan wanted to dispose of it. She saw it and I had first chance."

"I remember an incense burner that Sylvester was particularly fond of," I said. My voice faltered and Adam looked at me sharply.

"It's lonely here in this house for you," he said.

"I'm all right. I have Jason . . . and Lottie is a great comfort to me."

He looked gratified and nodded as though to remind me that he had brought her to me. "You are pale," he went on solicitously, almost tenderly. "Do you get out enough?"

"Why yes."

"But you can't take walks as you did in England. Would you like to take a walk now? We'll go round the gardens and to the pagoda. What do you think?"

"Yes," I said, "I would like to. I'll get a wrap."

I went upstairs, looking in at Jason who was fast asleep and came down to Adam.

Walking was always an interesting experience at The House of a Thousand Lanterns. In the courtyards were paths over which were arches covered in climbing plants; one could walk right round the house along these paths. But I always felt it was restricting within the walls, and I liked to go through all four gates and outside to the pagoda.

This we did and I could never step inside the place without thinking of Joliffe's waiting for me there and stepping out to catch me as I entered.

The pagoda was eerie by night. A faint shaft of light shone through the roof and fell on the face of the goddess.

"I should have loved to see it as it was when it was a temple," I said.

Adam agreed with me.

"What a still night. It will soon be the Feast of the Dragon. On the fifth day of the fifth month he is supposed to be in a cruel mood. You'll see some fantastic craft on the water and on land too. Dragons breathing fire, and gongs beating to divert him from his wicked purposes."

"Jason will be thrilled. And I must say I always find these processions exciting. I suppose I shall get used to them in time . . . if I stay here."

"But of course you'll stay here. Your life will be spent here . . . and at home. But that's how it is with all of us."

"How long before you go home?" I asked.

"It depends on so much."

"Shall you go before the year is out?"

"No," he answered firmly.

"Doesn't it depend on what happens then?"

"I know I shall be here for a while yet."

I thought: He will wait until the year is up and then he will ask me to marry him.

I looked at him in the moonlight. He looked strong, serene, and a man of dignity. He was as dogmatic as he ever was but I was no longer annoyed by that in him. It amused me. I liked to pit my wits against his. In a way he was a challenge to me as Toby would never be. Toby would agree with me almost always—or at least try to see my point of view; Toby was kind and good and reliable. I was not quite sure of Adam. I only knew that the more I was with him the more he interested me.

I said suddenly: "I woke up this morning with the conviction that the secret of the house is in the lanterns."

He turned abruptly to look at me.

"How in the lanterns?"

"I don't know. That's what we have to find out. It is called The House of a Thousand Lanterns. Why?"

"Presumably because the lanterns are a feature of the house."

"*A thousand* lanterns," I said. "I am going to count them. Has anyone ever counted them?"

"I don't know. And what would be the point?"

"I don't know that either. At least I would like to satisfy myself that the thousand are here. Will you join in the counting?"

"I will. When?"

"Tomorrow. When the house is quiet."

"It's a secret then?"

"I think for some reason I don't want anyone to know I'm counting."

"Tomorrow then," he said, "when the house is quiet."

It was afternoon; the house was silent; only occasionally through a window would one hear the tinkle of the wind bells. Adam and I stood together in the hall; he was holding a paper and pencil for we were determined to take careful notes. We started counting in the hall, and went into the lower rooms watching the total grow.

"I'm beginning to wonder," said Adam, "how they can possibly have crammed a thousand into the house."

"That's what we will find out."

Through the lower rooms we went; then through every room on the next floor. One of the servants saw us and must have wondered what we were doing but his expression was impassive, and we had become used to this seeming indifference to our actions.

We came to the top of the house which was used very little. There was nothing Occidental in these rooms which had retained their Chinese furnishings. There were Chinese rugs on the floor—in lovely shades of blue and almost all decorated with a dragon; there were paintings on the walls of delicate misty scenes such as originated in the paintings of the T'ang Dynasty and have been part of Chinese Art ever since.

"They are really exquisite," I said. "We should use these rooms."

"It's such a big house. You would need a very large family to fill it. Perhaps," he added, "you will have that one day."

"Who can say?"

He came a little closer to me and for a moment I thought: Could I wholly trust Adam? I would never really know him, but that could make life exciting. There would always be discoveries to be made about him.

He seemed to sense my thoughts. He touched my hand briefly and I thought then that he was on the point of asking me to marry him.

He withdrew his hand immediately and for a moment was almost aloof. He would be thinking that it was not seemingly to mention marriage until I had passed a year in widowhood. How different from Joliffe!

"Such a big house," I said lightly. "I wonder whether the house was built for the lanterns or the lanterns put in as an afterthought?" I hesitated for a moment, then I cried out: "Perhaps that's the clue. Was the house built to accommodate the lanterns?"

"Whoever heard of such a thing? Who would want a thousand lanterns?"

"The builder of this house did or he wouldn't have put them in. Adam, I am now certain that the clue to the mystery is in the lanterns."

"Well let us get on with the counting as the first step."

So we went on counting.

"How many now?"

"Five hundred and thirty-nine."

"But we have nearly been through the entire house and we're nowhere near a thousand. You see, it's a misnomer. It's not The House of a Thousand Lanterns."

I went to the window and looked out. I could see the pagoda which never failed to excite me. Adam came and stood beside me. "It fascinates me," I said. "I suppose because it's part of the old temple. Can you picture it, Adam?"

He nodded and half closed his eyes. "The pagoda with its three decorated stories and the decorations then would not have been crumbling away with time," he mused. "The temple itself . . . where this house now stands; the paved path leaing to the portico, colossal stone figures supporting each of the granite pedestals—terrifying guards to the temple probably representing Chin-ky and Chin-loong, great warriors of renown. We would pass through a door and the lay-out would be rather as it is now; we would step into a courtyard with trees and paths and then through another door and so on until we came to the temple. There the priests would be assembled; imagine the chanting and the sound of gongs as they kowtowed to the great goddess. Priests would have lived close to the temple for it would be their duty to tend it and worship daily."

"I can picture it all so clearly," I said. "I can almost see the priests wandering out from the pagoda and hear the sound of the gongs. But I believe you think I am too fanciful for good sense."

"What I do think is that you combine the two. The danger is that you let one get the better of the other and if that should happen to be the imagination you might make a false judgment."

"You are too prosaic," I said.

"Then if I am so and you err on the side of fancy we are well matched."

I moved away from him. "What is the tally now?" I asked.

He looked at the paper. "Five hundred and fifty three."

"There is not much left. Where are these thousand lanterns?"

When we had gone through the house the figure was five hundred and seventy.

"Of course," I said, "this would include the courtyards too. Come. We have to complete the list."

We went round the courtyards and into the pagoda. There were thirty more lanterns which brought our total to six hundred.

"There couldn't be any more," said Adam.

"There must be."

"Then where are they? We are still far off the grand total."

We stood in the pagoda and I looked up at the glint of sky through the roof. I listened to the faint sound of the wind bells which I fancied had a teasing note.

I said: "I am sure the solution to the mystery is in the lanterns. I know it is. It's almost as though the house is telling me."

"You're not like the famous Joan who heard her voices, are you?"

"Perhaps."

"Oh, Jane!"

I turned to him a little impatiently. "I don't expect you to understand. But I first heard the name of the house when I was a schoolgirl and I knew it was going to mean something to me. The house and I have a kind of . . . what do you call it? An affinity. You don't understand that, Adam, do you?"

He shook his head.

"But I believe it. I think Sylvester knew it. I'm determined to discover the secret of this house."

Adam laid his hand on my arm. "The secret," he said. "There is no secret. The house was given to my great-grandfather; it was built on the site of an old temple.

Legend grew up round it for this reason. Then someone had the idea to fill it with lanterns."

"And it became The House of a Thousand Lanterns. A thousand though!"

"It's clear that the house is crammed full of them and they couldn't have got any more in. No, a Thousand Lanterns was a picturesque name so it was used without relation to the actual fact which was that they hadn't quite reached that number."

"Your reasoning sounds logical."

"I'm always logical I hope, Jane."

"I suppose I'm not . . . always."

"It's said to be a feminine characteristic to be a trifle illogical at times."

"And you deplore this feminine trait in me?"

"Actually I found it not unattractive but . . ."

"But what, Adam?"

"I think that all women like you need someone to take care of you."

There is something about the pagoda, I thought. People grew reckless in it.

I said quickly: "We are some four hundred lanterns short. We must discover where they are. If we do we may have the answer to the puzzle."

On the way back to the house we argued a little. Adam was sure that the house had been given the name because it sounded poetic; I was certain that there was more in it than that. I continued to believe the secret lay among the lanterns.

Lanterns! I dreamed of lanterns. The first thing I saw on waking was the lantern which hung from the center of the room and in which an oil lamp burned all night. When the Feast of Lanterns came I was delighted with the varying kinds as I had been the previous year. Sylvester had been alive then and we had gone to the waterfront to watch the procession. What an array of lanterns of all kinds! Many of them made of paper and silk. Ours were of wrought iron and solid.

After the Feast of Lanterns I studied the patterns on ours and to my delight I saw that the scenes engraved on them were similar. They all depicted lovers. In the lower hall the lovers were meeting for the first time. There girls were dancing, throwing ribbons exactly as I had seen them do at Chan Cho Lan's house; all the lanterns on the first floor seemed to bear the same engraving; but when I went upstairs I saw that those on the next floor were engraved with two lovers hand in hand.

On the next floor the lovers were embracing.

It was exciting. It was a kind of story. They met; they fell in love, and I presume the last engraving suggested marriage.

This was interesting but when I told Adam he laughed at the idea. It was clever, he said, to have discovered that there were different engravings on each floor, but that seemed the natural sequence of events and he could see nothing in that which might lead to the discovery of the secret.

"Have you ever heard the maxim 'Leave no stone unturned'?" I asked.

"Many times," he replied.

"Then don't you think it's a good one, because I do and that's what I'm doing now."

He smiled at me indulgently; but I continued to be fascinated by the lanterns.

The time was approaching when the Feast of the Dead would be celebrated.

It was so like last year. I remembered well how the atmosphere in the house had changed; how duties were neglected and an air of excitement pervaded the house. Everyone it seemed had some dead relative who must be made aware that he or she was not forgotten.

From the windows I could see people making their way to the hills; riding near I saw the burial grounds where the mat houses were being erected beside the tombs which were all shaped like the last letter of the Greek Alphabet, Omega, which might have been significant. Food was being taken up to the hillside and soon the feasting would begin.

I was transported back to the day when Sylvester had died. I remembered our last conversation. I could not forget the sight of him, his face emaciated, parchment color, and he so certain that the end had come and so anxious that he should have left his house in order.

And on the night of the 5th April—the culmination of the Feast of the Dead—he had died.

It had seemed a coincidence at the time. Now the thought occurred to me more insistently that it was strange that he should have died on that night.

The day had come. There was tension throughout the house. All the servants had gone to the hillside.

"You will wish to be with your grief," Lottie told me before she went off. "You do not feast at his tomb but you will think of him."

"Yes," I answered, "I shall think of him."

"In China lady mourn for lord three years. Foreign spirits mourn only one."

"Sometime they mourn for a long time, Lottie."

"You say one year and you marry."

"I said I should not marry before one year."

"But you will marry. House want it."

"You are still worrying about the goddess losing face because a woman owns the house built on her temple?"

Lottie gave her enigmatic giggle. "House pleased now soon there be master."

She had a basket full of titbits from the kitchens which she was taking to the grave of her ancestors.

"Must take care of ancestors," she said. "It is the

greatest sin not to. Buddha says a good man cares for his dead. If I did not I should never go to Fō."

I nodded for I had discussed Fō with Sylvester. It was the paradise inhabited by the followers of Buddha—a kingdom of gold where the trees bore glittering gems instead of fruit. It was dominated by the magic seven. There were seven rows of trees, seven fences, and seven bridges and the bridges were made of pearls. Above it all presided the Buddha seated on a lotus flower. Everything in Fō was perfect. There no one was ever hungry nor thirsty; there was no pain and no one ever grew old. It was the hope of everyone, man and woman, to reach this paradise and only through good deeds could he or she achieve it. And as man's chief duty was to respect and cherish his ancestors one of the most important days of the year was the Feast of the Dead.

I went to the sitting room. There was Sylvester's empty chair. I wished that he were alive so that I could tell him how grateful I was to him, how I would never forget that I owed him everything.

I could not say that I did not cherish my possessions for I did. I was proud to be the head of the business he had built up. I was proud too to be the owner of The House of a Thousand Lanterns.

How still the house was! They would all have gone to the hillside. Ling Fu had taken Jason to the Go-Down; he and Toby were riding that afternoon. I should have accompanied them but I had a strange feeling that I wished to be by myself in the house on this afternoon.

No sound . . . only the occasional tinkle of the wind bells and every now and then in the distance the sound of a gong as some procession made its way to the hillside.

There was one thought which kept going round in my head: Your year is up.

As I stood there in Sylvester's room and thought of his last hours, there was great booming throughout the house.

It was as though everything had become alert suddenly waiting.

I felt my heart begin to hammer. I had an idea what this might mean.

It was the gong at the side of the porch and meant that we had a visitor.

I knew who it was and the familiar joy and apprehension fought with each other.

I went to the door.

He said: "I've come as I said I would."

Then he stepped in and shut the door behind him.

"I was determined not to wait a minute longer," he went on.

And he took me in his arms and I knew that I had never seriously considered Adam or Toby, for there was no one in the world for me—nor ever would be—but Joliffe.

The Money Sword

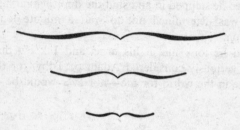

My calm calculations were swept away. I knew I could never have married anyone but Joliffe. I was as yielding, as eager, as much in love as I had been all those years before. I was reckless. I did not wish to look beyond the immediate future. I knew that I was not going to let anyone stand in my way.

I was living in the Paradise of Fō where every perfection conceivable to the desires and needs of man had been realized. Everything around me was beautiful. If the trees did not bear glittering gems as fruit, then the leaves and the blossoms were a hundred times more beautiful. Everything had changed. The world had become a wonderful place.

I was in love and I would allow no barrier to stand in the way of my happiness.

I was going to marry Joliffe.

Then I realized that there were people who had to be hurt by all this happiness. There was good Toby for one. I shall never forget the stricken look on his face when I told him.

"So he has come back," he said blankly.

"Yes," I replied soberly, "and as soon as he came back I knew it was inevitable."

Toby did not answer. He looked out of the window of his office onto the water scene, the sampans crowded together with the lines of washing stretched across them, the scurrying to and fro of the rickshaw men. He had seen thousands of them in his time but he was not seeing it then; he was seeing the dream he had conjured up of our being together; and Joliffe, returning to shatter that dream.

All he said was: "Jane, you should not hurry."

"I know," I answered gently. "I am not hurrying really. You know my story. Joliffe and I were together for three months and Jason is our son. It had to be, Toby."

He nodded.

"And Jason?" he said.

"Joliffe is Jason's father," I said.

He turned away.

"There'll be changes . . . here?" He waved his hand vaguely.

"You mean in the business? Oh no. I intend everything to go on as before . . . as Sylvester would wish it."

Toby shook his head.

"Toby," I said, "it will make no difference to you. Understand that. You were Sylvester's manager and you will remain mine."

But he only looked at me sadly. I felt angry suddenly that my pity for him had to intrude on my happiness.

Adam was less resigned. At first he seemed stunned; then he was angry. Angry with fate, with Joliffe and with me.

"So you are going to marry Joliffe!" he said.

"I thought I was married to him before," I replied gently. "And now that he is free and I am free . . ."

"You're crazy," he said.

"I don't think so, Adam."

"I should have thought you would have had the sense to know that it won't work."

"My instincts tell me it will."

"As usual you believe what you wish to believe in face of the odds."

"Joliffe and I love each other, Adam. We always will."

"Was that why he deceived you, gave you a child to bring into the world that had no name until you married my uncle to give it one?"

"It was not Joliffe's fault. He did not know that his wife was still alive."

"You are very innocent, Jane. That is why I fear for you."

"I'm fairly experienced of the world and capable of taking care of myself."

"It doesn't seem so. You got yourself into a mess and found a way out, and here you are ready to do the same again."

"I don't agree with you."

"No, of course, you don't. He only has to come back with his plausible tales and you are ready to give up . . ."

I was sorry. I knew he was hurt. I knew that over the last months he had thought it possible that I might marry him. I had even vaguely considered it might be possible myself. I should have told him right from the start what I knew in my innermost thoughts: that there would never be anyone but Joliffe.

There was something which disturbed me even more. I

was doing the very thing that Sylvester had warned me not to do. He had made it clear that he did not trust Joliffe. And surely he had indicated that he wanted me to marry Adam when he had made him Jason's guardian. He could not have spoken more plainly than that. I could not get Sylvester out of my mind, and the memory cast a shadow over the ecstasy of my reunion with Joliffe. In my sleep I could hear his voice. "It's like a pattern repeating itself."

"It's different now, Sylvester," I was murmuring one morning when I awoke.

It *was* different. Joliffe was free now, and I loved Joliffe so much that I could never be happy without him.

Even Lottie seemed dismayed.

"So the year is up," she said, "and you marry. The house not pleased."

"What nonsense," I retorted.

She lifted her hands in a helpless gesture; her halfmoon brows shot up. Then she put a finger to her lip. "You hear. You feel."

"I hear nothing," I said.

"It is here. The house not pleased."

There was fear in her eyes; she looked over her shoulder as though she really believed some deity might step out and strike us dead. "The goddess is warning," she said. "You hear it in the wind bells. It says: 'Not good.'"

"This is such rubbish," I said. "At one moment the goddess lost face because a woman owned the house; she wanted me to find a husband quickly—so you said. Well now I am going to be married and she is still not pleased. What *does* she want?"

Lottie shook her head helplessly.

"You not understand, Great One," she answered.

But if the goddess was displeased along with Lottie, Toby, and Adam, there was one who was delighted.

Jason placed his hands on my knees and looked up to me, his face glowing.

"I'm going to have a father," he said.

"Yes, Jason," I told him. "You'll like that, won't you?"

He laughed. Of course he would like it.

"I'll tell you something," he said, standing on tiptoe.

"Yes, Jason?"

"He was my real father all the time. He told me."

So we were married and I was happy as I had never thought to be again.

Joliffe had wanted us to have a honeymoon but I had refused this. We should have had to take Jason, I said, if we went away. He protested a little but finally agreed with me, for where would we have gone but into China? I did not think it was suitable to take Jason with us.

"What does a honeymoon matter," said Joliffe. "It's the marriage that's important . . . being together for the rest of our lives, Jane. What a prospect."

It was a glorious prospect. Now we could start dreaming and planning as we had years ago. We were taking up the threads of our story.

They were glorious days when sometimes he and I went out alone leaving Jason in the care of Lottie; at others we took him with us. We crossed to Hong Kong Island and picnicked on the sandy shore of Big Wave Bay. Sometimes we rode out and watched the workers in the paddy fields. We shopped in the Thieves' Market and peeped into temples where joss sticks gleamed on altars and incense hung in spirals from the ceilings; we had our fortunes told by the pavement seer and the trained sparrow picked out a lucky card for us. We took a small craft and sailed in the bay and threw coins to the small boys who delighted to dive down into the clear water to pick them up. Everything seemed beautiful—the rocking sampans on the water, the women with their little babies in slings on their backs, the rickshaw men in their coolie hats, the stall owners squatting on the pavements to make their bargains with those who bought their goods. It seemed a beautiful place with the smell of dried fish everywhere and the painted signs hanging from their shops adorned with the exquisite Chinese letters.

It was Paris again. It was the love haze which enveloped everything, heightening the colors, making the world dance, touching even the work-worn faces of the Hakka women with beauty.

One early morning when he lay awake and talked of the wonder of being together again Joliffe mentioned Jason, and how delighted he was in the boy, how he had thought of him constantly and had railed against a fate which had separated him from his son.

"And that will of Sylvester's," he said. "To think that Sylvester named Adam as his guardian. I don't like it, Jane."

"It is only in the event of my death," I said.

He held me tightly against him. "Don't mention such a thing.

"My dearest. It's something I won't think of. It's not going to happen anyway. I'm going to die before you."

"No," I said fearfully.

We clung together until Joliffe burst out laughing.

"Who's going to die? We're young, aren't we? We're healthy. We're going to live for years and years, both of us. In any case you're younger than I am, Jane. So I shall die first."

"I couldn't bear it," I said.

He stroked my hair. "What fools we are! Assuring ourselves that we are going to be the one to die first because we don't want to be the one who's left. One of us will have to be that."

For a moment we were silent then we laughed and made love and we were happy, but before we slept Joliffe said: "It should be altered, Jane."

"How . . . altered?"

"Easily. Sylvester nominated Adam as Jason's guardian. I couldn't tolerate my son's having anyone but me as a guardian. But that's what would happen if you . . . Jane . . ."

"If I were to die," I said. "Yes if I died tomorrow, everything would be in trust for Jason and Adam would be his guardian."

"Sylvester didn't know that you and I would be married," said Joliffe.

I was thoughtful. What had Sylvester thought? He knew of the sorrow I had endured when I had lost Joliffe. Had it ever occurred to him that Joliffe would come back, that we would be married? Of course it would have, yet he had appointed Adam—perhaps for that very reason.

Joliffe said: "It should be changed. It would be quite easy. You could do it. You have the power to."

I said: "I'm not sure. These were the terms of the will."

And I thought: Why did Sylvester appoint Adam? Because he believed that I would marry Adam? Because he had *wanted* me to marry Adam?

"Jane, you should do it. Jason is my son." He kissed my ear tenderly. "I cannot endure its being written even that someone else could be his guardian."

"I am not going to die for a long time, Joliffe."

"My God, no! You are going to live for years. And we will go back to England. Shall we go to Roland's Croft? I always liked the place. It's yours now. I wonder what old Mrs. Couch is doing? Wouldn't she be glad to see us. And wouldn't you like to go?"

"How I should love to be there . . . to go to the forest where we met! Do you remember that day? The rain . . . how we sheltered?"

"I shall never forget it."

"I don't think Jason remembers much of Roland's Croft now."

"He'll have to go to school. We'll all go back then."

"Yes," I said, "we'll all go back. Toby can look after things here. But first I want to discover the secret of the thousand lanterns."

"We'll discover it together . . . among other things."

"Such as?"

"You will have to learn how much I love you and how much you love me."

"Do you think I don't know how much I love you now?"

"These are far more important matters than this affair of the lanterns. And, Jane, just to put things right, step along to the lawyer and make it clear. I am my son's guardian and no one else."

"I'll go to see the lawyer tomorrow," I promised.

Mr. Lampton, who had looked after Sylvester's affairs for many years, listened intently to what I had to say. It was clear that he knew a great deal about family matters and I was sure Sylvester had discussed the advisability of making his will as he had.

"It was Mr. Sylvester Milner's wish that your son Jason should be cared for in the event of your death. It was a matter of grave concern to him."

"I know," I said, "but my son has a father. No father would wish to see someone else guardian of his son."

Mr. Lampton nodded. "It is the business which is really in question, Mrs. Milner. Mr. Sylvester Milner wished his nephew Adam to be in charge of it in the event of your death before your son was of an age to manage it himself. This nephew was the one he chose."

"I know he considered him to be steady and serious, which he is. But my marriage changes everything. My husband is working with me now. It would surely be wrong to put what he is building up into the hands of someone else . . . if I were to die."

"There is nothing, of course, to prevent your making a will in favor of your husband, but there is a possibility that in the event of your death Adam Milner might dispute that will. No court would give another man custody of a child when his father was living, but the business would provide certain complications. I repeat, though, that you could certainly make a will in favor of your husband."

"I will do that," I said.

When I went back to the house I told Joliffe what I had done.

"So you will make sure that Jason is not taken from me."

"I certainly will and without delay. Adam will be annoyed, I expect."

"Don't tell him."

"You think that's fair?"

"Look here, Jane, you aren't going to die. Things are going on as they are now for years and years. There's no need to make bad feeling."

"But he will go on thinking . . ."

"Let him. If he has any sense he'd know I'd never allow anyone to take charge of my son."

"Somehow I feel it's only right . . ."

He put his arms about me and laughed. "We don't want any bad feeling. Relations with Adam are fairly friendly just now. Let's keep them that way."

"And if I were to die . . . ?"

"You're not going to. I won't allow it."

He held me tightly and temporarily I forgot my qualms. But that night I dreamed of Sylvester. In the dream he regarded me steadily for a few seconds, just as he had all those years ago at Roland's Croft when I had told him I was going to marry Joliffe; then he shook his head sadly.

It was a few weeks later when I had the first of my dizzy turns.

I felt perfectly normal when I awoke but as I rose from my bed the room seemed to totter about me. It was only for a second, but as I sank back onto my bed I felt a wave of nausea.

I lay back on my pillows. Joliffe had left early that morning. He was going to see some ivory pieces some miles out of Kowloon.

I felt better as I lay back and I wondered whether I was pregnant. There were no other signs. I contemplated what joy it would be to have another child.

I had made the will nominating Joliffe his son's guardian and providing that he should be in charge of everything until Jason was of age if I should die. It was absurd but it gave me an uneasy feeling to think of dying and leaving Jason and Joliffe. I supposed most people felt that when they made wills.

Joliffe was working enthusiastically in the business which had been Sylvester's. He had said how could a husband and wife be business rivals? Toby didn't like it very much, although he gave no obvious indication of this, but I knew him well and I detected a certain sadness in his manner.

With some men there might have been a very difficult situation but Toby was not the sort to assert himself. He ran the business; he was the best manager in the profession. Adam would have liked to get him, but he remained loyal, even now when Joliffe had come in and was taking over so much.

Lottie came and stood by my bed.

"You not well this day, Lady?"

"I felt a little unwell when I got up."

"You stay in bed."

"I don't think so. I'll get up now."

She looked at me anxiously and brought my dressing gown to wrap round me.

I stood up. The room was steady. "I'm better now," I said. "It was nothing."

Yet all that day I felt listless and in the afternoon I slept.

I thought of Sylvester. He used to complain of feeling dizzy when he arose and on such days he would sleep a great deal and feel disinclined to do anything else.

It was a wretched feeling.

Poor Sylvester, I thought. I wish I could let him know that he is often in my thoughts.

A ship was in from England—always an exciting occasion. Then they would be busy at the loading docks and in due course goods would be brought into the Go-Downs. We were always interested to see what our London agents had shipped out to us.

There were passengers, too, and for so many it was a time of entertaining old friends. Joliffe had had hosts of friends and he liked to entertain them at the house. Social activities had increased since my marriage. Sometimes we would have dinner in the Chinese manner which was always of great interest to people who had just arrived, particularly if they had never before been to Hong Kong. The servants liked it too. They thought the house gained "face" when Europeans came and were entertained in the Chinese manner.

Joliffe was becoming more friendly with Adam. It was as though he wanted to make up for what he had done about the will, but I always felt uneasy in Adam's presence because of this and would rather have told him what I had done. After all, it was reasonable. Naturally I would wish my husband not only to be the guardian of my son but of his business interests, particularly as he was now working in that business. Adam was a logical man; I was sure he would understand.

A great deal of that reserve which had irritated me at the beginning of our acquaintance returned. I was glad, however, that he and Joliffe were on better terms.

When Joliffe wanted us to give a dinner party he always included Adam and he would say: "Is there anyone you want to ask? Let's make it a family affair." This was typical of Joliffe's free and easy nature, and consequently Adam was often at The House of a Thousand Lanterns.

One night a rather disturbing thing happened.

I opened one of my drawers and inside found an object I had not seen before. Puzzled, I took it out and examined it.

It was a number of old coins in each of which a square hole had been made; they were held together by a piece of iron which was shaped like a sword with a cross hilt.

I could not understand who had put it there.

As I sat turning it over and examining it, Lottie came in.

She said: "You wish to wear your blue silk dress tomorrow. I wash . . ."

Then she stopped short and stared at the object in my hand.

"What's the matter, Lottie?" I asked.

She stood staring; then she hunched her shoulders and giggled, but it was the giggle I had come to associate with horror or fear.

"You have money sword," she said. "Who gave?"

"It was in my drawer. Who put it there and what is it? What does it mean?"

She shook her head once and turned her face to the wall.

"Oh Lottie," I said impatiently, "what is it all about?"

"Someone put," she said.

"Undoubtedly someone has put it into my drawer. Do you know anything about it?"

She shook her head.

"It must have been one of the servants."

"It for luck," she said. "Should hang over bed."

I looked at the wall. "I don't think so," I said. "But I'd like to know who put it there."

Lottie picked up the money sword gingerly and looked at the coins.

"You see date on coin. If these hung over bed the Emperor who reign when coins made will watch over you. Keep evil spirits away."

"That's interesting," I said.

She nodded. "These always in houses where death come. If there is murder in the house . . . or someone take own life . . . then there must be a money sword to keep evil spirit away and protect."

"In a house where there has been murder or suicide . . . But . . ."

Lottie shook her head. "There are bad spirits when someone takes life . . . his own or someone else. So in such a house there is money sword. It protect."

"There has been no murder or suicide in this family."

Lottie was silent.

"All right," I said. "I'll wear the silk tomorrow. Good night Lottie."

She lingered. "You hang over bed," she said. "Keep good here, evil out."

I shook my head. "It's an interesting piece. I wonder who put it into my drawer?"

I told Joliffe about it.

"Joliffe, have you ever heard of a money sword?"

"Of course. Fascinating things. The Chinese are very superstitious about them."

"Lottie told me something about it."

"The old ones fetch quite a price. It depends on the date of the coins, of course. They hang them up over their beds as a sort of charm. They're used in houses where there has been violent death and particularly in case of suicide."

"One was put in my drawer. I wonder who put it there? You didn't, Joliffe, did you?"

"My dear, if I was going to make you a present of such a thing I wouldn't have hidden it in a drawer."

"But who could have put it there?"

"Did you ask Lottie?"

"She knew nothing. She was quite upset though. Apparently it's a sort of talisman."

"Interesting," said Joliffe.

Then we forgot it for we could not yet overcome the sense of excitement which being together brought us. I thought of the talisman later though.

We were to give a dinner party and had decided that it should be in the Chinese manner. All day long dishes were being prepared and there was a pleasant bustle of excitement among the servants.

Joliffe was eager that the dinner should be a success, and when Adam promised to take our guests to Chan Cho Lan's house afterwards for a dancing display, he was delighted.

"You'll meet the Langs," said Adam. "He's an old friend of mine. His wife died recently and he's remarried. It'll be her very first visit to China. She's said to be rather charming but a little emptyheaded. She'll be enthralled with everything."

Toby and his sister were invited and so there would be a certain amount of business talk. I was apprehensive to contemplate that the two men who had hoped to marry me would be there with my husband.

As I dressed for dinner in a green silk gown I looked at myself critically in the mirror and tried to see myself as Joliffe saw me. I was neither bad- nor good-looking; I had a certain vitality and a good deal of poise—acquired since my marriage to Sylvester and heightened during my year of widowhood. In the last months I had softened a little; I had become vulnerable, as one always must be when one loves.

I considered this as I studied my reflection. To love

was perhaps a mixed blessing. One could not have love without fear because one must always fear for the loved one. If Jason suffered from some childish ailment I suffered agonies in my imagination seeing him dead and following his coffin to the grave. All because I loved. And now Joliffe . . . I was terrified when he was not at my side. I visualized all sorts of dangers that could befall him in this country. To love was to suffer. I was indeed vulnerable.

And this ordinary-looking . . . no perhaps that was not fair to myself, perhaps I should say this tolerably attractive though not devastatingly so young woman, had had three suitors—all men of ability and some charm.

I saw the faint turn up of my lips; the flash of cynicism in my eyes. But then I was a woman of great means. I had so much more to offer than myself.

And yet I could not believe that these men were mercenary . . . not entirely so. Joliffe loved me; he had told me so a hundred times. And Adam and Toby? They told me too in a different way. Adam's aloof dismay and suppressed anger showed me; Toby's sad resignation.

It's strange, I said to myself. I'm sure they have some regard for me but my fortune may tip the balance in my favor.

In such a mood I went down to dinner.

Adam was right about Mrs. Lang's being a little feather-brained. She was a very pretty woman with fair fluffy hair; and she talked incessantly in disjointed sentences many of which she failed to finish.

Hong Kong was marvelous. She had heard of course . . . but had not guessed how truly wonderful. Darling Jumbo . . . that was her husband . . . had said she would be enchanted and, my dears, she was. All those boats! What a sight! Mind you she wouldn't want to live on a boat . . . And the little babies on their mothers' backs! It was a wonder they didn't fall off . . .

She was inclined to dominate the conversation with her

insouciant chatter which must have been very trying for those who were interested to talk of more serious matters.

Mrs. Lang had known Joliffe in London and was quite clearly more interested in him than in the other guests. She tried to talk to him all the time across the table.

I was trying to listen to Jumbo who was telling me about a vase he had found. It was of porcelain decorated in green and black enamel and might be of the Ch'ing Dynasty. At the same time Mrs. Lang was saying to Joliffe: "My dear, what a terrible time it was . . . Poor, poor woman. And all that fuss. So distressing for you . . ."

Joliffe said: "It's in the past. It's best to forget it."

"You are so right. It's always best to forget such unpleasant things. And now you have this marvelous wife . . . But my poor, *poor* Joliffe . . . So sorry I was for you. All that in the papers . . . and people being so unpleasant. They always are, I mean they always want to *blame* somebody, don't they? And if it's a wife . . . or a husband . . . the first thing they do is suspect the other one . . ."

I must have shown clearly that I was not listening to the description of the Ch'ing vase, for Jumbo said: "My dear Lilian, you talk too much."

"Darling Jumbo, I do, don't I? But I had to tell Joliffe how desolate I was . . . That terrible time . . . It's past now and he's happily married and I'm so . . . so happy for him."

Joliffe was looking intently at me. I lowered my eyes. I was afraid. There was something I did not know and it was about Bella.

The man called Jumbo must have become accustomed to rectifying his wife's blunders; he said smoothly: "I was explaining about this Ch'ing vase. I must show it to you sometime, Joliffe. I think I'm going to place it with the Comte de Grasse. He is most interested. Have you seen his collection?"

"Yes," answered Joliffe. "Magnificent."

"This will be a fine addition."

I looked up and met Joliffe's eyes. He was trying to soothe me. It was an expression I knew well. It meant: I can explain.

I had seen it before.

There was never such a long party. The guests came back to the house after the dancing display and it seemed hours before the last rickshaw had departed.

In our bedroom I waited for Joliffe. He seemed long in coming.

As soon as he came in I said: "What was that woman implying?"

"That Lang woman. What a stupid featherbrained creature she is! I wonder at Jim Lang's marrying her. He should know better at his time of life."

"She was saying something about . . . Bella."

"Yes about Bella. What did she say?"

"She said something about your being blamed. Bella *is* dead, isn't she?"

"Bella is dead," he said.

"Joliffe, please tell me what she meant."

He sighed. "Need we go into this? Bella is dead. That incident in my life is closed forever."

"Are you sure it's closed, Joliffe?"

"What do you mean? Of course I'm sure. Look Jane, it's late. Let's talk about it another time."

"I have to know now, Joliffe."

He came to me and laid his hands on my shoulders, wooing me with his charm. "I'm tired, Jane. Come. Let's go to bed."

I stood firm. "I should never sleep. I want to know what she meant."

He put his arm about me and drew me to the bed. We sat down on it together.

"She was referring to Bella's death."

"She died of an incurable disease. It was aggravated by her accident. That's what you told me. Wasn't it true?"

"It was true . . . in a measure."

"It must either be true or not true. How could it be true in a measure?"

"Bella died because she was the victim of an incurable disease. That's what I told you."

"But it was only true in a measure. What does that mean?"

"I didn't tell you that she took her own life."

I caught my breath.

"She . . . committed suicide. Oh, Joliffe, that's terrible."

"She had been to a specialist. She knew what was to come. She would get progressively worse and the end would be . . . painful. So she took her own life."

"Why didn't you tell me?"

"I didn't want to distress you. It wasn't necessary to tell you. She was dead. I was free. That was all that concerned you."

I was silent for a while and then I said: "How?"

"She jumped from a window."

"In the Kensington house?"

He nodded. I could see it clearly. The top room that looked out onto the paved garden with the solitary pear tree.

"Albert and Annie . . ." I began.

"They were very good . . . very helpful as you can imagine."

"What did that woman mean about the blame?"

"There was an inquest. You know how pontifical these coroners can be. It came out that we were not exactly living in harmony. There was a certain amount of censure."

"You mean you were blamed."

"Not by anyone who understood. It was just whispering and so on."

I shuddered.

Joliffe held me against him. "Don't take this so hard, Jane. It's over. It's nearly three years old. There's no point in raking it all up. I wish to God that woman had never come here." Gently he undid the fasteners of my dress. "Come," he went on. "It's no use brooding on what's past."

"I wish you'd told me," I said. "I hated finding out like that."

"I would have told you, in time. I didn't want to spoil things now."

I had heard him use almost those identical words. He had married Bella and thought her dead in the accident but he had not wanted to tell me, and I had had no notion that she existed until she appeared with her devastating news, just as now I had not known until I was told through the lighthearted conversation of a frivolous guest that Bella had taken her own life.

Joliffe soothed me. He loved me so much. He wanted our happiness to be perfect. Was he going to be blamed all his life for one youthful piece of folly? He had married Bella, thought her dead and married me. We had to forget the ugly tragedies which were behind us. All was well between us now.

He could always calm me; he would always make me see a rosy future. That was his power. He could show me that as long as I had him beside me and could keep him beside me, I would be happy.

So he lulled me to a sense of security. I did not want to look beyond this night with Joliffe's arms around me.

But later next morning when I was alone in our bedroom I opened my drawer and there was the money sword lying there.

I could hear Lottie's voice: "A protection against evil . . . the evil that comes into a house where there has been suicide or violent death."

Violent death, I thought. That could mean murder. Murder need not be violent. It could be a quiet slipping away.

I saw Sylvester's face in my mind—the emaciated face, the skin the color of parchment, drawn tightly over prominent bones.

Then I thought of him as he had been when I first saw him in the Treasure Room. He had been different then.

Violent death. Suicide . . . or murder.

I picked up the money sword. To bring good luck in a house where evil had been.

A talisman.

Someone thought I needed it. Who? And against what?

There was real fear in the house now. It was there like a presence. It was stalking a victim. Who was that victim? Was someone warning me that it was myself?

II

The question of who had put the money sword in my room continued to haunt me. It had become of increasing importance. It was no use asking the servants. I had come to realize the manner in which their minds worked. They wished to please and therefore it was a matter of etiquette with them always to give the answer which the questioner most wanted to hear. Truth was not as important as good breeding. They were docile, mild, and industrious; they wished to live peaceably; if I asked any of them to do something they would agree at once because not to do so would be bad manners. If it was impossible for them to do as they had promised they would smilingly lift their hands and invent some excuse, when they had not intended to do it from the start. To refuse was unthinkable.

It took me quite a long time to grasp this and to realize the difference between our Occidental and their Oriental ways.

I knew that if I asked who put the money sword into

my room I should be met by shakings of the head because whoever had put it there would sense that he—or she—had upset me by doing so.

I decided there was nothing I could do, but I could not forget the thing. Whenever I went into my room I would open the drawer to see if it was still there.

As I turned the money sword over in my hand and tried to decipher the date on the coins I was thinking of Bella, standing at that window. What must her thoughts have been? How desperate she must have been! How did people feel when they were about to end their lives?

Poor Bella! She had seemed so truculent when she faced me. Perhaps that very truculence was a mask to hide her misery.

I could see it all so clearly; the small garden with the crazy paving and the solitary pear tree; the windows of the mews cottage which faced the house and in which Albert and Annie lived.

And because of what had happened to her someone had thought I needed protection and had placed a money sword in my room.

Through the market I went with Lottie beside me. She bargained fiercely with the traders and ordered the goods which were to be sent to the house.

A mandarin's procession was passing by. Lottie and I stood watching it. There was the exalted gentleman carried in his sedan chair by four bearers. These bearers had their attendants, for this was a very grand mandarin. In two files his attendants marched beside his chair. Two at the head of the procession carried gongs which they sounded every few seconds to warn people that a great man came this way. Behind the men with the gongs came others with chains, which they rattled as they walked. Some in the procession shouted at intervals something to the effect that a very grand man was among them. Members of the mandarin's household followed, several carrying huge red umbrellas and others holding up boards inscribed with the mandarin's titles.

As the procession passed, barefooted men and women stood in respectful poses, heads down, arms hanging at their sides. Any who looked up and did not show the proper respect received a cutting blow from one of the canes carried by several members of the mandarin's household.

As we stood watching this show Lottie whispered to me: "Very great mandarin. He go to the house of Chan Cho Lan."

I was hailed suddenly.

"Why if it isn't Mrs. Milner." And there was Lilian Lang smiling at me, her china blue eyes dancing with curiosity.

"Did you see the procession? Wasn't it *fun?*"

I thought she should be wary for so many of the people spoke English and to hear a mandarin's procession called "fun" might result in a loss of face for the mandarin and his customs.

I thought then that Lilian Lang was the sort of woman who could always be relied on to find the most tactless remark and produce it at the most awkward moment.

"He's going to that mystery woman's house," she said in a loud voice.

Lottie was watching us with a smile on her face which could have meant anything.

I said: "Let us get into a rickshaw and have a chat."

"Come with me," she said. "It's not far and we'll have some of the ever-ready tea. It's quite a ceremony, isn't it? Never mind, I was always one for a cup of tea."

I told Lottie to go back in one rickshaw and I went in another with Lilian to her house.

There she talked interminably while we drank tea together.

I said: "You go out alone?"

She opened wide baby blue eyes. "But why not? It's quite safe, isn't it? Nobody would hurt *me*."

"I always take Lottie with me."

"The little Chinese girl . . . or half Chinese, isn't she? She's a pretty creature. I said to Jumbo: 'What an enchanting creature that little girl is . . . If I were Jane Milner I'd keep my eyes on her.' "

"Why?" I asked.

"These husbands," she said archly.

I felt resentful, and told myself she was a stupid woman.

"And particularly Joliffe."

"Why particularly Joliffe?"

"He's always so popular, isn't he? Poor Joliffe, that was a dreadful business. There was such talk. There always is, isn't there?"

I wanted to scream at her to be silent and on the other hand I wanted to learn all I could.

I said: "I was not in England at the time."

"That was a mercy because of what happened. They couldn't say you were involved, could they? Do you mind talking about it?"

I wanted to slap her face. Did I mind listening to insinuations about my husband! What was she suggesting? That people had thought *he* had killed Bella?

"You know what they are . . . the law I mean. And then the press. She had a sister who gave them her life story . . . and there was this about Joliffe's thinking her dead and marrying again. That was you, wasn't it? What a romance. Well, it looked as if . . ." She paused.

"What?" I said.

"Your being there . . . you see, and having married him . . . or thought you had . . . and then she died like that . . . and here you are married to him . . . and there's the dear little boy. It's a good thing you're here . . . far away. People *will* talk, won't they? Jumbo says I should keep quiet. I'm afraid I say things when they come into my head. But I'm sure it's going to be all right now. You're so happy, aren't you? So much in love. And Joliffe is so charming . . . quite fascinating. I always thought so . . . so did lots of others. Jumbo was quite jealous. Then I suppose lots of husbands have been. Joliffe is that kind of a man, isn't he?"

I just wanted to get away. I wished I had never come with her. But I had had a feeling that if I did not she would shout her gossip throughout the market.

I wished she had not come to Hong Kong.

She saw how distasteful I found the conversation so she made a studied effort to change it.

"That mandarin . . . what a sight! He has a high opinion of himself. It seemed a shame to slash the poor things just because they didn't kowtow. He was going to that Chan Cho Lan. She's supposed to be a very great lady. Her fingernails are four inches long." She giggled. "It seems an odd way to judge breeding. It means she never uses her hands. If she did those glorious nails would break even though they are protected by jeweled nail sheaths. They say she's a courtesan really. She and her girls whom she's bringing up to make great marriages . . . well, alliances. A sort of charm school! Jumbo says that what she does is train the girls and then makes bargains with rich men—mandarins and the like and some rich Europeans—and sells them for so many taels of silver. Poor girls, they don't have much to say in the matter. She's a sort of marriage broker . . . without the marriage. She's been a famous courtesan too . . . still is perhaps. Lots of men visit her. Isn't it exciting?"

I wanted to get away from her. I was more than ever sorry I had come. I could not think much about Chan Cho Lan. My mind was full of what must have happened in the house in Kensington when Bella's broken body had been found on the crazy paving.

About this time Toby fell ill. Joliffe took the opportunity of going into everything and was gratified by what he found.

"Sylvester was a good businessman," he conceded. "No doubt about that. And Toby Grantham was his good and faithful henchman. Your affairs are in excellent order, my darling."

"They're our affairs really, Joliffe," I said.

He shook his head ruefully. "Everything is yours. That was the stipulation."

"It's different with husband and wife. I hate to think we don't share."

He kissed me with great tenderness.

After a few days I called to see Toby.

His sister Elspeth opened the door for me and there was about her mouth that prim look of disapproval which I had noticed since my marriage.

The house shone and sparkled. No one would have believed it could have been in Hong Kong, it was so very Scottish in every way. Elspeth was the sort of woman who would not relinquish one of her customs. I was sure the house looked exactly as her home in Edinburgh had done.

There was crocheted macramé on the mantelpiece and some Staffordshire ornaments—one of a Highlander in his kilt playing the bagpipes. The cushions were of tartan which I knew was the color of their clan.

"Ee," she said, "so you've come to see Tobias."

"I hope he's better?"

"Aye, he's mending."

She had a rather delightful Edinburgh accent which was more pronounced than Toby's.

She took me to his bedroom. He was propped up in bed studying a batch of invoices.

He looked pale and tired.

"Hello, Toby," I said. "How are you?"

"Much better, thank you." His eyes showed his pleasure in my coming. "It was good of you to call."

"Nonsense. I was anxious."

"I'll soon be back."

"We miss you, Toby."

"He'll need to get his strength back before he returns," said Elspeth shortly.

"Of course."

"And it's far from strong he is now. He's been doing overmuch." She nodded her head, implying that he had worked too hard for those who didn't appreciate him.

She would never forgive me for marrying Joliffe when I might have had her brother.

I sat down and we talked of business for a time until Elspeth interrupted and said it was time he rested.

So I said goodbye to him and in her sitting room she boiled a kettle on a spirit lamp and infused the tea. She brought out shortbreads, homemade from a Scottish recipe, while she talked to me about Tobias who had been overworking. She scorned me for refusing what she believed to be the best possible match any woman could have made—and all in favor of a man who had already proved himself to be unreliable. At least that was how it would appear to her prosaic mind.

"He worries," she said, nodding towards the ceiling, indicating the room in which Toby lay. "I say to him: 'It's no concern of yours what others do. People make their own beds and must lie in them.' "

"That's true enough," I agreed.

"Tobias takes after his father. Gentle, too ready to take a step backwards. My mother used to say there wasn't a better man in the world than the one she married and there wasn't one more backward in coming forward either. I reckon you could say the same of Tobias. I wish he'd go back to Edinburgh."

"We couldn't do without him here."

"I was thinking of what *he* could very well do without."

"He wouldn't want to go, would he?"

"I couldn't be sure. All I know is that this life here is

not for him. He'd be better in a good Scottish warehouse. He never took to the way of life here."

"You've been here a long time, Miss Grantham."

"Oh yes. I came out with Tobias and that was fifteen years ago. He was a young man of twenty then. I was ten years older. I wasn't letting him come out to a place like this without someone to keep a home for him."

She was fiercely militant in his defense. That was why she was angry with me for hurting him.

"Being here all this time, you learn things," she said. "I know quite a bit about this place. It's not always what it seems."

"Is anything?"

"Perhaps not. But this is more different beneath the surface than most. I used to be afraid that he'd take a Chinese wife. I don't like mixed marriages."

"Did he ever seem likely to?"

"No. Tobias only seemed likely to marry the once. I used to worry though thinking he might take up with some Chinese girl like some of them do." She frowned.

"But he never did."

"He is a man who has the utmost respect for religion and marriage and all that goes with it. He's a very good man, is my brother Tobias. That's rare. So many of them here have their mistresses. It isn't always known. You've heard of Chan Cho Lan, the fabulous marriage broker, with her school for young Chinese girls?"

"Yes, I have visited her."

"These girls of hers . . . she arranges transactions for them . . . and not only with her fellow countrymen. Quite a number of European gentlemen keep their mistresses, you know. They say that matchmakers or brokers follow an old Chinese custom and it's an honorable profession. Of course it is all done with tact. A man has to pay at least twenty thousand taels of silver for a girl and give her a servant, and there is a clause in the contract that when he has had enough of her he must find a husband for her.

He must let her grow her nails and keep them four inches long—which is another way of saying she is not to do housework although how she could with her feet in the condition they're in I can't imagine. That is what happens and it is all glossed over and Chan Cho Lan is treated with great respect. People visit her and are her friends. I wonder why and what her business would be called in Edinburgh, or Glasgow."

"Different countries have different customs, Miss Grantham."

"Oh yes, there are excuses. What I'm saying is that my brother Tobias has never been near such establishments in all the years he has been here. He is a good and virtuous young man and one day, please God, he'll make a good husband for some woman who has the good sense to recognize this."

I found Elspeth Grantham as uncomfortable as Lilian Lang.

And I had the impression that they were both trying to warn me.

To warn me. First there was the money sword—now these two women.

Was I becoming fanciful? Was I looking for warnings where they did not exist?

Jason at least was happy. He had never missed a father but that did not mean he did not appreciate having one. He adored Joliffe. There could be no question of it. He spoke of him always as My Father. In fact he talked constantly of him and there was hardly a sentence in which "My Father" did not figure.

There was no doubt Joliffe had a gift with children. He never looked down on them and they never failed to look up to him. He didn't treat them as children; he could enter into a game as an equal. He seemed to be able to cast off the years and be a boy at a moment's notice, yet he was always the hero, the one who knew. He always made sure he had plenty of time for Jason. It was as though he must make up for the years of their separation.

They would fly their kites together, for Jason had never grown tired of his kite. Often I saw them high in the sky. No kites are quite like Chinese kites. I used to watch them from the topmost rooms of the house and all my fears would evaporate as I thought of them together.

They were often on the water. Joliffe used to take Jason out in his lorcha and they used to go out round the bays and across to Hong Kong Island. They knew many of the people who lived in the floating villages and sometimes when I saw Jason he would call a greeting to a woman with her baby on her back or some fisherman busy with his nets.

Joliffe made friends with the utmost ease. He was well known as Adam could never be. I thought Jason would be the same as his father.

Before my marriage I had been the center of Jason's life. It was to me he always came for comfort; he did often now, but there were two of us and I could see that Joliffe represented security to him as I could never have done. There had always been in Jason's attitude towards me a certain protectiveness. It strengthened now, but it was Joliffe who was the strong man to whom he himself would turn. I was pleased in a way. I suppose every boy needs a father and certainly Jason could not have had a more devoted one.

It was not only that Joliffe represented security; it was this ability to be a playmate which was so appealing. They played guessing games together; they shared secret jokes from which even I was shut out.

Watching them I used to ask myself why there had to be this nagging fear, this occasional awareness of impending disaster. Why did I have to think so often of poor Bella taking herself to the window and flinging herself down because life was so intolerable? Why did I have to think of Lilian Lang's gossip and Elspeth Grantham's covert warnings?

Joliffe and Jason used to play Chinese shuttlecock. In this, instead of batting a cork into which a circle of feathers had been stuck, the feet were used. They became quite adept at it and their favorite place for playing was just outside the walls of the house—near the pagoda.

It was while they were playing this game that they found the trap door.

They came into the house full of excitement. I was lying down.

I had felt a little unwell on rising. There had been a return of the dizzy feeling I had had before. It had passed, but always on such days I felt a certain limpness and a desire to rest for a few hours in the afternoon.

I heard Joliffe calling me, so I slipped hastily off the bed and went to meet him.

"Jane! Come and look. A most extraordinary thing. I'm sure it's a trap door."

I went out of the house with them; through the three gates to the pagoda.

The square slab of stone had been covered by bushes and Joliffe had to pull them aside to show me.

"Jason's shuttlecock landed right in the middle of all the bushes," he explained, "and when I hunted for it, I found this."

I was excited.

Since my marriage my enthusiasm for discovering the house's secret had been overlaid by other matters. Now it returned.

I was sure we were on the verge of discovery.

Joliffe was excited too. We must have the bushes cleared away. We must take up the paving stone. We had both made up our minds that this led down to a subterranean passage which would take us to the legendary treasure.

We were unsure what we should do. Should we try to

lift the stone ourselves or get others to help? Joliffe thought it would be unwise to call in outside aid. The House of a Thousand Lanterns had been a legend so long that it would attract much attention.

"I'm sure," I said, "that there is some other part of the house which we have to discover. It's The House of a Thousand Lanterns and we have only found six hundred."

Joliffe's enthusiasm was boundless. He was certain that we were going to find a fortune. He imagined the richest treasures. "You know what it's going to be, Jane. The original Kuan Yin. It'll be worth a fortune."

"We should give it to some museum, I suppose," I said.

"The British Museum," said Joliffe. "But what a find!"

"The Chinese might not wish it to go out of the country."

"They would have to put up with that."

"Well, we'll see, but we haven't found it yet."

We cleared away the shrubs and sure enough there was the slab of stone, but there was no indication of how it could be lifted up.

The only thing to do, said Joliffe, after we had thoroughly examined it for a secret spring, was to take it up and see what was below.

It was difficult to perform such an operation without attracting some attention. The servants were aware of what we were doing. Adam called and joined us.

"This could well be the answer to the mystery," he said, his eyes gleaming.

We were all visualizing a flight of steps which would lead us to vaults below the house in which the treasure had been hidden.

What a disappointment was in store for us! After a great deal of effort the men managed to move the stone slab. There was nothing but earth beneath it—the home of what looked like thousands of scurrying insects.

Joliffe and Adam lifted the slab between them and as

they did so it slipped from their hands. They jumped hastily out of its way as it dropped and fell crashing against the wall of the pagoda.

There was a rumbling sound of falling masonry.

We were all too stunned by the disappointment to see immediately what damage had been done, but when we stepped inside the pagoda to my horror I saw that the crash had broken off part of the crumbling stone goddess.

The top of her head lay in fragments on the floor.

Joliffe said with wry humor: "It seems the lady has indeed lost face."

It was inevitable that the damage to the statue should be considered an evil omen.

We—the foreign devils—had done this. The goddess would be angry with us. Carelessly we had allowed her image to be damaged.

Lottie said: "Very bad for house. Goddess not pleased."

"She'll know it was an accident."

She shook her head and giggled.

When I came in later that day I found the money sword hanging on the wall over the bed.

"Who put that there?" I asked.

Lottie nodded indicating that she had done so.

"Why?"

"Better," she said. "It protect. Is best place."

It was clear that she thought I was in very special need of protection.

I said: "Listen, Lottie. I didn't lift the slab. I was just looking on. Why should I be the one to need protection from the goddess' wrath?"

"You Supreme Mistress. The House belong you."

"So, therefore, I'm held responsible for what goes on in it?"

Lottie implied by a nod that this unfair assessment was true.

To please her I let the money sword remain where she

had put it. Yet I must confess I felt a little comfort to see it there. I was becoming superstitious as people often do when they fancy they are threatened.

III

Lottie and I had been to the market and were returning in a rickshaw when passing Chan Cho Lan's house I saw Joliffe. He had clearly come out of the house. I watched him walk the short distance to The House of a Thousand Lanterns.

I shrank into my seat. I asked myself why I should be so disturbed. I knew of course. I kept remembering scraps of conversation which I had heard at Elspeth Grantham's house; I could see the sly smile of Lilian Lang.

"What would you call that sort of business in our country?"

Why should Joliffe visit the house of Chan Cho Lan? I asked myself. Then it was as though Lilian Lang answered: She makes arrangements . . . not only for Chinese but for Europeans . . . And Elspeth Grantham: Many of the men here keep Chinese mistresses in secret . . .

I laughed at the idea. How could that be? I thought of the intensity of the passion between us. There was nothing lacking in that side of our marriage. Joliffe couldn't pretend to that extent.

Yet why would he be going to the house of Chan Cho Lan?

He had arrived home when Lottie and I returned. I went up to our bedroom. I knew he was there because I could hear him whistling the Duke's famous aria from *Rigoletto*.

I went straight to him.

"Hello, darling," he said. "Been shopping?"

"Yes."

I looked at him. One of the qualities about Joliffe was that when you were with him you could believe anything in his favor however incredible. It immediately seemed impossible that he could have gone to Chan Cho Lan's house for anything but business reasons.

I said: "Where have you been today?"

"Oh, I went to the Go-Down and then out to see an Englishman who is interested in that rose quartz figurine. You know the one I mean."

But I had just seen him coming from the house of Chan Cho Lan.

My apprehension was only faint because he was there giving me his frank open smile. But I knew my fears would grow when I was alone, and I had to say something.

"You've been to Chan Cho Lan's house." For a moment he looked startled and I went on: "I saw you coming out not very long ago."

"Oh that . . . yes."

"I thought you'd been to see about the rose quartz figurine?"

"I have. I called in at Chan Cho Lan's later . . . on the way home in fact."

"Do you often go there?"

"Oh, now and then."

I looked at him challengingly. "Why?"

He came to me and put his hands on my shoulders. "The lady is a power in Hong Kong. She knows a great many people."

"Rich mandarins who are anxious to make . . . alliances?"

"Exactly. Rich mandarins who are also looking for valuable pieces or perhaps wish to sell them from collections which have been in their families for centuries. This is how we find our most exciting pieces."

"So you go there to meet these people?"

"I seize every opportunity. So does Adam."

"Does Toby go too?"

Joliffe laughed. "Dear old Toby. Elspeth would never allow him to set foot in the place. She'd be terrified he'd be seduced."

"And should I be terrified on your account?"

He held me to him. "Not in the least," he said. "You know I'm completely yours."

Of course I believed him.

Jealousy is insidious. One laughs at the idea that the loved one could be unfaithful; one tells oneself that to have imagined it is due to an intensity of love. But the doubts would come to me suddenly, and I would ask myself how much I really knew of Joliffe. This much I did know: he was extremely attractive—not only to me but to others. Lilian Lang would make sly references to this fact whenever I met her; and in Elspeth's prim smile there was a touch of righteous pleasure because those who made their beds had to lie on them.

Joliffe's first wife was discussed. I knew these women half believed that it was not illness which drove her to take her life but some failing in Joliffe.

Elspeth believed that once marriage vows had been exchanged they should be adhered to, no matter what happened. In her eyes Joliffe was unreliable and the fact that I had preferred him to her brother meant that I was a fool.

She had no more patience with fools than with rogues and therefore she implied that I deserved all that was coming to me.

When Lottie came to me with an invitation from Chan Cho Lan I accepted it eagerly.

This strange woman was of greater interest to me than ever. I wanted to see her at close quarters, perhaps even talk with her.

"She wish you take Jason," said Lottie.

Jason was delighted at the prospect and we set out with Lottie.

The pigtailed servant opened the gate for us and there stood the house in its courtyard—charming in the sunlight with its three stories one protruding over another and its ornamental roof.

This was a different occasion from the last for we were the only visitors. I wondered why she had wanted to see me, and the thought occurred to me that Joliffe may have told her that I had been anxious to know why he came here.

In the hall we waited. We heard in the distance the tinkling indeterminate timbre of Chinese music and then a servant came to conduct us into Chan Cho Lan's presence.

She was seated on a cushion and rising, gracefully swayed towards us.

She joined her closed hands and lifted them three times to her head.

"*Haou? Tsing Tsing,*" she said in her soft musical voice.

She looked at Jason and gave him the same greeting. He now understood that he must return it in the same way.

She said something to Lottie who told me: "Chan Cho Lan say you have very fine son."

We sat down; she clapped her hands, the long nail shields tapping against each other.

A servant ran in and she spoke to him so quickly that I could not follow. I guessed she was asking that tea be brought to her guests.

But it was not tea that came in. It was another servant holding by the hand a small boy.

He was exquisite, that boy; his black hair was combed flat about his head; his eyes were bright and like Lottie's were more round than almond shaped; his skin was the same magnolia petal shade. He dressed in blue silk trousers and jacket.

Chan Cho Lan looked at him impassively.

Then she signed and he came forward and bowed low to us.

Jason and he studied each other curiously. There was a deep silence in the room. Chan Cho Lan was watching the boys intently as though comparing them.

Jason said to the boy: "How old are you?"

The boy laughed. He did not understand.

"Is Chin-ky," said Chan Cho Lan.

I said I had heard the name before.

"Is name for great warrior," Lottie explained. "He be great warrior one day."

Chan Cho Lan talked rapidly to the boys who looked at Jason rather shyly.

"Chan Cho Lan say Chin-ky should show Jason his kite."

At the mention of the kite Jason was immediately interested.

"What sort of kite have you, Chin-ky? Have you a dragon one? I have a dragon one. My father and I can fly them higher than anyone else."

Chin-ky laughed. He was clearly fascinated by Jason who seemed so much bigger than he was himself.

Chan Cho Lan spoke to Lottie who rose.

"Chan Cho Lan say I take them to play in the courtyard." She waved her hand and I saw the courtyard beyond the window.

I nodded and Lottie went out with the boys.

As she did so, tea was brought in.

Chan Cho Lan and I sat by the window. The boys appeared. They were carrying a kite which was almost the size of Chin-ky. Lottie sat down on a seat there and watched them.

My cup was brought to me by Chan Cho Lan's servant. I sipped the beverage. It was hot and refreshing.

She said: "Your son . . . my son."

"He is a beautiful boy, your Chin-ky," I said.

"Two beautiful boy. They play happy."

The dried fruits were brought to me. I helped myself to one with a two-pronged little fork.

"Play kite," she said. "East and West. Yet . . ."

She did not seem to be able to go on. Yet I had the idea that she was trying to tell me something.

Jason and Chin-ky were able to communicate better than we were. Their heads were close as they released the kite. They stood legs apart watching it as it soared upwards, and as I watched them I thought how much alike they were.

Chan Cho Lan seemed to read my thoughts. She said: "They look . . . one like other?"

"Yes," I said. "I was thinking that."

"Your son . . . my son . . ." She pointed at me and then at herself. She smiled nodding her head.

"Two boys . . . boys better than girl child. You glad."

"I rejoice in my son," I said.

She understood that and nodded.

Somewhere in the house a gong sounded. It was like a knell because her next words were: "My son . . . your son . . . both have English father."

She smiled nodding but there was a glitter in her eyes which was malevolent.

Oh God, I thought, what is she telling me?

And then far off in the house I heard the gong again.

I was not sure how long we sat there watching the children in the courtyard. Jason was shrieking wildly as the kite mounted and Chin-ky leaped about in an ecstasy of pleasure. Every now and then he would pause to look at Jason and they would both laugh as though at some shared secret.

I was so much aware of her—her delicate perfume, the graceful swaying body, the tiny tiny feet in little black slippers, the beautifully expressive hands. I felt awkward and clumsy beside her. She was exquisite; she had been trained to captivate men. Everything about her was alien. I thought of my mother who had wanted me to be big and strong and who had bought new shoes for me when she couldn't afford them so my feet would have plenty of room for growing. It seemed a strange thought to have on such an occasion but then I was trying to shut out that suspicion which had come to me.

She was trying to tell me something and I dared not ask myself too insistently what it was. I knew that Joliffe came here. I had seen him, emerging from this house. He had only told me he had been here when I pressed him to. How often did he come here? What was his relationship with this alien yet beautiful and fascinating woman? He had been in Hong Kong at intervals since he was a boy. He knew so much more about it than I did. He visited this woman. Why? Was he telling me the truth? How could I know?

And when he was not with me and I remembered what had gone before, hideous suspicions insisted on creeping into my mind.

And this strange enigmatical woman, why had she invited me here? Why had she arranged for her son to play with mine while we watched them? Why had she wished me to see them together? Was it to show me the resemblance—yes there was an undoubted resemblance—between her son and mine?

They both had English fathers. Was she implying that they shared the same one?

At last the visit was over. Chan Cho Lan sent a servant to bring Jason in from the courtyard. He came reluctantly. Gracefully, Chan Cho Lan was indicating that we were expected to go.

Jason chattered about Chin-ky as we went back to The House of a Thousand Lanterns. He was nice but funny, he commented. His kite wasn't quite as good as Jason's own, but almost. "He can't fly it as high as my father can," he said complacently.

Lottie was watching me covertly.

"You like visit?" she asked.

I said it had been very interesting. "Why did she ask me?" I said.

"She want show her son . . . see yours."

Lottie giggled and I asked myself: How much does Lottie know? Or does she merely suspect?

I brooded on that visit to Chan Cho Lan. I said to Jo-liffe: "Chan Cho Lan invited me to her house."

"Ah. She likes to be on good terms with the family."

"She has a son . . . a little younger than Jason. She seemed very anxious for me to see him."

"The Chinese are proud of their sons. It would have been different had it been a daughter."

"Then I suppose she would have trained her to make some . . . alliance."

"Doubtless she would."

"She said the boy had an English father."

"She should know," replied Joliffe.

He seemed imperturbable and I was ashamed of my suspicions when I was in his presence. It was only when I was alone that the doubts returned.

Soon after that visit my health began to deteriorate. The dizzy spells were more frequent, the listlessness more persistent. What's the matter with me? I asked myself. All sorts of fears obsessed me. Suspicions kept coming into my mind. Chan Cho Lan . . . and her son; Bella and her untimely end. What did it all mean? I didn't believe these suspicions and yet I couldn't rid myself of them.

Sometimes I tried to talk to Joliffe about them, but when I was with him I thought they seemed ridiculous. How could I say to him: Are you the father of Chan Cho Lan's son? That was the suspicion which had come to me.

But how could I say such a thing? When he was there, bantering, tender, his eyes full of love for me, how could I in seriousness ask such a question?

And there was Bella. I wanted to know more of Bella. What had been the true relationship between them when she had thrown herself out of that window?

Joliffe hedged away every time I got near the subject. There was one thing I did understand about him. He wanted to live all the time in the sunshine. He lived for the moment. Some people said this was how life should be lived. He believed that everything would come right in the end; he wanted to push aside difficulties, anything that might seem unpleasant.

I was different. I liked to look unpleasant things in the face and decide what to do about them. I would always be the sort of person who looked ahead. I had done this when I married Sylvester. I had been looking then to Jason's future. Perhaps the basis of our attraction for each other was in the difference in our natures. If I upbraided Joliffe for his rather reckless and impulsive outlook, he teased me about my careful one.

I didn't talk to him about the change in my health. I tried to ignore it; sometimes when the awful listlessness was creeping over me I would go up to our bedroom and lie down for a while. A short sleep very often was all I needed. But it was a strange feeling and I kept thinking of Sylvester and how tired he had been on some days.

Lottie knew about it. She would creep in and draw the blinds; sometimes I would find her little face creased into lines of anxiety. She would lift her shoulders; the half-moon brows would shoot up and then she would give her nervous giggle.

"Sleep," she would say, "and then better."

One afternoon I slept longer than usual and awoke with a start. Something had aroused me. Perhaps it was a bad dream. Then I was aware that I was not alone. Someone . . . some *thing* was in the room. I raised myself

on my elbow. A movement caught my eye. Then I saw
that the door was slightly open and something *evil* was
there.

I caught my breath. I was dreaming. I must be. The
thing was there at the door . . . and luminous eyes were
watching me from a cruel face.

It was not human.

I gave a little scream for I thought it was going to rush
at me. Time seemed to slow down and I felt as though my
limbs were paralyzed and I could not move, such utter
terror possessed me I was completely defenseless.

But, mercifully, instead of approaching me the thing
disappeared. I caught a flash of red as it moved.

I sat up looking about me. My heart was beating so
fast that it was like a drum in my ears. It could only have
been a nightmare. But what a vivid one. I could have
sworn I had awakened and seen the thing. But I was
awake now. I couldn't have been dreaming.

Was I becoming so vague that I didn't know whether I
was asleep or awake?

I got off the bed. My legs were trembling. I noticed that
the door was open. Surely I had not left it open?

I went to it and looked out into the corridor. At the
end of this was the figure of the goddess. I half expected
her to move.

I forced myself to walk up to her.

I put out a hand and touched her. "Nothing but an
image," I whispered.

It was a dream . . . a dream when I was half waking.
What else could it have been? I wasn't suffering from hallucinations.

No. It was a dream, but it had shaken me thoroughly.

I put on a dress and combed my hair. While I was
doing this Lottie came in.

"You sleep long," she said.

"Yes, too long," I answered.

She looked at me oddly.

"You feel well?"

"Yes."

"You look like you been frightened."

"I had an unpleasant dream, that's all. It's time the lanterns were lighted."

Joliffe went away for a few days. He was going to Canton to buy jade.

"I'm worried about you," he said. "When I come back we should go away for a while—you, I, and Jason." He took my face in his hands. "Don't take any notice of the old prophets of evil. They're bound to say that the goddess is displeased because part of her face fell off. That statue has been standing there for years and bits have been falling off for as long as I remember. But they'll make something out of it if they can."

"Don't be away too long," I begged.

"You can be sure I'll be back at the earliest possible moment."

When he had gone I went to the Go-Down. Toby was now recovered and was busy, he told me, catching up on everything that had piled up while he had been away. I tried to be animated about some bronze goblets we had acquired, but I obviously failed for Toby looked at me anxiously and said: "You're not well, Jane." His voice was tender. "Is anything wrong?"

I shrugged his enquiries aside. "I don't think it's anything. I just feel tired, listless sometimes, and a little dizzy in the mornings."

"You should see a doctor."

"I don't think it's bad enough for that."

"You should see him. You must."

"Perhaps I will."

"Is there anything else, Jane?"

I hesitated; then I told him of the figure I had thought I saw.

"You must have been dreaming."

"Of course, but it seemed so real and I actually thought I was awake."

"Some dreams are like that. It must have been a dream. What else?"

"I don't know . . . except that Lottie is always talking about dragons and I thought I saw one."

He smiled at me gently and I thought how kind his eyes were, how gentle and how I could explain to him what I could not to Joliffe.

With Joliffe I always wanted to be all that he desired me to. Joliffe hated sickness.

"It was a dream, Toby," I said. "It must have been for if it wasn't it was a hallucination. It seemed that I was awake. That's what worried me."

Toby smiled at me gently.

"Perhaps you had a high temperature," he said, "and this image came into your semiconsciousness. It's nothing, but I still think you should see a doctor."

"Perhaps I will," I said.

But I didn't. I couldn't bring myself to. It sounded so foolish. To be disturbed by a bad dream. The farther I grew from it the more it seemed like a dream on waking. That was what it was.

I did not need to go to the doctor: I could cure myself. I would cease to be afraid. That was what was at the root of my trouble. Fear. I had become too concerned about the legends which abounded here. This talk of bad joss, of goddesses losing face and turning their wrath on those who had ignored their code, had had its effect on me, and all because I could not stop certain questions coming into my mind. Sylvester . . . what had really been wrong with him? What had Bella really felt when she had stood at the window and thrown herself down? Why had her life become intolerable?

And now Bella was dead and Joliffe was married to me and I was a rich woman. I controlled many interests; and when I died these would pass into Joliffe's hands because he would hold them in trust for Jason. After I had made those arrangements in secret I had begun to feel ill!

These were thoughts that were chasing themselves round and round in my mind; this was why I had reduced myself to a state of nervousness as I asked myself whether it was true that I was threatened in some way.

Was the house really telling me this, or was it my ridiculous imagination at work again? And if I was threatened, who was threatening me?

"Go to a doctor," said Toby, his kind eyes full of concern for me.

I thought how easy it would be to tell him all that I feared. He would listen gravely. Strange that I should feel it might be easier to tell him than to tell Joliffe.

With Joliffe away it was easier to think. I tried to look at my situation dispassionately.

Words Adam had once used came floating back to me: "Do you realize the extent of your affairs? Do you understand all that Sylvester has left to you?"

I knew it was a great deal. I knew I had to hold it in trust for Jason, for that was what Sylvester had intended. Adam would have been his guardian and I had had that altered so that Joliffe should be.

And since I had made that change . . . ?

What is happening to me? I asked myself. Why should I feel ill? It is almost as though a curse has been laid on me. What have I done to deserve the wrath of Lottie's gods?

Or was it not the wrath of the gods I had to fear but the greed of men?

How long the days seemed without Joliffe! He was so vital that when he was with me my fears receded. I felt alive as I never could without him.

Even on this day when the terrible listlessness was upon me and if I sat down for a minute I found myself going off into sleep, I missed him terribly. How dull life would be without him!

Jason was restless too.

"How long is my father going to be away?"

"Only for a day or so," I told him.

"I wish he'd take me. He will one day. He said so."

"Yes," I said. "He's going to teach you about Chinese Art so that you'll be able to do what he does when you're grown up."

Jason sighed. "It takes such a long time to grow up," he complained.

He had gone to bed and I retired early. I was very tired and I took a cup of tea before I went to bed.

I had it in my room as I did very often on the days when I was not feeling well. I think some of the servants thought I was in the first stages of pregnancy. I myself had thought the strange sensations I was feeling might be due to this, but it was not the case.

It was something else.

Some strange malady. Toby had said that Europeans were often attacked by unidentifiable ailments when they lived for any length of time in the East. Our bodies would not always adjust themselves to the change. It was as simple as that.

As simple as that! I was just feeling an Eastern malaise and building up an atmosphere of tension and suspicion because of it.

But try as I might I could not shut out of my mind the thought of Bella. If ever anyone was haunted, I was by Bella. She was constantly in my thoughts. What agonies of mind must lead to suicide. It is the finality of life. Behind it is the decision that what lies beyond the grave is more bearable than one's lot in life. How desperate would one have to be to reach that conclusion?

I drank my tea and soon dropped into a sleep, from which I hoped there would be no dream.

But I dreamed vividly. When only half asleep I seemed to be plunged into some fantastic world.

Bella was there. She was saying: "It's easy. You let yourself fall . . . fall . . ."

"What happened, Bella?" I asked. "Were you alone when you stood by the window?"

"Come and see . . . Come and see . . ."

I dreamed that I rose from my bed. She turned and looked at me and her face was horrible . . . like the face I had seen in that other dream. I knew then what it was that looked at me. It was Death. Bella was going to her death. The face changed and it was Bella as she had been in the park. She said: "I have something to tell you. You won't like it, but you ought to know."

"I'm coming . . . I'm coming," I cried.

She held out her hand and I took it. She led me along the corridor and up the stairs. Her voice lingered in my ears: "You won't like it . . . but you ought to know. Come on," she whispered, "It's easy."

I felt the cold wind on my face. I felt myself gripped firmly. I was leaning out of a window.

I screamed: "Where am I?"

I was wide awake. I turned and saw Joliffe. He was holding me in his arms and Lottie was there.

This was no dream. I was in the topmost room. The window was wide open. I was vaguely aware of a crescent moon shining on the pagoda.

"My God, Jane!" cried Joliffe. "It's all right, I'm here."

"What happened?"

"We'll get you back to bed quickly," said Joliffe.

He shut the window firmly keeping one arm round me.

I saw Lottie, face pale in the moonlight. She was trembling.

Joliffe picked me up and carried me down to my room. There I sat on my bed and looked at him wonderingly.

"I'll get you some brandy," he said. "It'll do you good."

"I thought you were away," I murmured.

Lottie stood by watching with wide eyes.

"I came back an hour ago," said Joliffe. "I didn't want to disturb you so I slept in the dressing room." He was referring to the room which used to be Jason's, for since Joliffe's return Jason had moved to a room close by. "I was asleep, and something awakened me. It must have been when you walked out of the room. I was horrified to find your bed empty. I followed you. Thank God I did."

I glanced at Lottie. She looked like a marionette nodding there.

"I hear too," she said. "I come too."

I felt desperately weary. "What time is it?" I asked.

"Nearly one o'clock," said Joliffe. "Go to bed, Lottie. Everything will be all right now."

Lottie bowed her head and hurried out.

Joliffe sat on the bed and put his arm about me.

"You walked in your sleep," he said. "It's the first time you've done that, isn't it?"

"It's the first I've heard of it."

He took my hands and looked at me and I could have sworn that was real and fearful anxiety I saw there.

"I had a vivid dream," I said.

"You were at the window."

"I dreamed that Bella had taken me there."

"Oh God, no!"

"Yes, I did."

"It was a nightmare. You've been brooding on all that. It's over, Jane. It's done with. Put it behind you. You're letting it disturb you so that . . . this could happen to you. It's finished I tell you."

I looked up at the money sword hanging over the bed.

"Drink this now," he said, putting the brandy into my hand.

I obeyed.

"You feel better now," he said as though willing me.

"I'm tired," I said. "So tired."

"You'll sleep and in the morning you'll feel better."

It was true that I was exhausted. There was one thing I wanted and that was to sleep. Everything else could wait for that.

I was aware of Joliffe, bending over me, tucking in the sheets, tenderly kissing my forehead.

I did not awake until late next morning. Lottie told me that Joliffe had given instructions that I was to sleep on.

As soon as I awakened memories of the previous night came rushing back. I had walked in my sleep. It was something I had never done before. I remembered that night when I had awakened to find Sylvester in my room. I had led him back to his room and sat there watching him. "I walked in my sleep," he had said. "It is something I never did before in the whole of my life as far as I know."

I felt suddenly horrified. Sylvester had seen the Death figure. He had believed that it was a sign.

A cold shiver ran through my body.

What had happened to Sylvester was happening to me!

Those listless spells! He had suffered them too. They had been the beginning. And the doctor had found nothing wrong with him!

Sylvester had come to my room. He had wanted to see me so much that in his sleep his mind had been stronger than his body. He had wanted to tell me that he was going to die and that he was leaving everything to me. That was what had been uppermost in his mind. I had dreamed of Bella. That was what had been uppermost in mine. How had Bella died? That was what I had been asking myself. She had fallen from a window. Had she thrown herself down? Had she been led there?

No, no. I could not stop thinking of myself struggling in Joliffe's arms.

Lottie had heard me. She had come up too. Was that why . . . I would not think it even. Of course it had been as Joliffe had said.

"Of course, of course," I said aloud. "How could it have been otherwise?"

But how can one stop evil thoughts, fearful suspicions entering the mind?

Joliffe was solicitous. "My dearest Jane, you are not well. What is it? Tell me."

"I just feel rather tired," I said.

"But to walk in your sleep. You've never done that before have you . . . not as a child? Did your mother ever do it? Is it something that runs in families?"

"If I have done it I knew nothing about it."

"I think you ought to see Dr. Phillips. You need a tonic of some sort. You're run down. You've had a trying time."

"I came through my trying times. I should be all right now."

"But that's how these things affect people. Their nerves stay steady while they are going through their crises and afterwards when they've settled into a peaceful existence the strain begins to show. You need a pick-me-up!"

I shook my head. "I'll be all right, Joliffe."

Jason knew I wasn't well. He was worried too. I was deeply touched when he looked at me with anxious eyes. He feared he had neglected me. He had been so excited to have discovered a father that he had allowed his enthusiasm for one parent to submerge his care of the other. He had always looked after me, now I was ill.

He followed me around. He would come into my room in the morning and stand by my bed.

"How are you, Mama?" he would say and I wanted to hold him to me and hug him.

Joliffe understood. He always understood Jason.

"Don't worry, old chap," he said. "We'll look after her."

One afternoon he brought Dr. Phillips to the house without telling me.

I was resting on my bed as it was one of the listless days.

"Your husband tells me that you are not well, Mrs. Milner," he said.

"I feel quite well at times; at others there's a sort of lassitude."

"You have no pain of any sort?"

I shook my head. "At times I feel quite . . . normal. And then this seems to descend on me."

"Just tiredness?"

"And, er . . . rather violent dreams."

"Your husband told me that you had walked in your sleep. I think, Mrs. Milner, that you may not be adjusted to life out here."

"I have been here for nearly two years."

"I know. But this can manifest itself some time after the arrival. You are not apparently suffering from any malady except this lassitude and disturbed nights. The lassitude could be the result of the bad nights."

"I sleep most of the nights."

"Yes, but perhaps not peacefully, not deeply. And you have these nightmares. Perhaps you should contemplate a trip home."

"In due course, yes. At the time there is so much to be done here."

He understood.

"Still, I should think about it if I were you. In the meantime I will prescribe a tonic. I am sure that in a little while you will be yourself."

Afterwards I said to Joliffe: "You should have told me you were getting the doctor. Really, I felt something of a hypochondriac. There doesn't seem to be anything much wrong with me."

"Thank God for that."

"I'm apparently not adjusted to life in the East. He suggested a trip home."

"How would you like that, Jane?"

"I think I would like it very much but it isn't possible just yet."

"There's no harm in thinking about it."

"Would you like it, Joliffe?"

"I'd like anything that made you well . . . and happy."

He was so tender that my heart was touched. He had that power. He could make me happy by a look or an inflection of his voice merely. So much did I love him.

I started to think about home: Mrs. Couch getting the house ready; I could see her purring over Jason. She would hate it with the house deserted by what she called the upstairs folk. I thought of green meadows and the buttercups with the dew on them and the fields which looked like patchwork and the leafy lanes—the first primroses and the crocuses, white, yellow, and mauve peeping out of the grass. It all seemed so normal and so far away. I was sure I should be completely well there. And a great nostalgia swept over me.

I took the doctor's tonic and for a time it seemed to do me good. I became very excited when Joliffe found a Buddist temple gate which he was certain was of the ninth or tenth century A.D. Toby and Adam doubted this and I couldn't help feeling gratified when, after we had tracked down records, Joliffe was proved to be right. Sylvester had underestimated Joliffe, I told myself. He cared as passionately about the work as Sylvester had, and he would be as knowledgeable—perhaps even more so—when he reached his age.

I was feeling so well now that I laughed at my one-time fears.

Joliffe was delighted. "Old Phillips has put you right," he said, "and it's wonderful that you are quite well again."

But the listlessness came back. It was despressing after I had begun to believe that the doctor's diagnosis was correct and that I had not yet adjusted myself to life out here.

One afternoon I slept as I had before and awakened to that same horror. Dark shadows were in the room and I knew before I looked what I was going to see. A terror possessed me. This was real. This was no dream.

I raised my eyes and the horrible numbing fear swept over me for there it was in the open doorway, the hideous evil face, the frightful luminous eyes . . . and it was watching me.

In a few seconds there was the flash of red and it was gone.

I stumbled off the bed and rushed to the door, open as before but there was no sign of the thing in the corridor.

My nightmare again. And I had thought I was getting better. I tried to think logically.

I had imagined it. Sylvester had mentioned it and what he had told me had become imbedded in my mind to come out in this form when I myself was not well.

I shut the door and turned the key. I was alone in my room.

I looked over my bed. The money sword hung there as Lottie had placed it.

A Thousand Lanterns

The truth was brought home to me in a horribly disturbing manner.

The next day when I was drinking my afternoon tea in the sitting room, Jason entered the room.

He looked pleased to see me and came and sat beside me. He was being his protective self. He was very excited because the Feast of the Dragon was drawing near and Joliffe was planning to take us down to the waterfront where we would have a good view of the procession.

He chattered away excitedly and he asked if he could have a cup of my tea.

I poured it out for him and he gulped it down. He had

had fish he told me, which was very salty. He drank two cups of the tea.

That night my son was ill.

Lottie came and stood by my bed. She looked fragile and very lovely with her hair falling over her shoulders and her eyes wide and frightened.

"It is Jason. He is calling out strange things . . ."

I ran as fast as I could to his room and there was my son, his face very pale, his hair damp about his head and his eyes wild.

"He has nightmare," said Lottie.

I took his hot hand and said: "It's all right, Jason. I'm here."

That soothed him. He nodded and lay still.

Joliffe came in.

"I'll send for the doctor," he said.

We sat by Jason's bed—Joliffe on one side, myself on the other.

A terrible fear was with us that Jason was going to die. I was aware of Joliffe's anguish which matched my own. This was our beloved son and we feared for him.

Jason seemed aware that we were both there. When Joliffe had got up to greet the doctor he stirred uneasily.

"It's all right, old chap," said Joliffe, and Jason was relaxed.

Dr. Phillips was reassuring. "Nothing serious," he said. "Something he has eaten most likely."

"Could it have this effect?" I asked.

"It could have all sorts of effects. I'll give him an emetic and if that's all it is he'll probably be all right tomorrow—although perhaps a little weak."

I stayed with him all night—so did Joliffe. He seemed to be comforted while we were there and in a few hours had fallen into a deep sleep.

Strangely enough in the morning there was scarcely any effect of the previous night's indisposition. He was tired as the doctor had said he would be and I made him stay in bed throughout the day. Joliffe came and they played mah-jongg together.

As I watched their heads bent over the board I was so grateful that Jason was well and that we were together.

But later I began to reason with myself.

What had happened to Jason? Something he had eaten. The doctor's words kept coming into my mind.

And then suddenly, I remembered. He had come to the sitting room. He had drunk *my* tea.

Could it really be that Jason had drunk some poison which had been intended for me?

My son had been in danger and now I had looked this fear right in the face. It had been knocking at the door of my mind for a long time and I had refused to let it in.

Now it was there, and there was no turning away from it.

I had been ill—I who had never been ill in my life before. I had been listless when I had been noted for my vitality; I had had bad dreams, evil dreams, I who had previously been wont to put my head on my pillow and drift into deep and peaceful sleep.

And the reason: Someone was tampering with my food or drink. And when Jason had unexpectedly taken tea which was meant for me he had been ill.

I felt as though a light had suddenly shone in an evil place. But at least I could now see the evil when before I had been groping in the dark.

Someone was trying to poison me.

Who?

No. It couldn't be! Why should it be? Because if I were dead he would have control of what was mine and held in trust for Jason. Jason was very young; it would be many years before he could control one of the biggest businesses in Hong Kong. But Joliffe could advise me now. Advise. What was the good of that to a man as forceful as he was? I was always there to give the final decision and I

had Toby Grantham to back me up. If I were gone and
he were sole guardian of Jason, he would have the final
word. He would to all intents and purposes be master of
Sylvester's fortune.

I wouldn't believe it. But what was the use of saying
that when the thought had come into my mind?

The Feast of the Dragon was at hand. There were
many dragon feasts. It seemed to me that the people were
constantly trying to placate the beast or honor him. This
was in his honor.

Jason, completely recovered, chattered excitedly.

"My father is going to take us in a rickshaw. We shall
see it all. There are dragons who breathe fire."

Lottie was pleased we were going to see the procession.

When she was helping me dress she said: "When you
go away I go back to Chan Cho Lan."

"When I go away. What do you mean, Lottie?

She bowed her head and put on her humble look.

"I think you go away . . . sometime."

"What gave you the idea?"

"You go to England perhaps."

"You heard the doctor say that, I suppose."

"All saying it," she said.

"I hope you won't go while I'm here, Lottie."

She shook her head vigorously. "No leave," she said.

"Well I'm glad of that," I said.

"Chan Cho Lan say she may find union for me."

"You mean marriage?"

She lowered her eyes and giggled.

"Well, Lottie," I said, "that seems a good idea. Shall
you like it?"

"If I have good joss, I like. Not easy to find rich man
for me." She looked sadly down at her feet.

"You mustn't worry about them, Lottie. Your feet are
much more beautiful as they are than they would be
cramped and mutilated."

She shook her head. "No high Chinese lady has peasant's feet."

I knew it was hopeless to try to convince her on that point.

She told me that she had been brought up and educated with the high-born ladies. She had helped to bandage their feet with wet bandages and to keep them bandaged until the toes shriveled and dropped off. She told me how the little girls of six used to cry with the pain when the bandages dried and tightened. But in time they walked like the swaying of the willow and good matches were made for them.

"I used to think, Lottie," I said, "that you would be with me forever. That was selfish of me. Of course you want a life of your own."

She looked at me with mournful eyes. "Life very sad sometime," she said.

"Well, we'll always be friends, won't we? I shall come and see you when you marry. I shall give presents to your children."

She giggled but I thought she was a little sad.

"Hard to find husband," she said. "Only half Chinese and big feet."

I drew her to me and kissed her.

"You are as one of the family, Lottie dear," I said. "I think of you as my own daughter."

"But not daughter," she said, still sad.

She was merry though when we rode out in rickshaws to see the procession.

Jason sat with me and Joliffe and it was wonderful to see him jumping up and down with excitement. It seemed a long way from the night when I had feared he was going to die.

It was dark—the only time for such processions, for so much depended on the lighting. The sound of gongs mingled with the beat of drums. They sounded a warning note and always seemed ominous to me. There were lanterns, as always on such occasions, and they were of all colors, many of them with revolving figures inside.

Held aloft were flags on which were depicted dragons breathing fire. It was the dragons though which made up the procession. There were small ones and large ones— some held high like banners and others moving along on the ground. These were dragged along by men dressed as dragons and there were some men and women who made up other beasts—several of them to one dragon which appeared to breathe fire and shouted warnings as it trundled along.

The most attractive spectacle was that of two litters which were held high above the dragons and contained a girl apiece—two little creatures so lovely that it would have been difficult to match their beauty. They wore lotus flowers in their long black hair and one had a silk gown of delicate lilac color, the other was in pink.

Lottie called to me from the next rickshaw. "You see . . . you see."

I nodded.

"The girls," she told me, "are from Chan Cho Lan's."

I said to Joliffe: "Poor little things, what will their lives be?"

"Very pleasant, I imagine."

"I believe they will be sold."

"To a man who can afford to keep them and will give them the life of ease which they have been brought up to expect."

"And when he is tired of them?"

"He will keep them. He will not let them want. That would be to lose face."

"I'm sorry for them."

Joliffe said: "When you are in a foreign country you must adjust your ideas to those of that country."

"I still say poor children."

I started. One of the participants in the procession had come very close.

It was a man in a red robe and over his face was a mask.

I felt my heart begin to beat uncomfortably. I had seen that costume before—or something so similar that it might be a replica.

As he looked up at me I shrank back into my seat.

Joliffe said: "It's all right. Only part of the revelry."

"What a hideous mask," I said.

"Oh that," said Joliffe. "They call it the Mask of Death."

I had been well for some days. I had given up drinking tea since Jason's illness. I was certain now that what damage had been done had come through the tea.

It was a horrible realization. What should I do? I asked myself. If someone was trying to poison me through the tea and that someone realized that I had discovered this, would not the medium be changed? Would they not try something else?

I was in acute danger. I must turn to somebody. To whom? To my husband?

I shivered. There were times when I laughed my suspicions to scorn. That was when I was with him. It was only when he was not there and I looked facts in the face that I said to myself: He had the motive.

How is it possible to love someone and fear him at the same time? How is it possible to be so intimate and not to know the innermost thoughts of the other? We were lovers; our passion had not abated; ours was an intensely physical relationship. Yet in my heart the haunting suspicion persisted. Someone is trying to harm me, to kill me perhaps, but first to render me helpless, useless, to undermine my health. So that when I die no one is very surprised. And if this was indeed Joliffe how could he play the lover so wholeheartedly, so sincerely and devotedly.

Perhaps our need of each other was a thing apart—complete in itself. Perhaps our bodily union was quite

separate from that of our minds. Our attraction in the
first place I suppose had been a physical one, for my part
at least it had been what is called love at first sight and
that happens before one knows the other as an individual.
Had our love remained on that level all the time? Was it
indeed a fact that I did not know Joliffe any more than he
knew me? It must have been so for I could suspect him of
unimaginable horror. And he . . . could he really be capable of it?

Sometimes these theories seemed quite absurd. But at
others they were rational.

And now that I was feeling better they remained with
me, in fact were intensified. I had told myself that it was
because I was sick in body that my thoughts had been
sick too. My fevered imagination had built up a situation
which could not possibly exist.

But I was better and the stronger I grew the more convinced I was that I was in acute danger.

The old Jane was back in command. Jane with two feet
on the ground—logical Jane who liked to look life
straight between the eyes.

And what she saw was this: Someone is trying to harm
you, perhaps to kill you. And the reason could only be
because your death will give that one something that he
wants.

Joliffe on your death becomes the arbiter of a great
fortune. But Joliffe loves you, at least he says he does. He
was not too scrupulous as to how he discovered trade secrets. Remember his prowling in Sylvester's Treasure
Room? He was married to Bella and told you nothing of
this. Bella came back and you parted and then Bella died.
He lied to you about the manner of her dying. You married him and changed Sylvester's instructions that Adam
should hold his fortune in trust for Jason. And then you
began to be ill.

The case is black against him except for one thing: he
is your husband and he loves you. He says he does a

hundred times a week; he acts as though he does; at times there is a perfect accord between you and when he is not there life loses its savor.

It is not Joliffe. I won't believe it is Joliffe. It isn't possible.

It is someone else.

There is Adam. Adam, of the stern integrity. And what has he to gain? He does not know that the will has been changed and that it is Joliffe now who will take over. There would be no motive . . . if Adam knew. But Adam does not know.

How had you felt about Adam when you first knew him? There was something repellent about him. You disliked him. A cold man, you thought; but that changed. He wanted to marry you. He didn't say so but you sensed it. And if it had not been that you had loved Joliffe would you have considered Adam?

And now you are considering Adam. He was in the house when Sylvester died. Joliffe was not. But Adam does not live in the house now. No, but he is a frequent caller. And how did Sylvester die? It all seemed natural then . . . an aging man who had had a bad accident and gradually faded away, going into a decline until he died. And Adam had been in the house. But I could not believe that Adam was a murderer.

Surely Adam would have guessed that I would not allow anyone but Jason's own father to be his guardian. Yes, he certainly would; but he would also believe that Sylvester's wishes that he should be in control of the business until Jason was of age should be respected.

And Joliffe? I had made my will. If I died Joliffe would be in control.

Whichever way I looked it came back to Joliffe.

Each day I awoke to a sense of impending danger. I wished that I could have confided in someone, but who was there?

Lottie was no help. I loved the girl but it was so difficult for us to understand each other. I wished that I had a woman friend. There was Elspeth Grantham but she was scarcely that and I knew she disapproved of Joliffe if for no other reason that that I had married him instead of Toby.

It was indicative of my relationship with Toby that he was the one to whom I came nearest to confiding.

One day when we had finished our business he said to me: "You are better since the doctor's visit."

"Yes." I hesitated.

He looked at me earnestly and I felt a wave of affection for this calm self-effacing man, who was genuinely anxious about me.

"Sometimes," he said, "it is difficult to adjust oneself to a new environment."

"I have been here for some time now, Toby," I said. "I think I have adjusted myself."

"Then . . ."

My defenses weakened. I had to talk to someone and there were few I trusted as I trusted Toby.

He was waiting and I felt the words rushing out.

"I think something I'd taken was perhaps making me ill."

"Something you'd taken!" He repeated the words and there was incredulity in his voice.

"Jason was ill," I said. "He had drunk my tea. It seemed strange that he should have been ill after that. He had nightmares . . . and I am sure that his symptoms were the same as those which have been affecting me."

"Do you mean that there was something in the tea?"

I looked at him.

"It seems the last thing," he said, "unless . . ."

He did not need to say any more.

"I have always felt that strange things can happen in The House of a Thousand Lanterns," I went on. "The house affects me in an odd way. There are so many servants and even now I find it difficult to tell them all apart. Sometimes I think I am resented, Toby. Perhaps Sylvester was resented too."

"Who would resent him?"

I shrugged my shoulders. "You would think me fanciful if I said The House, wouldn't you?"

"Yes," he answered. His eyes were serious. "If it was the tea then you are in danger. For if you no longer take tea might something else not be used?"

"I can't really believe it, Toby. I think I've been run down and imagining things."

"And Jason?"

"Children have these sudden upsets."

"You've talked this over with Joliffe?"

I shook my head.

I could see that he was puzzled. "It's a lot of imagination," I said quickly. "I feel ashamed of my thoughts. I haven't told anyone."

I knew I had made some sort of a confession. My relationship with Joliffe was not what it should have been between husband and wife. If a woman feared she was being threatened wouldn't the first person she turned to be her husband?

"Don't treat this lightly, Jane," he said.

"No. I'll be careful. But I'm sure there's a logical explanation. I've been run down as they say. I've had bad dreams and even walked in my sleep. It happens to lots of people. All one needs is a tonic and one returns to normal."

"If something had been put in your tea," said Toby, "who could have done this? You don't think it could be one of the servants who has some crazy notion that you as a woman have no right to own the house? It's possible that one of them could get such an idea. I know how their minds work. Who would profit from your death, Jane?

There may be someone who would. It sounds mad. I wouldn't say this to anyone else. But you've got to be watchful. You've got to protect yourself. If you died Adam would get control of the business in trust for Jason. Adam could want that. Business is not good with him. I do know that. I think it would be very advantageous for him if he could get his hands on your affairs, which, of course, he would do in the event of . . ."

My heart was beating fast. I said: "I don't believe it. I don't believe it for an instant."

"Of course not. I'm sorry I mentioned it. It was just that I was looking for a reason . . ."

He trailed off miserably. He was worried about me. He would have been more so I know had I told him that I had brought about a change and that it was Joliffe who would now have control, Joliffe who would have the motive.

He said that Elspeth had mentioned the fact that she hadn't seen me for a long time. Would I call in to see her?

I said I would go now. Elspeth was a stern and practical woman; it was impossible to indulge in flights of fancy in her presence. I felt she would have a sobering effect.

"Ee," she said when we arrived, "so you've come for a cup of tea."

I said it would be delightful and she set about brewing it.

She had baked a batch of scones and Scotch baps. She made the tea at the table with her spirit kettle.

I drank it with relish.

"I wouldn't have any of the servants making it," said Elspeth. "There's only one way to make a good cup of tea and nobody seems to be able to do it here."

"Jane was saying the same," added Toby. "She likes to make her own tea. Have you got that spirit lamp you brought with you from Edinburgh? She could have that and make a cup when she fancied it."

"She's welcome," said Elspeth. "I don't use it now. But

they never will give it time to infuse. Only the Scots and mayhap the English . . ." she added grudgingly, "seem to know how to make a cup of tea."

She said she had heard I had not been well. She pursed her lips in the familiar manner. She was suggesting of course that I must expect ailments if I was so unable to take care of myself.

While we were having tea a visitor arrived. To my dismay and Elspeth's scarcely concealed annoyance it was Lilian Lang.

"I knew it was teatime," cried Lilian, "to tell the truth I couldn't resist coming. Those heavenly scones! And the shortbreads. What a cook you are, Miss Grantham, and isn't Toby the luckiest man to be so well looked after."

"I doubt he thinks so," said Elspeth, at which Toby assured her that he did.

She shook her head, half pleased and still resentful towards both her visitors—to me for refusing her brother and to Lilian for coming to visit her.

She poured out the tea and Toby carried a cup to Lilian.

"Delicious!" said Lilian. "Just like home. All this ceremony here makes me laugh. Jumbo is always telling me I mustn't laugh. They don't like it. But that tea ceremony really is too funny. When all you have to do is heat the pot and pour boiling water on the leaves. But what ones they are for ceremony! I think the women are rather pretty though, don't you? Now Mr. Grantham, you are not going to deny that."

"They have a certain charm," agreed Toby.

"You know the secret of this charm, don't you?" She was smiling archly at me. "It's the complete subservience to the male. They live to serve the man. They are brought up with that purpose in mind. Look at their poor little feet. I must say they do sway along rather gracefully. But fancy deliberately maiming oneself just to please some man."

"I suppose we have to accept the fact that it's an ancient custom," I said. "It's an indication of their social status."

"Of course. Things are different here. There is the mysterious Chan Cho Lan."

Elspeth pursed her lips. She did not like the way the conversation was going.

"I'll give you the recipe for my shortbreads if you like," she said to Lilian.

"You're an angel. Jumbo loves them. I don't know whether they're good for him though. He's putting on weight at an alarming rate."

"Good Scottish shortbread never hurt anyone," said Elspeth sharply.

"Nor good old haggis, eh! You must give me the recipe for *that*, too. What was I saying before we got onto this fascinating subject of food? Oh, Chan Cho Lan. Have you met her, Mrs. Milner?"

I said I had. She was certainly a remarkable woman.

"Beautiful in a way . . . if you like that sort of thing," said Lilian. She looked sly. "And lots of men do . . . Europeans, I mean, as well as Chinese. So feminine, so graceful . . . and with those inbred notions about the superiority of the masculine sex."

"When I met her she gave me the impression of having a high opinion of her own," I said.

"Of herself no doubt," retorted Lilian. "Then she sees herself as a liaison between male and female."

"I'll give you the recipe for the haggis if you like," said Elspeth.

"That's good of you, my dear Miss Grantham. Poor Jumbo. He's in for a treat. I wonder what my Chinese cook will make of it? At home we would probably call her a procuress."

Elspeth said: "I never heard such a thing."

"It depends on whether you call a spade a spade," went

on the imperturbable Lilian. "You know she has her school for young ladies. She has them when they are babies. Parents of unwanted children send them to her . . . if they are girls, and heaven knows in this place if a poor child happens to be a girl it's not wanted."

"I've seen them perilously wandering about the sampans," I said.

"You can be sure if a child falls overboard and drowns that child is certain to be a girl," said Lilian. "But she takes them in, teaches them to sing and embroider and some she makes into dancing girls to entertain her guests, clients perhaps one should say. It's quite a lucrative business I imagine."

"I suppose she cares for the girls from their babyhood."

"She does. It's not many years. Girls of twelve are ready to go into service as they say. It's all very honorable here and she's known as a matchmaker. Of course quite a lot of our gentlemen visit the establishment." She leaned towards me and lowered her voice confidentially. "We have to give them a little license, don't we."

"License!" cried Elspeth. "What talk is this!"

"Dear Miss Grantham. Your heart is in the Highlands but this is not Bonnie Scotland."

"I'm a Lowlander," said Elspeth tartly, "and I'm well aware of the location."

"Manners are different. These mandarins with whom our husbands do their business for instance. They live with a wife and their concubines all in one establishment . . . and it's all very amicable. The wife is happy to be Supreme Lady and the concubines are happy if they are visited by the master now and then . . ."

Elspeth was growing pinker every minute. She didn't like this conversation at all. Nor did I, for I sensed that it was full of innuendos and that she was trying to tell me something. I knew what.

Joliffe had visited Chan Cho Lan's establishment. I thought: Are people talking about Joliffe? This woman would see that if there was anything disreputable to be hinted about anyone, she would be at hand to do the hinting.

"Our husbands see the way these mandarins live," went on Lilian. "It's natural that they should attempt to try that way of life, European style of course. I can't see Jumbo bringing his concubines into our house. Can you see Joliffe?"

"No," I said. "It would not be permitted."

She seemed to be convulsed with secret laughter.

"But we mustn't grudge them their little visits, must we?"

"I don't know," I said calmly, for she was looking straight at me. "I think it would depend on the reason."

"Men," said Lilian waving a hand as though to include the whole sex. "They will always concoct a plausible excuse for anything, won't they?"

I said: "I think I should be getting back."

"Can I drop you in my rickshaw?" asked Lilian.

"Thanks, I have my own."

"I'll go back with you," said Toby. "You'll have Elspeth's lamp to take."

When we were in the rickshaw he said: "That's a pernicious woman."

"She's always hinting at something. She makes everyone so uncomfortable."

"I think," said Toby succinctly, "that that is the object of the exercise. Elspeth will give her short shrift."

I was sure of it.

We did not speak very much after that but when we reached the house and we said goodbye, he held my hand firmly. He said: "Any time you want anything send for me . . . I'll be waiting."

I thought what a pleasant comforting phrase that was as I went into the house. "I'll be waiting."

I was feeling better. I would pretend to take tea and when I was alone I never drank it. If there were visitors I did because I knew then that the tea would be untainted. I used to lock myself in my room and make myself tea on Elspeth's spirit lamp. When I had used the lamp I would lock it away in one of my cupboards. This little subterfuge in a way stimulated me. Or perhaps my natural vitality was returning. I had tried to make my mind a blank. I didn't want to suspect anyone, but I had to make every effort to find out what was happening and whether in truth someone was threatening my life.

What seemed so odd was the method chosen. I was not to be killed outright. I was to be made weak and then everyone was to believe that I suffered from hallucinations. There was a method in it for when I was very weak and had been so for some time my death would surprise no one.

This was what had happened to Sylvester. I was certain of that now.

He had had no idea. He had accepted the weakening of his body as a natural effect of the sedentary life he was forced to lead.

"Sylvester," I murmured. "What happened? I wish you could come back and tell me."

Whenever possible I directed the rickshaw man to take me in such a way that we passed Chan Cho Lan's house.

Sometimes I would say, "Slow down. We're nearly there." They were not suspicious because during my journey I often asked them to stop or slow down. I was so sorry for them, running as they did with their burdens. Sometimes I looked into their wizened faces and I seemed to see a certain hopelessness there. It was as though they accepted the fact that this was their lot in life. They were meek and uncomplaining, but looked so tired sometimes; and I had heard that the life of a rickshaw man was not a long one.

They were faintly amused by my concern, I think.

Whether they were grateful or not, I could not say. They thought me odd. I think perhaps I lost face with many of the servants by allowing myself to consider these menials. I didn't care. I was happy to lose as much face as they wished in such a cause.

It was on one of these occasions when I again saw Joliffe going into Chan Cho Lan's house.

When I reached The House of a Thousand Lanterns I went to my room and asked myself why Joliffe called there.

Chan Cho Lan and Joliffe. How long? I wondered. Lilian Lang knew. This was what she was hinting. She had told me as plainly as she dared that Joliffe kept a Chinese mistress and that mistress might well be the inscrutable fascinating Chan Cho Lan herself.

There was so much that I did not know. It seemed that often outsiders knew more of one's affairs than one did oneself. A man's secret life was often secret only to his wife. Others quickly learned about it, whispered about it and if they were kindly, kept it from the one it most concerned and if they were malicious they betrayed it.

Now I was building up the picture. Could it possibly be that Joliffe wished to *marry* Chan Cho Lan? That was not possible. He could not marry anyone because he was married to me. But if I were not here . . .

I tried to push such thoughts out of my head.

Joliffe came in.

"Jane, my darling, I wondered if you'd be in."

I was caught in an embrace. He smelled mainly of a mixture of jasmine and frangipani.

I did not have to ask myself where I had smelled that before.

"Do you often go to Chan Cho Lan's house, Joliffe?" I asked.

"I have been."

"Recently?"

"Yes recently."

"Do you have business with her? Is she interested in some collector's piece?"

"She is always interested in collectors' pieces."

"So that is why you went to see her . . . recently?"

"There is another matter, Jane."

My heart began to beat faster. Was he going to tell me now? Was he going to explain to me, confess that he had a mistress, that there was much I had to learn about life here, that I had to adjust my views . . .

That I would never accept, I thought fiercely.

"It's Lottie," he said.

"Lottie! What has she to do with this?"

"Everything," he said. "Chan Cho Lan is going to find a husband for her."

"Lottie mentioned something of this to me."

"She should marry. She is now of an age."

"Is it marriage . . . or a liaison?"

"Marriage."

"Lottie seemed to think that because her feet had not been mutilated this would be impossible."

"It would probably be so with someone who is entirely Chinese. The husband Chan Cho Lan has in mind for her is half English half Chinese like Lottie herself."

"So the reason you visit Chan Cho Lan is to arrange this?"

"Yes."

"I can smell the perfume of her house on your clothes."

"What a nose you have, my darling."

"You make me sound like the wolf in Red Riding Hood. All the better I should say to smell out your secrets."

He kissed me lightly on the nose. "What a mercy that I have none from you," he said.

"I should have thought that Lottie's matrimonial affairs should be discussed with me rather than you."

"Oh, you don't know the Chinese. It's the men who arrange these matters."

He was so plausible. When I was near him I believed him. How could I ever have thought that he would deceive me?

I was always swamped by my love for him, by my need of him; for that tremendous physical bond which held us together.

I would believe him now that we were together. Later perhaps in the night when I awoke suddenly and looked towards the door for fear that I should see the Mask of Death, the doubts would come back again.

Someone in this house had threatened me.

I would find out who, and in order to do so I must not allow myself to be deluded.

I had always known that Joliffe liked Lottie and she him, although I think she had been disappointed when I married. Not exactly disappointed but fearful. She knew of course that Jason was his son and that something had gone wrong. She probably put all this down to the inscrutable ways of the foreign devils.

Now I began to notice certain glances between them. A fondness in his expression when he spoke to her or of her; of Lottie I could not be sure. Those giggles which indicate tragedy or amusement had always bemused me.

I knew that she often visited Chan Cho Lan. This had been a regular feature of her life since she came to us, so there was nothing unusual about that. I asked her how she felt about this union which was being arranged for her.

"Very happy," she said dolefully.

"You don't sound it, Lottie."

"Shall wait and see," she said.

"You should be dancing with joy," I said.

"No." She shook her head. "Nothing all good."

"Have you seen this man?"

"Yes, I have."

"He is young ... handsome?"

She nodded.

I put my arms about her. "Is it that you don't want to leave us?"

She laid her forehead against me in a helpless gesture which I found appealing.

"We'll see you often, Lottie," I said. "I shall ask you and your husband to visit us. To come to tea ..."

She turned away giggling.

II

I was now feeling as strong as I ever had. My energy—both physical and mental—had returned. I now faced my suspicions squarely. Something mysterious was going on. Someone had attempted if not to kill me to harm me and when I thought of what had happened to Sylvester I believed that the same method was being used on me. Sylvester had died—whether as a result of these methods or not I could not be entirely sure, but if he had been poisoned however mildly this could not have done him any good.

He had had violent dreams. He had seen the Mask of Death.

And so had I.

I had been awakened from my sleep by it. I now believed that I had been awake when I saw it, and if this was the case then I must have seen someone.

I was going to discover.

The next day I feigned listlessness and retired to my bed. I spent two hours there watching, ready to leap from my bed at the moment the apparition appeared. Nothing happened. The next day I tried it again.

Just as I was beginning to despair I fancied I heard a

faint movement. I was tense, watchful, my eyes on the door. Then I saw it move . . . quietly, slowly. The face was in the doorway glaring at me from the gloom.

I leaped out of bed. The door shut but I was there in a matter of seconds.

I opened the door. There was nothing in the corridor. I ran to the stairs. I was just in time to see a flash of red on the curve of the staircase.

I started down . . . but as I got to the curve the staircase was empty.

I went on down. I was in the hall and there was no sign of an apparition.

Still, I had proved something. It did not vanish as such an apparition might be expected to. It had to run to get away.

Somewhere down here someone who had masqueraded as this thing must be hiding. I was going to search until I found out.

There were four doors through which it could have passed. I hesitated. Then I opened one door and went in.

The room appeared to be empty. I looked in the alcove, behind the draperies. Nothing.

Hastily I went from room to room. All were empty and silent.

I stood in the hall and once more the silence of the house enveloped me. Apprehension swept over me.

I knew that I would be doubly vulnerable now. Someone was threatening me, perhaps threatening my life. This person was a murderer. He had intended to kill me slowly, presumably to divert suspicion. But now I had betrayed the fact that I was suspicious. I had been lying in wait and had just not been quick enough to seize the dragon to pull off his disguise and expose him.

I had shown that I was ready, waiting.

The lanterns were lighted in several of the rooms. It was dark now. The house took on a different character with the fading light. At such times it seemed very quiet indeed, when a distant sound would startle one.

I had promised myself that by day I would examine those four rooms which led from the hall. It must have been in one of these that someone masquerading under the dragon's robe had entered.

The lanterns were lighted as they always were in these lower rooms, but even so the light was dim. I looked round the room. Where could the masquerader have gone to? Could he have hidden in one room while I looked in another? How could he have slipped away? He had his costume to dispose of.

These were the rooms with the paneled walls. The lantern threw a dim light on the paneling which was not what one would have expected to find in a Chinese house.

I examined the paneling. There had been something like it at Roland's Croft. And then suddenly as I stood there my heart leaped in excitement, for protruding from the panel was a tiny fragment of red cloth.

I stooped and examined it. I tried to pull at it but I could not budge it. Then I saw that it was wedged in the wall.

My heart began to beat very fast. I ran to the door and closed it.

I went over to that fragment of protruding cloth.

I should call someone and tell them what I had found.

Tell whom? Joliffe. But to tell Joliffe . . . I was horrified, for I was ranging myself against Joliffe. I had to face all the facts if I were going to discover what was going on. I had to stand outside my love for him. I had to be reasonable. I had to listen to logic.

I went to the wall. I took the material in my hand. There was very little of it. I tried to pull it out.

As I did so the gap in the paneling widened.

There was enough space now for me to get my fingers in and I pulled.

Very slowly the panel was drawn back and I was looking straight into that evil face.

I drew back gasping. The thing seemed to sway towards me.

Then I saw that it was a robe with a hood and on this hood was painted the face which had frightened me. The Mask of Death—luminous paint that shone in the dark. An evil expression which lingered long in the mind.

"You idiot!" I said aloud. "It's a robe of some sort, the sort they wear for processions. Somebody who knew of this secret place has been using it."

I forced myself to go right up to that yawning cavity to look the Mask of Death straight in the face. I touched the red cloth. That was all it was. And it was hung on a nail with the face showing so that a quick glance made it seem like a living image.

Inside that cavity was a musty smell. As far as I could see it was like a large cupboard. I could have stepped inside but I was not going to.

Nothing, I thought, would induce me. I had a horrible feeling that if I did the doors would close on me forever.

I ran out of the room calling: "Joliffe . . ."

There was no answer. This was the hour when the house was quiet.

I returned to the paneled room and waited. I was not going to leave it until someone else had seen that open cavity. I had a notion that if I did it would be closed and there would be no sign of it. They would think I was having hallucinations again.

I was glad when Adam called.

I brought him straight into the room. He stared at the cavity in amazement.

"How did you discover it? To think it's been there all this time!"

He stepped into the cavity and I followed him.

It was about six feet square.

"A sort of cupboard," said Adam disappointed.

"Look at the lantern up there," he said. "Quite a fine one."

"That makes six hundred and one," I said.

"Ah yes, we never got farther than that. This is an exciting discovery, Jane."

"You had no idea that it was here?"

"If I had I would have explored it."

"I think someone in the house knew."

"Why?"

"Because I saw a piece of cloth protruding. It was not there a few days ago. That's how I discovered it. Someone may have gone in hastily and come out hastily too, leaving a piece of the cloth of one of these garments betraying the secret."

"Who?" asked Adam in a bewildered way.

I looked at him steadily; his face seemed expressionless in the dim light from the lantern.

"It's interesting," he said. "There may be other such cubbyholes in the house. These paneled rooms would be ideal for hiding such places. I wonder if there are."

His face was impassive. One never knew what Adam was thinking. Watching him I asked myself: Did he know before? Was he the one who took the robe out and used it to frighten me? Was it Adam of whom I had caught a glimpse when I ran out of my bedroom?

"We'll have to have a thorough examination of these lower rooms," he said. "I think that's Joliffe."

It was. He called him.

"Look what I've discovered," I cried.

"Good God!" cried Joliffe. "A secret panel. What's in there? Nothing!"

I watched him closely as he stepped inside. How suspicious I was! What were his feelings? How much of his surprise was pretense?

"Another of them," he said with a grimace. "What a find! And you discovered it, clever Jane!"

And I looked from one to the other and I thought: One

of you perhaps is putting up a game of pretense. One of you perhaps knew of the existence of this place. One of you took the robe and came to my room because you wanted to delude me into thinking I was ill enough to imagine I saw what was not there. Hallucinations . . . the kind of visions people have when they are very sick or going mad.

I am afraid, I thought. I am threatened. But I am stronger than I was because now I know that I am in danger. I know that I must be watchful because someone who wants to be rid of me is under this roof.

Love is the betrayer and I loved Joliffe. Perhaps he was trying to kill me. I was not sure. Perhaps he wanted to share my fortune with someone else. I could entertain such fears; and yet I loved him.

I said to myself: I must watch him. I must discover why he really goes so much to Chan Cho Lan. I must understand whether he is trying to poison me.

Yet when he was near me I forgot everything but the intense joy of loving and being loved by Joliffe. My love and my fears were like two separate emotions. I couldn't understand myself, but when we were alone together I trusted him completely.

We lay in our bed and it was early morning and not yet light. I had awakened suddenly and this was, I think, because Joliffe was awake too.

"Jane," he said quietly. "What is it?"

"Joliffe," I replied, and the words seemed to rush out involuntarily, "I have such fears . . . They come to me sometimes . . ."

"You should tell me. You should always tell me."

"Sylvester . . . how did he die?"

"You know he was ailing for a long time. That accident was the beginning of the end for him."

"He was well enough in England. He had an injury but

it was not the sort of thing that kills. Yet he came here ... and suddenly he began to deteriorate."

"It's like that sometimes."

"He was listless; he had hallucinations; he walked in his sleep. The same thing happened to me."

"People walk in their sleep when they're run down."

"They can be ill because they are being given something to make them."

"What do you mean?"

"I mean that I sometimes think someone in this house is trying to kill me."

"Jane! You've been dreaming."

"It has been a long dream, going on for weeks. As soon as I saw that piece of red material in the paneling I knew. It was obvious. Someone was trying to frighten me, to undermine my health—in the way Sylvester's was undermined—so that in time I could pass quietly away and it would all seem inevitable."

He held me against him. I could hear his heart beating fast.

"You haven't been well. You've been working yourself up to a state of anxiety about something that doesn't exist. You saw the mask in the procession. It caught your imagination. You dreamed of it."

"I dreamed of it before I saw it in the procession."

"Darling Jane, it's in every procession. You've seen it right from the first."

"But I saw someone in it. It was in the secret cupboard. That was how I discovered the cupboard was there, because it was protruding."

"Oh Jane, who would do such a thing?"

"It seems very important to me to find out. There's so much I don't know."

"Understand this, Jane. I am here. No one shall hurt you while I'm here. This is not like you. You were always so bold, so brave. And you have me beside you."

So strange it was that there in the intimacy of our bed I believed him, I trusted him absolutely.

"You are close now," I said. "Sometimes you seem far away."

"You've been suspicious about things, haven't you? It started with Bella. I didn't tell the whole truth, did I, and you didn't trust me after that. I didn't want to tell you that she had killed herself. I knew how it would affect you. You're very sensitive, Jane. You brood; you look back; you remember."

"Don't you remember, Joliffe?"

"I remember what is good to remember and try to forget what is unpleasant."

"That's true enough."

"It's weak, selfish probably. But life is for enjoying, not for brooding. We had our tragedy. For all those years we were apart. I lost you and my son and now I have you back. I knew how you'd feel about Bella if you were aware of the whole unpleasant truth. You'd have some guilt feeling and imagine all sorts of things that were not accurate. So I didn't tell you all that happened."

"You said she died of her illness."

"She did. It was because she knew she was going to have a painful end and that it was imminent, that she killed herself. That was dying of her illness. It was her decision, Jane, and only she had a right to make it. I believe it occurred to you that I might have pushed her out of the window. There was that nightmare of yours. I feel limp with horror every time I think of it. What might have happened on that night if I hadn't found you?"

"How did you find me, Joliffe."

"I heard the sound of footsteps, as I told you. I came up to the room. I saw you there and Lottie had come up too. Because she had heard you . . ."

"So if you hadn't come, Lottie would have been there to save me?"

"She is so fragile and you seemed so determined. I

doubt if she could have held you back. I have never ceased to be thankful that I heard you, Jane."

"I have often thought of it . . . So you came up and found Lottie there with me?"

He kissed me. "Don't talk of it, Jane. Even now it terrifies me."

I believed him then—such was the magic of our intimacy.

"Tell me about Chan Cho Lan," I said.

"Chan Cho Lan!" He hesitated for a moment.

I went on: "You visit her . . . frequently. I have seen you going in and coming out of her house. I have been watchful."

"Jane!"

"It was wrong, wasn't it? Spying you might say. That's an ugly way of putting it. I had to, Joliffe. I had to find out what is going on."

"I should have told you. I am the one who has been in the wrong. Yes, I go to her house. I have been frequently. It's about Lottie."

"You are planning Lottie's future?"

"There's a reason for it. I should have told you before. It's ancient history now and involves others . . . but I should have told you. Chan Cho Lan as you know was one of the court concubines."

"I know of this," I said.

"My father was fascinated by her. She became his mistress. There was a child. That child was Lottie."

"So Lottie is your half sister then!"

"Yes. That is why I want a good marriage arranged for her. When Chan Cho Lan would have exposed the child to the streets where she would have shared the fate of many other girl children, my father determined to save her. Because he feared his wife might become suspicious if he were concerned in the affair he induced Redmond to rescue her and give her into the care of Chan Cho Lan and to be her guardian. Chan Cho Lan would have lost

face if she had had a child of her own that was only half
Chinese, but if this child was rescued from the streets and
she was implored and perhaps paid to rear it that would
be acceptable. Redmond continued to look after Lottie's
interests when my father died. He would not allow her
feet to be bound. Now you know the story. Our family
have always been on terms of friendship with Chan Cho
Lan. I should have told you all this in the first place, of
course, but it is a long ago secret and I did not want you
to think our family too disreputable. I thought it was best
forgotten. Adam knows this of course. That is why Lottie
was brought to you."

"Poor child, I felt drawn towards her from the first."

"What happened is due to no fault of hers. I want her
to make the best marriage possible. We shall provide her
with a dowry and this will ensure that she makes a good
marriage."

"I wish you had told me," I said. "I had visions of your
going to your beautiful Chinese mistress who was tempt-
ing you away from me."

He laughed and said: "No one would have the power
to do that, Jane. I love you and I know the value of that
love. Don't ever think otherwise."

How happy I was! How easy it was to slip into this
pleasant euphoria.

How I laughed at myself in the velvety darkness, with
Joliffe beside me.

But the doubts came back with the daylight.

Lottie was putting my linen into drawers.

I said to her: "I often think of that night when I
walked in my sleep."

She stood very still; she looked like a statue.

"Yes," I went on, "I think of myself walking up to that
room, to the window."

"You ill," said Lottie. "Better now."

"You sleep lightly, Lottie."

She looked blank as though she did not understand.

"I mean," I went on, "you heard me."

"I hear," she answered.

"Did you see me leave my room?"

She shook her head.

"So you just *heard*."

"Just heard," she echoed.

"And when you came into the room I was there at the window?"

"And Mr. Joliffe is holding you back."

"So . . . he was there before you?"

She nodded giggling.

"I always wanted to know," I said faintly, "but didn't want to think about it when I was ill. Now I'm better I feel curious. So he was there before you."

"He there before," she confirmed.

It was not what he had told me.

Oh God, I thought, what does it mean?

III

I went down to the Go-Down to see Toby. He took me into his private office and closed the door.

"Jane," he said, before I could speak, "I feel very uneasy about you."

"I feel very uneasy about myself," I replied.

"I have been delving into books on Chinese drugs and medicines and I have found something I must show you."

"Please do."

"The book is at home. You must come and see it. But briefly there is an account of an old Chinese recipe. It contains opium and the juice of some rare poisonous plants. It was used centuries ago by some of the most efficient poisoners. It produces certain symptoms."

"Yes?" I said faintly.

"The victim suffers first a listlessness, a lethargy. He is disturbed by dreams, hallucinations too. Shadows form into threatening shapes. While he is under the influence of this drug he will walk in his sleep. Gradually his health becomes undermined and he goes into what at home we would call a decline, until he eventually dies."

"Sylvester . . ." I whispered.

"And . . . yourself?"

"It seems as if someone is trying to destroy me."

"I'm afraid for you, Jane."

"I did not suffer from hallucinations. I saw the figure on the stairs. I found the robe in which someone was dressing up." I explained what happened.

"But you were in such a state as to *believe* it was a hallucination."

"At first, yes. Then I walked in my sleep. If Joliffe had not been there . . ."

I paused. Why had Joliffe been there? Why should he say that Lottie had been there when he arrived and she say that she had come into the room to find him there with me? What did this discrepancy in their stories mean? I was fighting the suspicion that he had administered that Chinese poison, that he had led me in my drugged state up those stairs and was attempting to throw me from the window when Lottie appeared. It was absurd. He would not have wanted to have two wives who killed themselves by jumping out of windows! I was however known to be ailing. Perhaps the idea was that the fact that his first wife had died in this way would have preyed on my mind.

I would not accept such wild reasoning. I could not mention it even to Toby.

He said: "Look here, Jane. This is very serious I believe."

"Who would do it, Toby?"

"Let's consider. Sylvester died and left a vast business to you."

"That would point to me then."

"No. It was a surprise to us all that it was left to you. It would have been imagined that you would have had an income for life and the business would have gone to the family."

"Adam and Joliffe . . ." I said.

"Joliffe was out of favor."

Toby looked at me intently. "Someone wants you out of the way, Jane. I know Adam's business is not good. And if you died he would take over, in trust for Jason. Jason is a child yet . . . there are many years ahead before he could come into his own . . ."

I blurted out: "Adam won't take over. I have had that changed. Joliffe, my husband, will be in command if I died. He will hold everything in trust for our son."

I saw the horror dawn in Toby's eyes and I couldn't bear it.

"Does Joliffe know?" he asked.

"Of course he knows," I blustered. "We discussed it together. It seemed only right as Joliffe is Jason's father that he should be his guardian."

"Jane, you are in danger. We have to look at every possibility . . . however distressing, however remote it may seem."

"Sylvester died but Joliffe was not there when that happened," I said triumphantly.

Then horrible thoughts like mischievous imps danced through my mind. I remembered how he had bribed one of Sylvester's clerks to let him know when I would be going to the Cheapside office. I heard Mrs. Couch's voice coming to me over the years: "Servants . . . he can get round them. They'd go and jump in the lake if he told them to."

Toby did not speak.

I found myself defending Joliffe as though I were a counsel for the defense. I went on: "Sylvester died in this way, after suffering the symptoms you mention. I've certainly been affected by those symptoms. And I've proved that it was in the tea. It's someone in the house. It's someone who was in the house when Sylvester was alive."

Because he still did not speak I grew frantic. I knew the meaning for his silence. He suspected Joliffe.

Joliffe's reputation would put him under suspicion. The wife who had died . . . mysteriously. The coroner's censure. The visits to Chan Cho Lan.

I could picture Elspeth Grantham's discussing the scandals with Toby rather triumphantly implying that I was now suffering for my folly.

I said: "Joliffe had been often to Chan Cho Lan's lately because he has been arranging a marriage for Lottie. He had told me the truth about Lottie. She is his half sister. That is why he takes an interest in her and wants to see her happily settled."

Toby continued to regard me sadly.

"What's the matter?" I cried. "Why do you look like that?"

"It's not true, Jane. Lottie is Redmond's daughter. He had always been secretly proud of the fact. Chan Cho Lan was his mistress and this was known in some circles. He saved Lottie and was her guardian until his death. Then Adam took his place in looking after her. His father had asked him to do this. Adam has been arranging Lottie's marriage."

I felt as though the world was shaking under me. I was numbed. I would not believe what was staring me in the face.

Toby put a hand gently on my shoulder.

"You should not go back, Jane."

"Not go back! Leave The House of a Thousand Lanterns. Leave my son."

"You and he could stay with Elspeth."

"Toby, you've gone mad."

"I'm just looking at facts."

"It's not true," I cried.

"Look at it calmly, Jane."

But how could I look at it calmly? Joliffe . . . trying to kill me! I wouldn't believe it.

"Elspeth will look after you. Go to Elspeth. Take Jason and go."

"I am going back to the house," I said. "I am going to talk to Joliffe."

He shook his head. "That will do no good. He will make excuses. When you told me that you had changed Sylvester's arrangement everything fell into place. Don't you see, Jane . . . the motive . . ."

But I loved Joliffe. I would not look at the logic of Toby's argument. I could only see the man I loved and would go on loving until I died.

"I'm going back," I repeated firmly. "My son is in the house. I must go back for Jason."

"I'll come with you."

"No. I'm going alone. I will get Jason and come back perhaps. I can talk about it . . . think about it more clearly when I know Jason is with me."

He could see that I was determined.

I walked out to my rickshaw.

I returned to the house. I walked through the courtyard vaguely hearing the tinkle of the wind bells. How silent was the house! I stood in the hall, and momentarily I thought of the figure in the mask which must have sped down the stairs and into the paneled room. Someone who knew that secret cupboard existed . . . someone who had known the house since his boyhood. Someone had staged my hallucination. I heard Joliffe's voice at the Feast of the Dragon: "That's the Mask of Death."

A slow lingering death. The safe kind of death. One went into a slow decline so that when the final hour came no questions were asked.

I should never have come to this house. There was

warning in the silence, the alien quality, the wind bells and the enigmatic lanterns. Six hundred and one of them —and where are the others to make up the thousand?

Perhaps I should leave, take Jason with me and go to Elspeth. That would be running away from Joliffe. I had done that before. It was like an ugly pattern. Perhaps that was what it was meant to be.

I felt a sudden urgency to see my son. For if I were in danger, what of him?

He was not there. I looked through the window. There was no sign of his kite in the sky. At this time he was usually in the schoolroom doing the lessons I had set for him. Lottie was generally with him. I went to the schoolroom, to find it empty.

And where was Lottie?

She had come into the schoolroom and was standing behind me. Her expression was impassive.

I said: "Where's Jason? I expected to find you both here."

"Jason not in house."

"Then where is he?"

She bowed her head and was silent.

"Come," I said impatiently, "I want to know where he is."

"At Chan Cho Lan's house."

"Chan Cho Lan's house! What is he doing there? Who took him?"

"I take."

"Without my permission?"

"Chan Cho Lan say bring."

"That's no reason why you should take him without asking me first."

"You not here."

"What happened? Tell me."

"Chan Cho Lan sent servant. Chin-ky wish to play with Jason. Send Jason."

"Lottie," I said, "we are going at once to Chan Cho

Lan. We will bring Jason home. And don't ever dare to take him there unless I say he may go."

Lottie nodded.

We walked through the courtyards and across the grass to Chan Cho Lan's house.

My heart was beating angrily. I hated the woman. How dared she send for my son in this arrogant fashion. I hated her because she was beautiful in her strange alien way and I believed that she was Joliffe's mistress and Chin-ky was their son. No wonder Joliffe called often to see her. Horrible suspicions kept crowding into my mind. Did he want me dead so that he could marry Chan Cho Lan? That could not be so. And yet . . .

Jealousy and anger overcame all fear.

The pigtailed servants sprang up to open the gate and with Lottie close behind me, I went into the house.

I was taken straight to Chan Cho Lan. She was waiting for me. She looked exquisite in pale mauve silk, jewels gleaming in her black hair, her skin delicately tinted and perfumed.

"You bring," she said to Lottie. "That good."

"I have come for my son," I said. "I did not give him permission to go out and I am surprised that he was brought here."

"Your son," she repeated smiling and nodded her head.

Lottie watched us breathlessly.

"Come," said Chan Cho Lan. "I take you to your son."

I said: "I know that he enjoys playing with your little boy. But I must impress on him that he is not to leave the house without my permission."

"It is good of great lady to honor my miserable house," said Chan Cho Lan. "Good of clever boy to fly his kite with my unworthy son."

It was difficult to respond to such talk. I knew it was only custom and that she adored her son and thought him perfect. For all the custom in the world I wouldn't pretend for a moment that my Jason was wretched and stupid.

So I merely nodded.

I followed her into a small room paneled like those lower rooms in The House of a Thousand Lanterns. She turned to smile over her shoulder and led the way to the panel. I was not altogether surprised when she touched a spring and the panel slid back.

"You look?" she said.

I was in a cupboard not unlike that in which I had found the costume. But leading from this were steps. She stepped daintily into the cupboard and started to descend the steps. Lottie and I followed.

We were in a room from which hung lighted lanterns. There must have been some fifteen of them. They threw shadows on the walls and showed us a narrow opening through which came the gleam of more lanterns.

Chan Cho Lan nodded to Lottie who went towards the opening.

"Chan Cho Lan wish me take you to Jason," said Lottie.

"You know this place then, Lottie?" I asked.

She nodded. "Chan Cho Lan show me."

I followed her as she led the way.

We walked some distance.

"What is Jason doing down here?" I demanded.

"He come to play with Chin-ky."

I looked around. There was no sign of Chan Cho Lan.

We were in a passage with a wall on either side. It was cold and the light from the lanterns was dim.

"Where are we going?" I said. "Jason is not down here surely?"

"Chan Cho Lan say is."

"Where are we?"

"We nearly under The House of a Thousand Lanterns."

"The lanterns are here, Lottie. This is where the rest of the thousand are."

She nodded. "Come," she said.

We had come to a door. There was a grille in this door. Lottie opened it and we went inside. Numerous lanterns were lighted. It was like a temple. And there I saw the statue and I guessed at once that it was the great Kuan Yin. Her kindly eyes were studying me; she was of jade and gold and rose quartz. A glittering beautiful figure.

"It's *the* Kuan Yin," I said.

And before the goddess was a tomb—of marble and gold on the top of which was a marble recumbent figure.

I thought to myself: This is the secret of The House of a Thousand Lanterns. I looked up at the ornate ceiling on which were depicted the delights of the Paradise of Fō. There were seven trees on which jewels hung, seven bridges of pearl and figures in white robes.

Then I said: "But where is Jason?"

"Over there," said Lottie.

I could see nothing but a long box on trestles.

"Lottie," I said sharply, "tell me what this means."

"Over there," she said.

I went in the direction she indicated.

There was no sign of Jason.

I turned to Lottie. She was no longer there. The door had shut and I was alone.

"Where are you, Lottie?" I said. My voice sounded hollow.

Panic surged up in me. The kindly goddess seemed to look pityingly and I knew that this was what the house had been warning me of.

I went to the door through which we had come. There was no door handle. I pushed the door with all my might.

It did not respond.

I was shut in this strange place.

I knew then that I had been lured here. That Lottie had lured me here. Why? I asked myself.

"Let me out," I called. "Lottie, where are you?"

There was no answer.

I turned and looked in panic about the place. A temple indeed—I noticed the beautiful mosaic floor; the tiled walls; it was a worthy setting for the tomb of a loved one, and presiding over it all was the goddess of tenderness, the goddess who never turned a deaf ear on cries of distress.

For what purpose had I been lured here?

I went to the tomb. There were Chinese characters on it in gold. I could not decipher all of them except that I recognized the word "love."

Then suddenly I knew that I was being watched. I turned round. There was a shadow across the grille.

Chan Cho Lan was there; her face looked infinitely evil.

"You have not found son?" she said.

"He is not here." My own fears were forgotten in those that I felt for Jason.

"You do not look," she said. "Is here."

"Oh God," I cried. "Tell me where?"

"You search and will find."

"Jason!" I cried shrilly: "Jason!"

My voice echoed in this chamber of death but there was no answer.

A terrible dread had come to me. I had seen the box on trestles and I had thought it was a coffin. I could not bear the thought. It was not possible.

I went to the box. I think I knew the utmost misery then for lying in the padded box, his face as white as the silk which lined it, looking so unlike himself in life, was my son Jason.

I don't know whether I cried out. I felt as if the world had collapsed about me. I could not imagine a greater calamity. I stood swaying looking down at the well-loved face.

Jason, my baby . . . my son . . . dead.

But why this senseless torture, this misery? What did it mean? "Jason," I sobbed. "Jason speak to me . . ."

I bent over him. I touched his face. It was warm. "Jason!" I cried. "My dear child."

Then I put my lips to his and joy of joys I could see the pulse in his temple. He was not dead then.

A voice said to me: "He not dead. I do not kill. My religion does not let me."

I ran to the grille. "Chan Cho Lan," I said, "tell me what this means. What have you done to my son?"

"He will wake up. In an hour he will wake."

"*You* have brought him to this state . . ."

"Had to be. He very lively. Must get him here for when you come."

"What do you want of me?"

"I want you dead . . . and your son dead, so that what is right may be done."

"Listen, Chan Cho Lan, I want to get away from here. I will give you anything I have if you will let me get out of here with my son."

"Cannot . . . too late."

"What do you mean? Explain to me. I beg of you, Chan Cho Lan, tell me what you want."

"You see altar behind statue of goddess. On it is two phials. You drink contents of one and son drinks other. You die."

"So you want me to kill myself and my son?"

"It is best. You must die."

"And what benefit will that bring you?"

"It will restore face to my ancestors. My grandfather great mandarin. Doctor save his life and he give him house, but first he builds beneath it tomb to beloved wife and gives her the great goddess to watch over her. He live in my house and visit tomb of beloved wife often. But you try to find secret and all foreign devils do. One day they might find. House should belong to rightful owner."

"So you want the house. Why did you not explain this?"

"Chin-ky will have house. When you dead and boy dead, House will be Adam's. Chin-ky Adam's son so it is right he have it. Chin-ky marry Chinese woman and they live in House of Thousand Lanterns and ancestors will rest in peace."

"Adam! I don't believe it."

"No. You believe he Joliffe son. Adam very clever. He hide much."

"The house will not be Adam's," I said. "If I die it will be Joliffe's."

"Not true. Sylvester make will. Adam know."

"It was changed. I changed it. Adam will not inherit it."

"Not?" she said, for the moment taken aback.

"My husband will have what was mine," I went on quickly.

She lifted her eyebrows. "If there is more to be done it shall be done," she said.

So she would murder Joliffe too!

"And Lottie," I said, "what part has she played in this?"

"Lottie my daughter. Adam father is her father."

"You deceived my husband. You told him that his father was Lottie's."

"To bring him here. Yes. I want you to know he come here. Best I think. For future."

"And you ordered Lottie to kill my first husband."

"I do not talk with you but to tell you that you must kill yourself and your son."

"Do you imagine no one will look for us?"

"They will find. In sea. You will be taken there and in time they find you . . ."

"You're diabolical."

"Not understand. Take draught. No pain. It will be over quick."

She had gone and I was left there in that chamber.

I went to the coffin and lifted Jason out.

I carried him in my arms and sat down on the marble steps of the tomb.

Silence, and Jason and I in the light of the lanterns—four hundred in this chapel and the labyrinth which led to it—waiting for the miracle that would save us.

A certain relief had flooded over me because Joliffe was not involved.

And I thought. What will he do when he finds me gone?

I looked up. Over my head was The House of a Thousand Lanterns. I was immediately under it. Somewhere above me Joliffe might be. He might be asking: "Where is the mistress? Where is Jason?"

Oh Joliffe, I thought, forgive me for my doubts and, oh God, let me get out of here.

I laid Jason gently on the floor. He had been heavily drugged and I was glad in a way that he was not aware of what was happening.

I went to the altar; there stood the two deadly phials. So she had ordered Lottie to murder Sylvester that her own hands might not be stained; and I was to kill myself and my son that she might be guiltless of murder. When she learned that the will had been changed and that it was Joliffe who would inherit she saw this as yet another obstacle which fate had put in her way to test her and she would set about eliminating him.

The goddess' eyes looked straight into mine. Kuan Yin who was supposed to listen to pleas for help. Never would she have heard any more urgent than mine.

I would not die. I would find some way out. But how? I had to save not only Jason and myself but Joliffe. I went to the door and pushed it with all my might. That was foolish. I could achieve nothing by that.

Oh Lottie, I thought desperately, how could you have been such a traitor? She it was who had tried to frighten

me in the Mask of Death, Lottie the daughter of Redmond—not Magnus as Joliffe believed. Lottie was
Adam's half sister who had been saved from the terrors of
the streets by her father. I saw now that Lottie had hoped
I would marry Adam and then I suppose Chan Cho Lan
believed that Adam would have had control over The
House of a Thousand Lanterns. How strange that Adam
should be so involved—Adam, the taciturn man who was
father of Chin-ky. And how deeply *was* he concerned?

Poor Lottie, she would believe that she owed an eternal
debt to her ancestors.

Would it really be that in twenty years' time little
Chin-ky would be installed with his wife in The House of
a Thousand Lanterns as both Lottie and Chan Cho Lan
believed the gods wished it to be?

I will give up the house, I promised the goddess. I will
never ask for anything else but my life with my husband
and child . . . if only I can get out of here.

I prayed: "Please, God, help me. And Kuan Yin, who
is said to hear the pleas of the helpless, listen to me now."

Jason stirred. The effects of the drug were passing. I
was relieved and yet frightened. I did not want him to
wake up in this place.

I called out: "Joliffe."

My voice echoed about the tomb. They would never
hear it overhead.

I thought of the ceremonies that would have gone on in
the place right beneath us. The ceremony of the dead. I
thought of the mandarin who had loved his wife and
buried her here that he might visit her grave and mourn
in secret.

I can't die here, I thought. There is so much I have to
live for. I must see Joliffe again. I must tell him of my
hideous suspicions and ask him to forgive me. I will tell
him that I love him . . . as he is. Whatever he has done in

the past, whatever he does in the future, nothing can alter that. I would love him forever.

And what am I doing talking of loving forever with death staring me in the face.

It was difficult to assess the passing of time. Jason stirred and muttered something.

I bent over him. "It's all right, Jason. I'm here. Your father will soon be with us."

I was trying to calm myself, to prepare myself for the moment when he emerged from his drugged sleep. He must not be frightened.

"Joliffe," I prayed, "come to me. I want a chance to tell you of what I have been thinking. I want to tell you how much I love you and always have loved you even when I believed you were trying to be rid of me. Could there be any greater proof of love than that?"

How quiet it was in the tomb! And how the mandarin must have loved his wife. I pictured his coming here to mourn for her.

And in this place, dedicated to love, I was to die.

Oh, Joliffe, you are just above me. Miss me. There may have been someone who saw me come here. Is it true that when a loved one is in danger there are certain premonitions? Your loved ones are in this tomb, Joliffe—your son and your wife.

Something, someone must lead you to us. Who? How?

Jason had stirred again. I took his hand and his fingers curled round my palm.

And if we drank the contents of the phials, what then? Painless sleep. And by night Chan Cho Lan's servants would come and take our bodies. They would put them into sacks and throw them into the sea. We should never be heard of again. It would be one of the mysteries of this mysterious land. I could hear Lilian Lang talking of it at dinner parties, and eyes would be turned to Joliffe. His first wife had died violently; his second had disappeared.

Oh, Joliffe, I thought, you are in danger too.

Thoughts were chasing themselves round and round in my mind and the minutes were ticking past. How much more time would be given me?

At any moment a face would appear at the grille.

Footsteps! I went to the grille.

I could not believe it. I was dreaming. It could not be. How could Joliffe come to me here?

But it was not a dream. It was his face—taut and anxious and then suddenly so joyous that my heart was filled with happiness.

"Jane!" he shouted.

"Joliffe," I answered.

The door swung open and he caught me in his arms.

Roland's Croft

Lottie had saved me. She had broken down and confessed everything to Joliffe. She had obeyed instructions and brought about the death of Sylvester. Chan Cho Lan had believed that The House of a Thousand Lanterns would belong to Adam when Sylvester died and that he would have left it in time to Chin-ky. Lottie had obeyed instructions not because she would gain anything by doing so but because she believed it was the will of her ancestors that Sylvester should die.

When it was revealed that The House was mine, Chan Cho Lan had thought that I should marry Adam who would be willing to return the house to its rightful owner who was after all his own son Chin-ky. When I married

377

Joliffe I was doomed and Lottie was ordered to remove me in the same way as she had Sylvester. Jason would have followed. But Lottie was in a quandary. She had grown to love us both but Adam was her half brother and so was Chin-ky and as the daughter of Chan Cho Lan she owed her duty to her family. She had been, Chan Cho Lan complained, dilatory in carrying out her task, and I had gone on living. Perhaps I was younger and stronger than Sylvester and better able to resist this slow poison. She had been commanded by Chan Cho Lan to produce the hallucination for me as she had done for Sylvester. Chan Cho Lan had known of the secret cupboard behind the panel and had put the robe there that it might be safe from prying eyes.

And Lottie had obeyed. Poor Lottie, torn by her emotions, had put the money sword in my bedroom to warn me that I must prepare for death. Half English, half Chinese, brought up to think as a Chinese and then to have been thrust into an English environment, she had been bewildered. She wanted to kill me and yet save me. Bemused, she had been afraid to carry out Chan Cho Lan's instructions and yet afraid to disobey them. Because I had not fallen so easily under the spell of the slow poison as Sylvester had, she had sought to hasten matters. That was why she had thought of throwing me from the window. She had heard of Bella's death and had thought it would please Chan Cho Lan if I died in a similar way. In desperation she had drugged me effectively and led me to the upper room. Perhaps that would have been the end if Joliffe had not come up in time. I liked to think that it was his love for me that awakened him at precisely the right moment. I believe it was so.

As for Lottie, I could feel no rancor towards her. I understood how her mind worked for I had learned something of Chinese customs and logic.

I was greatly relieved that Jason did not come out of

his drugged sleep until we were safely back in The House of a Thousand Lanterns. He was astonished to wake up to find himself lying on his bed.

"Where's Chin-ky?" he said. "She was going to take me to him. First she gave me tea . . . and then I fell asleep."

I said: "It's all right. You're back here now. I came to look for you and found you asleep, so I brought you back."

He accepted this and asked when he was going to play with Chin-ky again.

Joliffe and I discussed at length these strange events which had been going on around us and all my fears and suspicions had been revealed. He was incredulous that I could have believed such things of him.

So was I now that I knew the truth.

"I'm wild," he said, "I'm reckless. I haven't always told you all I should. I couldn't bring myself to tell you Bella committed suicide . . . but believe me, Jane, it was because she knew she was doomed. I knew you'd be distressed. I knew you might think that I had driven her to it and I took the easiest way out. I told you she had died of her illness convincing myself that in a round about sort of way that was so. I really did believe Chan Cho Lan when she told me that Lottie was my father's daughter. Listen, Jane, don't look for perfection in me. You won't find it. I'm devious, I hate trouble, I go to all sorts of lengths to avoid it. I'm wild if you like. I accept all this. You'll never be sure of what I'm going to do. There's only one thing in life you can be sure of, and that is that I love you."

"That's enough," I said, "while I'm sure of that I'll be ready to face anything that may come."

Chan Cho Lan took her own life by drinking the poison which had been intended for me. This was due to loss of face. She had failed to eliminate us and restore The

House as she believed to its rightful owners. She had produced a daughter who was half foreigner—it was different to have had a son—and that in itself was enough to create the wrath of the gods. Her daughter had betrayed her to the foreign devils just as she was about to expiate her sin in loving a foreigner. She had failed and in a way which meant she would never be able to bring about the desired result. In Chan Cho Lan's mind there was only one thing she could do. It was the classic solution when so much face that could never be regained had been lost. She could sanctify herself by joining her ancestors.

Adam decided that he would leave Hong Kong for a while. He had always hid his feelings and he did so now. It was difficult for me to adjust my view of him, so completely had I been deluded. And so, I assured myself, had Sylvester. Who would have thought this rather solemn man of apparently stern morals, was all the time the lover of the woman who had been his father's mistress, and that she had borne him a son.

He convinced us that he had had no part in Chan Cho Lan's schemes for murder. He had believed at first that he would marry me and so get control of the business and it had been a great blow to him when I had married Joliffe. Chan Cho Lan had kept her secrets even from him, for although he was her lover he was a "foreign devil" and she knew that he would never be reconciled to her reasoning.

He was without doubt deeply upset by what had happened and his great concern was to look after Chin-ky now that the boy's mother was dead. Before he left he put him into the care of an uncle, a respected mandarin of Canton.

There was Lottie. How sorry I was for her. She wept often silently and the manner in which she sat so still while the tears ran unheeded down her cheeks was more than I could bear.

I tried to make her see that I held her guiltless of Syl

vester's death and her attempts to kill me. Others had planned it and misled her into thinking that it was her duty. She declared that she was a miserable creature who had failed in her duty to her ancestors. She had betrayed her mother because she could not allow me and dear little Jason to die.

Joliffe and I set out to convince her.

We reiterated that she was not to blame. If Sylvester had died because of the poison she had given him, I and Jason were alive because of her. Did she not see that in saving two lives she had expiated her sin of taking one? It was an odd sort of reasoning but it worked. She was thoughtful. She confessed that she had meant to throw herself from the window from which she had planned to throw me, and we were afraid for some time that she would carry out her intention.

Adam, before he went away, joined his entreaties to ours, and I think his were the more effective. She was his half sister, and he commanded her to take notice of what he said. So strong was her feeling for her family that she would listen to him more readily than to me whom she loved.

Finally she was persuaded and she went away to prepare for the marriage which had been arranged for her in fact by Adam. Chan Cho Lan had pretended to consult Joliffe about the marriage and had led him to believe that his father was Lottie's also because she wished to call him to the house frequently in order to make me uneasy. She apparently thought it would be a good idea to make trouble between Joliffe and me in case my death could be made to appear suicide. It was for this reason that she had invited me and shown me her son Chin-ky. She thought it as well that I should have a reason for suicide in case there should be enquiries after my death, and as Joliffe's first wife had killed herself it could seem a good idea that his second did too.

Lottie's husband was half English and half Chinese and

had been educated in England. He was a good and intelligent young man and I believed she would be happy.

There was The House of a Thousand Lanterns. In the vaults below this, the mandarin had created a beautiful temple to his wife. There was no way to this temple through The House of a Thousand Lanterns; the only way was through Chan Cho Lan's house where the mandarin had lived after he had given The House of a Thousand Lanterns to Joliffe's great-grandfather.

His greatest treasure was the tomb of his wife and to her he had given the most prized statue of Kuan Yin.

The words he had had inscribed on the tomb when translated were:

> Through the changing scene I loved you.
> In life we were as one and death shall not part us
> For our love is everlasting.

We went down to look at it. There was a hushed feeling in the vaults. It seemed a different place from that in which I had been imprisoned.

The benevolence of the goddess seemed to be fixed upon me and I said suddenly as though prompted to do so: "This must always remain. This was what he intended. The Kuan Yin must remain here where the mandarin put it."

Adam said: "That statue is worth a fortune."

I said quickly: "It doesn't belong to us. We are aliens here. It is not for us to interfere."

I spoke with authority. The House of a Thousand Lanterns belonged to me and this was part of the house.

And there in that underground haven I knew exactly what I would do.

I was going to relinquish The House of a Thousand Lanterns. It could never in truth be mine. That was what it had told me from the moment I had entered it.

It must be restored to those who would have lived there but for the mandarin's quixotic gesture.

Adam would look after his son, and when Chin-ky was of age he should live with his wife and children in The House of a Thousand Lanterns.

There seemed to be a lightness in the air. The House had changed.

II

A few months later Joliffe, Jason and I left for England. I was pregnant and I wanted my child to be born at home. There was also Jason's school to be thought of.

It was a wonderful day when we arrived at Roland's Croft.

Mrs. Couch was at the door, fatter than I remembered, her red cheeks aglow, a slight glaze of tears in her eyes.

"Home at last then, young Jane," she said. "But I suppose I've got to call you Madam." Her eyes went from Joliffe to Jason and back to me . . . significantly studying me, knowing that I was what she would call 'expecting.'

"It's about time, too," she said. "Now the house will be a home again."